THE WANTON ROAD

J. C. Harvey is the fiction pen-name for Jacky Colliss Harvey. After studying English at Cambridge, and History of Art at the Courtauld Institute of Art, Jacky worked in museum publishing for twenty years, first at the National Portrait Gallery and then at the Royal Collection Trust, where she set up the Trust's first commercial publishing programme. The extraordinary history of the Thirty Years War (1618–48) and of seventeenth-century Europe has been an obsession of hers for as long as she can remember, and was the inspiration behind the story of Jack Fiskardo's adventures, which begins with *The Silver Wolf*, continues with *The Dead Men* and ends here with *The Wanton Road*.

THE WANTON ROAD

J. C. Harvey

ALLEN&UNWIN

First published in hardback in Great Britain in 2025 by Atlantic Books,
an imprint of Atlantic Books Ltd.

10 9 8 7 6 5 4 3 2 1

A CIP catalogue record for this book is available from the British Library.

Hardback ISBN: 978 1 83895 348 5
E-book ISBN: 978 1 83895 350 8

Printed in Great Britain

Allen & Unwin
An imprint of Atlantic Books Ltd
Ormond House
26–27 Boswell Street
London WC1N 3JZ

www.atlantic-books.co.uk

Product safety EU representative: Authorised Rep Compliance Ltd., Ground Floor, 71 Lower Baggot Street, Dublin, D02 P593, Ireland. www.arccompliance.com

This one is for Lydia and Rich.

Contents

Author's Note

THERE ARE TIMES when history makes a writer's life easy. There are many more when it doesn't (why couldn't so-and-so be in this place when it would be so handy to the plot to have them there; why couldn't this have happened when I want it to, not when it did; why was this marvellously evocative phrase not in use a hundred years earlier?), but sometimes the gods of history and of fiction sit down together and get along. Such is the case with the winding-down of the Thirty Years War in Europe, and the ignition of the Civil War in England, in 1642, and the many, many men of war who moved from one to play a part in the other.

So, gentle reader – and thank you so much for still being there, for completing this marathon through the first half of the seventeenth century with me – we come to the third book in the Fiskardo's War trilogy. And by now Jack Fiskardo's war is not only the one he fought in Germany, and the one between him and his sworn enemy Carlo Fantom, but also the one taking place in his own heart and head.

I always knew that I would bring Jack to England, to fight in the English Civil War; I always knew that his faithful troop of discoverers would join him; that I would make him the owner of Varney; and that, before any of this, he would lose his patient and loving helpmeet, Mirelle. And I always knew, in that evil writerly way, that I would present him with challenges that could not be solved by cunning or daring or strength of arm – such as caring for a child who has none of those resources to call upon, and never will.

But I also always knew that I would match him with a heroine who has wholly unexpected abilities of her own, who could be every bit as potent, within her female world, as Jack is within his. I knew this character's name, I knew her background was privileged but lawless, that she came from within London's underworld; I knew her spirit was indomitably confident and unquenchably selfish and venal, yet that this was going to be what ensured her survival, and the survival of (almost) all those she would come to love. And I knew that her appearance would need to be unforgettable and unmistakable. I knew there would be gowns. And then I came across the history of Bess Holland and Holland's Leaguer, and of Crossbones cemetery, and thus history became 'story', at a stroke.

And of course I knew that there would have to be a final reckoning for Jack with Carlo Fantom. The historical Carlo Fantom also came across from Germany to fight in the English Civil War – for both sides as it turned out – but for him, as for the 'Carlo Fantom' of *The Wanton Road*, it would be the last such war in which he, or Jack Fiskardo, would play a part.

And with that, read on…

THE WANTON ROAD

THE
WANTON ROAD
N
ENGLAND
R. Severn
Naseby
Hereford
Edgehill
Varney
Oxford
Bristol
Chalgrove Field
Roundway Down
Devizes
Reading
London
FRANCE
Border of the Holy Roman Empire
0
50
100 miles
0
50
100 km

NORTH SEA
THE DUTCH REPUBLIC
Haarlem
Amsterdam
Breda
Dunkirk
Antwerp
Brussels
THE SPANISH NETHERLANDS
HESSE
R. Rhine
Laon
St-Étienne-des-Champs
aris

Cast of Characters

PROLOGUE

At Crossbones graveyard, London, 1620

Bess Holland, proprietress of the infamous 'Holland's Leaguer' brothel in Southwark
Abigail Skinner, her maid
Miguel Domingo, Bess Holland's coachman, waterman and bodyguard, a native of Capo Verde
Walter Spikenard, an old soldier, now Bess Holland's doorman

PART I

In the village of St-Étienne-des-Champs, Picardy, 1637

Jack Fiskardo, notorious discoverer, one-time captain of a troop of military scouts known as 'The Dead Men', newly widowed
Mirelle, his late wife
Edouard, 'Ned', his oldest son
James, 'Demi-Cuit', his newborn
Robert, landlord of the Écu de France, Jack Fiskardo's brother-in-law
Cou-Cou, Robert's wife

Madame Bertin and Georges Artaud, neighbours
Père Hubert, the village priest
M'sieu, Jack Fiskardo's horse

In Paris, at the Palais-Cardinal

Armand du Plessis, Cardinal Richelieu
Achille de la Tour, the Cardinal's confidential agent

In a wood outside the town of Breda

Zoltan, the Dead Men's one-time lieutenant
The Dead Men: Thor, Ulrik, Luka, Jens and Per
Rupert, Count Palatine, later Prince Rupert of the Rhine
Fritzi, a dog

In the village of Teteringen, also outside Breda

The besieging army of Frederick Henry of Holland
Mr and Mrs Tobor Martlin of Haarlem
Floris, their horse

Within the town of Breda itself

Felipe Ortez, a clerk within the London office of the Spanish ambassador
Francis Hooley, his servant
Pris Holland, his mistress
Sister Albertine and the nuns of Breda's Beguinage
Carlo Fantom, 'Charles the Ghost', Croat mercenary and one-time assassin, Jack Fiskardo's sworn enemy

In the town of Haarlem, on the Dutch coast

Ava Franka, a businesswoman
Mungo Sant, a Scottish mariner, captain of the *Guid Marie*

In London

Aaron Holland, adoptive brother to Pris Holland
Greville Holland, Aaron's uncle, head of the Holland crime family
Mary Frith, Bess Holland's companion
Mr Sullivan, proprietor of Sullivan's tobacco shop
Sir Theodore de Mayerne, Physician Royal
Jemima, his maid
Sir Antony Wyncanton, MP, Pris Holland's admirer
Molly Tubb, Pris Holland's maid
Madame Oliphant, Pris Holland's dressmaker
Cornelius Vanderhoof of Amsterdam, Jack Fiskardo's oldest friend
Rafe Endicott, bookseller
Belinda, 'Belle', his wife
Mr and Mrs Butter, Belle's parents
Mr William Watts, a churchman, friend of Rafe Endicott
Lodowick Alembert, leading man at the Red Bull theatre in Clerkenwell
Ingram Skinner, head of the Skinner crime family, rivals to the Hollands
Ezra and Asa, Ingram's sons
Dilly and Flo, the Skinners' whores
Tucker Turnbull, a Skinner 'bangster', now well past his best
Mr Barlow, captain of the *Sapphire*
Abel Plumstead, a carrier and wagoner
Master Barnaby, 'Bug', a homeless urchin

Josh Arden, one-time pirate, now caretaker of the Dunqerqer tavern on the River Lea
Dash, the Endicotts' dog
Boy, Prince Rupert's dog
Helen of Troy, Bess Holland's cat

PART TWO

In and around the city of Oxford, 1642

Peter Topham, steward at Varney, an ancient manor house
Harriet Mayhew, housekeeper at Varney
Master Abram, Toby Dearlove, Old Henty, Lily – the household at Varney
Sir Joseph Astley, Major-General of the King's Foot in the army of King Charles I
George Digby, counsellor to King Charles I, rival to Prince Rupert of the Rhine
Joseph Cantley, captain of dragoons in the army of King Charles I
The Gemini, Kazimir and Konstantin – Latvian freebooters, also members of the Dead Men
Cicely, upstairs maid at Oxford's Spotted Cow tavern
Mr Unthank, proprietor of Unthanks' dressmakers
Miss Suzanne, his assistant
Colonel Ancrum, a Scot, Jack Fiskardo's one-time colonel in the wars in Germany, now of Upper Aston Hall, Buckinghamshire
Dorothea, his wife
The Reverend and Mrs Henry Gage, neighbours of the Ancrums
The army of the Earl of Essex, commander-in-chief of Parliament's troops

Ocker and Todd, Jack Fiskardo's dogs
Annie, a horse

At the Battle of Roundway Down, outside Devizes, 13 July 1643

The army of Sir William Waller, commander of Parliament's forces in the west
The army of Sir Ralph Hopton, commander of King Charles's forces in the west
Maurice, Prince Palatine, younger brother of Prince Rupert

PART THREE

Following the defeat of the army of King Charles I at the Battle of Naseby, 14 June 1645

Jenkin Holland, Greville's younger brother, usually to be found in Amsterdam
Will ('God's-Will-Be-Done') Franklin, Antony Wyncanton's lawyer
Lucius Symond, friend of Joseph Cantley and now a prisoner in Tothill Fields, Westminster
Oliver Cromwell, commander of Parliament's 'New Model Army'
Snowdrop, a bear

PROLOGUE

London, 1620

Crossbones

'... these single women were forbidden the rights of the Church, so long as they continued that sinful life... therefore there was a plot of ground, called the single woman's churchyard, appointed for them, far from the parish church.'

John Stow, *Survey of London*

EVEN DEAD, YOU don't want to end up here.

Ask any man what this place is, he'll tell you it's the burying ground for St Saviour's, ain't it? And if he's a native of Southwark, look at you askance for not knowing that in the first place. The burying ground for St Saviour's, he'll say, in a manner that leaves unspoken (but not unheard) the *What's it to you?*, because they are a tribe within a tribe, the people of Southwark, as those at the bottom of any such great place as London tend to be, and suspicious of strangers, as well as being most perversely proud.

Not that this is the proper burying ground, you understand. It's not that round St Saviour's itself, where you might already lie in company with such worthy souls as old John Gower the rhymester, or that mad lad Will Kemp, or even Will Shakespeare's little brother Eddie, and thus be as respectable as, in Southwark, you are ever like to be. No, this – this acre of wasteland, humpy and unmown, dotted with those lozenges of naked earth – this is St Saviour's other burying place. This is where they bring the outcasts, the nameless, the friendless, the penniless. Those who lived in sin, died in misery, and are buried here in shame. That's what a man will tell you.

But ask any woman you might find hereabouts – this woman, maybe, sat here in the yard of the George, just up the road from the boneyard itself, one of the three huddled together here this February morning, warming their hands round cups of buttered ale – and she'll tell you something different. She'll give this place a name, for a start. She'll call it Crossbones.

Why is it called that?

Because it always has been, that's why.

But who is buried there?

The women.

What women?

(It might take a moment for her to answer. Who are you, after all? But give her time.)

The women of the Southwark stews. Them, and their little 'uns what never grew up, or what died of being born, or whose poor mothers died with them inside. Hundreds of them. Hundreds of hundreds. All buried here.

And she'll give you a look, as she sips from her cup. That wrinkled mouth, those shadowed eyes… when you chose her to speak to, you did so because compared to the other two (one so humped she's almost doubled over; the other freakishly tall even sitting down, and with a strip of leather tied over her eyes) she seemed younger, she seemed almost comely, and now you see how wrong you were. Something to her, to all three of them, ringing that warning note: *These are not as you.*

And then she gives you the look, the look that dares you. Judge me not, the look says. This is our ground, not yours. Crossbones.

*

Old Bess Holland (and don't you ever let her hear you call her that), but Old Bess Holland all the same, she could walk here from her place, the notorious Holland's Leaguer, but will she? Will I my arse, says Bess. You don't work hard as Bess has done these many years, you don't get *rich* as Bess has done to inflict upon your petticoats the mud of Southwark's streets, and you don't get as old and canny as Bess Holland counts herself to be to chance yourself to some lurking plague-rat bastard Skinner for no good reason, neither.

So when Bess Holland leaves Holland's Leaguer, which is the finest bawdy-house London has ever seen, when she has its literal drawbridge lowered over its actual moat, when she processes through its gardens (noted for the arts of flirtation and arousal practised within their shady groves, although admittedly, not when the weather is as bitter raw as this), first there's the getting of her ready, which can take two hours or more; then there's the fanfare to warn all her girls to tumble out of bed and run to the stairs (Bess keeps a trumpeter on her staff – she does, truly), and then when Bess herself appears at her bedroom door, the cheering and applause. Abigail, Bess Holland's maid, is never sure how much of it is genuine, but cheering and applause, nonetheless. Then there's the processing outside, past old Spikenard, Bess's doorman, still as hefty as in his days trailing a pike, and out to Bess's carriage, waiting there at the garden gate. Then there's the bowing and the handing of her up into her carriage by that handsome young buck Miguel Domingo (coachman, waterman, bodyguard, all rolled into one) and only then does the journey proper begin; and only then can Abi let out her breath.

Don't *huff* so, you creature, Bess Holland says. All these years, ain't I taught you better manners than that?

All these years. Bess set up Holland's Leaguer the same year Old Queen Lizzie died and King James of Scotland came down to the English throne. 'Elizabeth was King, now James is Queen' was the joke in Southwark, har-har-har, when the first rumours of the man began to run about (and how Bess rubbed her hands together when they did!), but His Majesty King James is ageing now himself, and the years have not been kind. First he lost his proper heir, Prince Henry; then there came this hellish war in Germany that sent his daughter and her German husband scurrying from their thrones in Bohemia into exile in The Hague; and then the remaining son, Charles – God save us, the ninny, what poor watery shot was it engendered him? In his prime, Old King James, masqued up like Arlecchino with only his beard and that perpetually wet-lipped mouth of his left visible, would sit in the garden at Holland's Leaguer, whinnying with delight as the mimics, the molly-boys, waited on him dressed in nothing but vine leaves, and so Scots-drunk he'd topple right off his seat and lie there on the grass all happy and helpless, but his boy Charles? What a mullypuff. What a suck-egg. A pompous kill-joy of a suck-egg, what is more. The Hollands – Bess, and her unholy trinity of brothers, Cosmo, Greville and Jenkin – are already planning for times that may be nothing like as free and easy as those they've come to know, and there's been many a recent family council at Greville's house in leafy Rotherhithe, plotting how to buttress the family's interest in taverns and brothels and theatres with all those other bits of business that go on wholly out of sight. Ships that fly black sails, that appear at the mouth of the Thames only as daylight fades; rowboats (such as Miguel Domingo's) that creep out to meet them in darkness, and return with barrels of brandy and casks of Dutch gin; parcels of lace so thick and luxuriant it wheezes if you squeeze it; the commonplace of cinnamon and nutmegs; even (nowadays) the most radical of tracts and pamphlets, ending their journey bound face to face with such perpetual favourites as *Araminta in the Nunnery* or *Nights of the Emperor Tiberius*. Basically, anything (or even any*one*) you want to bring to or carry from London-town, with no-one knowing of the doing of it, it's the Hollands you require. All of which is most exciting stuff to listen to, at Greville's chamber's inner door, while minding Cosmo's young'un, little Aaron, who is already such a devil-cub you can't take your eye off him for a minute; and all of which is (in Abi's opinion) a far safer and *warmer* way to spend a Sunday than a goose-chase such as this – trundling along Bankside and past the Bear Garden and Winchester Palace and the evil old Clink and then bossing and fighting a way through the traffic coming off London Bridge – Lord! It's like being tossed about at sea! – and then right down Borough High Street and past the George and oh, thank the saints, we've arrived. Surreptitiously, under her cloak, Abigail draws a cross upon her bony bosom. Above them Miguel Domingo gets down from the coachman's seat, and the carriage rises on its straps. Abigail lets down the slide, Miguel's face appears (oooh, it still gives Abi such a *start*, to see an African as close to her as that!), and the door to the carriage is swept open.

'Out my way, you kipper,' says Bess, standing up. A nose-tingling waft of Hungary water, creamy with neroli oil, fills the carriage. Now the susurration of silks: silk chambray for the winter petticoats, silk brocatelle for the gown (textured like flock, and in that oh-so-fashionable colour known as dead Spaniard), silk velvet for the cloak and hood, chinchilla for the muff. Sheeny kid, the gloves and boots. Lace, lace, everywhere.

And pieces, to pad out the hair, and belladonna for the eyes, a wash of dew-and-white-ceruse for the face, mouse-skin for the eyebrows and a patch, to hide the scar that horrid chancre left upon Bess's forehead, long ago. It's such a playful disease, the pox. God knows what goes on underneath the silks these days – what ulcers, what yellowings, what wastings-away – but the Bess Holland that Bess Holland presents to the outside world is so richly, lushly fine she could walk unchallenged into Whitehall Palace.

Abi, in her wool fustian, the same brown-black as ink, gets down behind Bess and starts lamenting at once. 'Oh milady, 'tis so *cold*! Oh, that wind! 'Tis Arctic!'

Bess, striding away, ignores her.

'Oh milady, must we do this? Must we?' Abi gathers her cloak about her. It's a good thick cloak, but Abi's shivers come not from the icy air, nor the wet chill of the ground, but from the sense of being so exposed out here, at the mercy of every passing thing, be it keening disembodied spirits wafting about in that colourless sky or an all too embodied Ingram Skinner, or his boys Ezra and Asa, or their hireling gangs of clubbers and cutters. God knows, Miguel is a handy man to have about, but it is such a wasteland, this – haunted, unholy – a place where nothing but bad could befall you. Where ghosts seem to thicken the very air, and even as she thinks it, Abi seems to see, there at the edge of the ground, three smoke-like figures – one unnaturally tall (if they be human, to begin with), one bent double and one who might almost be blowing a kiss… She shakes her head, to deny them purchase in her thoughts; but even as she darts another glance at them the figures are gone, blown away by the knife-edged wind, less to them even than the flutter of that tattered ribbon, pressed into the earth. Or there: that pair of women's shoes, laid neatly side by side, all faded by the weather. Ghost shoes. Beside them, a wee cross of sticks, with a child's bonnet tied to it. Every place you set your foot in Crossbones, you're walking on the dead. Although the cold does at least keep down the lurking sewage-stink of putrefaction. When the Thames rises, in the lowest parts of Crossbones graveyard, your footsteps fill; when the river floods, graves pool with water even as they're being dug, that grey-blue London clay slumping into the rising seepage like rotting flesh detaching itself from bones. It has always seemed to Abi that some great, sad, relentless power lives under Crossbones, slowly pulling all that are put to rest here into its implacable embrace. If she stands here long enough, she fears to feel it pulling at her too.

She's falling behind. Bess, ahead of her, has turned, waiting for her to come up. 'What,' Bess calls back, 'you'd give Dainty Jane your word and break it, would you?'

Well, no. Even if the woman do be dead. Especially now she do be dead, truth be told. Sweet-faced as she was (and she was! Oh, she was!), no-one crossed Dainty Jane. If she could lay her hand on you and melt a cramp, fade a toothache, open your palm in hers and read it like a book, what else might she do, if you should sour her piss? Dainty Jane was a moon-girl, a Roma. No-one wants to get the wrong side of one of them.

'I promised her. First Valentine's after her passing. I'll be there, I said. I'll be at your graveside, girl. Just as you ask. And soon as she heard me give my word, she closed her eyes and was gone. Never saw so quiet a death. You have them flowers?'

Abi has, a great bunch of 'em, under her cloak. But it's February, so the flowers are all waxed silk, hand-brushed with colour – peonies and roses, irises and lilies, with paper stems and leaves, and all tied with a stiff-wired ribbon. Abi can't believe the cost of 'em. And all to moulder away out here.

'Now where's that place we put her?' Bess asks, looking about.

'There,' says Abi.

Where Abi points is Crossbones' only landmark: its yew tree. Or what was its yew tree. No churchyard is complete without a yew, but this being Crossbones, and unconsecrated ground, its yew was chopped down lifetimes ago to make good English longbows. The tree's roots, however, seemed to draw unnatural sustenance from this dreadful ground, so the tree grew anew – crabbed and hollowed and curved over its stump. Just to look at it makes Abi's skin grow goose-flesh. It's like the tree's grown carnivore, feasting on all of them sodden cadavers below. But that was where Dainty Jane wished to be laid, so that is where she—

'The devil in hell is that?' Bess demands.

There's something lying at the centre of the yew, within the hollow of the stump. All wrapped up like a pasty, cloth tucked in at either end.

'Oh, I don't like it!' wails Abi, at once. 'I'm not looking!'

'Abigail Skinner, how did your family ever produce such a mouse as you?'

Bess goes forward on her own. She bends over, hips a-creak, backbone protesting.

There is some point within the bend when she knows exactly what that parcel will contain, just from the size of it, the shape. 'It's a baby,' says Bess. There's every modulation in her tone – pragmatism (such things be), pity (that such things be), anger (that such things be) and then Bess's own habitual way of drawing a cover, at once, over anything you might call feeling, weakness, hurt. Her hand reaches the little bundle. Abi behind her is wailing, 'Is it perished? For sure it's perished of the cold!'

'No,' says Bess. 'No, Christ, it's warm as a new-laid egg.' She straightens up, holding the bundle in the crook of one arm, lifts the cloth laid over what she thinks to be its head. Peers down.

The bud of a mouth, bright pink and pouting. Such

well-marked brows too, for such a baby-thing. The tiny miracle of every single extravagant eyelash, swept over the plump cheeks, and then the eyes open and gaze straight up at her. Under the cloth, the child is naked. Kicking feet, soft fat arms reaching up. Cord dried up and gone, infant umbilicus a-wink in the round of the belly. No piddler. Little cleft. And green-eyed. Green as holly.

'She's bonny!' says Bess. She cups the infant's head. There's some few faint curls of hair, slick to the scalp. Darkish. Reddish. Dark amber, polished cherrywood. She holds the baby toward Abi, for her to see. 'Look at that!'

'Oh!' says Abi. She's a hand laid to her heart. 'Oh, the weeny worm! Oh, the duckling! Bless!'

The baby kicks and wriggles. Abi offers it a fingertip. Which is grappled onto at once and brought to the pouting mouth. 'Oh, she's *hungry*!' Abi exclaims, delightedly. 'Are you hungered, pipkin? We must find you some brekker! We need to find her some milk, milady! Yes, ducky, we must, we will!'

The baby kicks and squirms. Bess leans forward. There, on the fat little neck, a mark as if a moth had settled on the child, shaken the powder from its wings, a mark like a crescent moon.

'Abi,' says Bess, 'when did we bury Dainty Jane?' Something's prompting her, *Start counting backwards*. 'When was it we brought her here? When did we lay her to rest?'

'It was May-time,' comes the answer, in a coo down to the baby, 'May-time, wriggler! Nice and warm! May-time, milady. Sure of it. All them bushes in the garden was in bloom.' She looks up. 'Why?'

January, December, November... all through this last foul winter, back and back. Back to the autumn, back further yet. August, July, June... No, impossible. No, ridiculous. Unwanted infants crop up all over Southwark. Abandoned on the steps of

St Saviour's. Left on the foreshore for the herring gulls to deal with, the next high tide.

Even so…

'Abi,' says Bess. 'It was nine months ago we brought Jane here. It was nine months to the day.'

PART I

St-Étienne-des-Champs, Picardy, 1637

CHAPTER ONE

What Is a Man to Do?

'Our selves are ships launched forth for heaven; our tears must be the sea.'

William Worship, *The Christians Mourning Garment*

WHAT IS A man to do, after his wife has died?

He might sit beside her, holding her hand to his lips; he might sit there all night, in fact, bowing his forehead to hers as it chills, as her fingers stiffen. He might watch her face as dawn creeps its way into the room where she lies, on the bed that was theirs – the bed where they made the child that has now killed her. A boy, they told him, another son. He might note – vaguely, as if this is being thought by some other man entirely – how her face has relaxed, how the rigidity of pain has gone from her jaw, how one eye is that little bit more closed than the other. He might lift his head, and see how the window of the room is bright with sun, and flinch to find in his head the words *the first day without her*. And know – with a sensation like the iron on a plumb-line rattling through his soul, and finding no bottom anywhere – that all the days now will be without her, endlessly so.

There are birds singing in the garden, rustlings in the roof above his head, but not a single human sound from the rooms below, nor a voice from the street outside. News travels fast in a village as small as St-Étienne-des-Champs; bad news travels fastest of all. By now Robert will have tied black cloth to the door of the inn for his sister; they will be covering the mirrors; emptying anything with water in it, drawing the lid across the well. The soul, apparently, has an irresistible fascination with bright surfaces, will trail endlessly from one reflection to the next, dragging itself across them, and it cannot get to heaven with wet feet. Not even a soul as unsullied as Mirelle's.

Sunlight moves across the bed and spills onto the floor. He thinks how Mirelle's hens will be gathering at the back door; how the cat will be circling the kitchen, waiting for her to slip it some small treat; how M'sieu, out in his paddock, will be poking his mighty head over the fence. He looks down at her hands again, remembering how it was, watching her fold linens, as if the cloth flew to anticipate her bidding; how carrots rose from the earth at her touch; how she could knead dough, patch and darn with her head turned and her conversation somewhere else entirely. The cleverness in those hands, the knowing – where does it all go? How can it cease? Doesn't this have to be a mistake?

The pallor of her fingernails, no pink left in them at all; the way the sides of her fingers are hollowing, like those of an old, old woman, even as he turns her hands back and forth in his (that are so scarred, so ugly, and with so much blood on them to boot – how could she have loved him?). Somewhere in that dull, pained place within his head, that place that is like the spot on a forge where the hammer keeps hitting over and over again, somewhere in there it is as if he believes there must be an alternative to this, and if only he can find it, he can stop this in its tracks. Otherwise he feels nothing; nothing at all. He is inanimate, floating, but not at the surface – no, he is suspended, with fathoms above him, and fathoms beneath him still to go.

On her finger, the ring with the pale blue stone, the ring he gave her after their first night together, when odds were he would never see her again. He had to convince her to take it, to ward off the stares of the censorious, should stares there be; but she wore it every day since and now she will wear it for ever. Even in heaven, she will be his. Even up there, they will know she loved him.

Everything I love, I lose.

A scratching at the door. It opens by an inch or two, and Madame Bertin's face appears in the gap, eyes downcast. 'Monsieur Jacques,' she says, 'Monsieur Jacques, I have to make her ready. Please, Monsieur. You can sit with her again when I am done.'

Robert is waiting for him at the bottom of the stairs, holding a bottle of calvados.

Robert sits him on the window-seat in the parlour and leaves him with a brimming glass; goes back to the small group gathered round the fire. Cou-Cou is there, in the oak armchair, Ned circled in her arms, his head on her shoulder. When he sees Jack, his son twists his face away. He thinks of calling Ned to him, but no; what you want, when you're young as Ned, when the truly quite intriguing prospect of a sibling has ended only in this, all this adult panic and despair, is the softness of a woman's body to burrow your head into, even a woman as unmaternal as Cou-Cou. 'She is one of those,' Mirelle had once said of her sister-in-law, 'who will only have children if their hands are never sticky.' Christ, his wife is everywhere. This is the cushion she re-covered when she saw how fond he was of sitting here. That is her honeysuckle, tapping on the window. There the votive plaque to Saint Céline she brought back from Laon and set up on the mantelpiece – Why this saint? he had asked and Mirelle replied, 'Because she was a wife, and she was happy.'

He thinks Saint Céline's husband was the happy one. Was.

They are talking of Mirelle, over there, by the fire – her goodness, her kindness, her light hand as a cook; how she could pick up a hen and have it go broody at once; encourage a leaf to sprout out of anything. Robert has his head bowed; Georges Artaud's arm about his shoulders. He thinks how he has always been a stranger here, he from his *terroir* of battles and tumult and gold; and how she had stood like a good hostess between him and this world of neighbours and chickens; introducing him to it and it to him. He thinks of all the secret things a man knows about his wife – her naked derrière, walking away from him across their bedroom in the morning, imprinted with the wrinkles of the sheet; how she coiled her hair under her cap (one half twisted one way, the other, the other; 'for balance,' she had said); how she would sit the purring cat up on her lap, fold Minou's front paws and say she was having Minou pray for the souls of the mice; her exclamations of mock-horror changing Ned's napkin when he was still little enough to need them ('Oh, *mon Dieu*! It is the lava of a volcano!'). He thinks how she loved rainbows, would stop whatever she was doing, scoop Ned up into her arms and rush outside to see – '*Regarde! Ah, c'est beau!*' There should be a rainbow up there for her now. Is there?

There is not. Nothing but heedless blue. Only now above his head he hears the sound of muffled voices, and then the noise of wooden clogs ascending the back stairs and the group by the fireplace falls silent, grows still.

Madame Bertin reappears, a bundle of sheets in her arms, folded to hide the blood. He gets to his feet. 'No, Monsieur Jacques,' Madame Bertin says, 'give them a moment more,' and he understands the carpenter is up there with Mirelle, the carpenter and the coffin and the nails.

'No,' he says. At the note in his voice, Robert stands. Madame Bertin gives Robert a look of helpless entreaty – this is *le capitaine*, what are we to do?

'No, I will do it, I will move her.'

No man touches his wife but him.

No-one argues with her widower either.

They carry the coffin downstairs and set it up in the back parlour. There she lies, on her bed of bran; a rosary wound about her wrists. Madame Bertin had tucked Mirelle's scissors in beside her too. 'It is the done thing, Monsieur Jacques. For those who are lost in childbed.' Why? he had wondered, then worked it out – so that the soul of the mother might cut the cord, and her child might live.

Madame Bertin has dressed Mirelle in her finest – the quilted satin petticoat; the Haarlem linen cuffs, delicate as cobweb, which her husband had brought back for her from his most recent trip north; the necklace of opal beads Mirelle had declared too fine to wear but would hold up to the light, marvelling at the rainbows glimmering across them. Knowing his wife, he thinks Mirelle would have much preferred to be left in her ordinary kitchen gown and apron, but also that she would be far too polite to complain. In any case, this is no longer Mirelle. This is something doing its sad best to masquerade as her.

'Shall we let Edouard see her now, Monsieur Jacques?'

He is coming to realize how different civilian death can be. On the battlefield they die, you live, simple as that, hurrah, but this – this is something else entirely. The only choices it presents you with are between the bad and the worse. How at a loss he finds himself in telling them apart. 'If you think so, Madame.'

Madame Bertin lays a hand upon his arm. 'It will comfort him. To see her at peace.'

Astoundingly, it does. He lifts Ned up, to peek over the side of the coffin, and Ned looks his fill, considers, and announces, 'That's not Maman.'

No, he answers, it's not.

His son produces a deeply phlegmatic-sounding sigh. 'She's gone, isn't she?'

A realist at five years old. Yes, Ned, he says. She is. But what does 'gone' mean when you're five? Does it (for example) come leading along by the hand the word 'forever'? Jack Fiskardo was twice his son's age when he was orphaned, knew by then what death was, knew it all too well. Would it have made a difference to him, if he had been able to see his own mother in her coffin and at peace? Instead of as he found her, as she was left to be found, suspended from the ceiling like a huntsman's trophy?

The five-year-old realist's fingers consider stroking this-thing-that-isn't Maman's cheek, think better of it, return to the coffin's edge. Ned turns his face up to his father. 'Where's the baby?'

The baby is in the kitchen, in the warmest spot by the fire. It is far too small for a cradle, so Cou-Cou emptied out Mirelle's sewing box, padded it with hanks of wool and laid the child in there – if you can call this tiny, bright red, wrinkled scrap a child, with its eyes full of misery, wheezing for breath. The creased balloon of the stomach, the skin so thin you'd think you could see its organs; the butterfly flutter of the lungs. How can anything as fragile as this have killed her?

Ned kneels down beside this thing that is his brother. Extends a finger. Does stroke, this time, the skin of his brother's forehead, furrowed like that of an ancient senator. The skin is the size a child is meant to be. His brother fits it not at all. 'Was I like this?' Ned asks, in a whisper. 'When I was born?'

'No. You were born kicking and screaming and waving your fists. So Maman said.'

'But you weren't there,' Ned reminds him, seriously.

No, he was not. When Jack Fiskardo's firstborn came into the world, his father was hundreds of miles away in Prague, and best not to enquire in too much detail why. Came back to Picardy almost on a whim, back to the Écu de France and to its landlord's sister, opened the door to her chamber and walked in to find her standing there with an infant Ned cradled in her arms. The best and greatest surprise of his life. What, now, is he to make of that *but*? Is it a criticism? Or does it quietly contain the hope that maybe all babies start like this, that this trembling, wrinkled leveret might miraculously grow into its skin, become a proper baby brother, a changeling in reverse, instead of what it is now?

'Ned, your mother never told a lie in her life. If that's what she said, that's what happened. That's how you were.'

The baby shakes continuously, there in the box that looks destined to become its coffin too. As if with shock at finding itself here, but Cou-Cou maintains it is with cold. Hence the fireplace, hence the wool. When Mirelle's belly began to round, they told Ned that her belly was rising so because a baby was like a new loaf, swelling and growing. Ned gives a sigh. His unasked question hangs above his head: *If that's how I was, why is this one like this?*

'Babies need cooking for nine months,' his father tells him. 'He only had seven.'

'Why?'

'It went wrong, Ned, that's all. It just went wrong.'

He can still hear that scream from the garden. Out he had run, to find evidence of disaster everywhere – Mirelle's basket dropped, flowers scattered all over the grass; Cou-Cou on her knees and his wife sprawled half on the path, half off it, her skirts dark with water and with blood. It just went wrong. No reason, no warning; the capriciousness of God. 'This one, your brother – he was only half-cooked.'

He had raised Mirelle's head and known at once how grave this was. The eye rolled sideways, her mouth, opening, closing, but no words emerging, and then that fiercest of clenchings of her hand upon his arm, the unshakeable grip that said, *Help me. You must take charge. Everything has gone wrong but this is happening now.* All he can recall, as warning, is that once or twice, as her belly grew, Mirelle had complained of dizziness when she rose from her chair.

His son's small finger reaches out again. 'Poor Demi-Cuit,' says Ned.

It seems inevitable that Demi-Cuit will depart this world as rapidly as he had entered it, so the priest, Père Hubert, will come to the Écu to christen the child; then lead the cortège to the church to bury the mother. Père Hubert lets it be known that he will be doing this only in view of Mirelle's goodness and her family's great loss. He certainly won't be doing it out of any consideration for her husband, that godless English, or half-English, or whatever the man is, who has never had any time for

Père Hubert and made no secret of it, either.

Père Hubert arrives with his bottle of water and his little flask of oil; sets them up on a cloth on the table. Peers into the sewing box and seems pleased by what he sees.

Madame Bertin lifts Demi-Cuit out of the box, carefully, tenderly, carrying him on one hand, using the other to shield him. A spasm travels through the miniature body; as it does, Jack feels his heart contort. He has to lift his eyes away. Robert stands godfather, Cou-Cou, godmother. 'And the name?' Père Hubert asks.

The name. When Ned – Edouard – was born, Mirelle had named him after her and Robert's father. This time around, the fact that a name will be needed seems to have escaped them all. 'Perhaps another Jacques?' Père Hubert suggests, offhandedly, seeming also to imply it will not be needed very long.

'No,' he says. 'No, my son will have his own name. He will be James.'

The name – alien, yet close enough to his father's to make no difference – is pronounced, with faint distaste. Water is dribbled onto the wrinkled forehead; the tiny limbs react. Then the oil. Demi-Cuit is laid back in his mother's sewing box; his soul, if not his body, now secure and whole. Across the field the bell of St-Étienne-des-Champs begins to toll. Jack hears the carpenter returning, hears the man's clogs out there on the kitchen floor. The coffin must be closed now. There will be the sound of nails and hammering. It must be carried to the bier. The bier must be wheeled to the church. They must enter the church, they must stand round the coffin. He must stand there, knowing Mirelle is in that box, not beside him. It feels endless. It seems impossible. It must be got through. This pain will never cease.

The bell is still being rung as they approach, six times for a woman (for a man it would have been twelve), and then, with the church full, they begin tolling it once for every year of her age. Jack counts them, he cannot help himself, all the way up to twenty-six, and it is as the echo of the twenty-sixth dies away, when there is no twenty-seventh and now never will be, that he feels himself begin to lose connection with everything about him – the villagers standing with bowed heads, and as they follow the coffin outside, the whispering of the trees, the half-stifled sobs, even the feel of Ned's hand in his. Now it is the fact that this is coming to an end that is the worst thing in the world. He hears the earth spatter down upon the coffin – a handful from Robert, a handful from Cou-Cou – and in his head there is the image of something like a root-ball, thickly interwoven, and it is being torn asunder, ripped in two. Now it is his turn. They are all of them waiting. He lifts a handful of earth, and cannot do it. He cannot throw it into her grave. Instead he lets it dribble through his fingers and, as if his limbs were being moved by someone else entirely, walks away.

He walks around the church, away from everyone, into the shaded half of the churchyard, where the grass is left unscythed, where the dead have been lying long enough to have faded to almost nothing. This is where he was the first time he saw Mirelle, this is where he knelt, with his men around him; here at the mound that held Jean Fiskardo, here at his father's grave.

You had better look after her, he tells his father, in his head. Will they know each other? *Will you recognize her? The girl who waited on you, who was the last with whom you exchanged a living word?*

Or almost the last. The last was of course the man sent to kill Jean Fiskardo, who poisoned him, who watched him die. Oh, the length of history, the chapters in this tale.

She'll know you, for sure. All she'll have to do is wait for a man who looks like me.

Ned has his mother's eyes. Softly hazel; gentle of expression. Jean Fiskardo's – icily pale, balefully glittering, they are his son's alone.

'Jacques?'

It's Cou-Cou. Here she comes, holding her skirts away from the damp grass. She's cup-size, is Cou-Cou, and even her sister-in-law's funeral is an excuse to dress up, he sees, with a new way of arranging her hair on her forehead. 'Jacques,' she says again. For all the carefully arranged curls, there is a no-nonsense side to Cou-Cou. When she gives it expression, you see her father, Old Marin, in her: the peasant farmer with his gold hid up the chimney, under the floor; the man who never missed a bargain or a trick. There are no fists tighter; there are no souls plainer.

'We all loved her,' Cou-Cou says. 'We have all lost her. We all have to learn to guide ourselves without her.'

It's the first time he has ever heard Cou-Cou acknowledge Mirelle in such a way.

'Your son needs you,' she tells him. 'Your sons. You cannot hide here.'

Back to the Écu. The neighbours have gathered outside: he hears their voices, the loudness of relief that mourners always have once a funeral is done. Robert is walking about with a jug; Madame Bertin, pink-cheeked, comes up to Jack, lays her head against his chest, squeezes his arm, walks unsteadily away. When he was in Germany, in the army of Gustavus Adolphus, a life lost would be celebrated with too much to drink then, as well. But Gustavus Adolphus, the king who ever hazarded himself too easily, he too is now numbered amongst the numberless, and his one-time captain, Jack Fiskardo – hard man, discoverer, stealer of fortunes and slayer of princes of the church – he is here, instead.

In the back parlour, where the coffin stood, there is food – waffles, cheeses, little cakes. He wonders how long it is since he ate. He thinks of going to see if Mirelle needs help in the kitchen, and then he remembers, and it is as if he has been speared.

He hears Ned in the garden, a gang of children with him, hears them asking his son about his new brother, hears Ned putting some too-eager questioner in his place. 'No, you can't see him,' Ned is saying. His son's tone is fierce. 'You have to wait till he's cooked.'

He wanders into the kitchen. Georges Artaud is there, Cou-Cou, Madame Bertin too, and the priest. The fire has been banked up, despite the warmth outside; the room is hot enough to make sweat prickle under Jack's collar. There is a conversation under way: Madame Bertin, seated by the fire, has James once more in the crook of her arm, and is murmuring something to Cou-Cou about a wet-nurse, tomorrow, a wet-nurse; is dribbling sops from a spoon into the tiny open mouth. The spoonful dribbles out again.

'*Dommage*,' he hears the priest comment. 'But a seven-month child. It is no doubt for the best.' Père Hubert – you would almost call him jovial. His beard is trim, his eyes are eager; in public, and loudly, he likes to question his parishioners about their troubles, where plenty of others can hear. Despite being a dreadful shot, he likes to hunt as well, although Robert, having been out with him once ('Never again,' Robert had said), returned home convinced Père Hubert's off-target aiming was deliberate; there was far too much enthusiasm for snatching the limping hare from the ground, pulling the fluttering bird up by its broken wing. His eyes have always put Jack in mind of a crab, ceaselessly sidling about. Now, those eyes have sidled up to him. 'Ah! Fiskardo,' Père Hubert exclaims, advancing. 'Might we speak? The field?'

Georges Artaud attempts to interpose; Georges Artaud who knows *le capitaine* well enough to recognize the glacial chill in Jack's eye: 'Monsieur – Père Hubert, perhaps, if I might detain you a moment—'

Jack lifts his hand. 'No, by all means, Monsieur Hubert. The field. Let us discuss.'

Out they go, into the empty parlour. He sees himself reflected in the window as they pass – unkempt, unshaven, as if he was coming back into camp; heart as black and hands as red, no doubt, as ever.

'The field,' Père Hubert is saying.

The field sits on the other side of the road. It is handkerchief-size, no more to it than a stand of chestnut trees. In the autumn Madame Bertin grinds the chestnuts to make flour; her hog roots for left-overs. By repute, at this time of year, village maidens take their lovers there, to lie beneath the trees in the darkness, breathing in the unmistakable scent of the flowers. 'They smell like you,' Mirelle had whispered once, as she and he lay hooked around each other, the smell of spunk wafting up from the sheets and in through the open window.

'Indeed,' Jack says now. 'The field. What of it?'

'It was always Mirelle's grandmother's wish that the land should come to the church.'

'Was it so?'

'Certainly. It is well known. For masses, for her soul.'

'Odd, then, that she should have left the field and everything in it to her grand-daughter.'

Because you discuss such worldly matters, such disposals with your wife when she is with child. You discuss them in the same spirit as you would cross your fingers: to speak about the thing means it won't happen. Apparently, not so.

'An oversight,' Père Hubert assures him. The eyes tick left, tick right, as if checking there is no-one near to contradict him. 'It was always understood that Mirelle would follow her grandmother's wishes.'

'You must be mistaken, Monsieur. Mirelle's stated wish, to me, was that the field should go to our good neighbour, Madame Bertin.'

'To Madame Bertin?' Père Hubert is so unprepared for this that he falls back a step.

'To Madame Bertin. She makes good use of those trees already. Whereas you, Monsieur, as is also well known, seek only to cut them down for timber. Which is not about to happen.'

You can see the calculations taking place, the claws a-nip-nip-nip. 'If it is a matter of money—' Père Hubert begins.

There was, at one time, a deal of talk in St-Étienne-des-Champs, regarding Jack Fiskardo and his money. When he first came back here; when the entire village sought to make sense of him by whatever means it could. Was he a deserter? Had he committed some crime? Why did he keep going to Amsterdam? Far from the easiest journey to make, even on a horse the size of M'sieu, yet *le capitaine* is there regularly, two or three times a year. What did he do there? And where did he get the money for the gifts he brought back with him? Did he have a fortune? If he did, how much of a one?

Jack Fiskardo could buy St-Étienne outright; still be wealthy, even then. Mirelle had never asked, he had never explained. It was part of another life, in which he was another man entirely; one who, curiously enough, was also dead.

'It is not, Monsieur. Bad guess.' A smile. 'Are we done?'

It seems they are not. Père Hubert has his hand upon Jack's

arm, is gripping the sleeve. 'There is precedent!' he hisses. 'I will go to the courts, I will make a case—'

Jack's bark of laughter stops Père Hubert short. Instead he brings his face closer to Jack's, lifts himself up to do so. 'You will regret this. Who are you, to decide what happens here? You are *un vaurien, un scélérat*—'

A scoundrel. A scoundrel and a rogue. You're not supposed to behave like this as a civilian, he knows, but is he a civilian any longer? When she who civilized him is gone?

'No,' says Jack. 'I am *this* scoundrel, Monsieur.' And he puts out his hand, hooks Père Hubert with it, under the jaw, lifts him off his feet and puts him against the wall.

The eyes bulge. The hands come up, clawing at his. Jack tightens his grip. He feels the priest's windpipe, the rings of gristle. Père Hubert's heels kick the wall. 'In the army,' Jack begins, 'in Germany, someone would have done this to you years ago.' He holds up his other hand, tightens it finger by finger into a fist, the knuckles like a battlement. 'I am very angry,' he says. 'I am angry with God. I cannot get at him, but I can get my hands on you. Perhaps that will help sate me.'

'*Capitaine!*'

He turns his head. There is Georges Artaud, in the doorway, there is Robert; there is Cou-Cou; staring, open-mouthed, from behind Cou-Cou's skirts, there is Ned.

'*Capitaine*, please,' says Georges, coming forward. 'You are not your proper self. Think of Mirelle. Think of your children. Come away.'

Anger like this – you have to break it. Pain is the thing you break it with. He drives the fist into the wall, beside Père Hubert's head. Opens the hand around the throat. Père Hubert drops to the floor. Cou-Cou rushes forward. Ned is gone.

*

Robert sits him down in the kitchen, makes him put his swollen knuckles in a bowl of milk. 'We know you loved her,' says Robert, 'but you could have fooled anyone else.'

Georges Artaud summons Robert away. Jack hears them talking: '… a man such as Père Hubert,' Georges is saying. 'There will be trouble, perhaps for you as well. Maybe *le capitaine* could make one of those trips of his. A little time away?'

He goes up to their room – or at least, to the room that had been theirs. There is the bed, freshly made, no doubt by Madame Bertin. *Bit by bit*, he finds himself thinking, *bit by bit, my wife is being taken away.* He surveys the bed for a moment, then he falls upon it, as one might upon an enemy, tearing it apart – the bolster, the pillows, the counterpane, the sheets. The mattress underneath appears pristine – Madame Bertin must have turned it. So he lifts it up, throws it from the frame, and there, that's where Mirelle is hiding, that's where she waits for him, in that darkening stain on its underside – her blood, her pain, her courage.

He wants to get her body from the churchyard. He wants to hold it close, to keep her safe.

There is something on the floor, beneath the bed. He fishes it out.

It is one of her caps, a panelled coif, long since lost, long forgotten. Under the dust it is embroidered with lines of yellow ribbon, flowers of blue. Forget-me-nots. He rubs his thumb over the threads, then on impulse lifts the cap to his face and there she is – the scent of her, her hair, her skin, in the cap's linen panels even the shape of her head, and he feels himself buckling as he breathes her in, bent over this tiny shred of her. He can hear the sounds he's making – keening, keening, an animal in a snare – but they are in his head only. In this world, he is silent.

In the thin light of early dawn, so early that even the hedgerows are quiet, Jack Fiskardo lifts himself from the bivouac he had made on the bedroom floor, goes down the corridor and climbs the creaking ladder to the Écu's attic. Goes to the chest at the far wall, and lifts from it his long boots and his soldier's buff-coat with that grinning death's head painted on the back. Brings out his sword, hangs it over his head. Finally, there at the bottom of the trunk, wrapped in a screw of paper, the little silver pendant of an up-reared wolf, one that still bears a musket ball embedded in its breast. He never wanted it near him while he was here, never wanted it near any of them – not Robert, not Cou-Cou, Mirelle least of all. This was his curse, not theirs.

Holding boots and sword under his arm, he tiptoes along the corridor again, to Ned's room. Looks down at his son's face: the forehead dampish, the eyelids rippling with dreams, the eyelashes still spiky from their last watering with tears. Tucks in beside the boy his mother's cap. Then he goes down to the kitchen. There lies the baby, in his mother's sewing box, wheezing and spluttering.

The room is sweltering. The plaster of the walls is a-sweat, like the skin of a cheese.

He opens the window by half an inch, folds back the blanket binding Demi-Cuit in place. On the cloth below, a little squirt of shit.

He touches the hand. Fragile as a tendril, hardly bigger than his fingertip. It quivers at his touch. Hard not to see it as a quiver of horror.

'You are the last of her,' he says. 'You have to live.' Hunkers down, brings his face close. 'So I must go.'

And for those two great reasons, back he goes to the war.

CHAPTER TWO

Pistol Down, Hands Up

'Espionage is not for gentlemen.'

Lucius Cary, Viscount Falkland

AH, THE WAR, the war, the war; this same bitter conflict that has been rampaging across Europe for almost twenty years now. How did it begin? Who can remember?

Let us recap. The Habsburg Holy Roman Emperor, who is as Catholic as the Pope's tiara, is at war all up and down the lands of Germany with those heretic Lutherans and Calvinists, except when he's not, when he is at war with the French. Who are at war with the Emperor's Habsburg cousin, the King of Spain. Who is at war with the Dutch; which is where Dame Geography comes into this: France has Habsburgs beneath her, in Spain itself; she has them on her right hand, in Germany; and most annoying of all, sat on her head there is this slab of Habsburg territory, the Spanish Netherlands, with Brussels as its capital, shoved in between France and the United Provinces of the Dutch Republic, Holland proper. Meanwhile, the Queen of France, who happens to have been born an Infanta of Spain, is in constant secret negotiations with her homeland; when these are discovered she folds her famously beautiful hands together and swears her innocence, fooling no-one; and in response, Cardinal Richelieu of France, the wily old schemer, he puts together an alliance between Louis XIII of France and Frederick Henry of Holland, so that they may chip away at the Spanish Netherlands from top and bottom, both at once. Cities have been besieged, and won, and lost as fast; armies bubbling with the plague have left their customary dragon-trail of devastation behind them; there have been parlays and treaties and thunderous battles at sea. There is only one problem (thinks Richelieu as he sits in his office in the Palais-Cardinal): the Dutch – who enjoy a significance wholly out of proportion to their size and undistinguished geography – made peace with Spain before. What if they should secretly do so again? Is this what they are up to, with their agent in London?

An inward groan. The Cardinal is a sick man, his ever-restless mind battles against a strangury of the bladder, hopelessly incompetent digestion and most recently a mysterious little well of weeping discharge on his arm, but none of these cause him the pain occasioned by Frederick Henry's agent in London. An intelligencer known only by a nickname, 'Mercator', who is of such skill that apparently all he need do is walk about Westminster to soak secrets out the very air, as if he was clothed in blotting-paper. To whom all doors are open – even, apparently, those of the Spanish ambassador's ancient Tudor place in Peticote Lane. Who seems able to lure information from everyone, and be suspected by none. Indeed, there are those who maintain the mysterious Mercator doesn't exist at all; that an agent so adroit and subtle is no more than smoke, fuelled by every intelligencer's suspicion of every other; but the Cardinal is not amongst them. Mercator, to the Cardinal, is wax in a lock, is the retied tape about a document, is the faint scar in a letter's glossy seal; he is Frederick Henry's knowing tone; he is two plus two makes five; he is a flicker out the corner of one's eye, a creature whose trail blows away like dust; he is, in the words of the Cardinal's own most trusted intelligencer, one Achille de la Tour, *un putain de cauchemar* – to you and me, an utter fucking nightmare. He is – he is –

He is this: the letter the Cardinal pushes toward Achille across the table.

What is that? Achille asks.

The Cardinal views the letter, upside down. It is an offer, he says. An offer from London. From one of those young secretaries to the Spanish ambassador. One Felipe Ortez. He wishes to come over to us. And he says he will bring the identity of this Mercator with him.

Because once you have an agent's identity, you can control him. You can use him. You can, if need be, dispose of him. His true identity is the most precious thing an agent has. God save us, France's own agent in London – how much ingenuity has gone into obscuring his identity over the years?

Achille regards the letter more closely. It is poorly written, in faltering French, further garbled by its cyphering, but its import is clear. What does our man in London say? he asks.

The Cardinal tents his hands, fingertip to fingertip, flexes them, as if testing by this method the reliability of the offer. He says, replies the Cardinal, that it is possible. This Ortez was a go-between, apparently; he may have stumbled upon something.

But equally, we should be particularly cautious of Spanish trickery at present. With the ink on our treaty with the Dutch only just dry.

Indeed, says Achille. Beware of Spaniards bearing gifts.

So, the Cardinal continues, this may be no more than a trap.

Each man regards the other.

But what, says Achille at last, if this Ortez is in earnest?

That is a question, says the Cardinal, only a conversation with Ortez himself can resolve. You had contacts, I believe (and here the Cardinal does a splendid job of seeming to half remember), amongst a band of discoverers?

I have them still, replies Achille proudly.

They may be useful to us here. Annoyingly, this Ortez is no longer in London.

He has fled? He was compromised?

Apparently, he was in debt, says the Cardinal. The notion of selling a secret, it makes sense.

Ah. So where has he fled to?

This too is annoying, says the Cardinal. He has high-tailed it to the Spanish Netherlands. He is in Breda.

Breda?

Yes. It is annoying. As I said.

BREDA. IT HAS been Dutch, it has been Spanish, it has been Dutch again; then in 1624 General Spinola marched across the border from the Spanish Netherlands and retook the town for Spain. Diego Velázquez, that Spanish favourite, he concocted a famous painting celebrating the handing-over of the town, with Spinola to the right and the Dutch to the left and nobody looking as if they had endured anything worse than a bad night's sleep: there is no battle-dirt on the clothes, no blood; there is simply some smoke, spiralling away into the distance. In life (if not in art) Breda is a low, grey town; still modest, in that Dutch way, despite its present Spanish overlords; with winding river and winding streets, and a splendid Grote Kerk at its centre, its steeple pierced and bobbined like an ivory monstrance. And all the way around it, as with so many border towns, lines of earthworks, interlaced like Christ's own crown of thorns. Palisades, ditches, hornworks, redoubts, all laden with cannon and bellowing defiance. Why so? Because in this our summer of 1637, there is yet another army outside Breda's walls, this time that of Frederick Henry himself, intent on taking Breda back for the Dutch. Eighteen thousand men – Dutch, French, Scots, English, Germans, Polacks, Switzers, Swedish… the war has made soldiering a profession. By now, it's almost a nationality.

In which case, here comes one of its native sons. Jack Fiskardo, lifting himself up in M'sieu's stirrups, taking a prospect of the landscape and thinking, *What a God-damned mess war makes of everything.* Tracks run across it hither and yon; trees hacked down for fuel; reaching him on the breeze the flap of flags and whinnying of horses; and from Breda itself (that island of smoke there on the horizon) the endless pounding of cannon: thud, shake, roar. Just visible under the smoke, a telltale pair of zigzag lines, already being driven by the besiegers toward Breda's walls.

'And where the pissing fuck d'you think *you're* headed?'

The challenge scatters his thoughts like birds. Oh yes. One detail he'd forgotten. Guard posts and their sentries; bloody everywhere.

He slides from M'sieu's back. Jack Fiskardo's horse is eighteen hands high, the colour of a storm cloud and with the demeanour of a berserker; even now M'sieu is baring his teeth, as if personally affronted by the sentry's challenge. '*Vrede, vriend*,' says Jack, as the man levels his musket. Peace, friend. In Dutch, the salutation has a placatory sound, one matched not at all by the expression on the sentry's face, but then that might be more the result of the pistols the man is eyeing holstered either side of Jack's saddle, the weight of the sword at Jack's hip, the bandolier of cartridges bumping against his chest. Then there is his height, as he comes forward; after all this time in the saddle there is the scarecrow beard; and then that cold, hard silence in his eyes. Jack Fiskardo has long given up expecting his first reception to be either warm or easy.

'Out with it,' the man demands, squinting at M'sieu. 'Who the devil *are* you?'

'Looking for your scouts,' says Jack. 'Your discoverers.'

A second man emerges from the shelter of the guard post. He is of exactly the same type as the first – footslogging old cinquanters who somehow endure through everything. The second man opens his mouth to speak, waits for the roll of sound from Frederick Henry's cannon to pass, then asks, 'Woss 'e want?' He has a bottle in his hand, gripped like a club.

'Discoverer, ain't he?' the first man replies.

'Oh yeah?' The second man performs a tipsy rotation to face Jack. 'You with them others, are you?'

With any luck. In fact, why the hell not? 'That's me.'

'Them's gone thataway,' the man says. The bottle is jerked to indicate a farm track, running off the road.

Another boom, this time the Spanish guns on Breda's walls, replying in kind. Helpfully, you see them fire first, that quilt of dirty smoke spreading out; the boom of sound follows after.

''Arf hour ago,' the man adds, when he can once again be heard. 'An' you'd better shift, if you're with 'em.' He cocks an eye upward. 'Gerrin' dark.'

Jack remounts, tips his hat to them. He feels them nudge and comment to each other on the death's head on the back of his coat as he turns M'sieu toward the track. Yes, but so many stories have been told of the Dead Men, no-one knows any longer if they once were real, or are no more than another myth, engendered by this war – and in any case, what are the odds of one such being out here?

The track leads into a wood, the elbows of the branches low enough to have Jack duck his head. The air smells of wood-rot; it smells, to Jack, of loss. *What am I doing here?*

You are re-enlisting, he tells himself. You are going to find these discoverers, and offer yourself for hire. You will give them your story, because that is what you do: *I joined up at sixteen as a scout, and saw my first proper action on the field at Stadtlohn; then my regiment was sent to winter on the Polish border where this outlaw Swedish force, they all but wiped us out; only their commander, Torsten the Bear, he saw me fight, and let me enlist with 'em. I came back into Germany with the army of Gustavus Adolphus of Sweden, in an invasion financed, as it turned out, by France. I had my own troop of discoverers by then, and I led 'em on a mission down the Elbe, all the way to a stronghold of the Prince-Bishop of Prague; a mission for Cardinal Richelieu, so we discovered, where we retrieved a letter that would have ruined him and on the way netted ourselves a fortune, but it was a mission that saw half my men lose their lives. I may have gone a little mad at that, as in revenge I blew the palace of the Prince-Bishop sky-high and murdered the man himself in hot blood. Oh, and there is someone I am hunting for, have been hunting all my life: one Carlo Fantom, a man who also wears a silver wolf; but then as it turns out, the Prince-Bishop was his father, so it may be that the gods are satisfied and he and I are quits, although I doubt it. And back in Picardy, there is this tiny child, who is the last of the woman I loved, but everything I love, I lose, and if I stay with him and with his brother, and love them as I loved their mother, my greatest fear is I will lose them too. So here I am. Think you can make use of me?*

The path turns. From somewhere nearby, Jack hears a scampering, and then an unmistakable twiggy snap.

He hears M'sieu begin a low grinding deep in his throat; a sort of equine growl.

This, with M'sieu, can mean anything. That the planets have slipped into some alignment that displeases him; that a mouse just broke wind down there in the leaf litter; that M'sieu has spotted a goose (a particular hatred of his); that from somewhere the breeze has brought the whiff of a mare in heat. There are times when his horse reminds Jack of nothing so much as his lieutenant, Zoltan, in the days when the Dead Men adventured down the Elbe – both the man and the horse handsome as the devil and neither capable of believing they're not irresistible. Ah, but these days Zoltan lives in almost-wedded bliss in Haarlem, with one Ava Franka – not so?

He dismounts. He's thinking of that scampering sound, he's thinking of the snap. He curls a hand about the stock of one pistol. The grinding in his horse's throat is relentless.

'What's there?' Jack asks. It's long been a precept of his that any animal will spot a coming danger long before the sharpest-eyed of men, and while this wood is no great thing, as woods go, it's surprising how close it would allow you to get to Breda's walls, all unobserved. And now M'sieu has dropped his head, the way a horse will do, to bring some other creature into focus.

'What is it?' Jack asks again, and as he does –

– a dog comes bounding out of the bracken and onto the track. A dog the colour of a biscuit and as woolly as a sheep, with a blue and white rosette between its ears, holding back the wool on its head, like it's been put in regimental colours. There is a yell from behind it – 'Fritzi! *Fritz!*' – and then what Jack presumes can only be the creature's owner is there on the path behind it.

Pale face, black breastplate, dark hair, dark eyes, long nose. A well-made face, and its owner as long-legged as Jack is himself. Not often that happens.

The lad scoops the dog up and stands there, staring, with it in his arms. He is, Jack guesses, about the same age as Jack was himself when he joined up: sixteen or so, maybe a little older. The lad holds up a finger, very cool; bends, to put the dog down on the path behind him. When he turns around, he has of course drawn his sword.

'Well now,' says Jack, laughing, 'ain't *you* a cunning young whipster?' as he lines up the shot over the barrel of the pistol he now holds cocked between them.

The dog puts up a leg and scratches behind its ear. The lad looks at the pistol. Not one whit abashed, he declares, 'You do not know who I am.'

'Neither know nor care,' Jack informs him.

'Oh, but you *vill*,' says the lad, and at that moment Jack hears behind him the clunk of a musket being readied to fire, and a voice saying, 'Pistol down, hands up.'

Only a discoverer can come up behind a man as quietly as that. And there is something about the voice too, a sort of Baltic lilt. Jack turns. Five figures there behind him on the path – one the size of a Goliath; one, a titch; one startlingly freckled; and one lanky as a camel. And the musketeer, who has his hat pushed back, revealing the fact that he has one eye half the size of the other. And two more crashing through the bracken onto the path. The first is in a fancy doublet, striped up and down and beribboned at its points, and with the silliest damn haircut you ever saw in your life, up at one ear and down at the other, and he goes running up to the lad with the dog, calling out, 'My Lord! My Prince, my Lord! Are you unharmed?' The other, who sports moustachios like wings on his handsome face, has come to a halt, exclaiming, 'Jacques!'

Christ all-bloody mighty—

'*Herregud!*' the musketeer exclaims. 'It's you, Domini! We saw the coat, only we didn't believe it. But it's you! It's truly you!'

THE DEAD MEN. Thor, with his little eye, who came into Jack's troop in Germany as a conscript, hardly spoke a word the first month he was with them, then found himself behind a musket and showed them all exactly what that little eye of his could do. The Goliath that is Ulrik – even more of a giant now, thighs like veritable tree trunks. Half-pint Luka, a half-pint still, yet whose voice has dropped so deep Jack has difficulty believing it is Luka speaking at all. Ever-helpful, freckled Jens; lanky, conscientious Per. His old lieutenant, Zoltan, arms outspread, smile almost as wide. And there, with the lad on the path, that is Achille de la Tour, intelligencer to Cardinal Richelieu, whose secret mission sent them down the Elbe all those years ago. What the devil is this? Whatever it is, Achille will be behind it, that's for sure.

'What it is,' says Thor, 'is this.' They are walking single file through the bracken, Thor with his precious musket, with its rifled barrel, held on high; Achille and the lad with the dog bringing up the rear. Jack hears their low-voiced conversation, hears his own name feature in it.

'You see, we'd this captain, when we was first in Germany,' Thor is saying. He has dropped back into Rotwelsch, the soldiers' slang, that patchwork tongue of every territory marched through, every country fought across.

'Was he any good?' Jack asks.

Cackles of laughter all about him. 'He was a *bastard*,' Luka announces, in that new voice of his that seems to come out of the ground at his feet. 'A right leather-arse son of a bitch, and that monster horse of his, it was even worse. But what he taught us, it went in. Gave us a bit of a reputation, you might say. Did he not, lads?'

A growl of agreement. 'Yeah, we tried making a go of it back home,' Ulrik tells him, stomping along, making the ground tremble. 'But it didn't – it didn't—'

'Didn't fit?' Jack suggests.

'That's it, Domini,' says Per. 'There's a few of us found ourselves back in the life, truth be told. The Gemini—'

'The *Gemini*?'

'Yes, Domini. They're somewhere out there too. Leastways, that's what we heard. Only you'd never know with them, would you?'

No, you would not. The crazy, white-blond Gemini. A law unto themselves, as discoverers tend to be.

'So now,' says Jens, finishing the explanation, 'anyone who has some tricksy bit of business to be taken care of, we're who they go to. Get it done. Like our friend there, Monsieur Achille.'

Right. And that business would be?

'There's a Spaniard. Name of Felipe Ortez,' says Zoltan. He points toward Breda, from where he and Jack stand at the edge of the wood. 'He's somewhere in there, and Achille needs him fetched out. So that, my friend, is what he has brought us together to do.'

'A mere nothing,' Jack comments.

Another tidal wave of smoke breaks toward the town, followed by the roll of sound. Through it, the ruin of a hornwork comes in and out of view: lopsided where it took a hit; abandoned, and now, apparently, their way in. 'It seems the man has information to trade. Information vital enough for Achille to have set this up. The real unknown here, Jacques, is you.'

'Me?' But it is a question that he knew was bound to come.

'What are you doing here? Why aren't you home in St-Étienne?'

'I lost Mirelle.'

The shock, the stricken look. 'Oh, Jacques!'

You have to say something. You have to bridge this for others; he's learned that. 'And you? Why ain't you home with Ava?'

If a man about to undertake an enterprise such as this can be said to squirm, Zoltan is squirming. 'I lost some money. Fancied myself the businessman.'

Now it is Jack's turn to gape. 'How much?'

'Not *all.* Of course not *all.* But enough for Ava to throw me out, until I've earned it back again.' Jack hears the sigh. 'I think it is not that I lost the money. I think it is that I speculated with it without telling her.'

'You *idiot,*' says Jack.

The lad with the dog has been standing off to one side. Now he comes up, and Zoltan, Jack notes, gives a bow and immedi ately steps away. The lad still holds the little woolly dog in his arms. Jack never met a dog he didn't like, nor any man a dog would call its friend where he wouldn't do the same. He holds his hand out for the dog to sniff. Under the lad's arm, the woolly tail rotates. 'What breed is it?' Jack asks.

'A *pudel,*' comes the reply. 'They are water hounds. This one is my brother's, but it keeps company with me. You are Fiskardo?'

'I am,' says Jack, extending his hand.

The lad takes it, briefly ducks his head. 'I haf heard of you,' he says. 'I am pleased to know you.' Another nod of the head in acknowledgement, and off he goes.

'And who is that?' Jack asks, as the lad walks away.

'He's an interest in learning how we discoverers do what we do, apparently. And when we go in, it's his company of gunners will keep the Spanish too busy to notice us. We hope.'

'That infant has a company of gunners?' Jack asks, incredulous.

'And one of foot. And one of horse,' Zoltan replies. He lowers his voice. 'Don't dismiss the boy, Jack. He's more between his ears than most of his kind.'

'His kind being what?'

'Princes of the blood.'

'*Whose* blood?'

'Wittelsbach. You remember how this war began? The Emperor marching into Bohemia? Throwing out her king and queen?' Zoltan nods to where the boy had stood. 'Their son,' he says. 'Or one of them, at least. That, when it grows up, will be Rupert, Count Palatine.'

CHAPTER THREE

The Death of Felipe Ortez

'Grievous and hot was the service on both sides, and sometimes their aims so just, that they burst one another's cannon, for almost they never rested, insomuch that the crystal air and azure skies were rent asunder, and the people deafened and over-thundered with their reverberating echoes and tremendous noise...'

William Lithgow, *A true and experimental discourse upon... this last siege of Breda*

THIS IS THE plan. At midnight, the artillery company of Rupert, Count Palatine will rain furious fire upon Breda's walls, and under cover of the barrage, the Dead Men will scramble over Breda's earthworks to the point below that ruined hornwork. Ulrik throws a grappling hook to the top of the wall, with the ease with which another man might lob a fir cone, and up they go. Thor takes up position with his musket, Zoltan, Achille and Jacques lower themselves into Breda and, with Per and Jens left to guard the route out, make their way into the town.

'Señor Ortez,' says Achille, 'is lodged within a house of the Beguines. It is a type of nunnery—'

'A *nunnery*?' queries Jack.

'A *type* of nunnery. The sisters provide lodging for travellers. Care for the sick, that sort of thing. It is a mere hop from where we will make our way in. You yourself,' Achille declares, clapping Jack over the shoulders, 'could not have come up with a better scheme. But I see you have another question.'

'I do.' Several bloody hundred, in fact. 'The devil did this Ortez think he was doing, coming here in the first place?'

'Fleeing his London creditors, apparently. It seems he has a taste for the finer things in life. Unfortunately, by the time his letter reached us—' Achille waves a hand, to indicate Breda, the walls, the thunderous barrage. 'By the time it had, all this.'

The guns roll again. It has grown dark enough to make out the end of each length of burning match, down there in Frederick Henry's lines, as it is applied to the touch hole of the barrels. Like the eyes of tiny creatures. Then the rocket of flame, then the roar.

There is a mechanism in Jack's head that he thinks of as being something like an orrery, in that its function seems to be to rotate all possibilities until they align, and never to cease until they do. The possibilities here do not. 'And *how* did his letter reach you, exactly?'

'The way such communications always reach us. To Paris, carefully encyphered. You may be certain, Jacques, we have *inched* forward on this. One does not approach such offers of defection carelessly, no matter how enticing the bait.' Achille has pulled out his watch. It nestles in his palm, a thing about the size of a persimmon, flashily gilt; exactly the kind of trinket Achille delights in.

'That had better not have a chime, Achille,' Zoltan warns him.

'It had the prettiest chime in the shop,' says Achille, haughtily. 'It plays "Sur le Pont d'Avignon". And I have silenced it, of course.' He snaps the watch closed, restores it to his pocket. 'Gentlemen, it is almost time. Señor Ortez's servant, one Francis Hooley, will see to it that the door in the nunnery's wall has been left unlocked, and will put a lantern in the window. There Ortez will await us. We go out exactly as we came in, Ortez gives me the name of this pestilential Mercator, and there, gentlemen, our brave enterprise is done!'

It goes wrong almost at once. They get to the top of the hornwork and there is no simple drop the other side; instead, there is a scree of rubble down which they must tumble as best they can. The street before them has already been blown apart, nothing left of it but a sea of broken stone; timbers projecting from it like the masts of shipwrecks. The barrage ceases; behind them they hear faint shouts from Frederick Henry's lines, which seem only to underline how, here, they are in another world entirely. Ahead, the bobbined steeple of Breda's Grote Kirk looms up into the night, and somewhere beyond, there is the Beguinage, where they must go – only now, from behind them on the hornwork, Luka's hiss of warning: 'Cock-heads!'

There in the moonlight at the end of the street, beyond the hillocks of rubble, and wearing their unmistakable mitre-shaped helmets, a Spanish patrol.

To the left, as if a baton has been handed on, another barrage begins.

The patrol has that gappy, erratic look to it of men who would far sooner be back in their barracks than here. There is the sound of desultory chit-chat; there is what might be the sharing-out of tobacco; there is the lackadaisical behaviour of those expecting to encounter nothing whatsoever on their duties tonight. The patrol moves on. Per and Jens creep forward into position, one to one side of the ruined street, one to the other; pistols at the ready.

Thumbs up from both.

'Yes, and I would remind you, gentlemen,' says Achille under his breath, 'that Breda is a city under curfew. If we are spotted, it will be all up with us. Follow me.'

They follow. Another street, somewhat less ruinous; a market-place, ghostly with deserted stalls. That relentless barrage is on its circuit round the walls, and as it swings away from them, Jack becomes aware of something hovering just outside the compass of the orrery, something he's not sensed in years. His hand, his left hand, with its old white scars and dark tattoos, it feels as if it's seizing up. Ah, the body and its memories – who can make sense of them?

He glances back at the outlines of the stalls, the odd skirt of canvas aflap. 'Achille, we're being followed.'

'Impossible,' Achille declares, in a hiss. The guns sound again. They wait. The glow of cannon-fire fades from the night. Silence and darkness, all about them. Achille shakes his head. 'I fear you are out of practice, my friend.' They are in line beside a roughly plastered wall, with a door let into it. Achille leans against the door. 'Also, we are here.'

In they go. A courtyard, with the Beguines' church closing it off at one end; a courtyard divided like a chessboard with nigh-invisible, knee-high hedges of box. Achille catches his foot on one, and at the sound of his furious curse, a figure appears at a window on the right and there is a low, whispered, 'Monsieur Achille! Up here!' The voice has a noticeable brogue. But then the Spanish Netherlands is full of displaced Irishmen – indeed, Spain's most esteemed commander, one Owen Roe O'Neill, is reputedly a native of Armagh. *I never lifted my hand in any war*, thinks Jack, *did not have religion driving it on.*

They turn toward the voice. Now the darkness is pillared, with cobbles underfoot, then a stone stairway. At the top of it, a corridor. And a door, easing open.

'Señor Ortez!' calls a voice from within. 'Señor, Monsieur Achille is here!'

They enter. There stand two men, one a deal the senior to the other. The older man, who must be this Francis Hooley, has greying hair, dark brows, the nipped-in mouth of one who keeps his opinions to himself, and is quaintly old-fashioned in his hand-me-down clothes. The younger, by contrast, is plushly resplendent in striped doublet, with swirling cape and braid about his hat. As they come in, he pushes the long side of his crisp dark hair nervously behind his ear, revealing that not only does he favour a lovelock like Achille, but also like Achille, sports a pearl ear-drop. There is a peculiar stutter of a glance between him and his servant, a moment of *So it begins*, perhaps, then Ortez comes forward, sweeping them all a bow, hand flip-flopping over and over, like the loose sole on a shoe. '*Hola, mis amigos!*' Ortez declares. He peers a little closer. 'Señor Achille?'

'That is I,' Achille replies, stepping forward.

Zoltan forestalls him. 'Señor Ortez,' he says, 'if we might request, hands on the wall. You and your servant both.' He beckons to Jack. 'You care to do the honours?'

Ah, so like old times. Jack pats 'em down, even (for the hell of it) searches inside Ortez's fancy hat. 'Forgive my friends, I beg you,' says Achille. 'They have – they have soldiers' manners.'

'*De nada*,' Ortez replies, plainly not meaning it, and making great play of resettling his hair. 'Is nothing.' A glance at Hooley. 'We go now, yes? Is time we go.'

The glow of another barrage washes over the town. 'Zoltan,' says Jack, at the window, 'there are men in the garden.'

Yes, there are. Tripping over those same little hedges that caught Achille, by the sound of it; jocular, familiar, not a worry in the world. God almighty, it's the patrol.

'Señor Ortez,' says Zoltan, low-voiced, 'we require your silence.'

'Eh?' says Ortez.

'*Silencio*. There are men outside.'

'But that cannot be!' Achille exclaims. He tiptoes forward. He peers down; he lifts a face of horror toward Jack. 'What are they doing there?'

As if in answer to the question, the smell of tobacco smoke. Yes, of course. Where better to while away the time on patrol than in the Beguines' garden?

'Jacques,' says Zoltan, 'we are going to need another way out of here.'

This is what it is to be a discoverer: you reposition yourself continually to everything about you; but this is what it is to be Jack in particular. When he and Zoltan first encountered each other, Jack had been leading a crew of lads through a town up on that border with Poland with the streets going up in flames all about them; but Jack hunted out a way through, nonetheless – at least, until finding himself in a fight to the death with his own then captain. And who was it witnessed that fight? Torsten the Bear. Who came striding forward, clapping his hands in hefty applause: *this young one has fire, this young one deserves to live.*

This young one is here, fifteen years later. 'Follow the corridor,' says Jack. 'Get ourselves to the other side of the building. I'll find a way out from there.'

Ortez, suddenly galvanized, grabs at Hooley's arm. '*Nunca*,' he hisses. '*Nunca!*' Never!

'Señor Ortez,' Zoltan replies, 'the men below will no doubt be as ready to spill your blood as ours. It would oblige me greatly if you do as we tell you. Or, we leave you here. Up to you.'

On they go, along the corridor. Ortez, behind Jack, is in furious whispered conversation with Hooley. The baffling phrase *puta de Londres, mi puta de Londres* – London whore, my London whore – comes round again and again. The loudness of the complaint is increasing too.

Jack Fiskardo did not always have a fuse nipped short as this (but then, ruined farmland never used to trouble him either). He turns about, puts Ortez against the wall. 'Señor Ortez. *Cállate la boca*, or by God, I will gag you myself.' He looks over to Hooley. 'Did he understand that?'

'I do believe he did so, yes,' Hooley replies. Jack has the distinct impression that Hooley, too, is a man recalculating the odds. Ortez, pulling his collar straight, glares at Jack. Says Zoltan, 'There's a door.'

So there is. A sculpted Virgin spreading her cloak above, while patient angels wait to left and right. And if ever men needed the aid of heaven—

Zoltan steps forward. 'No,' says Jack, 'let me.' All his old instincts are stirring into life, and every single one of them is telling him there are warm bodies beyond that door.

He tries the handle. More darkness, but not so silent nor so deep as in the corridor. He sees windows, big as in a church, through them he sees starlight. He has his sword drawn for the first time in God knows how long, and at some lower level of his consciousness he makes a note: *that felt sticky, the blade needs an oiling*, but that is of no moment now. He holds up his hand to Zoltan. *Be ready.*

At that moment, a thin, high, human wail from the room beyond, a wail overlaid with tiny, individual sobs, and unmistakably a voice reciting an Ave Maria: *Ora pro nobis peccatoribus, nunc et in hora mortis* – Pray for us sinners now and at the hour of our death – *What*, the orrery demands, *is this?*

He steps around the door. A great high-ceilinged room, lit with candles, and then – what are they? Some monstrous form of bat? No, it is nuns, *nuns* – arms raised, headdresses bobbing like wings, and behind them beds, and women laid upon the beds, some with tiny infants in their arms.

She comes at him like a thunderclap. She even looks like a storm, a storm at midnight, a gown of billowing silk, but silk that keeps changing its colour, deepest blue to mermaid green, shot through with lines of lightning – pink like a sunrise, sulphurous yellow. The dwindle of a waist, a bodice strung about with pearly beads, beribboned as a Maypole, and above, the face – eyes ablaze, hair coiling about her naked shoulders in tendrils that look dark and red as blood. She is shaking with fury. Gown a-shimmer with it. Or (it may well be) with simple fright. And then, by God, he sees the gun, the end of its barrel flared like the mouth of a trumpet. A musketoon, the whole of it so heavy it's taking both her hands to hold it, and pointed, unwavering, straight at his face.

And her voice. Clotted with rage, nigh-on choked with it; roaring, in English, as the English do, 'You hold it *RIGHT* there! I will take the head off the shoulders of the first man to move!'

Christ all-bloody mighty, there truly is a *puta*. This is she.

QUESTION: WHAT DO you do if you find yourself facing a virago, a virago as terrified as she is furious, wielding a musketoon?

'Woah, woah, *woah*.'

He comes to a halt from the boots up: one hand out for balance, the other hefting the sword. One of those thin, thin slivers of time, with him staring at her and she at him. When he comes to look back on it, he will think, *surely there was more to it than that*, but no, there was not, just this silent percussion, like two bodies running into each other on some busy street, something that meant nothing to anyone but them: *bang*. Then the rest of the world shoves its way back in: the nuns a-whirl; the wailing, the sobs: the squeals of terror no-one has any control over whatsoever. And the musketoon, the fulcrum to this scene, if you like, its barrel shining. She lifts it higher. 'I *said*, hold it *right* there. Not one step further. Not *one*.'

Jack holds up his free hand, fingers spread. 'That's a wheel-lock.'

'I *know* what it *is*.'

'They are – temperamental.'

Yes, they are. Once a wheel-lock has been primed and wound, all you have to do is twitch. Or sneeze.

'And I *know* how it *works*. Stop talking to me like I'm some fucking *horse*.'

He raises his hand again, conciliating, placatory; lifts the scabbard for his sword; shows her he is sheathing the blade. Behind her he sees one of the nuns stoop to a woman lying there abed, take the woman's hand. There is something about the woman's shape beneath the bedcover, the animal force to her squall of noise—

But now the *puta* has spied Zoltan and Achille behind him. Her eyes come back to Jack. 'I promise you,' Jack assures her. 'No-one will harm you. You have my word.'

She looks, if anything, even more likely to pull the trigger than before. For the first time he sees how ragged she is, in spirit, nerve, everything; how creased her silks, how threadbare the ribbons holding her in place. How garish her paint, as well – the powdered face, the reddened lips, the darkness round those Pharos-like eyes. And a mark on her neck when she turns her head, a tiny thing, exact as a stencil, the shape of a crescent moon. Christ how must they appear to her – smeared with mud, faces blackened, reeking of smoke, swords drawn… How old is she? How *young* is she? 'What is this place?' he asks.

'A hospital,' she answers. 'For women.' She takes a step back, holding her skirts against her, so he can see. The woman in the bed wails anew. His interlocutor still holds the musketoon. 'For lying-in,' she says.

Of course it is. That's what's so familiar about the woman's shape, her noise. The woman is in labour.

He cannot imagine what his face is doing, but it's doing something, it must be, because watching him, the girl has at last lowered her musketoon, so it would merely blow his foot off, rather than his head. It's an enormous weapon; Ulrik would not look out of place behind it; the walnut stock ending in a knop of wood the size of a cooking apple. 'Who are you?' she demands.

Achille steps forward. 'Mam'selle,' he says. 'Achille de la Tour.'

Only Achille could conceive of this as being the moment for a formal introduction. 'You're a Frenchman?' the girl exclaims. 'The hell is a Frenchman doing here?' And then she spies Ortez. Her tone changes. Complete bewilderment. 'Felipe?'

Ah yes. *Mi puta*, of course.

'*Querida*—' Felipe begins.

'These men are with you?' She corrects herself. '*You* are with *them*?'

'*Mi amor*, I explain—'

Oh, now she's grasped it. 'They're taking you out of here, aren't they?' And up she blazes, instantaneous as a tinderbox. 'You – you *toad*, Felipe! You were *abandoning* me?'

One of the nuns has straightened herself in alarm. She calls out, 'Zuster! Zuster Albertine!'

From outside in the corridor, the racket of men in armour, the tread of booted feet. Sister Albertine – strong of feature, emphatic of movement – shouts across the room. Says the girl, 'They will try to come in here. They think the sisters welcome them. They do this to us every bloody night.'

The patrol. Now he understands. This is why the musketoon.

'They must not find you. You have to hide.'

Hide? Where?

Says she, 'Get down on the floor. Get under the beds.'

Flat to the floor, Jack watches as the girl takes up position before them, the musketoon hidden behind her back. He sees, too, Sister Albertine call to the woman in labour, and the woman press her head back into her pillow, open her mouth and roar. The babes-in-arms begin to wail anew. Under the next bed along, Achille has his head in his hands.

There is a banging on the door, a confident-sounding greeting, but Sister Albertine is more than equal to it. Jack Fiskardo spent part of his vagabond childhood in Amsterdam, within the household of one Yosha Silbergeld; Yosha's son, Cornelius, is still his oldest, dearest and most loyal friend, so while his Dutch may be dusty, it is still plenty good enough for this: No, says Sister Albertine, they cannot come in, there is a woman in childbed here, do they not hear her? Right on cue, an even louder roar from the bed, a chorus of prayers from the nuns. The wall of female noise in the room would have Gustavus Adolphus himself think twice before entering.

Sister Albertine, at the door, is shaking her head, the wings of her headdress flapping. '*Uit schaamte*,' Jack hears her declare, '*uit schaamte! Ga weg. Laat ons met rust!*' For shame, for shame! Take yourselves off. Leave us in peace!

The door is closed. The patrol goes back the way it had come, back down the corridor; laughing, offhand, the way men do. One by one, Jack and Zoltan, Achille, Hooley, Felipe Ortez, get back to their feet. 'Thank you,' says Jack to Sister Albertine. '*Hartelijk dank.*'

But Sister Albertine is opening the window, pointing down. Is making shooing motions at them with her hands. '*Gaan! Gaan!*' Is pulling one sheet from a bed, then another. Is tying the sheets together, and then about the central stone mullion. '*Gaan! Nu!*'

'What is she doing?' Achille asks, sounding baffled.

'The good sister is showing us how we get out of here,' Jack tells him, and Achille's face blenches white as the sisters' linen.

'*Nu!*' Sister Albertine insists. A quick glance down and she throws the sheets through the window. Now!

Says the girl, 'I'm coming with you.'

'*Querida!*' Ortez is aghast.

'Don't speak to me!' A snarl of fury. 'Don't even look at me! You think you're leaving me here?'

'*Es peligroso! Muy peligroso!*' Ortez appeals to Hooley: You tell her, it is too dangerous. '*Ella nos retirará!*' he adds, appealing now to Achille. She will slow us down!

She understood that. All her fury falls away. Her gaze comes round to Jack, and her eyes, in that moment, are of something finding itself cornered in a cave. 'You try to leave me here,' she says, 'I swear to God, I will scream so loud they will hear me in Brussels. Never mind the patrol, they will hear me in the fucking Coudenberg Palace.'

Damnation... 'Zoltan, we can take her with us,' Jack hears himself saying. 'What we don't have is time to stand here while they squabble.'

'No, we do not.' Zoltan is at the window, peering down. '*Zehr gut*, she comes too.'

The girl rounds on Ortez in triumph. 'There!' she says. 'Now empty your pockets.'

'*Che?*'

'Empty your pockets, Felipe! For the sisters, everything you have!'

'*Ma pero?*'

'Because they took us in, you *graceless* little turd.'

Felipe, glaring, muttering, hands over a clutch of coin. Sister Albertine cups the *puta*'s face in her hands, shaking her head, but at what? The girl's recklessness? Her nerve? The woman in labour lifts herself onto her elbows and roars anew – God damn you all, have you forgotten me?

'Mam'selle,' Achille begins. That circling barrage is returning, the wash of light outlining the roofs beyond. '*Donnez-moi vos mains—*'

'No,' says the girl. She points to Jack. 'Him. He speaks English. He can help me.'

Right. Hardly the moment to argue. 'What's your name?' Jack asks.

'Pris. Pris Holland.' Her eyes have that cornered look to them again.

'Don't be afraid.' He pushes the window open as wide as he can, holds out his hand. She edges closer, glances down over the sill; he sees her face get that sucked-in expression of one realizing this will be so much more than they had bargained for. 'Everybody ought to do this once,' Jack tells her. 'When you were younger, did you climb trees?'

She stares at him as if she thinks he has run mad.

'That's what this is like. Climbing down out of a tree.' He pats the sill, as if encouraging her to trust it. He feels ridiculously as if he were talking to Ned. 'Sit yourself here. Hold the sheet, get onto your knees, back yourself up and walk your feet down the wall. That's all there is to it.' The guns boom. He sees her flinch. 'How if I go first, and catch you?' He is already wondering how she will manage in those skirts. And with the blasted musketoon. 'And for Christ's sake, leave the bloody cannon here. You can't climb down with that.'

She puts herself up on tiptoe, brings her mouth to his ear. 'It isn't loaded,' she says, pityingly. 'It never was.'

One revelation after another with this little punk, ain't it?

Sister Albertine is making those shooing motions again. '*Mynheer! Nu! Nu!*'

Very well. Time to find out for himself what he remembers of climbing down out of trees.

What he finds out is that the last time he did this, it was before he snapped his left thigh-bone as the price for that stolen fortune. His leg reminds him with a sharp yip as it takes his weight. But there is the girl above him, already making ready to come down; Zoltan directing her how to take the knotted sheet, how to steady herself. Something impedes her. A muffled 'Pox!', and Jack is standing in a hail of pearly beads, bouncing about him; then she begins her descent. Looking up, he makes out the soles of her shoes, the ruffled edge of petticoats, the marbled midnight of her skirts, where she has them gathered up over one arm. A stockinged calf. A garter. *This is when I should turn my head*, Jack thinks, notwithstanding the difficulty then of catching her, but her waist finds his hands with no difficulty and fits as if made for them. For a moment he holds the ribbing of her stays and she herself within them, strong and warm; then he sets her on her feet, and she shakes herself back into order like a cat. Nicely done. Now Ortez. Now Achille. Now Hooley, who proves astonishingly inept at this – twisting about and finally losing his grip altogether, to land on his arse with a wail of 'Oh, Jesus, Mary and Joseph!' but the barrage has reached them, and the noise of that could cover almost anything – or at least, so one hopes. Zoltan comes down last of all. Two, three of those nodding headdresses at the window, watching his progress, and the moment Zoltan's boots touch cobblestones, the rope of sheets is being pulled back out of sight.

Zoltan dusts off his palms. 'Earn your corn, Jacques,' he says. 'Which way now?'

Where is that bobbined steeple? The girl is watching him. *Pris*, the orrery reminds him. *Pris Holland.*

Pris Holland who has the look of one who doubts any of them are up to this.

'That way,' says Jack. 'The marketplace. It's thataway.'

The guns are building to another crescendo. Zoltan gives the order: 'Go!'

They make so ill-assorted a crew you would think Fate would take pity on them for that alone. There is Achille, in his striped doublet, shepherding Ortez, in his (Ortez who makes no attempt to wait for his *puta* whatsoever, Jack notes); then Hooley, then Jack, on the lop, on his left leg, and the girl herself with her skirts still gathered up over her arm. The heels of her shoes chime on the cobbles, but the noise of the guns muffles everything. They pass houses dark and empty; they pass others with dim lines of light showing round the shutters of cellar windows. This is what life does, under siege, it burrows down, like an animal. How long before these streets too are seas of rubble—

Zoltan, ahead, has lifted a hand in warning – *Slow down.* The noise of the guns has circled past and gone on, into the night;

the street is quiet once more. Zoltan motions again – *Hide, wait.* Jack points the girl toward a doorway. Just enough light to make out her pale face, waiting, within the jungle of her hair.

Just enough to make out Zoltan, down the street, miming like a mariner the scanning of some far horizon. This way, that – then Zoltan turns and there is the flash of teeth, the famous smile that won over Ava Franka. Now he points. Now a thumbs up. The marketplace: *down there.*

Jack points toward himself, mimes a gathering-up. *You go. I'll bring them.*

He beckons the girl to come forward. Finger to his lips: *Quietly. Slowly.*

She comes forward as if she were on a tightrope. When she is near enough he points down to the marketplace to show her, whispers, 'Do you see the hornwork?' In the moonlight you can just make it out, the uneven outline of the platform, and the three figures – half-pint Luka, gallon-sized Ulrik, Thor – crouched and waiting.

Miss Holland nods her head.

'That's how we get out of here. One more circuit of the guns and we're there.'

Another nod. She is holding herself like a horse in a flat race, panniered with her skirts, ready to run. It makes him smile. 'You are a woman of spirit, Miss Holland, I'll say that for you.'

A swift, uncertain grin. It's the first time he's seen her face not blazing with fury or chilly with scorn; it makes a difference. *Oh, she IS young*, he thinks.

A shift of movement at the far end of the marketplace. Yes, Per and Jens, working a way toward them. And Zoltan moving forward as noiselessly as only a discoverer can. Wait for it, wait—

The scars across Jack's palm sing out as sharp as if they'd just been cut. A piercing shriek from up ahead, and Ortez staggers forward into the open, followed by Hooley and Achille. Ortez is holding his side like a man with a stitch; Hooley must support him; then Ortez seems to push Hooley away, and, canted over, falls toward Achille. Jack puts out his arm, holds the girl back. That shriek was loud enough to echo, and on the hornwork, one of the figures has jumped up in warning, but there's no need, they can all hear the booted feet running into the street behind them. That blasted, bloody patrol.

Now Per has reached Ortez – Ortez who is down on his knees but still seems to be reaching for Achille, to be trying to pull him close, as if he has something of the greatest urgency to impart. Hooley, standing over them, appears to be wringing his hands – but who can say, because that, when they come to look back, proves to be the last any of them can recall of Hooley whatsoever. The fiery light of the approaching barrage is coming closer, closer, is reflecting in the windows, but even so the marketplace beyond is still dark enough that if you didn't know what you were looking at, would you know there were men down there?

It seems the patrol is asking themselves the same question. Jack can make out the upward lilt of query, the irritation of their officer. Now one man, coming forward, but mighty cautious, keeping to the middle of the street. Moon-gleam on the Spaniard's helmet. He can feel, against his arm, the race of the girl's breathing. He can hear his own.

The Spaniard's step is faltering. They hear him call back, '*Nadie aqui!*' No-one here! And then from just ahead: *ting ting ting, ting ting ting. Sur le pont d'Avignon*—

A shout: '*Alla!*' There, there! The patrol, running forward. Another shout, and then a shot, but the shot must be Thor's, for one of the Spaniards drops to the ground and the rest scatter. Per is hauling Ortez, who is still doubled over, toward the hornwork, the ropes up to safety. Jack grabs the girl's hand, hauls her forward too. 'Run!' he tells her. He makes to do the same, then catches a movement out the corner of his eye—

The blade goes past so close to his head that he feels his hair move in its wake. Ah, yes. Señor Nadie Aqui. Forgotten about him.

Señor Nadie Aqui, unprepared for slicing empty air, is pivoting around. Jack's two hands, gripped together like a club, swing into the back of his neck. Señor Nadie Aqui stumbles forward. Jack hears a shout from Zoltan: 'Thor! Hold fire!' The girl skitters backwards, like you would from a pair of dogs in a fight. The Spaniard is coming at Jack again. But Señor Nadie Aqui is heavy on his feet, and has the look of a man still trying to work out what he has walked into here. His blade is thick-ridged down its centre, turned out by the dozen, unevenly weighted, Jack would swear; as he turns about, to Jack's merciless eye, the man is off-kilter too. So Jack kicks him in the knee, and down onto one leg he goes. There are swordsmen out there better than Jack Fiskardo, but this is not one of them. There are some few who have his trick of being just as lethal with left hand as with right, but this is not one of those either. As it always does in this moment, everything about Jack fades away; there is nothing but this, an enemy, in front of him, the geometry of blade and arm and feet and step, the dance of it, the explosion of movement, then the ensuing sack of skin and blood. He cannot keep his wife from death, he cannot make his youngest hale and whole; but this he can do. The thought strolls through his head: *I can just see the unholy fucken mess I am about to make of you.* He drops his shoulders, makes to draw his sword –

– and it sticks. That wondrous blade of Solingen steel, the first possession he ever looted; all those years in the attic of the Écu and now, it sticks.

Señor Nadie Aqui's face has the look of one who can't believe his luck. He swings his blade up, he makes a lunge. All Jack can do is dodge. A shot – Jack thinks from Jens – separates them for a moment, long enough for Jack to grab his old clasp-knife from his pocket, spring the blade. The caballero looks at it, and laughs. He lunges again. Jack feints sideways. He's thinking, *Get his sword-arm.* He's thinking, *Stab his sword-hand.* He's thinking a blade as heavy as the Spaniard's will shave muscle from bone like it was butter. Here it comes –

No it does not. A clang like a bell being dropped into a bucket. His assailant is on the ground, felled with one wallop from the stock of the girl's musketoon, swung into that helmet with the gusto of a woodsman swinging an axe. A Spanish bullet buries itself in the wall behind her. 'You *bastards*!' she screams. Jens is sprinting toward them; Jack all but throws the girl at him: 'Get her out of here! Get her up that wall!' And here comes the barrage again. As the street is once more lit by its glow he sees Ortez and Achille are at the scree with a rope apiece, Ulrik hauling them in like a fisherman landing a catch, and Thor, on the hornwork, is taking cartridge after cartridge from the bandolicr about his chcst. Ncvcr known a man rcload and firc as fast. But now the Spanish are coming down the street in line, firing as they go. Ulrik looks to be bellowing something to the Palatine gunners, cupping his hands about his mouth, then gesticulating with those mighty arms of his, over and over again. Jack has reached Zoltan, but as he does, he sees Zoltan reverse his pistol and hold it by the barrel, like a club. Out of bullets. This is not looking good. The two of them are like to be shot to pieces where they stand, for all that Thor or anyone else can do about it. Jack lifts his sword over his head, wallops the hilt against the cobbles, once, twice – finally it comes loose. *Right*, he thinks, readying himself. A glance across at Zoltan, also with sword drawn. *Take the fight to them.* It's all he and Zoltan can do – and then, above their heads, there streaks what, if you did not know what it was, you might almost take for a meteor; screaming like a soul in torment, trailing its tail of fire.

But Jack does know what this is; they all do. This is where they were at Stettin in Germany, seconds before that infamous bullet struck, the one the silver wolf now bears embedded in its breast: under the guns of your own side, when your gunners elevate their barrels and lob cannonballs right over your head. He has just enough time to holler to Zoltan, 'Turn your back! Cover your face!' and even as they crouch, there is the smack of impact, the pulling backwards, then they are both of them thrown forward into the rubble. The boom so close, so loud, your ears give up at once. The flood of heat and light, as from the opening behind them of a furnace; the air thick with grit, the earth resonating with the impact of thudding chunks of timber and of stone. Deafened and almost blinded, mouth full of dirt, Jack feels Zoltan push a rope into his hands, sees Zoltan mouthing, 'Go! *Go!*'

Up they go. The sky above the hornwork is red with cannon-fire. Zoltan has made it to the top already, but Jack's leg is slowing him, and there is rubble coming down beneath him in a landslide. He gets one knee, one elbow up onto the platform, pulls himself up, lies flat, hauling in the air. Turns himself over, counting heads – Zoltan, Thor, Ulrik, all on hands and knees; Jens, Per, Luka, looking stunned, as well they might. When he speaks – 'Where's Ortez? Where's Achille?' – he cannot hear himself. Zoltan is mouthing at him. Jack cups his ear. 'Hooley!' Zoltan is saying. 'Where is Hooley?'

Jack cannot remember having seen Hooley since Ortez staggered out into the open. He shakes his head. Fuck Hooley. *Where's the girl?* Then he spies her, kneeling beside Ortez. What, have the lovers made up?

He crawls across. Ortez, supported by Achille, has a faint smile upon his face. As Jack reaches him, he unclasps the hand from his side, displaying a modest bloodstain on his palm, a match to that on his fancy doublet.

'*Ah, non!*' Achille exclaims. '*Ah, non!*'

'*Verde,*' Felipe says, slowly and carefully, as the dying do. A bubble of blood on his lip. He looks up, he seems to be talking to Achille. '*Verde lagarto.*'

'Yes, my friend, yes,' Achille tells him, '*Verde lagarto*. What of it? What does it mean?'

The girl, on her knees, has taken Ortez's hand in her own. 'Felipe?' she says. 'Felipe?'

Felipe moves his gaze to her face, but as he does so his own goes strangely blank. He pants for a moment, like a dog. His head falls forward. The girl is still repeating his name, but Ortez is never going to hear it. Ortez is never going to hear anything again.

CHAPTER FOUR

The Problem of the Puta

'It shall be my study and endeavour to accomplish your intents and purposes…'

John Garfield, *The Wandring Whore*

'THIS,' SAYS ACHILLE, 'is a nightmare.' He lifts his eyes, blank with misery, to his listeners. 'What am I to tell the Cardinal? It is a catastrophe.'

He stands – he, Zoltan, Jack – within a cellar in the village of Teteringen. Or what was the village of Teteringen, but which is now home to four companies of cavalry, two of foot and a good thick slice of the staff of the quartermasters-general. The cellar itself was once home to barrels of good ale and casks of wine, all requisitioned long since, of course, but it is cool enough to function as a mortuary, so that is what it has become.

Felipe's body lies before them, on a trestle. His shirt has been lifted over his face, his pale smooth belly confronts them, complete with its tiny tear, which (the surgeon's probe confirmed) reached right down into the artery that sits behind a man's gut. Felipe bled out while hardly shedding a drop.

'*Ah, le malchanceux*,' Achille continues. 'For him to fall to a bullet, when we were so close!'

It is curious, the tear in Felipe's belly. Distinctly triangular in shape.

Zoltan puts a hand to Achille's shoulder. 'It was every man for himself. We're lucky any of us came out of that.'

'Although the watch-chime didn't help,' Jack points out. His leg aches, his hearing whines, he has one eye bright red… but then they are none of them at their best this morning. Zoltan's forehead has a blistering of scabs; Ulrik's palms are skinned; Thor's fingertips are raw from his constant reloading.

The din of Frederick Henry's cannon comes at them through the cellar walls. 'Did the surgeon find the bullet?' Jack asks. His thinking is unhelpfully slow this morning, but surely the firing began *after* Ortez ran out into the street?

'What else could it have been?' Achille demands, snappish. 'No,' he continues, sorrowfully as before, 'we are back at square one. It is a disaster. Alas, the poor Cardinal. What can I tell him?'

'At least,' says Zoltan, trying again, 'if you don't have Mercator's identity, no-one else does either. Assuming Felipe ever knew it in the first place. Ain't that so, Jack?' He waits. 'Jack?'

'Undoubtedly,' says Jack. Where had he just been, in his head? Thinking of Mirelle? No, he realizes, no, surprisingly, and for perhaps the first time, not – instead there had been something else in his thoughts, something twisty and elusive, like a loose thread. And who was the loose thread here?

All those Irish, in the service of Spain. 'What did you know of Francis Hooley?' Jack asks.

'What do you mean, know of him?'

'Just that.' He had been thinking of that moment of recalculation he had surprised on Hooley's face. Of the noise the man had made, climbing down. The girl had managed it perfectly well… What if – what if –

'He was a *servant*, Jacques,' says Achille. 'And now, poor soul, he is not even that. Why would I know anything of him?'

'You don't think,' Jack begins, 'that all this might just have been a ruse?'

'A ruse?' Achille repeats.

'You said that when Felipe wrote to you, it was before the siege began.'

Achille lifts his hands, palm up. 'And?'

'The treaty, Achille. The treaty between France and the Dutch. Could this have been no more than a means to lure you here? Into Spanish territory? Could Ortez have been no more than bait?' In Jack's head there is the image of Achille and Ortez, side by side, both in those striped doublets, hurrying down that darkened street, and there's something about it makes him restless – what was the target here? Or who?

The image fades. Achille is staring at him. 'Zoltan, did he take a blow to the head? That is ridiculous. *Impossible.*'

You said that before, thinks Jack.

'And to make matters worse, not only must I confess this failure to the Cardinal, I have to get word of it to London too. As a matter of *urgence*. Our man there, he must be warned, that all our hopes of Ortez have miscarried, and where this Mercator is concerned, we are as much in the dark as ever.' He peers at them. 'A matter of *urgence*,' Achille repeats.

'Don't look at me,' Zoltan tells him. 'I've a troop of discoverers to lead and a city to take.'

Achille transfers his gaze from Zoltan to Jack.

'Nor I,' says Jack. 'I'm an enlisted man, remember? I do as my lieutenant tells me.'

'You two are intolerable,' Achille tells them.

'Write to your man in London,' Zoltan suggests. 'Send him a cypher. We know how much you intelligencers love concocting those.'

'*Written* intelligence?' Achille sounds outraged. 'After everything we went through with the Prince-Bishop? No, my friend. Never!'

'Go to London yourself then,' says Jack. 'Forgive me, Achille, we'd miss you, but no-one else here would even notice.'

Achille shakes his head. 'There can be no contact between me and our agent in London. He is far too well placed to risk. For me to arrive on his doorstep? Heaven forbid.' He looks from one to the other. 'You have no idea how much of this goes on, have you? Spain, France, Holland, England – all of us striving and contending to know more than the next. There are enemies of enemies, there are friends of enemies, there are enemies of friends; there are those who may be either, or both at once. And tomorrow, it could all change anew. No, this wretched news must be got to London, but it must be done some other way than me. All I can do is take me back to Paris and throw myself on the Cardinal's mercy.' His shoulders slump. 'I tell you, it is a fucking *nightmare*.'

A LITTLE WAY outside Teteringen, there stand the remains of a windmill – sail-less, like a giant pepper-shaker on its tump. This is where the Dead Men have based themselves, and where Jack and Zoltan are making their way, edging past the traffic on the road: the wagons groaning on their axles, the lowing cattle, squealing pigs – the quartermasters up ahead have a welcome for all. Or would, save for some reason the line has come to a halt, and the air is thick with curses. Dutch is an excellent language for cursing: *Gods naam! De fuck!* (Extraordinary, how many languages that one word passes through unchanged.) *Wat is hier het probleem?*

The *probleem* is an ancient dobbin, pulling a brewer's wagon, who in the manner of such stolid creatures has dropped its head and nodded off to sleep. The brewer is tugging on his horse's reins, imploring it – 'Floris, Floris! Move!' But Floris is having none of it. Barely twitches an ear. In the barrels piled behind him, you can almost hear the ale souring. The barrels are lettered

TOBOR MARTLIN
HAARLEM

– way to the north, on the Dutch coast. No wonder Floris is weary.

On the seat of the wagon, a plump Dutch matron, presumably Mrs Tobor Martlin, is prodding at Floris's mighty rump with the end of her whip. She has a generously rounded face, and Jack approves of the way she is using the whip – to motivate, rather than chastise; and how she and her husband call their horse by its name. But the only effect such consideration has on Floris is to have him shake his ears, then go back to his doze. Tobor Martlin removes his hat and throws it to the ground, prancing about it like Rumpelstiltskin. Comes the bellow from up ahead, where the quartermaster awaits: 'What the bastard bloody bollocks is the hold-up here?'

'Give me a moment,' says Jack. He makes his way up the line, past the curses and gesticulations, until he gets to the Martlins' wagon. On seeing him, Tobor Martlin gives a startled jump. Ah, yes, that initial reception – never either warm or easy.

'Mind if I see what I can do?' Jack asks. Tobor steps back – as folk tend to do. A worried query floats down from Mrs Martlin. '*Vrouw, vrouw*,' Tobor tells her, soothingly. '*Wacht*.' Wife, wife. Wait.

Jack goes up to Floris's head (the size of an anvil, in itself), knuckles the star between the horse's eyes, rubs his hands together to bring up the salt on his palm, lets Floris get his taste. Goes to his pocket, brings out the candies. With some it's aniseed, with others, it's peppermint, but in Jack's experience there is not a horse yet born that wouldn't follow you right over the edge of the earth for fenugreek. Even M'sieu, at his most intractable, will mend his behaviour for one of these.

Floris's nostrils flare open, followed by his eyes. He lifts his head. '*Kom op*,' says Jack, encouragingly, holding out a candy in his palm. Floris takes a thudding step forward. The wheels squeak. The barrels knock, their contents slosh – Floris is moving. Up atop, Mrs Martlin gives a yodel of encouragement. From behind, rough applause. Jack and Tobor Martlin lead Floris, now drooling like a dog, up to the door of the quarter-master's depot. As Floris crunches through the candy, Tobor Martlin seizes Jack's hand. '*Bedankt, bedankt!*'

'*Het was niets*,' Jack tells him. It was nothing.

'Very clever,' says Zoltan, when Jack rejoins him. He points toward the mill. 'Now see what you can do about our other little problem.'

*

Ah, yes. The *puta*.

A run of stone steps gets one up the tump, and Felipe's mistress is sat to the edge of them. No mistaking the scarlet flag of her hair, even from the road. Ulrik, Per and Luka go back and forth, in and out the mill, ferrying their kit to shelter within, with Jens and Thor supervising operations, yet there she sits, unmoving, with nothing but her red hair and her tatterdemalion silks. Also, as Jack comes up, it seems to him both Thor and Jens are pointedly avoiding looking in the girl's direction. In fact, if you were being unkind, you would say they seem almost nervous of doing so. He beckons them over. 'Thor, Achille's turncoat Spaniard – it couldn't have been a shot from us that did for him, could it?'

'Not one of mine, Domini,' says Thor. 'My bullets are round.'

Good point. 'Is Monsieur de la Tour still all of an upset?' Jens asks, solicitously.

'He's all but inconsolable,' says Jack. He nods toward the girl. 'Is there some reason she's been put in quarantine?'

'She don't seem very keen on us,' says Jens. He sounds shamefaced.

'When all we did was put her under fire and get her lover killed? I wonder why.'

A silence. 'She is – she's kind of taking-looking, ain't she?' Jens comments. He sounds a little dreamy.

'She thinks she's a looker, she's mad,' Thor retorts. There is undisguised annoyance in his tone. 'Mad, as well as she's a *bitch*.'

A summons from Zoltan, from beyond the mill. Thor gives a heavy sigh. 'I ain't never going to get used to you not being in charge here, Domini,' he declares. 'It's right arsey-versey, this, the whole of it.' He stomps away.

Jack turns to Jens. 'Thor try it on with her?'

'She got a bit salty,' says Jens. He sounds apologetic.

'What did she say?'

Jens pulls a face. 'Told him to go fuck his fist.'

She did? Good for her. Even so, it's ridiculous to leave her sitting there on her own.

She glances up at his tread. She's purple under the eyes now, the way that young skin shows a night sans sleep; her tangle of hair in a knot at one shoulder. Jack sits himself down near enough for conversation, not so near as to be a threat, nods his head in greeting. Those great eyes of hers, hostile as a wildcat's.

'I am so sorry,' he says, 'for Felipe. We failed you both.'

'Oh, don't be.' She pushes her fingers into the knot of hair, undoing it, shaking it out. It reaches to her waist. It's like a live creature. Are those tendrils, or tentacles? 'Felipe and I were well on the outs before you arrived. It's why I took myself off to the sisters.' Yet even as she says it, she turns her head, as if hiding the fact that her eyes have grown wet. Jack has done the same himself, plenty of times, in the last weeks. This little punk in her carnival whim-wham – *Oh, you are not so tough*, he thinks. *You are nothing like the harpy you would appear.* Although Jens is right, she does have you staring. Every feature of her face is somehow out of balance with the next: the mouth is this bow of contempt, the nose, a bridge of disdain, the eyes would like you to drop dead. 'What did you know,' he begins, 'of Felipe's servant, this Francis Hooley?'

'Nothing.' Surprise in her voice. 'We arrived in Breda, and there he was. He knew nothing of me, either. He tried to make himself affable, but he was displeased Felipe had me with him, I could see that.'

Mystery upon mystery. He nods toward the musketoon, sat across her lap. 'You put us to the stop with a gun that wasn't even loaded.'

There's that grin again, swift as the sun between clouds. She lays her hand on the musketoon's stock. 'I found it in a cupboard,' she says. 'I suppose some traveller forgot it. I thought anything to stop those men in the damn patrol from harassing the sisters so.' Then out of that puzzle of a face, a glance as old as Cleopatra. 'I'm guessing, soldier, that in your world, everything is just as it appears. In mine, nothing is. Besides, you didn't know it wasn't loaded. Any more than I and the sisters knew you weren't about to ravish us to death.' And while he digests that: 'How is it you speak English?'

The languages were acquired in order, like the scars: English, French, Dutch, German, Swedish, scraps of Polish, of Spanish and Italian too, not to mention the salmagundi of Rotwelsch itself. After all these years he moves between these different tongues like a man walking from one room in his house to another.

'My mother was an Englishwoman,' Jack replies.

Her unblinking gaze. Jack finds he has the strangest urge to say more: my mother's name was Sally Arden; she used to make up tales for me, of how her own father was one of those pirating out of Dunkirk. She wed a Frenchman, my father, a captain of cavalry. And a man named Carlo Fantom killed them both. *It's looking into those eyes does it*, he decides, *you start blathering and can't stop.* Like a man thrown into some bottomless pool, helplessly swimming about.

'I was found in a graveyard,' she says next (like this was nothing). 'Crossbones. In Southwark. Do you know London?'

'No. But I have friends there.' Cornelius Silbergeld, for a start, trading in London under his mother's name of Vanderhoof; or Rafe Endicott, with his bookshop near St Paul's, who is another (his neighbours would be astounded to learn) from the days when the Dead Men went adventuring down the Elbe. *And to none of them have I as yet had the courage to break the news that Mirelle is gone.*

'Truly?' Her eyes widen. She tilts her head, the ringlets slide. 'What are you, here?' she asks.

Blunt as a spoon, this one. 'Nothing,' he tells her. 'A free-booter. I have no rank at all.'

That limpid gaze of hers is gone, abrupt as emptying a sink. 'Bugger,' she says.

'Why do you ask?'

'Because it has all gone to *shite* for me here, ain't it, so all there is for me is go back home and start again. Somehow or another.' The hand that had lain on the stock of her pistol now sweeps across the skirts of her gown. 'Only this is everything I have. Might I trade the pistol, do you think?'

'You want passage to London?' He gets to his feet. 'I have a way to manage that. Come with me.'

The brows lift once more. She gives him a look in which he feels every line on his face, every year, every mile, every act, every way in which he has spent his life that would appal her. There's almost a laugh. 'I think *not*.'

He is aware they are the subject of much scrutiny, he and she, from within the mill. 'Will you trust me,' he begins, 'to come with me, to Monsieur de la Tour?' *This is Mirelle*, he thinks. *This is her, wagging a finger at me: help this little one get home.* And perhaps assist Achille out of his predicament, to boot. 'Monsieur de la Tour has a message he needs taken to London. Perhaps you and he can help each other.'

Back to Teteringen. Jack is used to being stared at, but Christ, he never felt so many eyes on him as this: his companion draws attention like a magnet draws tacks. Even the Martlins, sat by the road with the remains of a picnic between them, even they point her out to each other; Mrs Martlin leaning across and whispering something in her husband's ear, something (Jack suspects) about the colour of his companion's hair. Yet the girl takes no notice of any of it. All this regard, all the stares, they break over her like water over a rock. There is only the slight curling of her lip (*the bow being drawn*, he thinks), an arch to her brow. In Prague a company of players had been a part – an unwitting part, true enough, but a part all the same – of the plan that brought about the death of the Prince-Bishop; Jack had been fascinated watching them move across their stage, as if it were the world and they its owners; here, swishing her bedraggled skirts toward Achille's tent, the girl is doing the same. It's as if all this attention is no more than tribute. The cloaks on which the Queen now deigns to tread.

They are at Achille's drum-shaped tent, the flap dropped across its door. Jack calls out, 'Achille? Are you in there?'

'I am musing,' comes the reply, 'on the utter futility of man's designs.' (The creak of a bedframe, the sound of one such man swinging his feet to the floor.) Achille appears in the doorway. The short side of his hair is sticking upward. 'What was the point of *any* of that, I ask myself? In the grand scheme of things, what possible purpose can it have served?' He looks from Jack to the girl. 'Yes?' he snaps.

'Achille,' Jack begins, 'you remember Miss Holland?'

'Pris,' the girl murmurs, stepping forward, eyes downcast. What a chameleon! Seconds before, nothing but disdain for everything about her, now all trembling vulnerability.

'Ah, my poor Mam'selle 'Olland,' Achille exclaims, taking the proffered hand and bending low. 'What trial, what tragedy this is for you, also!'

'Mam'selle Holland,' says Jack, his tone a little dry, 'is in need of passage to London. Perhaps Mam'selle Holland might undertake your commission for you?' (Mam'selle Holland murmurs acquiescence.)

'My commission?' Achille repeats.

'To apprise your London friend of your news.'

'My London friend?' Finally, the penny drops. 'Oh, *mon Dieu*, indeed!' Still holding the girl by the hand, Achille leads her forward. 'Mam'selle, please sit, sit.' He produces a stool. 'Do you – may I offer – I have wine?'

'No, nothing, sir.' Head bent, voice low. 'Only to be of service, if I may.'

'Why, yes, indeed. We shall discuss—' He glances up. 'Jacques, might I request…'

'You want me to step out?'

'If you would be so good.' Achille has already turned back to the girl. 'Mam'selle,' Jack hears him say.

He wanders back to the road. Mrs Martlin, seeing him, raises a hand in friendly acknowledgement. Well now. It seems he is made of good ideas today.

Entre nous, Achille has little experience of women. He assumes that at some point a match will be made between himself, as heir to the noble De la Tour family, and some daughter of some other house, just as noble and hopefully less impoverished; but until then, his work as an intelligencer is his everything and his all. And in this, women have a place. In fact, they often make the very best carriers in matters such as these, for no-one ever imagines they know a thing. Look at this one, for example, this little trembling doe. Whatever would become of her, if someone did not step in to assist? 'Mam'selle,' Achille begins, 'I have a friend in London—'

A sharp glance. 'Did Felipe owe him money? Because Felipe left debts bloody everywhere'

'I assure you, mam'selle, it is nothing of that sort,' says Achille. Bless the poor creature, such trivial anxieties! 'It is simply a message – very brief – to be delivered to Sir Theodore de Mayerne in St Martin's Lane. His house is the fifth, on the left hand, as one goes north. You know St Martin's Lane?'

A nod. She continues gazing up at him through her lashes. 'The smallest thing,' Achille continues, momentarily distracted. 'It is simply to say that our friend is in Hieropolis. Most sadly. And was taken there before he and I could speak.' Achille feels extraordinarily proud of himself here. Hieropolis was the place of death of Philip the Apostle. An intelligencer should always keep his messengers unwitting, if he can.

'Hieropolis,' the girl repeats, trying the word out.

'Exactly so. And if you would deliver this message for me, mam'selle, I would be honoured to pay you for your service. Certainly enough for passage across *la Manche*.'

She hesitates. 'Your passage and more.' Achille bends his head to hers. 'Five English sovereigns,' he says, pronouncing the words with grave respect.

He sees a start run through her. She lifts her head. 'Five sovereigns,' she repeats. 'For nothing more than to take a message to London for you.'

Achille inclines his head.

'And your friend must step away while we converse.' She meets his gaze with what one can only call masculine frankness. 'Monsieur Achille,' she says, 'I don't know what it was Felipe got himself entangled in with you, but Felipe was an idiot. I'm not. This is some sort of black work, ain't it?'

Achille is speechless.

'And I need not tell you, Monsieur, how dangerous a business that is to engage oneself in.' She puts her head back, as if assessing him. 'So if I am to take this message to London for you, Monsieur, I will do so for ten of those yellow boys. Not five. Agree to that, and we have a deal.'

A cough outside. '*Venez*,' Achille croaks. Ah, thank God, it is Jacques. Who looks from one of them to the other, as well he might.

'You quite done here? Because if you are, I've a means to get Miss Holland to the coast.'

THERE'S ALMOST A farewell party to see her off – he, Achille and Zoltan, and then Jens, pushing a knotted bundle into the girl's hands, where she sits, feet adangle, at the back of the Martlins' wagon. Jens unknots the bundle to show her: look – these are pancakes, here is cheese – and receives for it a pretty-enough thank you to put that dreamy look back on his face.

'Haarlem,' says Zoltan, with longing.

'It is welcome to her,' Achille snaps. 'What has happened to the fabled English rose? What is it they are breeding in London these days?'

From somewhere, the girl has acquired a cloak. Perhaps she indeed traded for it, as it seems the musketoon is gone. She sits wrapped within it, nose sunk in the curl of its collar. That hair of hers a beacon still.

'Hello, soldier,' she says, as Jack comes up.

'Fare ye well, Miss Holland,' he tells her. 'You will be in London in a week. I think you will do far better there than here. *Bon voyage. Bonne chance.*'

He lifts his hand. She looks at it, then at him, raises an eyebrow.

Ah. He still wears his gloves.

Jack Fiskardo removes one glove and tries again, and this time her hand emerges from the cloak and she lays her fingers across his. 'Mam'selle,' he says, and bows his head. A shout from Tobor Martlin, Floris strains forward, the wheels crunch.

Pris Holland lifts her nose from her cloak. 'And you should not be here either,' she says. 'You should be home with your sons.'

It's only later that the strangeness of it hits him. Lying wrapped in his blanket in that ruined mill, letting the thoughts come and go, drifting in that place he goes to, when sleep refuses to join him, only then does he find himself pondering, *How the devil did she know?*

Every war will show you things that are beyond belief. Cruelties that should be the work of demons, not of men. The bullet that should kill you, but does not. The man – the Roma – who held your sixteen-year-old hand, turned his blind eyes to your face and somehow put the picture in your head of the room full of gold, waiting for you at the end of all the years to come; and the old Roma woman, hobbling through the world with her equally ancient sisters, who warned you of the long and wanton road that lay ahead; yes, them – there had been something about the girl put him in mind of them. Something about her eyes. The moment of almost vertigo that returning her gaze seemed to induce.

And then he remembers. Jens, handing over the packet of food. Ever-helpful, ever-friendly Jens; that's how she knew. Jens told her. Simple as that.

You idiot. Jens, of course.

To be honest, it's almost a disappointment.

THE FRIENDS (IRELAND) of enemies (Spain). The things you can't believe are true. Such as a man you might have thought had been blown to rags, making his way along this humble little street behind the Coudenberg Palace in Brussels. Walking with the sort of briskness that suggests displeasure, if not outright anger. He turns to look about him, checking left and right, before opening the chapel door.

Good Lord. Francis Hooley.

In he goes. Even before the echo of the door closing behind him has died away, Hooley is raising his voice to address the man waiting for him, there in the front-most pew.

'Do you lose your touch, Captain?'

See this second man turn his head. A little top-heavy in his build, this one, especially now that he is, for the times, well into middle age. Still lardy-white as ever, however, still with those unsettling red-brown eyes, almost dead, save for the flicker of anger in them, at being so upbraided. Carlo Fantom. For anyone who knows the man, the fact that he still lives and breathes would be no surprise at all.

'And in God's house,' Hooley continues, striding forward, 'do you not rcmovc your hat?'

The hat is removed. The damage to Fantom's face is also older now, but it is evident, even so: the melted-looking ear, the shine of the burn across his cheek. As if licked by the flames of hell and then rejected, even by they.

'Your reputation, Captain, is that of a man who leaves no loose ends,' Hooley begins. Carlo makes as if to speak; Hooley forestalls him, holding up a hand, while with the other he crosses himself, for a moment bows his head. That done, he continues. 'Ortez is dead, yet De la Tour, even as I speak, is making his way back to Paris. You killed the wrong man, Captain.'

'You tell me,' Carlo begins, 'a striped doublet. You tell me, a lovelock. You tell me, wait in the marketplace.' The heat in his eyes increases. 'You do *not* tell me this De la Tour, he will have men with him. Nor that there will be a patrol.' Fantom lifts a hand, makes a bird-beak with finger and thumb. His fingers are small and pointed, almost as if they have been sharpened. 'This is not the way such business should be done, Mr Hooley. It makes for confusion. It is not – exact.'

'Achille de la Tour was our target,' says Hooley, 'Achille de la Tour, and the chance to show Richelieu he makes treaties with the Dutch at his peril. Ortez and his nonsense about Mercator, he was no more than bait for the hook.'

'Mr Hooley,' says Carlo, in placatory tone, 'consider this. Your dupe, your gull, your Spanish puppy, indeed, he is no more, boohoo, and your Frenchman, he goes back to Paris, but he goes back knowing no more than he did.' A smile; at least a baring of the teeth. 'There was time for only one, Mr Hooley. I make the right choice, I think.'

'Do you so?' says Hooley.

Carlo Fantom leans back, adjusting the angle of the panzerstecher at his hip – too long for a dagger, too short for a sword, and with its triangular blade capable of piercing just about anything, like a skewer. 'I do.' Another of those eerie smiles.

Hooley notes the leaning back. He notes the adjustment of the blade. 'Don't play your tricks on me, Captain,' says Hooley, slowly, carefully. 'You need me far more than I you.' He sees his point is taken. 'Tell me – what does the phrase *verde largato* suggest to you?'

Carlo shrugs.

'It means "green lizard". Something Felipe said to our Frenchman. He said it in extremis; he seemed most anxious to get the message across.'

Carlo pulls a face. 'A tavern? In London, perhaps?' As he speaks, he rubs the thumb of one hand against the palm of the other. 'Who were those men De la Tour had with him?'

'Rheumaticks?' Hooley enquires, sounding kindly. 'We none of us grow younger, Captain.' He stands. 'Those men of De la Tour's, they were hirelings. Freebooters. Exactly as you are to me.' He takes a bag of coin from his pocket, places it on the seat of the pew. 'Yours,' he says. 'And you owe me for my tolerance of your grievous error, this time around. You remember that.'

Carlo picks up the bag of coin, puts it in the palm of his hand with something of the same care as one placing a dummy in the mouth of an infant. 'I miss my time as a soldier,' he says, with feeling. 'Life was simpler then.'

'There will be other wars, Captain, you may be sure of that.'

'I hear talk of war in your England. Rebellion in Scotland, against the stupid English King. Maybe I mend my fortune there.'

'Not my England, Captain,' Hooley informs him, evenly. 'And the stupid English King? He too is a Scot. The time may come for me to send you into England, it may indeed, but if I do, you will be better briefed than that.'

Carlo gives a shrug. In front of him, suspended above the altar, a man hangs from nails driven through his wrists, feet crossed, blood dribbling down his face – a death that, for the simple, is supposed to be the worst there ever was. 'God's will be done,' says Carlo, baring his teeth at it.

Says Hooley, 'I would not be so quick to mock, if I were you.' A pause. Francis Hooley, confidential agent to the Spanish court, thins his lips. 'Felipe Ortez,' he repeats, as if to himself.

'What of him?'

'Ach, no matter,' Hooley replies. 'A foolish notion. I was wondering how it would be if Ortez did know something after all.'

CHAPTER FIVE

Home Again, Home Again

'Salute from a hundred paces off that woman who hath red hair…'

Diego Howell, *A New English Grammar*

BREDA TO HAARLEM, three days at Floris's steady plod. We will need some means to while away the journey. Let me tell you a little of Pris Holland.

To begin: one of her earliest memories. Imagine, if you will, a four-year-old Pris, at play in the garden of Holland's Leaguer – the infamous Holland's Leaguer, but at four years old, who knows or cares? It is Sunday, the Lord's Day, and Southwark is as peaceable as Southwark knows how to be. No noise from further along the Bankside of the baiting of bull or of bear; no yells for business from the watermen at Paris Garden's Wharf; the bells of St Mary Overie and of St Olave's are all that disturbs the shimmering air. It would amaze the patrons of the Leaguer, if they were ever to know how many children live within it, yet so they do, and here are two of them, carefully hidden amongst the greenery along the bank of the moat: Miss Pris and a playmate, Little Nan. Strewn about them on the grass, tiny pots and bottles: Indian kohl, Egyptian green, miniature vials of cochineal from the coast of Mexico; all purloined from dressing-tables and cosmetic boxes within the Leaguer itself, and evidence of the kind of childhood larceny that would see any other culprit locked in the cellar – but no-one ever punishes Miss Pris. Here she is, rose-coloured taffeta over her knees, coppery ringlets piled on her head, spangled collar raised on high, painting Little Nan's face to look like a lady. It is her first attempt at such, and Little Nan, who is dressed in boiled white linen and who waddles devotedly after Pris all day long like a small white puppy, now greets the world with cheeks zebra-striped with kohl and a mouth like she had been eating beets.

And a man had appeared on the opposite bank, a man with his breeches flapping open and something sticking out of them that he held grasped in his hand. Pris had stared at him, much less interested in what the man might be doing than by the almighty roiling she saw going on in the man's head, like a stew of live serpents.

They were there for less than a moment. Pris blinked; by the end of the blink the serpents were gone, and there was the man and his hat and the something sticking out his breeches as before. It never occurred to her that the snakes might not be real, or that Little Nan would not have seen them too. All Pris knew was that there they were, all spitting and hissing in her direction, and that she did not care for them. So she picked up a bottle of cochineal and hurled it with all the might in her four-year-old arm. Good shot. The man gave a yell, then he cursed the pair of them, as godless poxy crossbit pugs who would die as their mothers had done.

Little Nan of course at once burst into tears. Not an hour later, Little Nan went quiet, then waxy pale; her head fell forward on her breast; she closed her eyes, set up a constant fretful moaning, and by sunset Little Nan was gone.

Two: Losing Little Nan, dopey wee grub that she was, cast something of a pall over the Leaguer, so come September, with the same sharp distemper that had sent Little Nan to her maker still stalking Southwark's streets, Bess Holland took her household off to the open fields of Cambridge, for Stourbridge Fair. Holland's Leaguer needed new linens (no-one will pay to fuck in a bed where the linen is holed, or not at the Leaguer's prices, that's for sure); it needed new piss-pots and warming pans; so off they all went: Bess and Abi, the girls and their babbies, old Spikenard for muscle, and that bright-eyed limb of Satan, nephew Aaron too. Ah, but while you may leave London, London never leaves you. In amongst the excitements of jugglers and tightrope-walkers and roast goose for sale by the slice, Miss Pris dropped Aaron's hand, exactly as she had been told *never* to do, and wandered off; and a man named Tucker Turnbull – a braggart, a bangster, one of those who made his living under the Skinners' table – threw a sack over Pris's head, right over her octopus of ringlets, and made to carry her off. And had it not been for a Cambridgeshire farmer and his family, who spied this wriggling, screaming, sackful hoisted to Tucker's shoulder, this story might have ended very differently indeed.

Three: and this time it wasn't a Puritan nor a Skinner broke the world apart, it was the London apprentices, who chose Shrove Tuesday 1631 to riot over London's bridge and down into Southwark. The London apprentices lived miserable lives of servitude and want; riot was their only pleasure and they indulged it every chance they got: breaking windows, kicking in alehouse doors, hauling prisoners out of the stocks, and beating to within an inch of their life anyone they decided had a Papistical look to them. And on this particular Shrove Tuesday, plunging through the moat of Holland's Leaguer (this place that would in any otherwise have been as much out their reach as was the moon), swarming across its garden, and surrounding its spectacular dovecote, lofted on its pole. Of course Holland's Leaguer had doves, the birds of Aphrodite, it had coo-ers and tumblers and pouting fantails, all as pretty as if folded out of marbled paper, but the apprentices didn't care. The apprentices rocked the pole back and forth until it rose from the ground and brought the dovecote down with it, then they began seizing the doves and wringing their necks.

The doves were Aunt Abi's particular care; she would go out in the evening and coo for them and fret till they were all safe home, which was but one of the things the girls of Holland's Leaguer mocked her for, but not Pris. Pris spent more time with Abi than she did any other living soul: Abi dressed her, sang her to sleep; taught her the ABC; told her over and over how she was the cleverest, beautifulest child who ever lived; and Pris, now eleven, understood in turn that for all Abi's fears and flutterings, for all the sorrows of her past (including trying to make away with herself in the river, forsooth), the instinct of love burned as fierce in Abi as a lamp in a temple; and that this should be respected, not have the life wrung out of it and be stomped into the mud. So never mind that the women of the Leaguer had all been told to hunker down indoors, to wait it out as they had done before; when Pris heard Abi's wail of horror, and saw what the 'prentice boys were doing, she tore out of the door and across the garden, and straight into the neckerchiefed, hobnailed mob. The swarm of apprentices parted before her and she found herself confronting their leader, a thick-bodied lad whose uneven beard was garnished with pimples, and who stood there goggling at her, limp of arm. Pris felt her own serpents rise and hiss; she lifted one hand and told the pimply one, with awful earnestness, 'I will kill you.' Only at that moment Walter Spikenard came thumping up behind her, and Miguel Domingo and the watermen burst into the garden from the Wharf and laid about the 'prentices with their oars; otherwise, God knows what might have ensued.

What did ensue, in fact, after the riots of '31, was the closing-up of Holland's Leaguer altogether. The authorities stepped in; the Leaguer was denounced as a place of perpetual disorder and notorious ill-repute; the soldiers of the London Trained Bands were sent to turn the women out; and despite all Bess's girls did to defy them (emptying their chamber-pots over the soldiers as they massed on the drawbridge, hurling their bloodied napkins with their monthly soil at them, even raising the drawbridge and tipping the soldiers into the moat), within a year, the famous Holland's Leaguer was no more.

Yet it is certain, in truth it is spoken,
That Holland's Leaguer up lately is broken

as the song went. The Leaguer's memory even inspired a play, a most excellent comedy, so its dramatist called it, written in the Leaguer's honour that very year. Meanwhile the girls shared 'emselves round the other brothels on Bankside – the Castle, the Antelope, the Lion, the Heart – and Bess Holland went into retirement, down in Chelsea, taking Pris and Abi with her. Nothing lasts. 'There is a reason to everything,' Aunt Abi told

Pris, consolingly. 'There is a reason you was left in Crossbones; there is a reason we was there at just the time to find you. Providence, my sweetheart. No matter what twists and turns along the way, there is a path for us all.'

Yes, I know, the adult Pris might now reply. *That's exactly the problem, ain't it? What if one wants to make a path for one's self? Is that too much to ask?*

There, do you see how sandy the road has become? And how huge the clouds – so enormous you would think you must surely hear them as they sail by overhead. And that vast block on the horizon, which Mrs Martlin is now pointing out to you? That is St Bavo's church. Haarlem – we've arrived!

Haarlem too was once besieged, but that was sixty years ago. What Haarlem is about these days is the making of money – from the linen bleaching in its fields, the silk being woven on its looms and, increasingly, from the skills of its plantsmen. And plantswomen. Haarlem is not especially bothered if you wear skirts or breeches, to be honest, nor does it care overmuch if your Bible is that printed in Geneva or if, in private, you still get down on your knees to the Virgin; it can't afford to be distracted by such petty considerations as that. The salt-laden North Sea, which even now is quietly eating away the glass in St Bavo's windows, might overwhelm the city any time it likes, as Haarlem knows only too well, so in the business of business, there is never a moment to lose. Leisure is forced upon you; as here, as now, waiting in the front room of the Swan, with a glass of ale, spiced with ginger and caraway, in your hands. Ava Franka lifts her glass and finds in her line of sight a girl, sat at the window, twisted in her seat, looking out over the quayside.

Wie is dat? she asks the landlady, *sotto voce*. The woman shrugs. *Geen idee.* No idea. But she is English.

– She is?

When the girl moves, the play of colour across the front of her skirts is mesmerizing. Three things every citizen of Haarlem knows – good beer, fine linen and silks. The peacock silk gleaming and glimmering over the girl's legs comes only from Milan, and costs a veritable fortune. Yet the cloak the girl wears is old and rough and stained, and the girl herself needs some attention too – disordered hair, and so pale she almost seems to glow.

And she pays in gold, the landlady adds. (She dips her hand below the counter, comes out holding a coin, revealing it to Ava like a magician revealing some sleight of hand.) We could hardly make change for her. In fact, we were a stuiver short. But we had opened up for her, so she said to keep it.

Indeed? Ava asks. She drains her glass. But what is she doing here?

– The same as you, comes the answer. Waiting for the *Guid Marie* to take her on to London.

Here she comes, the *Guid Marie*, pilot at her prow, the currents and contrary winds across the dunes of Haarlem being almost as unpredictable as those of the Thames. As the first of Haarlem's defiant little windmills comes in sight, as the bulk of St Bavo's lumbers up, her captain, at the pilot's shoulder, lets out his breath. Another crossing, safe accomplished. No small thing. Out there, beyond the deepwater cut that is Haarlem's access to the open sea, all the way up and down this coastline is the hunting ground of the infamous Dunkirkers.

You can call the Dunkirkers what you like – privateers, pirates, rovers, raiders – they won't care. You can even call them traitors, in that so many of them are outfitted and paid by Spain.

They prey on fishing boats, laden with silver herring; they harass merchantmen; the boldest will set off after Dutch East Indiamen too, can be seen harrying them across the horizon like dogs running after a bull. They sneak their loot – barrels of herring, of tobacco, sacks of spices, casks of brandy, rolls of cloth – ashore by moonlight, wherever they please. They ferry supplies to Spanish galleons out at sea; they raid the vessels of the Dutch, the French, the English, the Danes, the Balts, without compunction. It is supposed to be a mark of shame, to be a Dunkirker. But –

But, the sea is the sea. Those who brave it share an understanding of each other at least as strong as any loyalty to some power on land. If you capture a Dunkirker, you can drown its crew, as according to Dutch law you are bid, or you can set them off on some handy sandbank, where they may wade ashore. If they later find themselves hot on your tail, it might be they will fall off a little, let you get away. If you criss-cross the North Sea often enough, you may find it's worth paying them off altogether, in which case those who would otherwise pursue you become almost an escort, until Margate comes in sight – Margate, the Isles of Sheppey, and the great jelly-bag of the mouth of the Thames. Of course you need to be a particular kind of mariner to square such an arrangement with your conscience, let alone to have the nerve, the reputation, to put it so regularly to the test. Before Dame Fortune found you, perhaps you were one of these pirates, these privateers, these smugglers yourself.

Meet Mungo Sant.

He's rather greyer these days, is Sant, than when he too sailed as a privateer, even more bowlegged, but in compensation he wears gold on all eight fingers and boots of such fine Cordovan leather that as he hops from gangplank to Haarlem quayside, they utter not a squeak. As always his first act, come safe to shore, is to go up to the prow of the *Guid Marie*, remove his hat and sweep her salt-stained, sea-cracked, dark-as-bog-oak figurehead a bow. However hideous she may be, she has preserved Sant through Baltic storms and mid-Atlantic hurricanoes; and borne him safely down the Elbe and then back up it, with a stolen fortune hidden in her hold, what's more. 'Yon's the only woman,' Sant is fond of telling his crew, 'ye'll find aboard mah boat wi' mah blessing on her.'

All the same, crewmen must be paid. There stands his passenger, proud as a figurehead herself, glossy mink framing her face. There waits her carter, with his hat tied down over his ears; there stands the cart, with its usual peculiar cargo – bell-jars hiding hints of green; crates like those in which you'd transport wine bottles, but with canes poking up from them rather than bottle-necks; box after box of seed packets, filed like correspondence; and then one single smaller crate, bearing the sternly lettered warning:

VENENUM

Poison. 'I take that,' the passenger announces, picking the crate up as Sant's first mate approaches. 'Our little friend in there, one touch of her would haf you seeing horrors such as you would not *belief*.'

'Get yersel' aboard, Madame Franka,' Sant tells her. 'You know the way.' It's one of Sant's private pleasures, watching his passenger stride her way up his gangplank, like an admiral going aboard a flagship. But this time, as she comes up to him, she pushes back that mink-lined hood and says, 'You haf one more, this trip.'

Well, well. So he has.

She comes forward hesitantly, this second passenger, holding her over-long cloak about her with one hand, keeping the hair from her face with the other. By God, Sant has not seen hair that red since he was a boy on the streets of Dundee. It disposes him rather better toward this unexpected extra than might otherwise be the case. 'Are ye looking for passage over, lassie?' he calls out.

'I am,' she calls back. 'For passage to London.'

English. No sign of any baggage. Nor of a companion. 'Do ye travel solo?'

'I do,' comes the answer. 'But I can pay.' She comes nearer. The wind makes her cloak beat like a sail. Sant sees a flash of silk. 'I thought if your boat was safe for one woman travelling alone, it might be safe for two.'

Sant's passenger – his regular passenger – gives a laugh. 'The beds are hard like rock, the food inedible, the cabins so small you can keep the door closed with your foot. But yes, you will be safe.' She jiggles the crate into position against her hip and, freeing one hand, extends it. 'Ava Franka,' she says. 'Vat do they call you?'

The girl comes forward further still, wrapping her hair into a coil against her neck. Pale as the moon. Shadows like thumb-prints under her eyes. She says, 'They call me Pris.'

Those who have never been to sea, thinks Ava Franka, as she sits in her cabin on the *Guid Marie*, listening to the North Sea thump along the keel, to the deck creak above her, the squeak of the rigging and the hollerings of the crew, they would not believe how noisy a business it can be. Nor how uncomfortable, as the sea tips your cot on its ropes first one way, then the other. Ava has surprised herself with her excellence as a sailor, but this crossing might test even her, and it sounds as if the girl in the cabin next door – *Jesu*, it sounds as if it might finish the girl off altogether. Above the squeaks and thumps and groans, even above all that, she can hear the girl retch. What can so young and tender a creature be doing travelling on her own?

Ava waits a moment more, then one especially brutal thump has her on her feet, doing that arms-outstretched, stilt-walker lurch from one solid vertical to the next. She swings herself out from her own cabin door, steadies herself at that of the girl's, waits for a lull between the swells, and raps upon it. The door swings open on its own. There lies the girl, on her cot, hidden under that great cloak of hers, skirts spilling down to the floor; no more of her face visible than the eyes – wet with misery, dark with fright.

Ava takes a small silver flask from the pocket tied about her waist, and waves it encouragingly. The only response the girl makes is to cover her mouth.

'Come,' says Ava, going forward, slipping one sinewy arm under the girl's shoulder. 'We will go up to the deck. Fresh air. Also, the tipping about – it is so much less troublesome when you are on top of it. Trust me. Come!'

Above the figurehead of the *Guid Marie*, where the only thing between you and the horizon is her bowsprit, there is a nest of coiled ropes. You may sit on one, and rest your feet upon another, and with petticoats to cushion you, it is about as comfortable a place to sit as you are like to find on deck. Also, the tipping of the sea is indeed less troublesome up here; also the sea itself, now they are properly out in it, has quietened down, and the wind has dropped, as it so often does, come sunset; and there is the sunset itself to calm you even further. Fresh air has put a little pink back into the girl's cheeks – fresh air, or the heat of the good Dutch genever in Ava's flask – and she has even induced the girl to eat a little nuncheon of the undemanding sort will cause no trouble later. Hard rusk, sweet raisins, a handful of nuts. 'You must keep your belly just a little full at sea,' Ava assures her. 'Not too much, but enough to give it something else to think on.'

'Thank you,' says the girl. A moody glance to the horizon. 'I hate crossing water.'

'What brought you here in the first place?' Ava asks. Whatever the story might be, she is longing to hear it.

The girl takes another sip of the flask before handing it back. 'Because I listened to my heart and not my head.' A weary sigh. 'There was a man. Well, a boy, really. We eloped. Or we sort of eloped. I was so sure we would be wed,' she continues, mournfully. 'I suppose I forgot to check he was of the same mind.' She turns to Ava. 'But isn't that what you are meant to do, if a woman consents to give up all she knows and to run away with you? Instead he just grew peevish.'

Ah. Ava might have guessed it would be something like that. 'And he abandoned you?'

'No,' says Pris. Another sigh. 'Well, yes, he did, but then he died. He had himself caught up in something or other, and it was the end of him.' A moody picking at a stain on her skirts. 'I knew it would come to naught.' She taps at her forehead. 'I knew so early. Here told me so, over and over again. Only here –' (and the girl puts a hand to her breast) '– begged me to believe otherwise. But we always know, don't we? Even if we tell ourselves we don't.'

Ah, so true. They stare in silence at the evening star. 'Do you ever vunder,' Ava says at length, 'vot it is the gods are at? Do you?'

'All the time,' says Pris. 'How is it that you know this ship? This Captain Salt?'

'Sant,' Ava corrects her. 'It is my business, do you see? I am plantsvoman. Bulbs and seedlings. The English are all *mad* for gardens, even madder than the French, so I grow my stock in Haarlem and then ve must ship it across. Sant is my shipping man.'

A little cough. Sant is also the man who sailed Ava and her brother and her father away up the Elbe, away from the clutches of the Prince-Bishop of Prague, in company with a band of Swedish discoverers and their captain, one Jack Fiskardo, and a fortune in stolen gold. 'Of course,' Ava continues, 'it is not me who ordinarily accompanies, but ve haf one special London customer, and he vaits for this little plant – Moon-flower, it is called, or Angel's Trumpet, very special, but so dangerous, *mein Gott*. And my partner – my voman partner – she is about to bring forth another baby, and my other partner –' A huff of displeasure. Ava too takes a sip from the flask. ' – my other partner, he and I are no longer… as we were.'

'You were abandoned too?'

A snort of contempt. 'No, I throw him out.'

Pris stares at her. There is a hint, in the stare, of admiration. 'Why? What did he do?'

'He *lies* to me.' There, now Ava's story must be told as well. 'Do you hear of this tulip business? Everybody buying tulips. Tulip, tulip, everywhere. Crazy prices. Like the bulbs were *diamonds*. I said, we do not do this. I said, this is madness, it will all come crashing down. But my man and my brother Otto, they think they are clever. They think they are more clever than anyone.'

'They bought tulips?'

'*Worse*,' says Ava, with heat. 'They buy the seeds. Not bulbs, the tulip *seeds*. Six hundred guilders' worth of these tiny, stupid little tulip *seeds*. You know how long it takes a tulip seed to grow into a bulb? Ten years. TEN! And now of course the market goes phut, no-one vants even to *see* a damn tulip again, and my six hundred guilders is all in little trays in the cellar, in the dark.' A sigh. 'Even then, I will never get six hundred back. I tell him, *go*! He is soldier. I tell him, *go back to war*! Now, I do not know where he is.' Ava fixes her eyes upon the horizon and sniffs. 'I do not even know if he is still alive.'

Pris places her hand on Ava's arm. She waits a moment, then she says, 'I am sure he is alive. I am sure you will see him again.'

'Well,' says Ava, chasing a fingertip across her cheek, 'so I hope. He is very *beau*. But he is young – younger than me – so he is also very *stupid*. He thinks he will show me, this way, that he is in charge. *Eeedeot*.' A sniff. 'I was very angry.'

'And you feel bad for that?' Pris suggests. She has turned to face Ava, widened her eyes.

'Yes, I do,' Ava admits. 'Very bad.'

'And that is why you are being so kind to me, perhaps? To make up for it?'

Ava draws her head back, narrows her gaze. 'Hah,' she says. 'You are one of those with sharp wits, yes?'

'So I'm told,' Pris replies. Then she says, 'I think the gods take note of kindness. I am sure they will bring your man back to you.'

A moment's silence. 'You see, this is the problem,' says Ava. 'We get our wits and our good thinking so much younger than our men.'

'Well,' says Pris. 'We have more need of them. Not so?'

THOSE BRISK NORTH Sea winds, if they let you cross at all, they do it speedily. Two days more (salt-stained and much in need of fresh linen), and they are at the mouth of the Thames, waiting for the tide; the day after that, riding at anchor off Blackwall. Ava's cargo is unloaded and ferried to the shore, and a wagoner is found to take her, and it, and Pris, to London Bridge.

It seems brutal, to Ava, to leave the girl there on her own, amongst the jostling crowds. 'I will stay with friends,' Ava tells her. 'The Endicotts. He is a bookseller, they haf a house in Coleman Street. By your Guildhall.' She has had the wagoner halt at New Hythe, just along from Pudding Lane, and just above the bridge. 'Are you *sure* you haf a place to go?' The wrinkles between Ava's brows are pleated like a fan.

'I do,' says Pris. 'And friends, myself.' *And family*, she thinks. A smile, to put her companion's mind at rest. 'Also, I am a great deal better at looking out for myself than I appear.'

'Yes,' says Ava. 'This is vot I fear.' She holds out her hand. '*Tot ziens, juffrouw Pris.* Take care of yourself, yes?'

Home again, home again, jiggety-jig.

There before her, London Bridge.

Home. Pris reaches out a hand, places it on the stone of the parapet. Oh, the grind of the waterwheels under the bridge, the burr of their vibration through the stone. Oh, to hear folk speaking English once again. Oh, the coal-smoke stink of the city, and oh, the river, like beaten metal, sunlight in its hammer-marks; and the scream of gulls and the cries of the street-sellers, London's music – *Hot codlings, hot! Old doublets, old and good! Sweet milk for little babes! Sweet milk for all!*

For an instant, she lets herself drift; and there, it happens, as it has done so many times before: there is the world as it is, as it appears to everyone else, then there it is with this overlay that no-one seems to see but Pris herself. That comfortable housewife, for example, standing with a basket over her arm, tallying her purchases, while all the while there is a sort of miniature of the woman herself, stamping back and forth across her brow, shouting, *It's not enough! It's never enough!* And there, the couple in their carriage, which has come to a halt, and the man tells the woman to cease looking out the window, put up the slide, and the cloud that passes across the woman's face, it is as if the carriage fills with fog… And there, that old man, so mild of feature and so rheumy of eye, in old-fashioned breeches like unstuffed cushions, and what does he see as he gazes out over the water? Is it the many boats? Is it the boys there larking in the shallows? Or is it one figure, falling, falling, like Icarus, lost so long ago but falling still, down into the rush of muddy blue—

Pris gives herself a shake. At the far end of the bridge, the tower of Southwark's cathedral sticks up like some great Elizabethan salt – *Enough of this*, she tells herself. *What you need now, girl, is a plan.* The world as it is will present her with troubles enough, God knows. Out into it she goes, joining the rivulets of pedestrians nudging their way around the carts and carriages; dodging the urchins who live and sleep upon the bridge, poor little sods; avoiding the rats that scamper in the gutters – everything pushing and shoving and striving against everything else. Of course you are meant to pass over the bridge to Southwark on the right, and come up into the City on the left, but that is such a quaint idea, and some of the carriages are too wide, while all contest their right of way, and in any case, when did Londoners ever take notice of rules such as that?

Pris has hardly gone ten yards when she feels a hand laid on her arm. She spins about, ready to slap.

A fly-looking lad, very fly, in his suit of mulberry stuff with its turned-up collar and cloak, and his hat with its pheasant feathers pinned to the side. Grey eyed. Curls upon his forehead. He is smiling broadly. ''Ullo, little sis,' he says.

Aaron leads her down the stairs to where the watermen tie up beside the bridge; Miguel Domingo hands her to her place in his wherry and waits as Aaron Holland takes his seat beside her, making sure, first of all, that there are no spots of wet upon it to spoil his velvet. Miguel, Pris sees, has that same expression on his face as ever, as if he is simply waiting for the world to catch up with him. 'How goes it, Miguel?' she asks, in greeting.

Grave as a magus. 'Miss Pris,' Miguel replies. 'Welcome home.'

Miguel Domingo's wherry is one of those with fancy woodwork behind the passenger's seat that the weary may lean back upon. Pris does so now. But then one of those puckish swells at which the Thames excels lifts the nose of the rowboat just that bit higher than before and has it fall back with a splash, and Pris seizes the gunwale with one hand and clutches at Aaron with the other.

'Miss Pris,' says Miguel, 'I never lost a passenger yet. I am not about to start with you.'

'No,' says Pris, white-faced all the same. An attempt at swallowing her fright. 'How did you know to look for me?' she asks, turning to Aaron.

'Oh, we'd our spies out. We figured as either you'd write to tell us you was rich and wed, or you'd be coming home with your tail between your legs. When the one didn't happen, Miguel and I, we started watching for the other. We had eyes on Gravesend, in Blackwall… Even had that old bastard Josh Arden watching on the Lea. We been watching for you for *weeks*,' says Aaron. He peers into her face, as if inventorying every tangle in her hair, every sour thread in the linen under her arms, every inch, around her ankles, of her draggled hem. 'Christ, sis,' he says cheerily, as brothers will, 'you ain't half out your looks. Tail well between your legs, I'd say.' An even sharper study of her. What Aaron and everyone else will be waiting for, as Pris knows full well, is to hear if there is still a maidenhead tucked underneath that tail.

Let them wait. 'Is she –' says Pris (she means Bess; there is only ever one *she*, for any member of the Holland family), '– is she very angry with me?'

'I've seen her worse,' says Aaron.

'Truly?'

'*No*,' says Aaron, rounding his eyes at her in disbelief that she might have thought otherwise.

On they go. The prow lifts, the oars groan against the tholes. Blackfriars is to the right, which means that Holland's Leaguer itself is to the left – Holland's Leaguer with its garden now as overgrown as Sleeping Beauty's, and planks nailed across its windows. 'It's all right, the old place,' says Aaron, seeing how she turns her head. 'Walter Spikenard, he's there. He keeps a watch on it. Him and Josh Arden, they sit on the jetty and fish.'

But there is no-one on the jetty now, no sign of life at all. Westminster is creeping into view on the right, the low-lying ground between it and Charing Cross milky with mists, as it always is. 'Where are we going?' Pris asks.

'Chelsea,' comes the answer. 'The Pightle.' Naming the house Bess had built for her retirement. It's a pretty house – brick-built and dry, a neat three storeys with a twist of chimneys either end, and glass in all its windows, windows that on the first floor are big enough to stand at, looking down. Inside the rooms are light, the floors polished, the chairs plentiful, the wainscots painted.

'Oh,' says Pris.

The tide is at its height by the time they reach Chelsea; the blushing sun, by contrast, dropping in the sky. Miguel draws the wherry in toward the bank, gets out, pulls it up high enough that Pris can step onto dry land. With Aaron in the lead they make their way to that pair of chimneys. In at the gate, into the garden.

The first person Pris sees is Mary Frith. Mary Frith, in Pris's view, worked out fifty years ago that Mother Nature had made her plain and unlikeable, so made herself noisy and boorish and irksome too, as if in revenge. She has no utility whatsoever, in

Pris's view, and her hearty presence about the Pightle is a source of constant irritation. 'Oh, fuck *me*,' Mary Frith exclaims, as she sees Pris walk in. 'Look what the tide washed up!' The second person Pris sees is Abi – even skinnier than Pris remembers, but otherwise unchanged: a cry of delight, then Abi comes running from the kitchen door, wailing, 'Oh, my ducky! Oh, my ducky! You're come home!'

The third person Pris sees is Bess Holland herself. Bess, up in her lighted chamber on the first floor, stood in all her chilly splendour at the open window, which, on seeing Pris stood below her in the garden, she bangs shut.

Yes, welcome home indeed.

CHAPTER SIX

The Prodigal Daughter

'Must you be prying into a woman's secrets?'

Thomas Middleton and Thomas Decker, *The Roaring Girl*

SO. OUR HEROINE, awakening, and for a moment caught in one of those mental cobwebs where you cannot remember where you are nor imagine how you got there. The door is in the wrong place; surely the window too; if that is the ceiling, it is the wrong colour and too low. There comes an unpleasant scratching of claws somewhere above her head, then the unmistakable Cockney yawp of a London seagull. *Now I know where I am.* Chelsea. Bess's house, the Pightle. Up in one of its attics, where (being in such deep disgrace, as she is) Bess had put her to bed, like a servant.

There is some other sound in the room with her, a light and happy humming. Pris is no morning flower, to open with the sun. With her arm over her eyes, she gives a groan.

'There she is!' Abi's voice. Now Abi's presence, standing over her, Abi's hand, folding down the sheet, brushing back the hair from Pris's brow. 'There you are, sweetling. Feeling better, with a bit of rest?'

Not especially, no. Pris need only open her eyes for all she has awaiting her to fill her skull like a swarm of bees. And one bee, bigger and buzzier than all the rest – this undertaking to get herself to St Martin's Lane. She sits herself up, bunching her ringlets out of the way. 'Oh, such a tangle!' Abi comments fondly, reaching out a hand toward her head. 'The faeries have had a high old time of it, tying knots in that. Shall I comb 'em out for you, my ducky? Like what I used to?'

It was a childhood ritual, to have Abi comb out her hair. It was a childhood verity that the reason it tangled so was because (according to Abi) Queen Mab was jealous of it, so she and her cohorts rode back and forth in Pris's hair all night, knotting it up on purpose. Pris spent hours of her young life blinking back the tears, as Abi did morning battle with the worst Queen Mab had inflicted on her overnight. It would be wonderfully soothing to have Abi do so now. 'Yes,' says Pris, meekly. 'Please, Abi, if you would.'

Abi takes up position behind her. Abi's arms may put one in mind of the handles of wooden spoons, so thin are they, but she has tended the female body times without number, and the arms, the hands, have skill. The comb is flourished. A faint scent of beeswax: the teeth of the comb have been drawn over a block of it to make it slide more easily through the hair. Abi is humming once more, as she works, as she grips the curls, so as to pull as little as possible. '*Lady Margaret*,' she sings, beneath her breath,

Lady Margaret at her window, a-combing of her hair,
She saw Sweet William and his bride, unto the church repair.
Down she cast her ivory comb, and up she tossed her hair.'

Doing justice to Lady Margaret's misadventures takes a while; by the time Lady M, wretched creature, has died for pure true love, there is not a tangle left. It used to puzzle Pris greatly, when she was small, why every song Abi knew was about men and women in some mighty falling-out, which always seemed to end with the woman dying, at the man's hand or her own. *Well*, she thinks, *that's one puzzle puzzles me no longer, any rate.* This is simply how it is. Constant battling.

Up above, the seagull rattles its claws once more along the roofline. 'There,' Abi says, with satisfaction. She draws the comb from scalp to tip, from head to waist. 'We'll give you bit of a wash, my darling, then let's get you dressed.'

The peacock gown (complete with the nine remaining sovereigns craftily inserted into the seams of its bodice) lies draped across two chairs in the corner of the room, the green contending with the blue. While Pris slept, it appears it was brushed free of the worst of the stains it had collected on its travels, and its draggled hem has been sewn up. 'So beautiful,' Abi comments approvingly, seeing where Pris's gaze has gone. But something has also been laid on top of it, something so dark and solid-looking, at first Pris thinks it must be Helen of Troy, Bess Holland's immense black cat. 'What's that?' Pris asks, getting to her feet.

Abi has put her hands up like she's praying, like her answer will require forgiveness. 'Bess says we must make you seem ill-used and contrite.'

The thick pile of black is a costume, one of the get-ups the girls of Holland's Leaguer used to don for those of their clients needing the tang of make-believe. It's the widow's weeds, the garb of the virtuous woman left penniless at her husband's death, so what else can she do but go a-whoring? It laces up the front – for when did a poor widow-woman have a maid to help her dress? – but is nonetheless cut almost to the nipple. There is a gauzy black *thing* (thinks Pris, shaking it out), to cover and of course draw the eye to the slope of the breasts. There are unstarched petticoats that flop. There are black linsey stockings; there are shoes without rosettes; there is a heavy black veil. *God a'mighty*, thinks Pris, viewing herself thus arrayed in the mirror Abi holds up, *how the gods do mock us. I'm in mourning for Felipe whether I wish it or no*, and then to her amazement finds she has begun to weep.

'Oh, my honey!' Abi exclaims. 'Oh, my treasure, don't! That wicked lad, to take you away from us! You must have been so frightened and alone!'

No question whose part Abi takes in this. 'I was,' Pris admits, wiping her cheeks. 'I was.' For a moment she contemplates saying more, but Abi's face, with its palimpsest of worry-lines, is not that of a woman to have yet more horrors put into her head. Besides, how do you explain any of it to one who wasn't there? The roar of cannon, like a thousand lions all at once, the terrible light with which cannon-fire fills a street, the running through those streets with a man with a death's head on his coat; the watching your lover die – did all this truly happen? To the same girl who stands here now? 'Abi, I am so sorry I ran away, and was such trouble to you all –' (Abi is mopping round Pris's nostrils with her kerchief; Pris takes Abi's hand and holds it away) '– but why does Bess want me dressed like this? Why must I look contrite?'

Abi's hands are all twisted up together. 'Because,' she says, as if this is being wrung from her, finger by finger, 'because Greville is on his way.'

Greville Holland. Dark hair, close-cropped, coming down to a point on his forehead and tipped at its edges with grey; dark beard edging his jaw, also close-cropped, and as elaborately shaped as strapwork. Greville Holland, son of old Aaron, may he rest in peace (however unlikely that might be). Greville Holland, patriarch, fetched from his house in Rotherhithe by Miguel Domingo, and striding back and forth across his sister's Chelsea drawing-room with such anger in his heavy tread, he sets the Chinese tea-bowls on her mantelpiece a-rattling. What a fate: to survive throwing and painting and firing, to make it all the way downriver from Jingdezhen to the sea, to be stashed in the belly of an East Indiaman, one bowl atop another, one crate atop another; to be taken across the South China Sea, the Bay of Bengal, the Arabian Sea; all the way round the entire continent of Africa; up past Spain, up past France, avoiding all those damn Dunkirkers on the way, and into Tilbury; to be loaded onto a wagon, to be jolted across the Essex marshes into London proper; to be set up on display at Gresham's Royal Exchange, to catch the eye of Bess Holland, to be borne home in her lap, only to leap to your death on the granite of her drawing-room hearth all because Greville Holland will not stop striding about. 'Greville!' his sister snaps. 'Will you sit down!'

Greville sits. From the corner of the room, Mary Frith watches.

Pris enters. 'YOU,' Greville bellows on sight of her. He strides up to her, arm raised.

'Greville, *please*,' his sister says. 'You are not about to beat her, and you know it.'

'No,' Pris puts in, coldly, 'he is not.' Greville's temper is how he rules his family, how he keeps all Southwark in thrall; but Greville acts his anger; in any situation where he feels threatened or inadequate, this is the part he hops into. On first working this out, Pris had explained it to Greville, patiently and at great length, which was how she discovered that, far from welcoming the truth about themselves, people can react very badly to it indeed. She'd thought Greville would be impressed with her acuity; not a bit of it. Greville had her locked in her room on bread and water for a week. The problem here for Greville, as Pris knows full well, is that she has defied him, and defied him in such a wise that there is nothing he can do about it.

There is a chair in the centre of the room, clearly put there for the accused, so Pris seats herself upon it, those ugly shoes set square together. 'Had I come back here a *condessa*,' she says, calmly, 'you'd all a-been kissing my hand.'

'Hah!' says Greville. 'But as it is, you can kiss my arse.' His wit delights him. He looks up, to see if it has delighted anyone else. He catches Mary Frith rolling her eyes. 'I suppose it would be too much to hope that she still has her maidenhead?' Greville demands.

'Yes, it would,' says Pris. No point making a pretence of it.

Greville had topped off his attire for travelling upriver with a hat of beaver fur, pinned up at the side with an ostrich plume, whose journey to Greville's hat-maker had been almost as epic as those of his sister's tea-bowls. Now he takes the hat from his head and throws it to the floor. 'Is she mad?' he demands of Bess. Then he rounds on Pris again. 'Do you know how much you were worth?'

'I was glad to be rid of the thing, the fuss you all made about it,' Pris replies. She absorbs herself in arranging her skirt. From behind, she hears Mary's snort of laughter.

'Greville, a maidenhead can be counterfeited a dozen times over, you know that as well as I,' says Bess. There is the swish of silks as she moves behind Pris's chair. 'Our problem –' (her hands descend to Pris's shoulders) '– our problem is her being away, that's what we must account for.' Unseen by Greville, Bess's thumbs move back and forth on Pris's shoulder-blades. *I'm here*, is what those thumbs are saying. *I'm here, you're home and you behave.*

'Wash of alum,' Mary Frith puts in, from her corner of the room. Mary was a madam too, once, she knows almost as many tricks as Bess. She gives a wink. 'Wash of alum, tighten her up, and a clyster of cochineal. Or a good ripe raspberry, up the bum. That'll do the trick too, if the girl can squirm about.'

You come near me, thinks Pris, *with your wash of alum, you'll regret it, promise you that.* She is in no mood to be winked at by Mary or anyone else.

'We'll say she was took sick,' Greville suggests. 'Took sick and was sent into the country.'

'Don't be a fool, Greville,' his sister snaps. 'Anyone hearing that will think a pregnancy for sure.'

'Or the pox,' Mary puts in.

'By God.' Greville is the kind of man will give his grievances their due, no matter what. 'That dog Tom Howard, Dudley North, old Wyncanton – we could have named our price with any of 'em. Or Robert Essex – an Essex in our pocket, think on that!'

The eyes of all three women turn upon him. 'Not Robert Essex, brother,' says Bess, pityingly. 'Not he.'

'No,' Mary puts in. A suck on her pipe. 'Old Essex has to splint his cock to do anything with it at all.'

'A challenge for her!' Greville declares, pointing at Pris. All this damned secret knowledge women share! 'Something for all them gowns and graces—' *God give me patience*, he's thinking, the hours Bess had the girl stalking about with a book on her head, the gowns, the gewgaws; the dancing-master, the calligraphy-master, the lessons in Latin, the lessons in history, the lessons in French ('What sort of French?' Greville had demanded. 'The worthwhile, or the other?'), the fortune that was spent on her; when all you need teach any of these girls is how to fuck, and that they can learn any old how—

He is pulled up by Pris's hoot of laughter. 'Do you hear yourself?' she asks. 'How is the trade in maidenheads this season, Unc? Are prices good? Is the market up?'

For a moment it looks as if he'll make that rush at her again. Pris meets his gaze. 'Have a care, brother,' Bess says, quietly, above her head. 'Bruises would be no help to us at all.'

Greville takes his eyes from Pris, glares at Bess instead. 'I blame you for this,' he says. 'All this patting and cosseting, and what is she? Nothing but a witless little punk!'

I will kill you. Pris shakes herself free of Bess's hands, gets to her feet. 'I tell you what,' she says. 'Why don't you decide, between you, where I've been these last weeks, and who you're going to auction me off to now I'm back, and when you've got it sorted, you do let me know.'

An exit line if ever there was one. As she slams the door, she can hear Greville again: 'Anyone would think the bloody girl imagined her maidenhead was her own!'

What does a girl do, after she has been called a witless little punk? Throw herself upon her pillows in a passion, as the infant firecracker that was Pris was so wont to do? Not any more. Pris sits on that bed in the attic, head bowed. *Think*, she tells herself. *Think.*

From the floor below, the sounds of continuing debate. Greville's voice. Then Bess. Then Greville again. The phrase 'some BASTARD bloody Diego' finds its way upward.

Oh, to have Greville's power. Oh, to decide your own life, for yourself. Even Mary Frith has managed that. London has its roaring boys – a few steps up the ladder from the 'prentices, but otherwise like them exactly – in Mary it had a roaring girl, a sort of mimic in reverse, in that where the mimics of Holland's Leaguer costumed themselves in veils and vine leaves, Mary tricked herself out in breeches and doublet; dressed so, rode a horse all the way to Shoreditch for a bet. When she was made to stand public penance for it outside St Paul's, the crowd in its perversity threw flowers at her feet and sang her name: 'Mary Frith! Roaring Moll!' There was a play writ in her honour too. And what is it Mary has, and Greville has, and Bess has, that Pris does not?

Money.

I can't live like this. I can't go back to being their dolly, being hawked about.

Or perhaps that is a *won't*. Pris looks over at the peacock silk and scowls. She could take that to Unthanks, Unthanks in the Strand, with its drawerfuls of lace and ribbon, Unthanks with its gowns hanging in its windows. Oh, but how it would hurt her heart to go in there as a petitioner, holding out her hand, and not as some fine lady with money coming out her ear-holes!

Think. Money. Think.

Achille de la Tour, is what Pris thinks, him and his lopsided hair. Achille de la Tour – and then from nowhere that other one is there in her thoughts, him with those pale eyes and that slow smile, and she's thinking of how he strode ahead of her toward Achille's tent, of how the loiterers skipped out his way. What wicked pleasure it would be to have Greville confronted by a man of that… that *unarguability*. Yet at the same time, something in her revolts at it – *why should we have to have a man to fight our battles for us? Why can we not do so on our own?*

In any case, he was a nothing. Said so himself. No rank at all.

Achille de la Tour. St Martin's Lane.

I'll bet Monsieur de la Tour would have paid Felipe a deal more than he has paid me.

She picks up the mirror, unpins the hideous veil, teases out a ringlet or two. There. Ill-used and contrite, but a little easier on the eye. Goes to the door of the attic. The Pightle has a servant's stair; Pris creeps down it on her toes. If she can only get to the back door—

'And where might you be headed, little sis?'

Aaron and Miguel are sitting at the kitchen table, a jug of beer between them, but Aaron is already getting to his feet. *Pox.* Time was, she and Aaron were so thick, Pris would have given half those sovereigns to him just to see the delight on his face; time was, she might have given him them all.

'I've a – I've a hankering for Covent Garden,' says Pris. 'It's been so long, Aaron. I thought I'd take a peek around the shops, that's all.'

Aaron is somewhat pink-nosed. 'Oh no, you don't. No more slipping off on your own for you, missy. You want to go somewhere, you go with me. We'll take a hackney. As it happens, I've an errand that way meself.'

Bess's drawing-room is quieter than it was. Nothing now imperils the Chinese porcelain upon the mantelpiece, no loud male anger sends the mice behind the wainscot scurrying. Greville, Bess and Mary sit at the room's gate-legged dining table; Bess with her ebony moggy, Helen of Troy, upon her lap, the crackle of whose purr is the only sound in the room. On the table itself there reposes a bottle of dryly flavoursome Xeres sack, and the remains of a plate of fried oysters, the shreds of a sallet of carrots, the crumbs of a venison pasty, the bowls that held an apple-custard, a burned cream.

There is narrow, sallow Abi stood there in the corner, holding the tray on which she brought the meal into the room flat against her, as St George might hold his shield; and as silent as if she was one of those painted figures of a servant cut from wood. Inwardly, glancing at her, Greville shakes his head. The Hollands are a handsome family, always have been, hard-featured but handsome – Bess, even in retirement, has the presence of a duchess – but Abi is as ill-favoured as all her tribe, wrinkled and sere and fleshless as an Egyptian mummy, and what is a Skinner doing in his sister's drawing-room in any case? This – this specimen, who came here as a dripping rag, dragged from the river by Walter Spikenard, and who never left – human flotsam, that's all Abi is to him. The only reason to keep her here at all is the thorn she must be in Old Man Skinner's thoughts, when he remembers how he once had a daughter. *If* he ever does, thinks Greville, scowling.

Do we judge Greville too harshly? Let us remember, there were once three boys in the Holland family, three sons of old Aaron: Greville himself, the plotter and planner; Jenkin the merry-maker, transplanted now to their bureau in Amsterdam; and then there was the firstborn, the oldest of the three, brother Cosmo, the man who pursued everything – wealth, reputation, this enterprise, that, and finally the pretty face sent to lure him out one frosty night, and who was never seen alive again. Cosmo who, in the innermost chamber of his heart, his brother grieves for still. It is a lonely thing, to become the oldest, a lonely and a thankless thing, but does his sister ever think of this? Does she offer understanding and support? No, all she wishes to talk about is that shrew of a foundling of hers. Oh, the ghosts that float about a conversation, even this.

'Brother,' Bess is saying, 'you must remember, this is Pris.' She pauses, choosing her words. 'She will not be bossed and bullied. It's unwise.'

Greville sits back, as a man does when he has dined well; he looks on his sister with a lordly eye; he glances at Helen of Troy on his sister's lap, a cushion of black velvet. *Another bloody female*, thinks Greville. And a man-hater, to boot. Greville can still find the place where Helen of Troy as a kitten sank her fishbone teeth into his thumb. 'You filled the girl's head with airs, Bess; this is the result. To me, she's nothing but a hoity mort who needs to learn her manners. Some bobtail's bastard, no more.'

A glance exchanged between the women in the room. This is what they have always said: that Pris must be the by-blow of some London light-o'-love, left her infant on Dainty Jane's grave in hopes of bringing the poor mewler a bit of luck. But do they believe it? Bess's little copper-headed foundling, there was something unsettling about her from the start. Let's begin with that business of the Puritan – you know the one, ran mad in St Olave's, right in the middle of the service. Not a moment before, Bess had caught her foundling glaring at the man with such intensity it was as if the fellow could feel it, began rolling his shoulders, weaving his head, and when Bess plucked at Pris's arm – *Stop that!* – Pris had raised her prayer book to cover her mouth and whispered, 'He is afraid of us.'

Bess had lowered her head. 'What say?'

'He is afraid of us. Us, in our petticoats.' A tiny nod of satisfaction. 'That's why he has his snakes.'

'What snakes?'

'The ones in his head.' Another nod. 'They are going to be the end of him.' And not a moment after, the man ran screaming down the aisle, shrieking how he was damned, damned, damned; straight out the church and threw himself under a wagon coming down off the bridge. All but chopped the crank in two. True, the man was known all up and down for his nastiness and unpredictability, but even so. 'It ain't my fault if no-one else sees what I do,' the infant Pris declared in her own defence. 'Why shouldn't I say what I see?'

'Because you can't,' Bess told her, stakes and gallows erecting themselves with horrid speed across her imagination. 'Because you mustn't. Because I say so, is that clear?' The same for Pris's conviction that there were three old women living in her looking-glass, or the places she said she went to in her dreams and walked within. 'A forest,' she told Abi. 'It was all snow. There were people dancing. I danced with them. Feel how cold my feet are, Abi!' And indeed the child's feet were like little bricks of ice. 'She seeped into her,' was Abi's verdict, voice a-quiver. 'The hours Pris lay on Dainty Jane's grave, Dainty Jane's spirit seeped inside her.' And oh, the saints, that temper, if the little miss was crossed! 'You will better any woman you are put beside,' Bess told her, 'but you must be better, not different. Difference is dangerous. Do you understand?' So instead, as she grew, Pris learned to hide, to dissemble, to pretend, all of them skills that a woman must master, in any case; and year by year the oddness was submerged, the charm came bobbing to the surface; and soon it was all about how Miss Pris looked, and thus, her worth. Because that was one matter they were all agreed upon – the finding of a protector, so called, a man with status, wealth, position to take Pris as his mistress; and the grander the better.

Because men have the power. Women have the secrets, but men have the power. Because that is how the world is, that is all.

The sherry sack has made Greville expansive. 'Take the fire out her eye, let those little titties of hers drop, she'll be no different to the rest, you'll see.'

Then Abi speaks.

'She called the dead,' says Abi, from her corner. She lifts her eyes to Bess, sat there at the table, glass of sherry halted halfway to her mouth. Greville is staring at Abi as if he could not be more amazed if one of those same wooden figures had begun to speak, but Bess remembers, Abi knows she does, Bess was there, Bess heard it too: Little Nan still warm where she lay and Pris's flare of temper at being told her playmate was gone: *Gone where? I want her!* and then that thin, lost cry; fretful, wavering, and unmistakably Little Nan. Bess had pulled Pris to her, clapped her hand across her foundling's mouth. A pause, in which Abi could hear Bess's own heartbeat, the room was so still. The cry came a second time, but smaller, thinner now, as if from further off; then a third, even weaker; it did not come again.

'She called the dead,' Abi repeats. 'She was four years old and she called the dead.' She darts a glance at Greville. 'And what is more, they answered.'

Outside the room, a floorboard barks. Unless of course it is the ghost of Dainty Jane.

'Oh, for the Lord's sake!' This from Mary, sat there waving her pipe. 'For the Lord's sake, Abi, all this nonsense – is it any wonder the girl's turned out a baggage?'

CHAPTER SEVEN

St Martin's Lane

'Never were cheeks of roses, hair of amber,
Ordained to live imprisoned in a chamber.'

John Gough, *The Academy of Complements*

A HACKNEY. IN AARON'S childhood these little carriages were such a novelty; now you find them all over, but even so, they still produce in Aaron a pleasing sense of self-importance: the way they tilt when you climb in; the way the driver holds the door. He'll have a carriage like this one day, a carriage of his own, and horses, and stables, and a coachman – no, coach*men*, and a prodigious great house in Rotherhithe, just as Greville does. He'll be in charge. He'll be the one to sort out everything, Pris included. He glances over at her, sat in her corner, gazing out. She's come back into her looks a bit, he sees – those goose-gog eyes of hers (although to be fair, their colour is darker than that), as always watching, watching. And that hair… you have to say, she can be a looker, his sis, when her mood is right. Even a brother (a sort of brother) can admit that. 'You'd make a good little Puritan, you would,' says Aaron, jocularly. 'You oughter wear more black.'

She, a Puritan. What a notion. 'Thank you, no,' comes the reply.

He edges closer to her. 'Go on then,' he says. 'What was he like?'

You can follow her gaze, arcing over the Westminster rooflines, taking it all in. She loves London, does his sis. Mad, that she ever took herself out of it. *That God-damned princock, Ortez.* Aaron had only seen Felipe once, spying on the man as he walked with Pris in Westminster Hall, where all the young bloods go to strut. He had guessed there was something up with his sis, some fledgling intrigue under way (the pollen of suppressed excitement she gave off, her pushing dishes away at table, her inattention, all the signs), and he had taken against this blade who had Pris on his arm at once. Everything about the man: the curls of his hair, the extravagance of the lace about his collar, the way he bobbed up and down when he walked to make himself seem taller. 'What was who like?' Pris answers, from the midst of her daydreams.

'Your bingo.' He nudges up to her. 'Your lover-boy, Ortez.' He grins. 'You know.'

She glances back at him, half amused, half outraged. 'I ain't discussing that with you, you're my brother!'

'No, I ain't. You're me little sis, but I ain't your brother. We don't share a drop of blood, we two. Go on then. You can tell me. Was he any good?'

A silence. Pris lets her gaze drop. 'Christ, I hope not. If that's how it's meant to be, henceforth I'll be a nun.'

Aaron, in his way, is every bit as proprietorial as Greville where Pris is concerned. Privately, he is hugging himself. Outwardly, he's all solicitude. 'Bit of a disappointment?' Pris is contemplating sharing something, Aaron can tell.

Here we go. 'He always said the same thing. When he – when he—'

'Pissed his tallow?' Aaron suggests. 'Emptied his bag?'

That green glare. '*Oh*, you men are foul.'

Aaron is delighted. 'Go on then. What did he say?'

Now she makes a face. '*Aqui es para ti.*'

'And what's that mean, when it's at home?'

'It means – it means *here, this is for you.*'

'*Here, this is for you?*' Aaron is incredulous. 'Oh, little sis.' He's wiping his eyes. Young as he is, Aaron has had his share of such pleasures, but even so, none of the gentlemen with whom he has consorted (with utmost caution, and greatest secrecy) has ever delivered themselves at the magic moment of such a line as that. 'You do pick 'em, you truly do.' He reaches over, pats her shoulder.

Pris allows herself a sniff. 'All I wanted,' she begins, 'all I wanted was that first time, it should be with a man who didn't have wrinkles on his thighs.'

'Of course you did,' Aaron tells her, consolingly. 'And the thought of coming back here a *condessa* never once entered your head.'

Those eyes, how they can flash. 'You can go to hell,' says Pris, with dignity. ''Tis all a silly game in any case, and love a mockery. I always knew it. All I have done is prove myself right.' She turns her back on him.

The wheels of the hackney crack against cobblestone. There is the King's new Banqueting House (younger than either of them; its marble glaringly white), there is old St Martin's, and now the road is full of builders' carts, the pavements blocked with piles of stone. 'So much *new*,' says Pris, as the half-finished houses go by, workmen on their roofs.

'Ho yes,' Aaron assures her. 'It's all to be Eye-talianated hereabouts, I tell you. Covent Garden, *quite* the place to be. These –' (he waves out the window) '– these is all to be let out, floor by floor.' Aaron likes to hold forth; doing so reminds him of his father, Cosmo, makes him feel a little as if his father was still about. Instead of lying in Borough Market, surrounded by sawdust and blood. 'It'll be shops on the ground floor, where the big windows are – all the best, little sis, hairdressers from Paree and mercers from Venice and I don't know what besides; and up above, nothing but fine feathers. You wait and see.'

The house they are passing is a storey taller than the others in the row. A pillared line of triple windows rises up through its façade; at its top storey it is paired with an open space for sitting out, on the leads of the roof. 'I like that one,' says Pris, dreamily. She imagines sitting up there, breakfasting, in morning-robe of kingfisher blue; she imagines a place – any place – of her own. Ah, money. Money, money, money. What she could do with it. Why does she have *none*?

Her daydreams are knocked flying. Aaron is hammering on the front panel of the hackney, yelling at the coachman. 'Hey, stop! This is where!' He turns back to Pris. 'Out you get, little sis. We're here.'

*

The shop where the hackney has come to a halt has what might be taken for bulrushes carved on either side of its door. In fact, they are meant to be sotweed, tobacco plants, and just in case the passer-by should be as unfamiliar with their appearance as was the sculptor, an enormous white-painted wooden pipe has been hung over its doorway. 'Mary says as *I* should try a pipe,' Aaron tells Pris, nonchalantly. 'Says it makes one look quite the man.'

'And she would know,' Pris answers, stepping down.

'Now, now, little cat,' Aaron admonishes her. 'No more hissing from you.' He turns about. 'Mr Sullivan!' he calls out, entering the shop. 'Do you have me order, sir?'

Sullivan's Tobacconist is one of the many enterprises in which the Hollands have an interest; one of those – along with the Red Bull theatre in Clerkenwell, and the old Dunqerqer Tavern way out on the River Lea – that have been placed in Aaron's particular care. The Red Bull teeters forever on the brink of closure by the city fathers, the tumble-down Dunqerqer on the brink of sliding into the Lea for good; in Aaron's portfolio of responsibilities, Sullivan's is easily the most respectable, and certainly the only one where he is greeted with such enthusiasm. Mr Sullivan trots himself over to shake Aaron's hand. 'Mr Holland! Welcome, welcome!' He sees Pris. He stares. The other customers also turn and stare. Good God, a woman, in a baccy shop! What is the world coming to?

Pris retires to the back wall, stands against it, holding her shawl over her nose. The smell of tobacco – part vegetable, part mineral, dark as earth – is strong enough to taste. 'Me sis,' Aaron announces, cheerily, to the starers. 'I'm a-minding her; you don't have to.' He eyes the other customers, who take the hint and look away. Sullivan, meanwhile, at the corner of his counter, is prising the lid from a canister of tinned enamel. 'There you are, Mr Holland,' he declares. 'Finest Virginian.' The smell of tobacco is joined by a tendril of something else: part ambrosial, part faecal, wholly alien. 'And packed with a nub of ambergris, to boot,' says Mr Sullivan. 'Now ain't that good?' He and Aaron bend their heads over the canister and take a deep, appreciative sniff. It is extraordinary how great the trade in sotweed has become; these days London has almost as many tobacconists as it has taverns. And how it does garnish your accounts, as well, if the odd barrel of baccy comes onto your books via the River Lea, and the trapdoor in the Dunqerqer's floor, rather than via some bonded warehouse and the blasted excise men and their tariffs and taxes.

And if it does, why, may it not carry within it some other little item, best kept from curious eyes? Aaron glances behind him, sees no other customers within earshot, sees his sister take herself off into Sullivan's back room. Lots of pretty things to keep her occupied in there. He turns back to Sullivan. 'And it made it here *intacta*, I would hope?' Aaron enquires, lowering his voice.

Sullivan casts an eye to left and right, then reaching down the side of the canister produces a folded envelope, of yellow-stained canvas. It bears a glossy seal. 'Safe and sound,' he murmurs, 'safe and sound. All ready for our Mr Vanderhoof, when he do next pass by. He is a great one for the correspondence, our Mr Vanderhoof, ain't that so?'

Aaron casts an apparently careless eye across the seal. Hunting horn and lion, just as they should be. 'Bill of sale, that will be, I dare say,' he tells Sullivan. 'You know the Dutch. Love their paperwork, they do. Tell you what, I'll take this for him.' He tucks the envelope, and its seal from the private office of Frederick Henry, safely within the mulberry velvet. 'Get to him quicker that way.'

The back room of Sullivan's is devoted to the business of snuff. Shelf after shelf of blue and white jars, the smell of tobacco overlaid with that of mint and liquorice and camphor. Pris wanders past them, idly reading their labels: *Fennel. Attar Ros. Fr–Cognac.* Then a display case of snuff boxes – burled walnut, lidded cowrie shells, even one of Chinese jade. It is while she is perusing the snuff boxes that she sees the door set into the panelling in the corner.

Well, well. She wanders casually toward it, tries its handle –

– and it opens, into a high-walled yard. But a high-walled yard with a gate.

The gate too is unlocked. It gives onto one of London's many narrow lanes, almost a tunnel, it is so overhung with jutting gables. But which way – left or right?

Left it is. Left to the end of the alley. There's the steeple of St Martin's, and then –

The gods are smiling. St Martin's Lane.

More masculinity. A street full of houses no doubt every bit as high and mighty as their owners; all set to face east, where their windows may catch the morning sun, and grand enough to have smaller houses of their own behind them, places where live their coaches, their horses, their laundry… On she goes, this widow-woman, so pale, so heartbreakingly young (Pris is practising her effect on those she passes – *dauntless,* she tells herself, *dauntless yet sorrowful*), and it must be said, it is a damn sight easier to play that part in black than it was in her peacock silk. That man – not Achille, the other one, the one with the face like an intelligent hound – he's back in her head again. *See?* she tells him, or the memory of him. *Your friend's precious message is about to be delivered, safe and sound…*

Not another woman in sight. Nothing but the steady tread of menservants, in their heavy shoes, and the tippy-tap of the finer sort of gentlemen in theirs, with their fashionable canes to hand, marking their progress up the street the way a sea captain might swing a set of dividers over a map. The gaze of each man goes over her like a curious hand, much as an interested buyer might stroke the buttocks of a horse. This mourning black, thinks Pris, is going to need an explanation. *Señor Ortez and I, we were affianced…* the lesser the lie, the stronger it is, and she truly had thought they were to wed, she and Felipe, for a little while at least. Or she had told herself that she did. It had seemed inconceivable that so much excitement could come to nothing, fizzle out.

I loved him, yes, I loved him dearly.

She rehearses the feel of the line. What she had loved was the headiness of it all, the daring of those first meetings. What she had loved was the sense of power, of defiance, of taking charge of her own future. Hah! How wrong can one be.

And now he is no more, and my family has utterly cut me off. I am without a penny.

It is such a complicated business, the falling out of love. The anger, the ruefulness, but it is the anger that stings the sharpest now. It is possible the girl she is might find the Ortezes of this world rather less impressive than the girl she was. *Live and learn, Miss Pris*, she hears Bess intone in her head, *live and learn.*

She had been counting the houses as she walked along, now she tilts her gaze up. The house before her seems to tilt its gaze down, to frown, to draw its stuccoed brows together. Who is she, to climb the steps to its front door, to pull on its bell?

The echo of footsteps. The hall within must be cavernous.

The door is opened. The girl standing there is no older than Pris, and wears almost as much black as she, although her maid-servant's dress is stolid wool to its high neck, with a collar plain as milk. She looks Pris up and down, and her eyebrows seem to ask the same question as the house had done. Even so, it is almost as if the two young women are looking into a mirror: *This could have been me.*

Noises arrive in the hall from the floor below it: kitchen items being banged about in temper.

'Good day to ye,' says Pris. 'May I speak with Monsieur de Mayerne?'

The girl looks her up and down once more, her gaze slowing when it reaches the gauzy black net over Pris's breasts. Oh, she's the real thing, this, the real true dyed-in-her-Calvinist-wool thing. 'Are you consulting?' the girl enquires, frostily.

'Consulting?' Pris repeats. She is at a loss.

'Are – you – a – *patient*?' the girl asks, putting those pauses between her words that you might if you were dealing with a half-wit.

Ah, Monsieur de Mayerne is a *physician*. 'I am not,' Pris answers, smiling, showing her teeth. 'I have a message for Monsieur de Mayerne.'

Says the girl, 'You may give that to me.'

'I think not,' Pris replies. 'Since it is for Monsieur de Mayerne.' Another smile. There never was a woman yet, came out of Holland's Leaguer, let herself be bossed by a housemaid.

'Sir,' the girl says. '*Sir* Theodore de Mayerne, that 'ud be.' Having cocked her little snook, she points to a single bench, all on its own in that cavernous hall. 'You sit yourself there, and you *wait*.'

Pris waits. She hears more noises from the kitchen, but they are of small interest. Of much more note the wide-planked floor, the soft sheen of the walls, the amplitude of the stairs, the sparkle to the lantern hung above them. Every surface, polished, dusted, swept, kept clean with money. It's as if she can see it – the brush with which the floor is scrubbed, the bucket, the dusters, the brooms – golden, all of them. How Greville would relish such a place as this!

The sound of footsteps. The maid returns: coming down the stairs you see her feet the first, then the black, the collar, then the sour little face, like a crab-apple. 'Up,' she says, ungraciously, 'up, and go you left.'

Up, and left, and a double door of shining mahogany. It invites the gentle knock. 'Sir Theodore?'

Within, at first she thinks it is a library. Mahogany bookcases, all of 'em grilled to keep the books safe, but Pris cannot resist a book, never could. On her tiptoes, she examines them through the grillwork: an atlas in three volumes, all the works of Master Shakespeare, the essays of Montaigne. Herodotus's *Histories*, Cicero, Aristotle, Galen, Avicenna… Mr Harvey's *Anatomia Sanguinis*, then a herbal, then another, and another after that – *The Great Discovery of the Plants of New Spain*, Pris reads, New Spain being the Americas. How wonderful, to have such a wealth of books, and such a room in which to keep them, with that mighty great window, paned in roundels, to the side; and a surprise – beyond where she stands, as much green as in an orangery. The outside has come within. Above her head, odd items hanging from the ceiling: what must from its tiny fins and expression of astonishment be a fish, yet one covered in spines and round as a puffball. It has been varnished, perhaps. A turtle-shell, the whole thing, big as a Moses basket. Something with a snout upon a shelf, a snout, but armoured like a giant woodlouse. Next to it – now *that* she knows, that is some sort of crocodillo. A stick of coral, the size of a fallen antler; a collection of eggs in every size and colour, all laid on straw as if still in a nest; beside them, a miniature skeleton, its bones turned ivory, its joints hinged with silver. Beyond, the greenery lifts and stirs, there is a breeze. One pane of that window has been left open. The puffball-fish rotates; the skeleton trembles on its stand. There is a table at the centre of the room, with books piled about its legs. Ink pots, pens, notebooks as big as ledgers. An invoice from Endicott's Booksellers at St Paul's – 'Your earliest convenience will oblige,' she reads. An invoice for twenty-two pounds! Twenty-two pounds, on books! And then a jar, filled with amber liquor, in which there floats – in which there floats –

– a pair of human ears. 'Oh God!' says Pris, jumping backwards.

'Madam?'

He emerges from his indoor garden, moving frond and creeper gently aside. He seems to have been examining a small pot, raised on a stand for comfortable perusal and protected under a glass cloche, very much as Aaron and Mr Sullivan had been bending over their tobacco jar. A portly gentleman, very portly indeed, also dressed in black, his top-clothes with the proportions of a smock, yet the gleam of satin. He uses a stick to carry his weight as he comes toward her. A white beard, rilling down his chest; white hair, close-cropped as Greville's, smooth pink cheeks, and an expression that begins as innocent as a cherub, then shades into something shrewd as a vizier. He hardly makes a sound, as if his portliness is padding. She had no idea he was there. She has no idea how long he had been watching her, as she perused the spines of his books, the papers on his desk.

'Madam,' he says. His voice is soft as well. 'Sir Theodore de Mayerne. Jemima said you bore a message. How may I assist?'

Sir Theodore sits her down, and to help her get over the ears, presents her with a glass of sprits. Of his own distilling, so he says. 'I am much occupied in the study of the botanicals,' he tells her as she sips. 'Of the ingenious power of plants.'

'Whose *are* they?' Pris asks, indicating the loathsome jar.

'A Mr Henry Burton,' comes the answer. 'My patient, once. He referred to His Majesty's Archbishop as a caterpillar of the church, rather than its pillar.' A sigh. 'The joke was not got. I think the ears came to me in the hope that I might provide them with a more honourable home than some Newgate midden. How is that, madam? To your taste?'

The spirit is something like Dutch gin, but has a spicy heart. Pris gives herself a cautious reminder; her stomach is empty as can be, and it would not do to let oneself get bowsy. 'It is – it is most restorative,' she says.

'It is part-brewed from the pepper plant,' her host informs her. He has seated himself down in the leather-backed chair behind his desk. 'The capsicum, of the Americas. A plant of splendid calefaction.'

Calefaction. To make hot. Pris nods toward the specimen up there on its pedestal, under the cloche. Anything rather than look at those ears. 'Is that such a one?' she asks.

Sir Theodore shakes his head. 'That is a native of New Spain, indeed, but you would not wish to sample it, in any distillation whatsoever. That is the Angel's Trumpet, also called the Moonflower. The Spanish missionaries christened it the Floripondio, and say the Inca used it on their enemies to bring about visions of such terror men would dash their own heads upon rocks to be freed of them. I must construct some experiment to see if such is true. Now, madam –' (and he tents his fingers) '– if you are restored, your name?'

'Pris.' She looks him in the eye. His scrutiny of her is mild and calm. It is as if he is contemplating what kind of an anatomy she might make, if boned and with her own joints hinged with silver. 'Pris Holland.'

'As in Holland House, in Kensington, no doubt?'

'Not *quite*, Sir Theodore.'

Now he smiles. 'And your given name – as in Priscilla?'

'As in Cupris. Like the metal. I believe I was named for my hair.'

'Ah!' Sir Theodore exclaims. 'Cupris. From Cyprus. The place of copper mines. And, of course –' (a twinkle. It is as if he is proving he can flirt, like any other man.) '– Aphrodite's isle.'

The noise of female dispute from below. A door slams, the noise is cut off. *This*, thinks Pris, *is a house full of angry and unhappy women. And one man, sat up here in his own private kingdom.*

He is speaking again. 'So, Miss Aphrodite of the copper hair, what is your message for me?'

'It comes from Achille de la Tour,' Pris begins.

Instantly, the sharp-eyed vizier is back. 'I was anticipating such a message. But not such a messenger.' He scrutinizes her anew; he seems for the first time to see the blackness of the mourning. 'And it is?'

'I am to tell you that the person you were waiting for is in Hieropolis.'

'Ah,' says Sir Theodore. 'A pity. A great shame.'

'And went there,' says Pris, being exact as she can, 'before he and Monsieur de la Tour could speak.'

Beneath the silver-white beard, Sir Theodore has thinned his lips. 'An even greater shame,' he says.

'Exactly so.' She smooths her skirt. 'Sir Theodore, Monsieur de la Tour made mention of a commission. For the carrier of his message.' Pris tilts her head; lowers her lashes, gazes up through them at Sir Theodore.

Sir Theodore seems surprised. 'He did?'

'He did. He was most emphatic on that point.'

Sir Theodore stands. 'I see,' he says. He opens a drawer in the table. She hears the turning of coins. Sir Theodore's hands are laid upon the tabletop, one with something in it. 'Perhaps it is as well. London is a city full of whispers. Whispers and whisperers. Even if my unhappy patient –' (a nod toward the jar) '– no longer hears them. We are a divided country, Miss Holland. I hope you will take care.' Again, that sharp look. 'Shall we call it two guineas?'

SO THERE SHE goes, back into St Martin's Lane, lighter by the weight of one message, heavier by that of two guineas, but when you come down to it, how much further along in the world does two guineas get you? Two months' rent, perhaps, on rooms such as Felipe's, and that would be without coal or candles or, come to that, *food*. And where would those rooms be, exactly? Anywhere south of the river, she'll have Greville on her doorstep before she's even hung up her cloak; she'll have changed nothing – still a Holland, still at their beck and call; and anywhere north of the river she'll need a bully-boy to keep the Skinners at bay, two bully-boys, and even that wouldn't be enough. Oh, pox, pox, pox. There's no escape, declares the voice in her head, even as Pris the firecracker stamps her foot and roars, *But there must be!* The glow of the sovereigns is fast being cooled by the breeze – the same that has just taken the hat from the head of the gentleman in front of her and sent it bowling along the pavement to her feet.

It is a splendid hat, quite of Greville's quality. Pris picks it up and is brushing it off as its owner comes up to her. A right sparkish old blade, this one, his greying hair carefully set a-curl, although with the roundly undistinguished features of some village beadle.

She knows that face. She remembers it from the Leaguer; from Greville's carefully cultivated circle of the men who might be interested in her.

'Why, Wyn!' she says.

St Martin's Lane is so newly incarnated as a London street that deer have been known to wander in from St James's Park. It is certainly too new for anything as vulgar as a tavern to have taken root, but at its southern end, it does have Hopgood's Chop House, the kind of place where a man such as Antony Wyncanton can command a table merely by clearing his throat. Even if the first table they are shown, it sits in a draught ('Pris, my dear, do you not feel it?'), the second is too public by far, the third too draught-*less*, and all this fuss, fuss, fuss, that would once have grated on her soul like very shark-skin now feels to Pris like the essence of being home. There they sit, he one side of the table, she the other; with Wyn gazing at her with that mixture of amazement and delight Pris remembers so well. Here is her welcome; finally!

'My dear,' he says. 'My dear girl. Now you must tell me. Where have you been hiding?'

Wyn has also been considerate enough to order up a meal – a chicken, carbonadoed, buttered leeks, a tansy tart. The fire lit in Pris's belly by Sir Theodore's liquor is being assuaged, the belly itself, filled. She is ravenous. She has to school herself to eat in ladylike bites; left to herself Pris would lift the chicken from its plate and gnaw it off the bone. She dabs at her mouth, puts her hands with her napkin in her lap. 'It was Greville,' she begins. 'Uncle Greville.'

'Greville?' Wyn has been wined and dined many an evening by Greville Holland; the note of reservation to his tone suggests he now regrets them.

'He sent me away,' says Pris, dropping her gaze. 'To Breda.'

'Breda? The Spanish territories?' Wyn is amazed. Amazed and outraged. *Good*, thinks Pris.

'To people he did business with,' she adds, crossing her fingers out of sight.

Another hat, with cockade of pheasant feathers, is going back and forth outside the window. The window, fortunately, is too high for the wearer of the hat to be able to see in, and in any case, judging by the speed with which it goes past one way, then comes back the other, the wearer is either hopelessly lost or is in something of a panic. Far too busy to peer into Hopgood's, that's for sure. She glances at Wyn. No, Wyn sees nothing, indeed the very notion of doing business in the Spanish Netherlands has him canted back in his seat. Contact with the Spanish is as appalling to Wyn as would be trafficking with the Devil. *That's my finger in your eye, Uncle Greville*, thinks Pris; and then, inspiration!

'I believe I was to wed,' she says. 'The son of the family.' She lowers her eyes. 'There was nothing I could do.' She sniffs. She lets the phrase sink in; as it does, Wyn's expression of outrage deepens. 'But then he died, so…' A hand across the widow's weeds, coming to rest upon the net over her breasts. Oh, Pris, Pris, you are too good at this by far!

From leaning back, Wyn is now upright with indignation. 'But my dear, Breda is under siege—'

'I know,' says Pris. 'I was trapped.' A tear rolls down her nose. The tear, to her surprise, is genuine. 'I thought I would never see London again.'

'My dear,' says Wyn. 'My dear girl! We cannot have this. We cannot have you sent about the world in this manner.' He reaches across the table for her hand (the one that is not now perjuring itself in her lap). His own is neatly manicured, and it reaches for hers with real affection, and now she looks, she sees that same true feeling in Wyn's face as well – the bulbous nose, the small and honest eyes, the eyebrows where the hairs of one turn up, the other down; the kindliness of him, the old-fashioned gentlemanliness that is Wyncanton, all there, all unhidden. 'Oh, Wyn,' she says. It quite surprises Pris, the warmth with which the words come out of her mouth. 'It is so good to see you again!'

CHAPTER EIGHT

A Good Face for Bad Weather

'... then beat they their drums upon the walls, for a general parley to all quarters, and about seven o'clock on Tuesday morning October 6, the cannon ceased on both sides and there was no more shooting, invasion, nor resistance.'

William Lithgow, *A true and experimental discourse upon... this last siege of Breda*

IT TOOK GENERAL Spinola more than a year to take Breda by siege, but Frederick Henry is having none of that. His army arrived outside Breda's walls in July; their zigzag trenches are at those walls by the end of August. The outer walls are mined, then the inner – by October it is obvious to all within the town that it is only a matter of time. Then a ravelin collapses, with a crack loud enough to be heard in Teteringen. There is a terrible animal groan from the defenders within the town, wholly drowned out by the roar of the besiegers; then the English, the Scots, the Dutch, the French, swarm up the slope of mud and broken stone, and lo and behold, there is Breda, laid before them. So now, señores, you have a choice – surrender, or we take you by force. And you don't want us to take your town by force. Remember Magdeburg?

Magdeburg. A city of twenty thousand reduced in a single morning to a plain of ash. Rafts of corpses, floating down the Elbe; a bridge where the water turned red. Jack was there, Zoltan too, and Ulrik, and Thor; and it was so much worse than anything the ballads or broadsheets or tales told since can convey. It was like hell had broken open, risen up through the surface of the Earth. You bring out the name of Magdeburg like Perseus producing the Gorgon's head.

It works. At sunrise the Spanish drums on Breda's walls begin to beat a parley; a flag of truce appears above its gates, the gates themselves creak open. The commander of the garrison bathes and shaves for the first time in weeks; Frederick Henry's army breaks out its mighty regimental flags, there is an exchange of hostages, paradings back and forth. So famous a victory must have its due.

And then, with a shrug, the war moves on. Frederick Henry is rumoured to have Antwerp in his sights, soon as the spring arrives and drier weather hardens the roads. All that remains is the work of throwing down Breda's fortifications. Flattening those ramparts, filling the ditches with spoil, disassembling the trackways so recently built across them, and at such cost. Shearing the horns from the hornworks, untangling that crown of thorns. No-one, thinks Jack (up to his ankles in the mud of the Marck), will ever know how much of a soldier's time is spent with a spade in his hands. Bucketful by bucketful; dig, dig, dig, dig, dig. But the Marck will flow once more through the channel God made for it, when he dragged his finger through the batter of this land, and no future enemy will find Breda so easily defensible, that's for sure. And winter is waiting. The veterans warm themselves by telling tales of winter nights in Germany where you found sentries frozen upright at their posts, where men's fingers snapped off in their gloves; your beard beads with moisture if you stand talking out of doors, and in the cold of the early morning the scars on Jack Fiskardo's face – two above the left eye, one below – declare themselves like he'd been clawed by something as he slept. 'Made for this shit, weren't he?' Thor declares, almost proudly.

You should not be here.

Don't I know it, he thinks.

They collect the cannonballs they find buried in the mud, or rolling along at the bottom of the ditches; build them into ziggurats. Waste not, want not. '*Jä-ä-ävlar-r-r-r*, Domini,' says Ulrik, throwing six-pound cannonballs up to the top of the heap one after the other. 'To think as we survived all them!'

But they did. Damnation, but they did.

They find bones in the sides of the ditches, scraps of cloth, pads of leather that were once the heels of boots. Teeth. The skulls of horses. They are digging through the remains of soldiers from Spinola's siege of the city in '24. Are the bodies Spanish? Are they Dutch?

'They're dead, is what they are,' says Thor.

The provost-general pays a farmer for his field, and they dig yet another pit and throw the dead in there: these, their own, the Spanish caballeros; a jigsaw waiting for the Day of Judgement, and good luck with that. No-one wants to be bothered with this any more.

Says Luka, 'Ain't it the strangest thing, Domini? How battles get fought on the same ground, over and over?'

There's a couple of things that should tell you. One: that no war is ever truly won; and two: we never learn.

In Breda itself, life begins to settle. Greenery is brought into the Grote Kirk, stalls appear, selling mulled ale, so the air smells as if you had put your nose into a plum-cake, and one enterprising soul puts up a tent, sharpens his pens, and sets himself up as scribe to all those casting down the defences outside the town, to send a new year's thought or two back home. Two penningen a sheet, that's all he'll charge, and he'll undertake to carry every last letter to a posting inn.

Says Jens, 'We should do that. We should all do that.'

'Yes, we should,' says Zoltan. And by Christ, if he can get up the nerve to send a word to Ava, then Jack can send word back to St-Étienne-des-Champs. So you might say he is bullied into it, or you might say he allows himself to be. Whichever, it finds him sat in the tent one side of the table with the enterprising scribe the other, and the man asks, 'What should I put?' and Jack's mind goes blank as the sky.

Says the scribe, encouragingly, 'Shall we start with a wish for good health to all?'

What can he do but nod?

'And the weather?' says the man. 'It's always good to put in a bit about the weather.' So he nods again. The stool on which Jack sits (no bigger'n something a milkmaid might use) gives a groan as he shifts his weight.

'And reassure all those good souls at home that you are well?' the scribe continues, looking doubtfully at the beard, the wild-man hair, the scarred face. Jack glares back at him: Mr Clean Shirt, Mr Soft Hands.

'Make your mark there and all done,' the scribe says, hurriedly.

His father used to do this, send word back. Nothing for

months, then a brief *All's well*, and one time, with it, a purse full of gold.

You should be with your sons.

Forgive me, that was what he had wanted to tell the scribe to write. Forgive me, Demi-Cuit, but I am a coward. I keep telling myself that maybe, when I go back, you will be stronger, you will be grown. I am too much of a coward to face anything else.

The longest his father had left him and his mother on their own, in a village in Poitou, was three years. Three years! It would have seemed inconceivable to behave so before; now, though, he can see how easily it can be done. When you are a soldier, his father once told him, trying to explain, *eh bien*, life is – it is very simple, do you understand?

Yes, he does. So much simpler than that same life at home.

Sometimes, in the streets of Breda, he sees the sisters from the Beguinage. You spy them by their headdresses, the wings outspread. They always seem to move about in pairs. He wonders sometimes if they have heard from the *puta*. He wonders how her journey was; if she made it home. No, of course she did. Survivor writ all over her, that one. Then he wonders who, these days, she might be scowling at.

God a'mighty, a reply.

He has to have Zoltan read it to him. Sometimes, Jack is vexed he could never learn how to do this, but not this time. He has to lock his hands about his knee, to stop their trembling.

'This comes from a Georges Artaud.'

Jack nods his head. 'A neighbour.'

'*Good Captain*,' Zoltan begins. '*We send you our wishes for your good health. We are glad to hear of you, and that you do well. Your boys do well—*'

'Wait, stop. Go back. Boys? It says boys?'

'It says boys,' Zoltan replies. 'Shall I go on?'

Boys. Two of them. He is still a father of two.

'*Our summer here was dry, and the apples were small* – Why is this idiot writing to you about apples?'

'Cider,' says Jack, grinning. 'Picardy's life blood.'

Zoltan rolls his eyes. 'To continue. *Your man of business, he has been with us a month—*'

Now Zoltan looks up. 'Your man of business? Who the devil is that?'

Jack spreads his hands. 'I've no idea.'

'*He has took a room at the Écu and says as he will stay until you show your face. Cou-Cou says he is your man and so she will not charge, but still, she says, it is a room* – I hope all this means something to you, Jacques, because it sounds like the purest nonsense to me.'

Something, yes. That is Cou-Cou all over – the caution around any stranger from the world outside, let alone one describing himself as Jack's man of business; the resentment at not charging for a room. But who is this?

'*And she does say so twenty times a day, so it will please myself and Robert greatly if you would return and see to your business here with Monsieur Vanderhoof—*'

Mystery solved. 'Cornelius? Cornelius is at the Écu?'

'So it would seem,' says Zoltan, folding the letter. 'I give you leave, Jacques. As your officer, I give you leave to leave. Go rescue Cornelius from the cider-people. Go home.'

HE HEARS THE village before he sees it, and M'sieu scents it even earlier than that, snorting into the breeze as the singing of those strewing new seed in the fields is carried past them. As Jack dismounts, tethering M'sieu outside the Écu in the springtime sun, he can hear Robert, off-key as ever, warbling away in the stables. He walks into the garden and for one moment of almost joyous agony, his memory tells him it is Mirelle sat there, winding wool, outside where the light is best – but no, it is Cou-Cou, Ned sat at her feet with his hands upraised, a hank of the stuff stretched over them, dipping obediently left to right as Cou-Cou winds and winds, and sitting opposite –

– that is Cornelius.

And on Cornelius's lap, this little thing – these great blue eyes as big as ponds, a head as bald as a mushroom, a sort of kink between head and neck.

'You,' says Cornelius, standing, 'you are a terrible father. And an even worse friend.'

'How could you not tell us?' Cornelius asks. 'How could you not tell us you had lost Mirelle?'

They sit in the back parlour, Jack with Ned asleep in his lap and his son's breath warm on his neck. Robert and Cou-Cou have taken themselves off to bed, left Jack and his man of business to it. Stars peek in through the window and Demi-Cuit gazes silently up at them from his bed on the table; no longer his mother's sewing box, his father sees, but an old apple crate. Still too small for a cradle. Demi-Cuit has made a distinctive shape in the padding of the crate – one long straight furrow for left leg, one rounder for right, where he draws it up at the knee; left arm thrown out, the fingers opening and closing like a sea anemone; the right held tight to the breast, as if keeping a secret. Maybe he is.

Says Jack, 'Because I couldn't begin to work out how.' *Because every time I have to tell someone, it's like I lost her only yesterday.*

'Yosha wrote to me,' Cornelius is saying. 'He was distraught. He said it was months since you had been to Amsterdam, and not a word from you, nothing.'

Yosha Silbergeld, Cornelius's father. A man of business of the calibre to leave all others standing. 'I find it difficult to imagine Yosha distraught,' Jack points out.

'You have *never* understood how much you mean to him,' Cornelius says. 'How much you mean to all of us.'

Yosha Silbergeld, who took this scapegrace lad in off the docks in Amsterdam and made him a home. But what waif and stray ever truly thought they were worth anything to anyone? Except on the battlefield. Or here, with Mirelle.

'So I come all a-ways to Picardy, and what do I find? Mirelle in her grave, and you gone back to the wars. I hope this time,' Cornelius continues, 'you weren't trying to get yourself killed.' He sweeps out an arm: Ned, James. 'Not with these two waiting for you. Or I assume you weren't, at least.'

God forgive him, yes, there had been a time when Jack Fiskardo did all he could to force the gods to exact upon him the punishment he thought he deserved. But those thoughts had been leavened with madness, with fury, with revenge, revenge, revenge; Jack thinks he had hardly known what he was about, back then. There was one anguished night when he had sat on the edge of his bed in Yosha Silbergeld's fine house, sprung the blade on his old clasp-knife, the same that he had carried since he was no more than a child himself, and watched one after the other as the lines of blood bubbled up on his forearm. There were days and days after that of which he has no memory at all. This time, though, what he feels is leavened with nothing. There is just the great ache of grief, the background to everything. You carry it away with you; you bring it home.

From the apple box, the sound of humming. The same few notes, up the scale, then down. A fragment of something? Or nothing at all.

'Ned was almost walking at a year,' says Jack. 'I remember him, pursuing the cat.' He rubs a hand over his son's head. 'He could da-da-da with the best of 'em.' He glances over to the apple crate. 'Cou-Cou says James has yet to utter a word. It makes me – uneasy.'

'Listen, Jack,' Cornelius begins, leaning forward. 'There is a man in London, a physician. He is renowned. He has a specialism, in the ailments of children. He has produced improvements that are almost wondrous. Why not take James to him?'

'To London?' This tiny scrap, to make a journey such as that?

'Yes! You, Ned, James – come back with me. You could stay with the Endicotts, with Rafe and Belle. They would delight to see you again. We'll take Ned to see the lions in the Tower, and you can consult with Sir Theodore. Theodore de Mayerne. He is a Frenchman, like you. Well, a Swiss. Almost as good. What do you say?'

At mention of his name, his son's head has come up. Jack feels the damp little cheek detach from his neck. Ned looks over at his brother. Again, the tiny hum, up then down. For a moment it's the only sound in the room.

'I wonder if he hears it,' Jack says. 'I wonder if he knows what he does.'

'*Il chante*,' says Ned, rubbing his eyes, looking from one man to the other. He says it as if this is the most obvious thing in the world. 'When Demi-Cuit is happy, he sings.'

He's up at first light, to go to the churchyard. He stands at the grave where he had last stood a year before, hat in hand, heart twisting. Something has made itself a home here, some brave and early flowering thing. Little chequered bells. Fritillaries, of course.

Someone planted that. Brought the bulb back from Laon, dug a hole, tapped it in. Who would that have been – Robert? Madame Bertin?

Are you there? he asks. *Are you there, or are you gone too far away?*

The dead move on from you. His father did, his mother too. The men he lost, the loss that almost sent him crazy, even they.

Mirelle, what do I do? What do I do with our boys? With the little one, with Demi-Cuit?

Might there be something to be done? Some cure, some way to reach whatever is inside that tiny, bent-legged form?

But to risk such a voyage…

He looks up, as if to find her watching, but there is nothing. Nothing but clouds racing behind the steeple, on, on, on, over that distant blue.

Back to the Écu. Cou-Cou is in the kitchen, slipshod and harassed. Men are not supposed to be up and about as early as this. 'Will you look to him?' she says, pointing. She has lifted James from the crate, made a sort of nest for him with cushions before the fire. 'He's all of a wriggle this morning.' The sound of *bok-bok-bok* outside, querulous in tone. A hand laid to her forehead. 'I must see to those hens.' Her slippers smack across the brick of the floor. The back door closes. She is gone.

Jack gets down onto the hearth with his son – the usual growl of warning from his leg, but he's getting used to that. Pulls Demi-Cuit's camisole straight, where it has been rucked up over the child's bum-cloth. His hand looks like a giant's against the boy, an ogre's. Christ above, to think of taking this fragile grub all the way to London. He is almost scared to touch his son as it is.

He puts the pad of one finger against his son's forehead. The blue eyes – the skin about them so pale and thin, the blue seems to bleed into it – pass across his face, and focus on some place beyond his shoulder.

'Demi-Cuit, do you know who I am?' Jack asks.

The gaze is intense, but not at him. The left hand grips at the edge of a cushion, gripping, then pulling away.

The cushion shifts. A shudder of effort.

'Do you want this gone?' He moves the cushion. But his son keeps reaching and grasping, as if it were still there.

'Do you want – do you want to turn over? Is that it?'

He puts his hand against the boy's chest, against almost the entire length of his body, turns him onto his front. A moment to recover, as if to reorient himself, then James's head lifts, albeit shaking with effort once more. The bent right leg, the knee, comes up, to push against, the left leg does the pushing. Right elbow. Left arm. Push, stretch, push. It's like watching someone try to swim in sand. The head goes down. It is a mighty effort, clearly, to keep it raised. The face turns, the eyes still fixed on something. Jack, lying flat to the floor, looks where his son is looking and there, under the coffer, there's a glint.

On hands and knees, he crawls across the floor. He can feel those blue eyes on him, all the way. Reaches beneath the coffer, and there it is, the bell from the hat of the Pulcinella doll he had brought home for Ned, years ago, when Ned was still small enough for such things to be a wonder; a tiny silver bell, pulled from Pulcinella's hat within minutes of the doll's arrival. He remembers now, it had been the cat's favourite toy; he and Mirelle would sit in the parlour listening to Minou bat the bell back and forth across the kitchen, go skittering after it, mewing when she'd batted it some place she could no longer reach.

He lifts James onto his lap. The head flops backwards, but the eyes are on his hand – the hand holding the bell.

'Did you spy this? Is that why you were wriggling?' Jack holds the bell between finger and thumb, shakes it, rings the silvery chime –

– and the left hand comes up at once. Grab.

James holds the bell against his cheek, rolling it up and down. There's the jingle.

There's the hum.

Oh, God above. A *smile*.

Cornelius's bed in London is of feather, here it is straw. His sheets in Green Dragon Court are thick and soft; those at the Écu (at least, those the landlady has given him) are cicatriced with darns. Falling asleep takes what feels like hours of concentration, and waking is like climbing your way out of a pit. And *oh mijn God*, the noise out there! The squawks and twittering above his head; the bellowing and braying from the fields; the barking dogs, the blasted cockerels, from hours before the sun has even thought of rising. And something in the woods that had exploded in a scream of torture just as he began to drift away to dreamland. *Give me London*, thinks Cornelius, *give me the shouts of watchmen and the turn of wheels*—

'Cornelius!' Jack's bellow. Another bang-bang-bang upon his door. 'Cornelius, are you awake?'

'The devil is it?' Cornelius demands. His nightcap has swivelled around overnight, all he can see is its tassel. 'Is the place on fire, or what?'

'Get yourself up. Get packed. We're headed to London.'

CHAPTER NINE

On London Bridge

'Speculation… a spying, a watching in an high Tower or open place, a discovery, a considering, or observing.'

Thomas Blount, *Glossographia: or a Dictionary*

LONDON. HERE SHE comes, street by street, wharf by wharf, spire by spire. 'What is zat?' Ned wants to know.

'That,' says Cornelius, their guide to all things London, 'is the Tower. I will take you there.'

Standing between Jack's knees, Ned is on tiptoe with excitement, tilting as the boat rocks, as the tide runs them forward. 'And what is *zat*?'

'That is St Paul's. London's great church. I will take you there too.'

'And what is *zat*?'

His son has an accent. The *zis*, the *zat*. But then, thinks Jack, no doubt his father has one too.

'That,' says Cornelius, shifting his shoulder to shield Ned's eyes from the curious blackened lumps, like some hellish version of candied apples on their sticks, raised aloft at its far end, 'is London's Bridge.'

Ned's eyes are wide with wonder, his face open with delight. 'But it 'as *owsis* on it!' he exclaims.

That feel of the water beneath you; the sound of it under your keel. 'This brings back memories,' says Jack.

Their boatman takes note. 'You have a boat, Captain?'

'When I was his age,' Jack replies, indicating Ned. 'A sail-boat. On the Charente, in France. A long time ago.'

'A long way away,' the boatman offers.

'I think your journey will have been longer,' says Jack, and the man laughs, bistre-coloured skin wrinkling about his eyes. 'Yes, indeed.'

'Jack,' says Cornelius, 'meet Miguel Domingo. A champion amongst the watermen.'

The bridge is almost above them, the river growing that deep new note beneath its arches. Jack, seeing the speed with which the water runs between the starlings, comments, 'This must make a rapids, when it's on the ebb.'

'Indeed it does, Captain,' Miguel replies. 'Shooting the bridge, we call it. Not recommended.'

Onlookers idle along the parapet; fishermen dangle their lines. On the stone steps of a wharf, a gang of barefoot urchins, ragged as Jack once was himself, squabble and squawk. More squawking – a barge, unloading crates of fowl. A riverside tavern. And somewhere, even if Jack can't spot them, a pair of eyes taking note of it all.

'How safe will London be?' he had asked Cornelius as, finding themselves in some new place, fathers of small children have to do.

'Safe? Almost perfectly,' Cornelius had answered. 'But uncontested, no. England is – England is like a dog, turning about on its bed. London, particularly so.'

And there, they are through, the bridge behind them. And now on the south bank, another clot of folk: two women, one sat with head in hands and an infant held against her, just as Jack holds James; the other with a little girl leaning into her, as if to comfort; and a group of men, gesticulating, angry. All of them darkly dressed, and cloaked as if for some long voyage, yet one now come to grief, perhaps. There is also a rowboat drawn up to the bank, the boatman dragging bags and belongings from it to be laid at the men's feet. Jack turns to Cornelius. 'What's going on there?'

'Ah,' says Cornelius. 'That is an all too common story, sad to say. There is some disagreement, just at present, between good King Charles and his subjects. He would rule one way, unquestioned; they would question. They would worship one way; he will not have it. He is intent upon a war against the Scots, but his pockets are empty, and his Parliament will not line them without he deal with their grievances first. You know the English. You may push them thus far, and no further. There are some who would depart for the New World as a result, to show the King what they think of him, but if they wish to do so, they must have a licence. Such licences are frequently denied, and at short notice. I would say such a miscarrying is what we witness there.'

'Why not let them be gone?' Jack asks.

'Well, yes. I can only say that it seems His Majesty cannot countenance the fact he is not beloved by all.'

At his father's breast, tied in a sling, James sleeps on. It is as if (thinks his father) he has decided *London? All in good time.*

But that sense of being over-watched has gone.

Of course it has. One of those same urchins has lifted himself up from his raggedy elbows, cantered up the steps of the wharf on his scabby legs and set off at a trot through the thronging crowd. He makes good progress – so vermin-ridden is his appearance that even a crowd as thick as that on London Bridge gives way. Besides, no-one knows the bridge better than Bug. This is his acre; its wind- and rain-free corners his bedchambers; where the shopkeepers throw out the most palatable leavings, it is his pantry and his table too. Bug's current destination is his office, midway down the bridge, where stands an immense and unmistakable building, Nonsuch House: four storeys high, cross-hatched with timbering and gaudy with paint – red, gold and green. It marks the one place where in all the bustle, the cram of buildings, you may find a little light, a little air, as right before Nonsuch is London Bridge's solitary drawbridge, which is also where, if the weather be fine enough, you will find Tucker Turnbull. Tucker with his belly, like a toad had learned to walk upright; Tucker with the pennies and ha'pennies from Old Man Skinner in his pocket.

It's Tucker's favourite spot, in fact. When the drawbridge is lifted, all traffic on the bridge must stop, perforce, and as the crowd thickens, Tucker will give any standing near his views on who sails past and why, complete with many a dark and beery hint (if his audience is male) that his knowledge is some secret, arcane matter, which will this very night be shared with others great in power. If his audience should be female, Tucker will leer upon her, and endeavour to work into his conversation some favourite pun upon the word 'seamen'. In truth Ingram Skinner has Tucker waste his time in watching from the bridge because he can think of nothing else to do with him. Tucker is a drunkard; cannot be relied upon these days for anything. See him now, leaning back, elbows on the bridge's parapet, head full of beer-smoke, gazing up at Nonsuch's glinting casements till it makes him dizzy.

'Mistah Tucker!' Bug yells, arriving in front of him.

Tucker opens one eye, then the other. He sees before him a frantic puppet, with an open sore upon one cheek, topped with a shock of hair so thick with dirt it stands up like a crest.

'Mistah Tucker, tide's come in!' Bug informs him.

Tucker swings his gaze river-wards, as if checking that Bug has this right. He sees how the river laps against the walls of the Tower, how the weed-washed stairs of the Bear Garden are wholly underwater, how ducks and geese and London's famous swans throng up against the terraces of the riverside taverns, as those on the terraces throw out crusts of bread and apple cores to them. 'So it has,' Tucker agrees, grandly. 'And what has it brought us, eh?'

This is what Bug excels at. This is what Tucker pays him for.

'There was another bunch of radicals got sent back from Tilbury,' Bug begins. 'I saw 'em, they got dumped off by the Clink. Right twisted up about it, they looked.'

Tucker sniffs. 'Sod 'em.'

'An' there's a fine big merchantman moored off Lion Quay,' Bug announces. 'You can see her masts from here. Reckon she's from Virginny. Baccy, Mistah Tucker. Sotweed. Beaver skins and sugar-cane. Have her holds packed full, I'll bet.'

Tucker gives a grunt. That's more like it. Full holds mean full warehouses; mean bribing of watchmen and scaling of walls and barrels and sacks handed down to vanish into the dark of London's streets.

'An' Miguel Domingo says the *Guid Marie*'s come in again.'

This time, no grunt. Tucker salts this news away in silence. There is little love lost between Tucker and the captain of the *Guid Marie*, that whoreson Mungo Sant, who not only (in Tucker's younger days) refused Tucker a place in his crew, but is well known along the river as the Hollands' man. 'Go on then,' Tucker says. 'That all?'

'And she brought news, Mistah Tucker. The French 'ave laid an action against St Omer, and all the ports that way is shut to us. That's Calais, Mistah Tucker, Calais an' Dunkirk both. Don't Old Man Skinner have the *Sapphire* in Dunkirk? Coz if 'e do, she's stuck.'

Fuck, Tucker thinks. The way the world is, everybody has to pick a side, and whereas the Holland family favours business with Amsterdam and the Dutch Republic, Ingram Skinner does his trading with Brussels and Antwerp. And did indeed have the *Sapphire* in Dunkirk. ''Ow come,' Tucker begins, with all the clumsy doggedness of one pursuing something through a fog, ''ow come the *Sapphire*'s stuck, yet the *Guid Marie*'s safe 'ome?'

'Dunno, Mistah Tucker,' answers Bug, and then, cheekily, 'Mebbe it was Mercator! Don't'cha think? Mebbe it was Mercator warned 'im, Mistah Tucker!'

'Don't you start on that with me,' Tucker growls. 'Fucken Mercator. He's a fairy tale, he is. A will-'o'-the-wisp. He's an 'erring, and e's *red*.' He surveys Bug from on high. 'That's it, is it? That's all you've got?'

Bug rubs a hand under his nose. 'An Mistah Vander'oof is back,' he finishes. 'I saw 'im land at Churchyard Stairs. He'd another with 'im.' Bug lifts himself up onto his toes, raises a hand as high as he can above his head, indicating this other's height. 'Sowjer, I reckon,' Bug says, knowledgeably. 'Had that milit'ry look. And a death's 'ed on the back of 'is coat.'

'Mr 'oo?' Tucker asks.

'Mistah Vander'oof. You know. Got an office in Green Dragon Court.'

Tucker gives a snort. 'That's it, is it?' he asks. 'That all you've got for me?'

'Thass a lot, Mistah Tucker!' Bug declares.

'An 'apence, that's all that's worth, and you're lucky you're getting that,' Tucker tells him. 'Now gerrout me way. I gotta make me report.'

Bug watches him go. For once, having his intelligence rated so cheap troubles him not at all. Bug, in his tiny and unheeded way, is a consummate double-agent, and he is delighted Cornelius Vanderhoof is back.

'WE ARE IN *shreds*,' Cornelius declares. 'If it was not James needing to be fed, it was Ned needing to be plucked down from the rigging. No sooner did we have him corralled in our cabin, than James would need his bum-cloth changed. With our cabin at a slant like this,' says Cornelius, leaning his forearm at forty-five degrees. He nods to where James slumbers in his sling against his father, right hand as ever curled beneath his chin. 'And my God, you never saw such needing to be cleaned and changed!'

'They are prodigious shitters, my boys,' says Jack, mildly. 'Both of 'em.'

'So *somehow* we would change his cloth,' Cornelius continues, 'without James rolling away from us altogether, and when we turned about, Ned would be gone again. Shreds, I tell you. *Shreds*. This, dearest Belle – ' (he lifts his glass of malmsey by its foot) '– this was never so welcome.'

Belle tips her head in acknowledgement. 'And yet,' she comments lightly, 'women somehow manage all their duties to their children on their own. I wonder how?'

Rafe's sleek little wife – she puts Jack in mind of a seal. The swiftness with which she had disposed them about her house, readied her table, summoned them to eat. Disposed her parents at her board as well: her mother, who (from behind the fortification of her gown, which is swagged and braided like the royal box at a tourney) sits gawping at Jack as if he had two heads; and Belle's father, at the far end of the table, who sits looking as if the very invitation to dine here had been an insult.

'Mirelle used to say that was why you needed a man, to have a child,' Jack says, and even as he says it, finds himself thinking, *Good God, this is the first time I have used her name like that. As someone gone.* 'Apparently, we are good practice for 'em.'

A whinny of laughter from Mrs Butter. Mr Butter, at the table's end, stares on, pop-eyed. Jack has a sense Mr Butter reckons his place should be up here at this end of the table, where Rafe stands, wielding a carving knife over a fine-looking saddle of beef. Who would have thought the wandering scribbler, who became so unexpected a member of Jack's troop of discoverers in Germany, would ever be sat here, in this house in Coleman Street, with its panelled rooms and canopied beds, and its pretty garden visible there through the window: Crown Imperials raised on high, tulips nuzzled beneath them… 'Oh forgive me, Captain,' Mrs Butter is saying. 'You are so exactly as our Rafe described. To meet the man who made his fortune –'

At the far end of the table, Mr Butter's pop-eyed glare grows froggier still.

'– and yet you are so wholly different! I never thought,' says Mrs Butter, flapping a hand, 'I never thought you would be a man with children, for a start.'

Mr Butter clears his throat. 'And it would be the usual thing,' says Mr Butter, 'here in *England*, for children to dine *separate*. Don't y'know.'

'Not in this house, Pa,' says Belle, a gentle warning in her tone.

Beside her, Ned is sitting up so straight, and with so angelic an expression it can only mean (thinks his father) that under the table he is feeding the Endicotts' dog. 'Who is this?' Jack had asked, as the animal came trotting down the hall to meet them, tail a-wag and an oddly familiar pair of eyebrows raised on high. 'This is Dash,' Rafe had told him. 'Daughter of Dart.'

'And what do you make of London, Captain, on your first visit here?' Mr Butter asks, ignoring Belle. 'A splendid city, yes?'

'London seems somewhat at odds with herself,' says Jack. Now it is Mr Butter's eyebrows that lift. A critic?

Cornelius steps in. 'We saw a family of Puritans, most unhappily disembarked, as we came upriver,' he explains.

'Those,' says Mr Butter, at once. 'Those like the Scots, who would have God's house bare as a stable!' He turns back to Jack, and as he does so, gives a curious little wiggle of excitement, like a dog with a stick at its paws. 'What are your views on that, I wonder, Captain?' ('Now, Natty,' puts in his wife. 'There is more than enough talking of politics in the world at present. We don't need more.') Mr Butter ignores her too. 'Well?' he demands. 'Well?'

'I have no views,' says Jack. 'I have none whatsoever.' *And I just trod upon your stick.*

'None, sir?' Mr Butter looks as if he can hardly conceive of such a thing. 'None, Captain? A man who has fought his way all through Germany, and back again? Is not that a war of politics? Of faith?'

'Mr Butter, I hate to be the one to disabuse you, but on the field, politics and faith come very low on the list. The only man

I ever followed out of conviction was Gustavus Adolphus of Sweden –' ('Hear, hear,' puts in Rafe) '– and he we would have followed into hell. Whatever his religion.' Jack lifts his glass in a toast to the departed; he sees Rafe and Cornelius do the same. 'Men may fight because of many things, but they only ever fight *for* one. You fight for what you love. Whether it is your brother-in-arms beside you, or your family, or your home.' He shrugs. 'Unless, like me, you become a soldier because it is the only trade you know. And now I am not even that. Now I am here for this one only.' And he nods down to James, in his sling, who slumbers still.

'Our captain is here to consult with Sir Theodore,' Rafe puts in.

A small mean light glints into life in Mr Butter's eye. 'Well,' says he, 'I wish you good luck of it, sir. The man was of no use to Belle and Rafe, no use at all!'

And why did Belle and Rafe consult with Sir Theodore? Why, for their childlessness, of course. Six years they have been wed, six years, and not once has Belle missed her monthly courses. Not once has that river held itself back to build into something more.

'You mustn't fret, lovey,' her mother told her. 'Fretting will help not at all.'

She did not fret. Instead, Belle walked about with a clove of linen-wrapped garlic inserted in what the bawdy would refer to as her book of two leaves, this being how one ascertained there was no internal blockage to conception. 'Oooh yes, lovey,' her mother assured Belle that evening, sniffing her breath. 'That's risen straight up through you. You reek!'

Still no child. They took further measures, with Rafe anointing what was also known as Belle's contrapunctum with oil scented with balsam before they made love, this being reputed as a sovereign cure for infertility; they both enjoyed this very much, but still no pregnancy as a result. He took to anointing his own member with the same, then with civet and with musk – the female womb, they were told, delighted in sweet scents, and would thus open itself to his seed as well. Still no. He ate oysters. She ate oysters. Rafe ate lampreys, though they made him gag, but why would Nature create such a long, firm, muscular creature if not to bring vigour to the male organ? Yet even that brought no result. They consulted amongst their friends. The tulips and lilies in Belle's garden came from Ava Franka, that splendid plantswoman; and Ava's business partner, Rosa, suffered years of babies lost almost before she knew they were there; then she met Ilya, sergeant to that notorious discoverer Jack Fiskardo, in an army camp in Germany and now, in their house in Haarlem, Rosa and Ilya have three daughters, one after the other, came into this world with no trouble at all. 'Your child will come when it will come,' Ava had assured her. 'You are still so young, Belle. You haf more than enough time.' And yes, she did – she and Rafe had wed when Belle was scarce sixteen – but still no child came. Even Dart – beloved Dart, who was Rafe's companion all the way through his adventures in Germany and whose bones lie under the pear tree in Belle's garden – even Dart had puppies; Dash is the proof of that.

So they had consulted with Sir Theodore. Sir Theodore questioned Belle about her courses, listened to her belly through an ear trumpet, swirled her urine about in a bottle and peered at it with the light behind it; he took Rafe away into a corner and examined Rafe's cods, he questioned Rafe as to whether he gave his wife pleasure in the act, that too being needed for conception to occur – 'Yes,' Rafe told him, remembering the anointing, 'most definitely.' Sir Theodore pronounced them both healthy and exactly as they should be, yet still the most that has ever happened to Belle is that she has been late, once or twice, by a week or so, as her clock for some reason reset, and then matters went on just as before – the ache, the bleed, her tears, Rafe's loving arms about her; the hope bravely renewed. Until the hope did not renew. When Belle thinks now of the child that might have been theirs, a thing she strives her hardest *not* to do, she imagines it as a little plant, all alone, starved of sunlight in some room to which they cannot find the key, its existence hardly mentioned. Except in circumstances such as this evening, when her father forgets himself.

'You must forgive Mr Butter,' says Rafe. He and Jack sit together in Belle's garden, another bottle of malmsey between them. 'He was so long the master, and I the humble clerk. It grinds him that my name is with his above the bookshop now, even more so that it was my German booty paid his debts. When he speaks so I think it is because it makes him feel he is the master still.'

'A pompostous little fart of a man, all the same,' says Jack, in the same mild tone as before. Rafe splutters with laughter. 'Ah me,' he says. 'Indeed he is. Although since he became my father-in-law, I find I become almost fond of him. *Almost.* I grow mellow, Domini. I mean, look at this,' says Rafe, putting down his glass to squeeze the roll of podge above his midriff in both hands. 'I fatten. The fat bookseller of St Paul's, that is what they will call me. You look ready for action as ever.' He taps the side of his own face to indicate the scars, above Jack's eye, below. 'Although these are new.'

'My last encounter with Carlo Fantom,' says Jack.

'The last, as in final, do you mean?' Rafe sits forward. He bears his own souvenir of his time in Germany, the middle finger on his left hand ceasing at the first joint, and he knows full well the depth of Jack's hatred toward Carlo Fantom, and all the reasons for it. 'Do we dare to dream the man is gone?'

'I doubt it. Something tells me my ghost is still not in his grave. But I'll happily drink to him finding it, nonetheless.'

From the window above their heads, the sound of Belle settling Jack's sons to sleep. She is singing to them. The words come drifting down: *Sleep, pretty baby, do not cry, And I will sing a lullaby…*

'Your wife,' says Jack, 'is a jewel. Ned is half in love with her already.'

'She loves to have your boys here, that is sure. I know she pines for one of our own. As do I. Ah well. We try.' He reaches across, places his hand over Jack's. 'Jack, my friend, my brother – I am so sorry. We both are. There is so much in this world at present, should not be as it is. And losing Mirelle is the greatest wrong of all.'

Later, Jack will stand at that same window with James in his arms. Ned snores behind them in his truckle bed, but James has been wakeful, that one small fist appearing again and again at the edge of the basket in which Belle had laid him, the wicker all a-creak. Now, in his father's arms, against his father's heartbeat, James is quiet again. 'Of course you are,' Jack tells him, wearily. His son has a habit of carrying his head to the right, and then looking back at you, as if viewing the world askance is the way to do it. In the light of the moon, Jack sees for the first time that there is hair coming in on James's head, fine as spider-silk. 'You growing feathers, chick?' he asks. *All my force*, he thinks, viewing his own body there in the moonlight – the muscles lapped about the bone, the flop of his cock against his thigh (*and when am I ever going to need you again?*), all the scars, the battles won – all that, and I make this tiny, fragile thing I cannot seem to reach at all. 'You are at least a most peaceful companion,' he tells James. 'Your brother would have had the whole house wakened with his roar by now.'

Those great blue eyes, so great the stars are there, reflected back at him. What goes on in that head? He puts his nose down close to James's scalp, breathing in that mix of milk and linen. He whispers to the curve of the head, 'Is all this making sense somewhere in there?'

That gaze. Dark as the heavens, deep as an ocean, and just as unfathomable. Jack gives a sigh. *Zehr gut.* Tomorrow, Sir Theodore.

FAR TO THE west of Coleman Street, where the great flinty bulk of St Bartholomew's blocks out the stars one way, and the jumble of the roofs of Newgate prison do so the other, where the air at sunrise echoes to the squeals of pigs and the lowing of cattle being driven to Smithfield Market and the gutters by evening are sluggish with their blood, there is an alleyway, Turn Again Lane. At the end of it, should you be rash enough to proceed so far, you will reach Hag Place. No-one knows or remembers who was the hag, but by God she must have been an evil bitch to make this well her home – hemmed about on all three sides with houses as ancient as St Bartholomew's, and as dark, and as flinty, with overhanging upper storeys and windows thin as arrow slits, like they were making some mean assessment of your chances of getting out of here alive. The walls around you lean both in and out, as if you were making your way through some perpetually tumbling house of cards; they are patched here and there with a series of iron S's, like brands, and the ground is as uneven as if caught in the effort of shrugging all this dirty dereliction from its back for good.

Tucker hates to be here; but Tucker has no choice – Hag Place is where the Skinners hold court; Ingram, and his lumpen sons Ezra and Asa, and their scurry of whores – creatures who even to Tucker seem to have no more agency over their lives than the animals led every day to slaughter up the street. One time there was that poor wretch of a daughter too, but no-one speaks of her no more – wouldn't dare. Sat in the midst of this protean darkness, Ingram Skinner himself, a man who looks as if, should he see daylight, he would bubble and rot. Lean as an anatomy is Ingram, fatless, fleshless, white as a root; old enough for his knuckles to show purple, with a face like rolled-out pastry draped over a skull and eyes as hard and dark as obsidian. Tucker cannot be in his presence without having fortified himself with strong drink, and as a result is sometimes unsure, when he finds himself back on the streets of Farringdon, whether he has just survived an interview with Old Man Skinner or simply had a nightmare about it.

'Well now, Tucker,' Old Man Skinner begins, cracking those purple knuckles of his, as the light from the fireplace in his chamber leaps about him. From somewhere, outside in the courtyard or up on the roof, the sound of what must surely be a madwoman, or the spirit of the hag returned, screeching out a song.

'Well now, Tucker,' says Skinner again, leaning forward into the light of the flames, 'tell me what you've got.'

'Fine big merchantman, moored off Lion Quay,' Tucker begins. (Start with the good stuff.) 'I reckon I could get you in there, Mr Skinner.' He taps the side of his nose. 'I've a mate who's watchman.'

Skinner waves a hand, dismissively. 'Ezra will see to that.'

Knowing Ezra, this may well mean Tucker's mate the watchman ends up with his skull broke. Tucker swallows nervously.

'And there was more dissenters, sent back ashore. His Majesty has sealed 'is heart against 'em, no mistake.'

Skinner sits back in his chair. Those dark eyes glow. 'Trouble,' he says, with pleasure.

'And – and,' stammers Tucker, 'there's news of St Omer.'

Ingram Skinner cocks his head, indicating Tucker should proceed.

''Tis all besieged,' says Tucker, breaking the bad news fast, and spreading his hands as if to say *What can you do?* 'So's all the coast to left and right, Mr Skinner. Calais, Dunkirk – bit of a nuisance for us, I know.'

'The *Sapphire*?' Skinner says at once.

'Caught there, sir. Stuck. As I understand.'

'We had intelligence the Channel ports would be clear,' says Skinner, slowly.

'Yeah, so we did,' says Tucker, rubbing at his forehead, which has begun to bead with sweat. 'Must'a been put out falsely, Mr Skinner, sir.'

Silence. Then Ingram Skinner sits back. 'Mr Tucker,' he says. 'Who pays you?'

'You do, Mr Skinner.'

'And who pays me?'

Tucker drops his eyes. 'Mr Hooley,' he mumbles.

'What was that?' Skinner cups his ear.

'Mr *Hooley*,' Tucker repeats.

'That's right. Mr Hooley. And who pays Mr Hooley, Mr Tucker?'

'The Spanish,' Tucker answers, eyes still on the floor.

'Right again, Mr Tucker. The Spanish. The very same who were waiting for the saltpetre, and the cartridge, and the woolly wadding, that is even now a-sitting in the *Sapphire*'s holds, and which it would seem we have just made a present of to the bastard fucken *French.*' Ingram Skinner closes his eyes and takes a breath. 'Now what do you reckon Mr Hooley will think when he hears of that? Will he be pleased, Mr Tucker?'

'No, Mr Skinner,' says Tucker, looking at the floor.

'Will he rub his hands with glee?'

'No, Mr Skinner.'

'*No, Mr Skinner*,' Ingram parrots. 'He will not. He will think we are lax, Mr Tucker. He will think we are not up to the job. And what might he do, then, Mr Tucker?'

A mumble.

'Will he come amongst us his good self, Mr Tucker? Will he hazard his own skin, as he did in Breda? Speak up.'

'I don't know what, Mr Skinner,' says Tucker, miserably.

'Then I will tell you. He will send amongst us his contractor, Mr Tucker. You know who I mean.' Ingram is enjoying this. Of course, Hooley's dreaded contractor actually setting foot over here would be a very different matter indeed, but it is wonderful to use the man's reputation to discomfit Tucker so. 'His contractor who is such a man as even I would hesitate to turn my back upon. A man such as even Death itself will have no truck with. And believe me, Mr Tucker – we do not want no such murtherous fucken *Fantoms* here.'

CHAPTER TEN

The Wooden *O*

'Love, madam, has eagle's eyes; it can beget acquaintance even in a moment…'

Henry Glapthorne, *The Tragedy of Albertus Wallenstein*

'FISKARDO,' SAYS SIR Theodore. He leans forward. 'Where would I have heard that name before?'

'My father,' says Jack. 'Jean Fiskardo.' (It is always his father.)

'No, no, I think not,' says Sir Theodore. 'It was a Jack Fiskardo, I am sure. Who was I speaking to? What was I speaking of?' He taps his fingertips against his mouth; small and neat against the spread of his jowls. 'I have it,' he says. 'It was in correspondence with my fellow physician Felix Stromberg. He told me of a most curious case of his, in Germany. A captain of a band of discoverers, who took a bullet to the heart, yet lived to tell the tale.'

He raises an interrogative eyebrow. Jack, sitting at the table's other side, with James cradled against his arm, says nothing.

'Herr Stromberg described a belief there is amongst the soldiers over there, of warriors who have rendered themselves bulletproof. "Hard men", I believe, is the term used. Would I have that right?' Another interrogative glance at Jack. 'Such men wear the symbol of a silver wolf, apparently, to mark themselves out.'

'Herr Stromberg is mighty well informed,' says Jack, at last.

'And do you wear it still, Captain? Might I see the fateful object?'

With his free hand, Jack takes the silver wolf from around his neck and hands it across. Sir Theodore, rising slightly from his chair, brings it close to one eye, runs a finger across the disc of the bullet, flattened on its impact with the body of the wolf. 'Most extraordinary,' he says. 'One of the most extraordinary things I ever saw. Captain, I believe if you were a cat, you would be described as having eight lives left.' He hands the silver wolf back almost regretfully. Against Jack's arm, the movement of James's head tracks its return. 'If you were ever to consider selling it…' Sir Theodore raises a hand to indicate his choice of furnishings: the potted jungle, the turtle-shell, the ivory skeleton. 'I have a taste for curiosities.' He settles himself again. 'Did I also notice, as you entered, some slight claudication of the left leg?'

'A fracture,' says Jack. 'Some years back. I had a sergeant at the time, was something of a bone-setter.' He spans his leg above the knee. 'Although I do feel it still.'

'The thigh-bone?' Sir Theodore shakes his head. 'Seven lives,' he murmurs. 'Herr Stromberg tells me His Majesty Gustavus Adolphus held you in high esteem, sir.'

'As I did him,' says Jack.

'You were perhaps at Lützen, where he fell?'

'I am both full of regret and most heartily glad I was not,' says Jack. 'I had ended my time in the army by then. It was he made me a captain, on the field, in Poland. Long ago. It would have broke my heart had I been on the field with him again, yet unable to save him.'

'A true warrior-king,' says Sir Theodore, shaking his head. 'I think we will not see his like again.' Then he brightens. 'Now, let us turn to the reason for your visit, Captain. My patient, there in your arms. If you would be so good as to unclothe him and place him upon the table, for examination?

HE COMES DOWN the stairs, those great wide stairs with the lantern above; James re-dressed and cradled against him. That same thin-lipped maidservant there at the door. She bobs a curtsey – later he will worry, was he too abstracted to respond? Beyond the door is Cornelius, waiting in one of those idiot little carriages Londoners have dashing back and forth across their city.

'Well?' says Cornelius, coming forward to take James from him. 'What did the good doctor have to say?'

'BORN AT SEVEN months, I believe?' As he spoke, Sir Theodore had been palpating James's right arm, bending the right knee up and down. 'And does not as yet speak?'

'Barely a sound. He hardly even cries.'

'And did the mother survive the delivery?'

'She did not.' Watching Sir Theodore with his son, Jack had found he had to put a hand to the corner of his eye. It was an unwelcome surprise.

'I too lost a wife,' said Sir Theodore, almost pleasantly. He had been rustling a screw of paper against James's ear. 'It is a matter of no small consequence that your child is with us still. Such infants all too often follow the mother to the grave. My patient's name?'

Demi-Cuit, thought Jack. 'James. We called him James.'

More rustling. Then a goose-quill, waved back and forth across James's vision; James's gaze investigating some point beyond Sir Theodore's shoulder the while; James's expression one of polite forbearance. 'Clearly I am of no interest whatsoever,' Sir Theodore had commented.

A pigeon took off from the windowsill outside, the *woot-woot* sound of the air under its wings so like the call of the bird itself; and James's eyes moved, locked onto it, followed its path across the window.

Sir Theodore snapped his fingers before James's nose. James at once moved his deep blue gaze back to that point beyond Sir Theodore's shoulder.

'And if I might now investigate inside your mouth, young Master James,' said Sir Theodore, 'and then we are done.'

'So,' said Sir Theodore. 'My verdict. Are you based in this country, Captain, may I ask?'

'We are not,' Jack had replied. 'Home is across the Channel.' (*If it is anywhere.*)

'A pity. You should perhaps consider it. Not in London, however – the air here is too befouled with smoke for one as small as this. Although small as he is, he has great fortitude, I think. I would be glad to see him again. There is a deal that could be done to overcome the physical infirmity. Nor do I find any evidence of tongue-tie, and so far as we may judge, his other faculties, of sight, of hearing, function as they should. But—'

And that *But* the only hint whatsoever of what was to come.

Sir Theodore had leaned onto his elbows again, pushing his slab-like head forward.

'But, such children who lose the protection of the womb so early often pay a price. In effect, your son is in a world of his own. It is as if he sits behind glass.'

Jack had looked down at James, restored to the crook of his arm, right hand as ever folded beneath his chin, and said, 'Indeed. Yes, I see that. Marry, that is – that is an excellent descriptor.' He was already thinking, *A hobby-horse to strengthen the leg, maybe; a cup and ball for the arm…* 'So how do we bring him out from it?'

'Captain,' said Sir Theodore, slowly, 'he is what, a year upon this earth? You must accept he may still be as he is at five years old. At ten. At twenty. I would advise you to make peace, sir, with the possibility that young James will be in this world of his for ever.'

'I AM A bad father.'

Cornelius shakes his head. 'Jack, you are not.'

'I am a *terrible* father. I have failed her.'

'Jack, that is ridiculous.' This is Rafe telling him so. 'You have done no such thing.'

'She left our son in my care. What have I done for him? Did I ever truly take stock of him? I did not. Christ almighty, this feels as bad as losing her.'

'But you have done *everything* for him,' says Rafe. 'You brought him here, to Sir Theodore—'

'After a year. After more than a year, and only when Cornelius suggested it. First I ran away, like some fucken coward; then when I did come back, did I ever ask myself why he did not wail and cry like other children do? No, I was *grateful* for it, Rafe. Grateful!'

Those great blue eyes, moving from one face to the next. 'Husband, tell him,' says Belle. She has James propped against her, and is chasing spoonfuls of pap – oats and cream – around the bowl in her hand. 'Open wide now, bunny. Open wide,' she tells James encouragingly, that sticky little face but inches away from the corded silk over her breast. She waves the empty spoon for emphasis. 'James is a wonderful little boy. And he is only an infant, there is plenty of time for him to grow—'

'He will never grow as he should. He will always be small; he will always have this weakness on one side – how will he live? How will he make a way in this world?'

'Not as you have done, true,' says Rafe. 'But there are other ways, and there are other lives to lead – you must trust to Providence, Jack, to the grace of God—'

'Providence?' Jack feels his fury rising like the spouting of a whale. Of a sudden the ceiling is too low, the well-meaning faces round him not well meaning but obtuse. That should be Mirelle's breast, rounded against his son's face, it should be she, holding that spoon. 'Is that what I must do? Trust the fate that made him so? I would not trust Providence with the fleas on a dog. Providence decreed my son must be motherless. Providence decided he must live with the world perpetually shouldering him aside. Why should any child be treated so? Providence can go fuck itself. And it can take the grace of God with it!'

The door slams behind him. In the silence that follows, Rafe sits himself down. 'He did not mean that.'

Says Cornelius, 'I rather think he did.'

Belle finds him out in the garden, resting his forehead against the pear tree. 'Forgive me,' Jack tells her. 'I am fit company for neither man nor beast.'

'Then you must mend yourself,' says Belle, briskly. 'Rafe and Cornelius are going to take you out. Ned and James stay here with me; you big boys are going to the theatre. The players at the Red Bull are putting on *Holland's Leaguer*. No, I am not listening to a word of argument.' This tiny, silken person, standing with hands on hips. 'It is the silliest stuff, and lewd with it. It is *exactly* what you need.'

THE RED BULL. 'It is very quaint,' says Rafe. 'It was nothing but an inn-yard for generations. Like Mary and Joseph took to the boards, don't you know. But it is where our Master Alembert has set up anew a company of players—'

Jack's thoughts had all been full of James. He comes back to the here and now with a bump. 'Alembert? What, the same Alembert I knew in Prague?'

'The very same,' says Rafe. 'What is more, when he is done with his strutting and fretting, we will take you backstage. We will have a reunion.'

'I'm not so certain he would welcome that...' Alembert's performance in front of the Prince-Bishop of Prague had ended with Jack blowing the Prince-Bishop's castle up to heaven, and sending the Prince-Bishop down to hell.

'No argument, Jack,' says Rafe, seeing his face. 'He will be delighted, I know it. After all, it was you sent him back to London with enough gold to reopen his theatre.'

Well, yes. He did do that too.

Their carriage bumps off cobbles, down into dirt. They are already so far north as to be beyond the city walls. 'I think this is the only way the Red Bull survives,' Rafe says, merrily. 'Out of the eye of the city fathers.'

There are windmills. Orchards. Feathers of vapour rising into the air. Vapour?

'Hot springs,' explains Cornelius. 'This is Clerkenwell.'

A line of folk along the grassy edge of the road, the women holding nosegays, the men with picnic baskets on their arms; and rising above them a half-timbered wall built all in the round, like a Roman circus. 'The wooden *O*,' says Rafe, in high good humour. '*Holland's Leaguer* sells out every time. It is a London favourite. An event.'

They go in through what is clearly still a tavern, and thronged this evening, wall to wall. 'I'll catch you up,' says Rafe. Out and across a yard, and it, too, thick with folk, then in again, up and along, around the curve of the seating, edging past feet and knees. A scrap of a boy with a coxcomb of hair springs into view, like a Jack-in-the-Box. ''Ere you are then, Mistah Vander'oof!' this apparition declares. 'Saved you yer seats, just like you said, and got you cushions too!'

'Thank'ee kindly,' Cornelius replies, proffering a coin. Bug weaves his way back into the crowd, scanning for pockets to pick.

'Who was that?' Jack asks.

'A friend of mine,' says Cornelius, blandly. 'Shall we sit?'

They sit. They are at the front of the curve of seating and Jack's knees are under his chin. But there is a wall to lean on, and once Rafe has rejoined them, three stoneware bottles of beer. 'Now,' says Rafe, settling into place, 'this, my friend, is an object lesson for you on the condition of England. D'you see in the boxes there, above the stage?'

Indeed he does. To left and right, a run of little rooms. Unlike the noise and crush all about him and Rafe and Cornelius, these hold no more than two or three folk apiece. The men lean around the divisions between the boxes to converse, the women hide their faces with their fans.

'It has become the fashion for the grandees to slum it with the rest of us, so here you have it – the court to that side, and Parliament to the other. Land to the left, law to the right. These are the forces that contend in England now. And that – that young monkey, stood there at the corner of the stage, that is Aaron Holland, who is the Pilgrim Players' landlord, if you like,' says Rafe, pointing.

The lad at the corner of the stage, seeing Rafe point him out, removes his hat and sweeps them a bow. Then an individual salutation to Cornelius as well. 'We know each other,' says Cornelius, as mildly as before.

'So I see,' says Jack. There is something about the noise, the press of folk, Rafe's ebullience, that is encouraging his spirits to rise. The world outside will still be there, he tells himself, the world and all its troubles, but it is not here.

'It was grandfather Holland built the Red Bull – hey-ho, Cornelius, do you see that? By God, that's bold. D'you see there? The fellow with the bully-boys on either side of him, just come in?'

'He who is the colour of celery?' Jack asks. Aaron Holland, he sees, has turned about as well.

'That's him. See the hush there is around him? That, my friend, is Ingram Skinner.'

'Lord have mercy,' says Jack, drily. He sizes up the bullies, is unimpressed. '*Who* is Ingram Skinner?'

'The commander, the suzerain, the head,' says Rafe, with massy significance, 'of the Skinner family.'

'Who are...?'

'Dear Lord!' Rafe exclaims, while Cornelius claps hand to head in mock-despair. 'Very good. Listen to me, you unremitting alien. There are two families in London run every crime, every caper, every swindle, every smuggle, nigh-on every tavern and for sure every bawdy-house in London. One is the Hollands—'

'As in Holland's Leaguer?'

'Exactly so. The other is the Skinners.'

Ingram Skinner has, at this moment, doffed his hat to Aaron Holland, then to the upturned faces of the groundlings below. Aaron Holland returns a stiff-armed bow. As he withdraws the hand across his waist, it is evident to the whole house that he holds two fingers up and apart, pointed in Ingram Skinner's direction. The groundlings roar.

'They are as Montague and Capulet,' Cornelius says.

'As Athens and Sparta,' suggests Rafe. 'Or as –' (he drops his voice) '– as Parliament and the King.'

Two men have appeared on stage. They might almost have wandered onto it by accident. They bow. Some of the audience bow back, laughing, others shower the stage with a confetti of nutshells that rattle like applause.

It is indeed the silliest stuff, as Belle had warned. There are two friends, one worthy, one a nitwit. The sweetheart of the first is the sister of the second, and at the worthy one's behest, undertakes to have the nitwit fall in love with her. 'But he does not know who she is, d'you see?' Rafe whispers.

'Not know his own sister?'

'Exactly! This is theatre, Jack. The wooden *O*. Anything can happen here!'

'Of course,' says Jack, with a sigh. But he finds himself ambushed by the odd smile, all the same. There is a woman in one of the boxes with a particularly confident, pleasing laugh; he finds he is listening for it. Then the nitwit is sent off to redeem himself through noble service in the Netherlands (much grabbing of the crotch and grievous punning on the perils of 'the *Low* Countries'), and arrives on stage so bedecked with weaponry they hear him clanking toward them from the wings, and then Jack laughs, for how many tyros has he seen arrive in camp looking exactly so? Next it seems we are in the famous Leaguer itself, for two winsome, sinuously seductive figures arrive on stage; to all appearances stark naked. They sashay their way forward, gloriously slowly, as if their limbs were full of heavy oil. It is only when they are at the front of the stage that you can see the nakedness is in fact tight vests and stockings of flesh pink. They sport gauzy robes that flash and shimmer. Beneath them, at the top of each pair of stockings a heart-shaped merkin; above, fulsome breasts. The crowd is whooping so loudly that the whole action on stage must pause. Cornelius is blushing. 'Are they…' says Jack, 'are they – forgive me being such an innocent, but are they *boys*?'

'The mimics!' Rafe says, wiping his eyes. 'In old King James's time, the Leaguer was famous for such!'

And with them their bawd, in a gown of silvery brocade, with powdered face and crowned with a confection of snow-white hair tall as a sugar loaf. 'God above!' Jack exclaims. 'Alembert!'

'Exactly so! Oh, he used to fancy himself as Hamlet or Macbeth, I know, but it is in these dame parts he excels! No-one does them better!'

The bawd swishes her way to the front of the stage, to the

shouts of the groundlings, opens her mouth, catches sight of Jack, and for a moment stops dead. The groundlings turn to peer. Who's that? Who's so put Alembert off his stroke? Then she throws back her head. 'Well,' she shrieks. It is a prodigious shriek. It could cut stone. 'They may talk of Dunkirk, or of Calais, enriched with foreign booties—' and after that not another word is audible, so loud are the cheers, the stamping of feet on the hard-packed floor. 'Bess 'Olland!' comes the yell. 'Three cheers for old Bess!' – and as the cheers rise up, then die away, Jack hears that woman's laugh again. Not a giggle, not an *Oh my* titter, such as he has been hearing all round him since the mimics took the stage, hidden behind hand or fan, but a gurgle of a laugh: frank, knowing, wholly unashamed. He leans forward to see if he can make the woman out, but she is in shadow: all he can see is the swell of her sleeve laid along the edge of the box, and a bracelet on her arm, catching the light. Now she leans further back, as if reassuring her companion on some small matter. The bracelet is dazzling. Now she leans forward again, turned to see the stage; he makes out the round of her bared shoulder, the curve of her cheek, the slender colonnette of neck and throat. It is the contrast between the delicacy of her quarter-profile and that gurgle, that knowing almost-cackle of a laugh. He finds himself thinking, *Show me your face.*

Her companion has claimed her once again. There's something a little fussy, a little admonitory in the way the woman's attention is requested. She leans back, once more out of sight, and Jack hears himself asking, 'Do you know who that is? In the box to the left?'

Cornelius and Rafe both peer, then Rafe answers, 'Antony Wyncanton. Sir Antony, I should say. Another of Parliament's men. He has an estate in Buckinghamshire. A good fellow, a moderate. He comes into the shop.'

'And with him?'

Cornelius leans forward again. 'Ah, that,' he says, sitting back with a smile. 'That is Pris Holland. Daughter of the house. Do you see her diamonds?'

'Can hardly miss 'em,' says Rafe, and then, 'What, did they come through you?'

Cornelius's tone is modest. 'There are those in Amsterdam prefer to do their business here through me.'

'I always forget,' says Rafe, heartily, 'that you are a Dutchman.'

Cornelius smiles. 'I do not. Ah, there, see – she leans forward.'

They sit and watch. 'It does one good,' says Rafe, at last, 'to know such creatures walk the earth, not so?'

It does. Says Jack, softly, to himself, 'She cut her hair.'

Yes, she did. No more those mermaid tendrils; as Wyncanton's mistress, Pris Holland's curls have been smoothed and sleeked and gather on her shoulders in docile biddability. No more the gaudy peacock silks, either; nor those ropes of beads. All such have been put away. These days Pris wears gowns of dusky rose, of amethyst, of the green of shadows in a forest; gowns that announce the cost of their deep-dyed pigment as discreetly as the clearing of a throat. About her neck she wears a single modest string of pearls, no larger than peas, any of them, but each one with the glister of the real; while the diamonds that flash upon her wrist came from Golconda. And in the evening a hackney, or even Wyncanton's own carriage, takes her to her apartment in Covent Garden, up above King Street, with its parlour and bedroom and the cushioned alcove Mam'selle Pris has filled with books; and the little place for sitting out, high on the roof. The apartment where a man such as Wyn may stow his mistress, and where Pris even has her own Jemima; only hers is called Molly, and frequently forgets to open the door to callers altogether. Oh, Pris has such pride in it, her King Street roost – the lease signed right in front of her by

Wyn and his funny little lawyer Mr Franklin, the key put into her very own hand. Every three days her hair is dressed by Monsieur Vigne, down on the ground floor; every fortnight she is visited by Madame Oliphant, with her silks and ribbons and her book of all the latest fashions; and if Wyn's weekly visit and his stolid love-making is the price she must pay for all this, fair enough.

It has taught Pris much, these months with Wyn. She has learned, for example, that if (remembering her first explorations of such activity with Felipe, not to mention the thoroughness of her reading-up on the subject under Bess) she attempts some little thing that might make matters in the bedroom more interesting for them both, Wyn's only response will be a puzzled 'My dear – what are you trying to do?' *Concerning the bigness of the Yard, it is by most esteemed to be of a just length, when it is extended the breadth of nine thumbs....* Yes, and does not the ridiculousness of that as a measurement tell you everything about the control men exert upon the business? And all of it so much less than a woman may manage on her own! *The Clytoris is a certain substance in the upper part of the great Cleft, where the two wings concur. This in Women is the seat of Venereal pleasure...* No, it has taught Pris the virtues of pragmatism, this new life of hers, pragmatism and good sense. For we must all be mindful of which side the bread is buttered. Therefore, when she finds herself aware, from the seating opposite, of that deep male gaze, she does not sit forward as she would once have done, to spy out who this might be; and when Wyn, in his fussy way, frets to be gone ('My dear, remember – we must still bespeak a carriage'), even though, as the audience files out, she can hear backstage the kind of gathering it would delight her to be a part of once again, all she does is pick up her shawl and fan and answer meekly, 'Yes, Wyn. I am ready.'

*

This is the wooden *O*, and anything can happen here. You might, for example, if you are Aaron Holland, take yourself backstage to congratulate your company upon so good a house tonight, only to find already there, and raising toasts, all your players, plus Cornelius Vanderhoof (who, thank God, plays your connection to him as discreetly as ever), plus that bookseller-fella, Endicott, and at their centre this great rangy stretch of a man, with eyes like lenticles of sea-ice and a trio of scars upon his face. *Lawks*, thinks Aaron. *That's the real thing, no mistake.*

'Master Holland!' Alembert declares. The white on his face is running with sweat; he swings a bottle in his fist. 'This is our captain! Our captain from Prague!'

The stranger holds out a hand, hieroglyphic with tattoos. 'Jack Fiskardo,' he says. He has a grip that makes the strings of Aaron's cods contract.

'And pleased to meet ye,' Aaron manages. Alembert has swung his arm about the bookseller's shoulders. 'By God, Endicott,' he is declaring, 'you have quite took my breath away!'

'I knew I would!' Endicott replies. He too is grinning wildly, clearly every bit as well afloat as Alembert this evening. Cornelius has drawn himself a step or two away. *Ah*, thinks Aaron, *Signior Light-Touch. Signior Subtlety.* He sidles across. Behind him, he hears this Fiskardo asking after other members of the company: 'But there were more of you, I'm sure of it.'

In the wings, Cornelius has drawn a paper from his breast. 'Usual destination?' Aaron asks.

'If you would be so good,' comes Cornelius's reply.

On stage Alembert is going through the cast list, if you like: Henry Kempwick – 'performs now for the angels, bless his soul. But our dramatist, Andrew Frye – he, Blanche and Lucy, do you remember them? The last we heard, they had a company of players in Italy! You gave them a taste for adventure, Captain.

And Andrew did always say, nothing on earth could ever frighten him again, after his time in Prague with you.'

Aaron lifts the letter to the light. There is a single hair, stuck north to south across the wax seal, which shows that same combination of lion and hunting horn as before. 'You don't miss a trick, do you?' Aaron comments, smiling.

'Oh, I don't know about that,' Cornelius replies, modestly, then, holding Aaron's gaze for a heartbeat longer, 'You managed to surprise me.'

Behind them, Aaron hears some member of the company enquire, 'So, Captain – does your presence here mean you think war is on our horizon too?'

'I hope to God not,' this Fiskardo replies.

'Be damned if it is,' Alembert declares. 'I've had my fill of cabbage leaves from the cunts and cuntesses up there in their boxes. I am all for some new order of things. If war should come to England, I will be first to enlist, you see if I do not!' He has taken up a pasteboard sword, is using it to demonstrate his proficiency with the real thing. The mimics are beside themselves with laughter. 'D'you see, Captain? I could swing a blade with the best of 'em!' He swings. He staggers. His audience ducks. This Fiskardo lays a hand in friendly fashion to his own more than serviceable-looking weapon, there at his hip like some well-trained dog. 'A pass or two with me, friend Alembert?'

'*Christ*, no!' says Alembert. 'I am nothing *like* drunk enough for that!' And another roar of laughter, and this time, this stranger, this Fiskardo, he joins in. It's not at all the laugh Aaron would have expected from one who looks as he; it's brimful, unfettered. 'There!' they hear Endicott declare, sounding delighted. 'And now I have an even better idea. Tomorrow, Jack, Belle and I will make a trip, and you and your boys must come with us, and we will all of us go to Oxford!'

CHAPTER ELEVEN

Varney

After youth in travel spent
Let man be with his home content

Guillaume de la Perrière, translated by
Thomas Combe, *The Theater of Fine Devices*

AND WHY OXFORD?

Because there is a house, says Rafe. He is being very careful to keep his eyes shaded by his hat this morning, and every time Belle looks at him, she tuts and shakes her head. Or rather there is a library in a house, and Rafe has undertaken to price it up. 'The house is almost ruinated,' says Rafe. 'But the library, in its day, was very fine.'

The carriage bumps its way over a pothole. Ned is delighted. '*Oop*-la,' he tells James, '*oop-LA!*' Rafe gives a groan. 'I think,' he says, 'when we change horses, you must excuse me for some little while.'

Says Belle (rearranging her skirts in the way women do when they wish to make a point), 'We are never letting you three out again on your own. Are we, Ned?'

In Oxford they lodge at the King's Arms. The bed the King's Arms finds for Jack and his boys creaks with age; Jack lies awake between his sleeping sons while his thoughts circle with the relentlessness of crows over a carcass. *How do I do this? How do I care for James, how can we get to see Sir Theodore, where can we live?* Through the wall he listens to the soft domestic burblings of Rafe and Belle, as they ready themselves for bed. *Mirelle, help me, I am adrift. How shall all this be done?* He has never felt more lonely in his life.

'It has an interesting history,' Rafe tells them, as yet another coach carries them out of Oxford, into the green and gold of fields and woods and farms. He throws down the slide on the window to bring in the air. 'The first owners, they were great builders, but Catholic. What the fines under the old Queen did not take from them, the passion for building and collecting did. The last died years back; the estate has been in limbo ever since. Meantime, the roof leaks, the windows fall from their casements – I swear, the woodworms hold hands to keep the panelling on the walls. In the library there are the handsomest bindings, slowly being ate alive. Yet you will see, there is a housekeeper, a Mrs Mayhew, who always meets me at the door, and wine will still be brought up from the cellars, as if we were invited guests, rather than the prelude to the bailiffs.' He shakes his head. 'It will be a sad day when the place is finally pulled down, but no-one will take it and so I fear it must be.'

The carriage is rounding a curve in the road. Jack, who is heartily tired of being sat in a seat rather than a saddle, takes the chance to peer out and sees something coming into sight, above the cushion of trees. There are chimneys – one, two, three, four; there is the crest of a gable, there are spindles on the roofline, all of it gold-grey stone. A wide but weedy gravelled drive, a front door big enough for a cathedral, worn stone steps rippling up to it. The shine of water beyond. There is – later he will think how even at first sight, the place had the feel of an answer; that gentle murmur: *If you want me, here I am.*

'There,' says Rafe, sitting back in his seat. 'Varney.'

There is a woman stood upon the steps, waiting for them. She lifts her head as the coachman from the King's Arms pulls his horses to a halt. A wide nose, an undershot chin. The face of a kindly duck, shuttered by her cap. He wonders what on earth she, this Mrs Mayhew, will make of them: he, the boys – James, carried on his father's hip, Ned, released from his seat and running back and forth like a hare; Rafe with Belle on his arm.

It seems she makes nothing of them at all. 'Mr Endicott,' she says, coming forward. 'Welcome.' The smallest suggestion of a smile. 'How good to see you again, sir. Thc books are waiting.'

There is a steward ('Peter Topham,' Rafe had said, making introductions), who leads their horses and the coachman out of sight; there is a boy ('Toby Dearlove' – Rafe again), brings water in a basin, to wash the journey from these visitors' hands. For good measure, Jack scrubs around Ned's face and neck as well. 'Let me take your little one a moment, sir,' says Mrs Mayhew, seeing how he struggles to hold James at the same time, and to Jack's amazement, James suffers himself to be handed over without demur. Mrs Mayhew peers into James's face; James peers back. It seems she has caught his interest. 'How old is this one, sir?' she asks.

'A year and some.'

James, in his skirts, is handed back. 'He is very winning,' she comments.

Toby Dearlove is trying not to stare at the tattoos on Jack's hands: the criss-cross for the battles, the lines of waves for each crossing of the seas, the narrow black band for old Torsten the Bear. 'The wars in Germany,' says Jack, tersely, holding his hands up for show, and the boy blushes, lowers his head.

'My captain, from those hectic times,' says Rafe, by way of explanation. 'Fiskardo. Jack Fiskardo. He visits, with his boys. As you see.'

There is an old serving woman, humped with age; a wordless girl to assist. 'Old Henty, and Lily, I think,' says Rafe, out the corner of his mouth. They bring wine, which has sweetened in the cask till it runs like syrup, and flat-footed glasses with trumpet-shaped bowls. Jack lets Ned take a sip from his; then a drip off his finger onto James's tongue.

'Well,' says Rafe. 'Shall we to it? Belle, will you come with me, or shall you take the tour?'

'I will assist you, husband, of course,' Belle replies, demurely.

Says Mrs Mayhew, 'Would you care to see the house, Captain? You and your boys?'

She leads them into an even greater hall: a barrel-vaulted space with ribs in a honeycomb across its ceiling and panelling marching along its walls. Many of the panels are slipped, others discoloured with mould, but it is as if the house has hardly noticed. Sunlight brightens the wide boards of the floor; just as at the Écu, a honeysuckle taps against the leaded panes of a window; outside, clouds romp across the sky.

'Dada, *regarde*!' Ned exclaims, pointing to where, above the panelling, the wall is decorated to the ceiling with the painted scene of a garden and a kneeling unicorn, humbly laying its head in the lap of a wary-looking virgin. 'It's M'sieu!' says Ned, delighted. Mrs Mayhew looks enquiring. (*Oh, she is so very like a duck!*)

'My horse,' Jack explains. 'He languishes in Picardy.'

She leads them down the length of the room, their footsteps echoing. Occasionally, there is some piece of shrouded furniture. Occasionally, the walls are marbled green with damp. 'Varney is an old house, sir, and shows its age,' says Mrs Mayhew, seeing he notices the marks, and already he wants to say *Yes, but...* as if he were defending it. Now they come out of the hall and there is another space, with rooms off, and a stairway – stone, swinging round and out of sight, but instead of a banister, the most curious deep groove carved into the wall, like the house itself would put its hand in yours to guide you. Everywhere, light. Now the sudden patter of rain; the sky outside still blue. Not one single doorway yet where he has had to bow his head.

Through the door behind them, the sound of Rafe's voice, as its owner works his way along the library shelves. 'Pliny's *Historia*. The *Theatrum Orbis Terrarum* of Abraham Ortelius. And another Pliny, this one Englished. Belle, how many was that?'

'Shall you walk into the solar, sir?' Mrs Mayhew asks.

The solar? But as soon as he enters the room, he sees why it should be so called: another window, immense, but rounded, and so generously glazed it is as if the wall dissolves before you. Twenty feet high and curved like the stern of a ship, so you stand looking out from it as if looking out over Varney's wake. Extraordinary. He has never before seen a window so tall, or curved so. There is a tapestry upon the wall beside it, faded where the sun has been stroking it for years; he makes out a jostle of figures, the winding shape of water behind them, which seems to echo that visible from the road; and birds, hiding in beds of rushes. Hounds nose with undiminished eagerness through the woolly marsh in search of them.

'A gift, sir,' Mrs Mayhew informs him. 'From Venice. The first builder of Varney was there some years. He took the notion of our compass windows from there. There is another, in the bedchamber above.'

Ned has collapsed, cross-legged upon the floor, as children do to give notice they are bored. He sits James down carefully beside his brother, goes forward to the window, stands in the light with the sun's warmth on his head. Closes his eyes. What a marvel this house is. How gently its age sits upon it. How *at peace*. And then a shouted salutation from outside and when he opens his eyes, it is to see a quartet of men, gaitered to the knee and with rakes over their shoulders, making their way past the house. Their hands are raised familiarly to Mrs Mayhew; then they see him, and the hands drop, to be replaced with frank and curious stares. Does the house have land?

'Mrs Mayhew, do the fields come with the house?'

'They did, one time, sir. But all was sold, to pay the fines.'

Hah, Jack finds himself thinking. *So a new owner would have no need to be a farmer, then.*

He hears Rafe approach from the library. 'Mrs Mayhew,' Rafe begins, 'would you have—' and then an abrupt, 'Oh – *Ned – James*!'

Jack spins about. There is Ned, standing. There is James, also standing, held up by his brother, left arm out and pointing, smiling – a true, wide, eyes-lifted smile, and maddest of all, somewhere in Jack's head, the tiny echo of a voice, like two notes on a piccolo, uttering a single word: *Ma-man*.

'Ned, did he speak?' Jack crouches down, as you might to some creature so fleet and uncertain you scarce dare approach it at all. James is still smiling, right arm half extended, as if in a magician's *ta-da!* 'Ned, *a-t-il parlé*?'

'*Bien sûr, il a parlé*,' says Ned. Of course his brother spoke. He sounds as if the question has annoyed him.

Jack is on his knees before them. 'But what did he say?'

'*Il a dit* Maman,' says Ned, as if this was the most obvious thing in the world. '*Regarde!*' he tells them (these foolish adults), pointing at the compass window. And there, right across its circumference, against the blue of the sky, a rainbow, a beauty, distinct as if painted on the glass. '*Maman aimait les arcs-en-ciel.*'

'But how—' Jack reaches toward his youngest, who is still standing, smiling at the rainbow, oblivious to them all. He is aware Belle has joined her husband at the door. 'Ned, how would he know that?'

'Because I *taught* him,' says Ned. 'He can say *Ned* too. Demi-Cuit,' Ned continues, and snaps his fingers in front of his brother's nose. The head moves, the right hand goes back under the chin. 'Say *Ned*,' says Ned, encouragingly. 'Nnnn. Ned. You know how.'

James draws in his breath. '*Nnn*ed,' he says. There is a bearing down on the first letter, an effortful *nnn*, then it is said, as if this was the simplest thing in the world.

'*Voila*,' says Ned, to Jack. Then back to James: 'Now say *Dada*.'

'Oh, sweet heaven,' Jack hears Rafe say, at the doorway.

James's gaze shifts from his brother, comes in a line straight to Jack. '*Ddd*ada,' says James, with that same bearing down on the first letter as before. The left hand moves through space, touches his father's scarred cheek. '*Dd*ada,' James says again, with an upward lift of pleasure.

'Oh, Jack!' Belle exclaims.

Ned lowers James to sit upon the floor. 'See?' he says. '*Il parle beaucoup*. You only have to listen.'

Jack pulls them to him, buries his head between theirs. His thoughts are whirling. He has no idea what he's about, yet at the same time he knows exactly what's he's doing, all at once. *I will need to go to Amsterdam.* He hears Rafe murmur, 'Wife, forgive me, I am quite unmanned.'

Ned is already squirming to escape. Jack lifts his head. 'Rafe,' he begins, 'the deeds to this place. Who holds them?'

'What?' Rafe is wiping his face. 'The Exchequer, I think. The debts, you know…'

'Could my boys stay a while with you? With you and Belle? I will need to go to Amsterdam. And then to Picardy.' That engine in his head, laying it all out: the plan, the campaign. *Amsterdam. Talk with Yosha. Then Picardy. Retrieve M'sieu.* A glance at Mrs Mayhew. *Yes, speak with her. The steward too. I will have the panelling remade. And the damp – get that attended to. Is the roof weather-tight? Will those chimneys draw?*

I will have us in by All Saints. I will have a household. I will make a home.

'Rafe, you must finish your inventory of the library for sure, but any books you have crated up, they must go back upon the shelves.' He looks down at his boys – Ned, who has clearly worked out something is afoot here; James, who is still smiling as before, as if none of this is any surprise to him whatsoever. 'And I'll need a lawyer. Cornelius must know a lawyer. But can the boys stay with you?' And now he laughs. He hears himself, his hoot of laughter. 'Oh, Scribbler – you should see your face!'

CHAPTER TWELVE

How it Begins

'It is a thing most horrible that we should engage ourself in war…'

Henry Slingsby, *Diary, 1642*

IT IS THE fashion for a man to have a mistress, and Wyn has ever been a man of fashion.

What pish and piffle, Bess Holland would say. Antony Wyncanton was born the second son of a second cousin, with no hope whatsoever of anything from the Wyncanton fortune; does he think the world will have forgotten that? But one by one, all those who stood between Wyn and those acres in

Buckinghamshire, that seat in the Commons, turned up their toes – a sweep of the plague-brush, a hunting mishap, the quinsy, a tissick, the flux… Wyn had awoken one morning in his forty-fourth year, surrounded by mortality, and found himself rich.

He has never wed. No wife has ever gone with him to his tailors, to twitch a coat about his shoulders and tell him he looks better in green than in brown. His country place, his manor house of Goodwins, has never seen itself decked out for a wedding. But his wines come from Beaune, his cologne from Florence; his books are from Endicott's, and his mistress –

Ah, his mistress. What a puzzle she is. What pleasure in her company; what mortal terror in the remembrance of it. (In his imagination at this moment, to Wyn's intense delight and almost as intense discomfort, Pris is lying back on the bed in that King Street apartment, the ribbon of her shift unlaced, her pretty breasts within his hand, her fiery crotch awaiting.) And what satisfaction – God save him! – this second son of a second cousin finds in the covetous glances of other men, when he has Pris on his arm. A man of worth, of proper character, would never feel so, would have no mistress at all. Yet God (another puzzle!) has cursed man with these needs of the flesh – so how much better to assuage them with those women whose living it is to see to such matters?

In particular, Wyn recalls an evening in the chamber of one Yellow Katie, a terrible lickerish harlot of the most worldly sort, but exactly the type to make a young man's first steps into the Court of Venus as easy as possible. She had a painting above her bed, he remembers: Zeus, showering Danaë. And a pair of ivory figures, he remembers them, of Adam and Eve, but Eve with her legs boldly splayed, and Adam with his yard sticking out like a fishing rod. Wyn had been the most bashful visitor to Holland's Leaguer for weeks before it occurred to him that the purpose of the figures was to allow Yellow Katie's guests to demonstrate what they desired from her. The memory of the moment makes him blush even now.

And this extraordinarily graceful child had waited upon them, carrying in her tray and decanter with all the solemnity of a butler at the Lord Mayor's banquet. 'Who's this?' some wag had asked, and Yellow Katie flipped her golden hair, its colour ripened with chamomile, over one shoulder, and answered, laughing, 'Oh, just another little gosling.'

The child had turned her immense green eyes on Katie, on all of them. 'I am not a gosling,' she said, solemnly. 'I am Miss Pris.'

Who else had been at the table? As Wyn walks toward St Paul's, he recalls many of his neighbours from the benches of the Commons – there we were, ponders Wyn, with an inward sigh, all in our yeasty youth, all such innocents, and where are we now? Half trumpeting the rights of Parliament, half bellowing the prerogatives of the King, and as for the Commons itself – we are a Parliament of *England*, Wyn thinks, shaking his head, yet we spend all our time arguing about her monarch. There has been war with the Scots, which saw the English army bested on its own ground, God above; heads have rolled – literally, the Earl of Strafford, up on Tower Hill – and still riot and disorder spark up across the country like moorland fires. Ah, the times, the times – how unsettling they are! Here is Endicott's. Gratefully, he steps in.

And more to be grateful for: Endicott himself is there, as the price of having to listen to old Butter's views on the state of the world would, Wyn feels, be too high a price to pay. 'Ah, Endicott,' he says, stepping forward. 'I am here about a copy of – ahem – Carew's verse. A pretty one, if you have such a thing. 'Tis to be a gift.' (Wyn has no taste for poetry, but he is due to hold a supper in the King Street apartment tonight, a supper of the sort he knows Pris objects to, and the book is a bribe, to have her hold her tongue and mind her manners – which means, not thin her lips or roll her eyes when he introduces her as his ward, be pleasant as she serves the wine, and then disappear to her bedchamber.) The versifying of Thomas Carew is a favourite of hers, immodest as Wyn holds the man to be. All that talk of panting and perspiring, let alone of lips sliding down smooth alleys – what is the fellow whiffling on about? But he is most anxious for the supper to be a success. Goodwins has recently acquired a neighbour, a Scot (that doughty race), one Colonel Ancrum, a veteran of the wars in Germany and a man Wyn finds most pleasing deferential and whose politics align thrillingly with his own. The supper will be an opportunity for the two of them, as men of the world, to explore those same politics, perhaps to set their little patch of Buckinghamshire to rights – he stops. He sees now that the shop has another customer, a gentleman in a long, dark clerical gown, a man of the same full years as Wyn himself, with an expression of much resignation, yet no little humour.

'My Lord Wyncanton,' says Rafe, turning about with a bow, and then, 'May I present to you Mr William Watts?'

The name means something. Wyn hesitates, unsure what. It is getting so a man must be careful whom he gives his hand to. 'Mr Watts has recently been returned to us from his duties as chaplain to our army in Scotland,' Rafe adds, cheerfully, then seeing Wyn's face, realizes his error. 'A circumstance forced on him,' he adds, hastily.

The King's man, thinks Wyn. He keeps his hand at his side.

'It was he who turned my untidy correspondence from Germany into the thing that was *The Swedish Intelligencer*,' continues Rafe, with no idea the dilemma this now places upon Wyn, as *The Swedish Intelligencer* lauded that godly monarch Gustavus Adolphus of Sweden in his battles against the very popery Wyn and his ilk now fear to be claiming the English church. What to do, what to do?

Good manners trumps all, in Wyn's view. He holds his hand out.

It is taken. 'I am honoured,' says Mr Watts. A smile to Endicott. 'They were simpler times.'

'Indeed, sir,' agrees Wyn, with feeling. 'I hope you are settled safe again here in the city.'

Mr Watts lifts his hands in resignation. 'My Lord, who can say? Providence plays with unhappy England the way a child plays with a top.'

Whipped this way and that. 'Indeed, sir,' says Wyn. 'You have the right of it. You put it well.'

'Small comfort in that,' says Mr Watts, sadly. 'By your leave, sir.' He moves toward the door. 'Ah, Rafe, my friend, before I go – how does our friend Fiskardo?'

'*Entirely* rusticated,' Endicott replies. 'You would scarce know him. Or the house. It has been transformed. And he and his boys, I am most happy to say, they *thrive*.'

TAKE A WALK through Varney with me. Even better, take it in the company of Ned, clattering down Varney's stair with all the heedlessness of ten-year-old boyhood. Here he goes, across the inner hall, past the dining-room, past the door to the solar, through the great hall and on toward the kitchen. It is nothing at all to Ned that every fireplace he passes now draws and burns. It is nothing to him that the panelling in every room is new and sound, that the cracked panes in the windows are no more, that furniture has appeared all through the house – cabinets, mirrors, tables; all the things a place such as Varney should possess. To

Ned, Varney is home, that is all – both everything, and everyday. Here is the kitchen. Here are the dogs, Ocker and Todd, named (so Dada says) after his general in Germany, bounding from their habitual spot before the fireplace in the kitchen as he enters. Here too is Old Henty, at the kitchen table, polishing their heavy silver punchbowl and the ladle with its handle twisted like the horn of the unicorn. 'I'm told 'tis of a fish,' Dadda had said, as the punchbowl was carried into the house, Topham one side of it and the carrier, Plumstead, the other. 'It grows with that spike on its nose.' Old Henty is in love with their punchbowl. 'Who does that remind you of?' Dada had whispered to Ned, as Henty exclaimed over the bowl's heft, its lustre.

'Aunt Cou-Cou,' Ned had whispered back, lowering his face to hide his grin.

If Old Henty is polishing the punchbowl, it might mean the Endicotts are coming for another visit. Ned goes out into the garden whistling happily, Ocker and Todd at his heels.

Out through the door and into the garden. From the front of the house, Ned hears the screech of the pair of Indian pheasants that had arrived shortly after Ocker and Todd – the dowdy brown wife, the cock with his Byzantine train. 'Noisy old buggers,' is what Abram the gardener calls them, dismissively, and Ned is inclined to agree. Dogs matter, dogs and horses. And look – here's M'sieu in his paddock, who on sight of Ned goes charging round it in his usual show-offery: a circuit of the paddock at a speed as breakneck as anything Ned has ever achieved down the stairs, then M'sieu comes to a halt and does his favourite trick, of springing straight off the ground, all four feet in the air at once, head back, snorting, back legs kicking out behind. 'You might train a horse for months to do that,' Dada had told him. 'You might train one for years. It's how to break free in a mêlée, but he does it simply because it pleases him.' By way of reward, Ned holds out a heel of bread, cunningly purloined as he passed through the kitchen; M'sieu takes it; Ned continues on his way. Past James's play hobby-horse, discarded where his brother left it, the last time James came outside, past the set of skittles that should also have been put away, but somehow weren't. No time for them now. Ned is on a mission, aiming for where the bridge in the garden crosses the river. His head disappears down amongst the reed-mace. There are splashes; the ducks, lined up as brown as coconuts along the bank, begin a noisy protest, then Ned reappears, holding something carefully in his knotted handkerchief. Back he goes to the house, the dogs with their noses raised, trying to investigate whatever it is he carries. 'Not for you,' Ned tells them. 'This is for James.'

In at the door to the solar. Past the table that lives in the solar, with its kaleidoscope top of hardstones, and the plant Dada had placed upon it, with its flowerhead like a spray of sugared butterflies. 'An orchis,' Dada had said. 'A gift from Haarlem. Don't water it overmuch.' James adores the orchis; will spend hours examining the tabletop, hunting down slivers of blue lapiz, of cloudy agate, until he has found a pair, but for Ned the only item in the solar deserving of attention is the tapestry Dada brought back from Amsterdam: the explosions in the sky; the surge of men; the push of pike; the lobster-carapaced heavy cavalry. Breitenfeld, Dada told them. The greatest fight I was ever in.

'*Dddada*,' James had said, pointing at the figure at the front, on rearing steed.

'Not quite, chick,' Dada had replied. 'That is Gustavus Adolphus. But thank'ee, all the same.'

The foreground of the tapestry displays the dead. Ah, the variety of it – the bullet holes, the shorn-off limbs, the thick dribblings of blood. Even now, looking at it makes something strange happen low down in Ned's stomach. Lily had turned her head against Mrs Mayhew's shoulder when she first saw it, which was when Ned privately decided Lily might be very pretty, but she was plainly one of those who quaked in her breeches, as Dada would say.

'Come now,' Mrs Mayhew had said, patting Lily's back. 'This was all in Germany! Not here!'

On Ned goes. Across the inner hall, past its lacquer cabinet, without a glance, past the dining-room, its walls now panelled with gilt leather. He hears his father's voice. He hears Peter Topham. He pauses, to listen at the door. '… a Colonel Ancrum…' Supposedly there is a new landowner out Aylesbury way, another soldier, so it's said, and Topham has been out, gathering the local gossip. No, not gossip, intelligence, is what we call it, his father had told Ned. Now Ned hears his father exclaim, 'Ancrum? That's the newcomer?' A pause. 'Do we know if he's a Scot?'

Peter Topham knows everything. Ned tells the dogs to shush, creeps closer to the door. 'Yes, sir,' he hears Topham say. 'Another out the wars in Germany. He has wed a widow-woman, with an estate at Upper Aston.'

'God above,' says Dada. 'I think I know this Ancrum. When we were first come into Germany, his aide-de-camp tried to give us away to the Imperialists.' Through the crack in the door, Ned sees his father has lifted his hand to the scar on his breastbone. 'There was an attack. Ancrum was dismissed, in deep disgrace.'

'That will be the man, sir. A discontented soul, by all accounts.' Ned can hear the worry in Topham's voice. 'Will Colonel Ancrum be a trouble to you, sir?'

'Not I,' Dada replied. 'If he don't bother me, I most certainly will not be bothering him.' Ned makes to move away. Upstairs, James will be waiting.

'Ned?' His father's voice. 'What are you up to out there?'

Damnation, thinks Ned, as his father would say. In his handkerchief, now in his pocket, there is a determined squirming. He enters, followed by the dogs. 'Good day to you, sir. Good day to you, Mr Topham.' Topham, as ever, is in his outdoor clothes, his face seamed by wind and sun and a permanent russet, whatever the season, but his father sits at the table in his velvet coat, the one he wears of a morning before the day gives him his marching orders, as he puts it. 'Where have you been?' his father asks.

'To see M'sieu,' Ned answers, with perfect truthfulness.

'And where are you going?'

'To see James.' And watches as the expression on his father's face alters, which makes Ned feel uncomfortable not in his belly this time, but up in his chest. His brother has been in bed a week, beset by sweeps of fever and pains in his legs, and at such times Ned feels acutely how his father must bear all such worries for them on his own; and how unfair this is, and how helpless he, Ned, feels in the face of it, yet how he yearns to help bear the burden. But all his father says now is, 'Tell him I will be up to see him presently,' and Ned understands he is dismissed, and that his mission may continue.

'Stay,' he tells the dogs. Back up the stairs and to his brother's room. There lies James, propped up on pillows and the quilt to his chin. 'How's your leg?' Ned asks. He has his fingers crossed.

'It's good,' James replies, impatiently. '*Ddid* we get one?'

'Of course we did,' his brother replies. It was Toby showed Ned how to make the trap that caught the creature now wriggling in his handkerchief, and Toby's knowledge of such things is peerless.

'Put him in his house, then.'

In the corner of James's room is a half-barrel, and in it, presently, there lives a newt – a lady newt, James had ascertained. When he found her she was on the grass, being pecked at by a crow, but James brought her inside and had Topham provide the half-barrel, and made a grotto for her in it and fed her caterpillars, until the damage done by the crow had healed. He is always introducing creatures to the house – harvest mice in their nests, rescued ahead of the reapers, a baby rabbit that lived in a basket by his bed. The lady newt is the latest. She has moss to lie on, and ferns to hide under, and a little dish of water for a pond, but she has no companion. Now Ned upends the trap into the barrel, and Mr Newt, astonished, falls from it and skitters away, out of sight. James says, 'We will see if he likes her. If he does, he will grow a crest.'

WELCOME TO KING Street, in the fashionable west of London, where the morning is so well advanced it is almost done, and where Pris Holland, in a morning-robe of, yes, kingfisher blue, has wandered through to her parlour. The table here still bears the unlovely litter of the supper held by Wyn the night before – empty bottles, smeared plates, the mortal remains of a salmon. Snapped-off bits of pipe stem all over the hearth. Pris regards them sourly. These suppers are happening over and over again. 'Why can you not entertain in your place, in Lincoln's Inn?' she had demanded the first time Wyn did this. Ancrum, in her view, is a mealy-mouthed hand-washer, 'a bad penny,' Bess would say, 'with a good print.' She cannot think why Wyn should be so taken with the man.

'May I remind you, madam,' Wyn had replied, 'that this place is mine also.'

She goes to the door of the parlour, swinging it back and forth to encourage the smell of pipe smoke on its way. Madame Oliphant is due today, with a sample of silk-satin she has been talking about for weeks – come from Lyons, Madame Oliphant says, dyed with cinnabar, and the very colour of Mam'selle Holland's hair. 'Molly!' Pris yells as she wafts the door. No answer. Plainly her maid has slept even later than Pris herself. She goes to the head of the stairs, cups her hands about her mouth: '*MOLLY!*'

A commotion from below. Molly sleeps on what is in effect a shelf in a cupboard; once she has gained her roost at night one almost needs a shoe-horn to dislodge her. At last Molly sticks her own head into view, shawl about her shoulders. 'Yis, mam'selle?' she calls.

'Get yourself up here. We must set this place to rights.'

'Yis, miss!' At that moment there is a rat-tat-tat upon the knocker from the street. Molly's head disappears, then returns. ''Tis Madame Oliphant, miss!'

It would be, thinks Pris. 'Send her up, Molly, and beg her pardon – it smells like a chimney shat itself in here.' She crosses to the door of her balcony, walks through onto the leads. Closes her eyes. There is a tiresome blurring to her vision – or is it only the smoke from the room behind? *When I* was *Miss Pris*, she thinks, *not Mam'selle Holland, this was all I wanted: my own place and a man who could get it for me—*

And then it happens. Eyes closed, she hears screams from the street below. Her eyes fly open, she looks down – no, nothing. No crowds, no panic, and with her eyes open the noise has ceased. She closes them and at once the same chaos assaults her – bells pealing, the cries of some terrified press of folk—

She opens them again. She is gripping the rail so tight the skin over her knuckles is bloodless. Her heart is walloping against her breast. There is a shimmering curtain between her and the world; beyond it, all the colours are wrong.

The first time Pris had known this happen, she had only been a tot. It was so long ago she remembers it now only in swoops and falls. She had been looking out over a brown field, with nothing beyond it but hedgerow, and nothing about her but cow parsley. There was a man stood above her, a farmer, the very same who had rescued her from Tucker Turnbull, and who was still, days later, endeavouring to find who, at Stourbridge

Fair, had mislaid this child. 'We will find them, your people,' he had assured her. She remembers his face, latticed with shadow from his straw hat, so country a thing that in London it would have been worn by a donkey as a joke, and his reddish hair (although nothing like so red as hers). He was the first ever to call her 'Miss Pris'. She had called him her Uncle Nol. She had felt dizzy, she had closed her eyes, and in an instant, thunderously loud, coming across the field directly toward her, there had been horsemen, dozens of them, row upon row. One swoop of memory brings back to her the horses' teeth, streaming with saliva; another, the plunge of their hooves. She had been so terrified she had let loose a little bubble of urine, then she had fallen down in a faint.

When she woke, she was back in the farmhouse, laid upon a bed, being fussed; and her Uncle Nol was telling her how those like her and him, who God had touched with his very ruddiest finger, how they must be wary of too much of that pagan miscreant the sun. It was said in fun, she knew, but only partly so, for this was a man locked in fierce, perpetual debate with his unbending Creator, she knew that too. Yet when she asked about the horsemen, no-one could tell her anything. No-one else had seen them. Only her.

The megrims, Bess had told her, dismissively. The shimmer, the colours going awry, the noises, all of that. ''Tis part of the curse of womanhood. They come with your monthlies. You'll see.'

Yes, but they don't, thinks Pris. *Not mine.*

'Yoo-ho,' trills Madame Oliphant, behind her. 'Yoo-ho, Mam'selle Holland, I have it! The cinnabar silk!'

She turns about.

'Oh, my dear!' Madame Oliphant exclaims. 'Come away from the edge, my dear, you are white as Castile soap! Come away, come away!'

ALL THE DISORDER in the streets, all the noise in Parliament, and this thing, when it begins, it begins so small. For Belle, it starts on a January afternoon with the sound of a galloping horse. Rafe is gone over to Westminster, making deliveries; Belle is in the shop with her father; they are dusting the books, the sort of comfortable task they always used to do together, and one that seems to bring her father a measure of peace as well. Mr Butter has become a man of strange obsessions, most recently a conviction that Anabaptists are sending plague sores through the mails. 'But Natty, how?' her mother had asked. Answer came there none, only another of his outbursts of temper. Belle hears her mother now in the kitchen, drawing something from the fire. Belle and her father have been at their task for hours; she is about to ask, 'Are you peckish, Pa?' when the noise of a horse comes drumming through the shop. Who gallops down a city street? Belle goes to the door, peers out. Nothing untoward; in fact, it strikes her outside as being strangely quiet. She is about to speak again when she is once more interrupted, but this time by the sound of church bells – far off at first, but coming nearer, across the city. Her father has straightened up, as startled as she. 'What is it?' Mr Butter asks. They hear her mother's voice: 'Natty?' Belle raises a finger. She can hear something more. She can hear –

– she can hear not an earthquake, not a landslide, but perhaps in the city, the nearest thing. She can hear London's 'prentices, on a roar.

All winter there have been riots, and rumours of rioting. 'Get the stock!' Mr Butter shouts, pointing to the table on the pavement. 'I'll do the shutters!'

Belle pulls the table in through the door. Her father clanks past with lock and chain; the tumult now is close enough to make out yells of 'Tyranny! Tyranny!' The bells are in awful cacophony from every steeple, and outside every shopkeeper in their street is doing the same as they, hauling their stock back inside and chaining shutters into place over their precious windows. Her mother is calling from the back of the shop, 'Natty, come in! Come in!' Between them, Belle and Mr Butter lift and chain the final shutter into place, then run back inside. Mr Butter locks the door with trembling hand. They stand together, the three of them, at the centre of the shop. They hear feet running past, then more. Still the yells of 'Tyranny!' The crash of breaking glass from somewhere close by, and then one of the windows shatters upstairs. Mr Butter puts his arms about his weeping wife; all Belle can think of is Rafe, somewhere out there, in all this. 'NO POPERY' has taken its place amongst the shouts outside. And one single bellow, of 'NO KING!'

'My God!' Mr Butter whispers. He holds his women close. The tumult in the street sweeps past. 'My God, what is happening?'

'Natty!' Mrs Butter exclaims. 'I smell smoke!'

Mr Butter once nearly lost the entire shop thanks to a candle left upon the stairs. They rush out into the yard. What is on fire? Where is it? There, there in Cheapside, smoke is rising, and almost as soon as they see it, they hear the noise of the mob returning. They run back inside. Bodies barge against the shutters, shadows dart like evil spirits across the ceiling. Belle knows only that at some point they hear a single set of running feet stop at their door and then a thunderous knocking upon it, and her husband's voice: 'Belle! Belle! Open up, my darling, open the door!'

She runs to do so. There stands Rafe, his jacket torn, his collar all awry, a contusion on his cheek. 'Oh, my darling!' he says, on seeing her safe. He stumbles into the shop. 'I was there,' he tells them. 'I was there. Westminster. The King – an army. He came with an army. Five hundred men, Belle! He came to take away those in Parliament who opposed him, but they were warned, they were gone – I never thought I would get home to you. There are barricades thrown up everywhere.'

They tiptoe out into the street. Glass from their top window crunches underfoot. Further up the street, one of their neighbours, not as speedy with his shutters as they, stands before the wreck of his windows, wringing his hands. Books have been thrown into the gutters, loose pages blowing up and down the pavement. In Cheapside, a street away, the twirl of smoke is now a roar of flame.

'Mr Endicott,' says Mr Butter, drawing himself up, 'our women cannot stay here.'

'No, Mr Butter,' says Rafe. 'I wholly agree with you. It is the mob – London is in *ferment*.'

'Where is the mob?' Mrs Butter asks, with fearful, brimming eyes.

'They are gone to the Tower. They are bringing out the cannon.'

'Where is the *King*?' asks Belle.

'Whitehall. He is gone back to Whitehall.'

Then he is not at Whitehall. He is gone to Hampton Court. Then he is no longer anywhere near London at all – London has been abandoned; no, London has been freed! Now he is meant to be in negotiation with Parliament. 'Negotiation?' Mr Butter asks, dumbfounded. Months are wasted in this – yes, but surely there will be a resolution? No, surely there will not! Now the King is outside Hull. The armoury at Hull is full of weapons, all the arms brought north to fight the Scots. Charles demands admittance; the governor of Hull tells him to fuck off; Hull closes its gates. Then he is in Nottingham. Then, he raises his standard. Then, England is at war.

PART II

Oxford 1642

CHAPTER ONE

The More the Merrier

'Are you for King or Parliament?'

Civil War pamphlet

JACK FISKARDO, STANDING at the compass window to his bedchamber, narrowing those pale eyes of his toward the horizon. The trees are bare; the choices facing England just as stark. There is a broadsheet, brought to him by Mrs Mayhew, in his hand. Its lettering is emphatic, and you have no need to be literate to con its meaning. Above the blunt demand of its title, there canters the Earl of Essex – England's most famous cuckold, now commander-in-chief of Parliament's troops. *And make what you will of that*, thinks Jack. The artist has depicted Essex looking put-upon as ever; and with a bloody awful seat upon his horse. Facing Essex, on the King's side, as

General of His Majesty's Horse, that beardless youth Rupert, Count Palatine. There has been a battle. Popular wisdom had been that after one engagement on the field, both sides would sit down and treaty with each other, but since both sides claim the victory, such, it seems, is not to be. Edgehill. Where the devil is Edgehill?

Warwickshire. Nothing like as far away as one would bloody wish. When Topham, leading the household in their morning prayers, bade them pray for the peace of our well-beloved sovereign Charles. Jack had to hide his disbelief in a cough. But then it was the same growing up in the village in Poitou. The King was incapable of doing wrong; it was everyone else who offended.

'They say the armies barely found each other,' Mrs Mayhew tells him. 'That when they met, it was almost by accident. Can that be true, sir? Can that happen?'

All too likely, if you lack discoverers. Years back, in Germany, when he was still as new and raw and green as it was possible to be, Jack had been one of those hunting the army of Christian of Brunswick right up to the Dutch border, across country as flat as a rug. It still took days to find them. A wrinkle in the landscape can hide one army from the other; rain can do it; dusk; a stand of trees.

His face is set, in a manner his men in Germany would have recognized at once. The lines that time has bracketed round his mouth are doing their job, of holding everything in. Damnation, this was meant to be his past. The future was to be those fields to the horizon, his boys kicking up a rumpus downstairs – 'Give it back!' he hears Ned roar, then James's squeak of defiance: '*Nnno!*'

'They say the King's horse chased Parliament's men from the field with a tally-ho, sir, like they were chasing no more than a fox.'

He thinks of Rupert, Count Palatine, now Rupert of the Rhine in popular parlance. He thinks of the lad's insouciance. *Yes, all too bloody likely.*

'They say the King will come to Oxford. They say he will make his headquarters here. They say Parliament will send my Lord Essex and his army against him.' A pause. 'Do you think we will be safe, sir?'

There are crows hopping across the field nearest to the house. In Germany the crows were the old women, went among the fallen, stripping and robbing. Field to battlefield, how hideously fast that transformation can be.

You will be safe as I can make you.

'Mrs Mayhew,' Jack begins. 'If I wished to get a letter across to the Low Countries, to Haarlem, say, how would I go about such a thing?'

IT TAKES FOLK different ways, such news. Pris Holland, for example – fury, is what it engenders in her. Not even in Breda was she as incensed as this.

'Soldiers on our doorstep, Wyn, armed men, right *there*,' Pris declares, throwing out an arm to indicate Covent Garden and its piazza. 'They broke up the market. We could not even get bread!' She pulls Molly over to stand beside her. 'Moll's nose was blooded—'

'But you should'a seen the other mort,' Molly puts in, stoutly.

'And a curfew, Wyn – a curfew, here in London! Is this England or is it –' (she racks her brains for the opposite of England, some place where freedom is unknown) '– is this England or is it Tartary?'

Never so angry, nor so – yes, say it. Afeared. She has to stop to take breath. 'They broke into St Paul's, did you know that? They shot at the statues.'

'Shot the Christ-Child,' says Molly, with a nod of the head. 'Our Saviour, and they shot 'im.'

'My dear,' says Wyn, 'I am sure that is not so—'

She hardly hears him. 'You never saw a war, Wyn. You cannot think how bad this will become. All of our neighbours downstairs are fled, and have you seen what they are doing to the park? They are *digging* across it, Wyn, great earthworks, already – we will be in the *front line*.' Her voice trembles. Wyn is looking from her to Molly and back again, as if Molly will have some explanation for her mistress's behaviour, as if it is she, Pris, who is at fault here for making such a fuss.

'*And* Monsieur Vigne's buggered off,' Molly puts in, gaily. Such excitement! 'Put a notice in his window, took himself back to Paree.'

'Exactly, Wyn!' her mistress exclaims. 'Who is to tend my hair? *Look* at it.'

The copper curls, at present, are bunched about Pris's head in a manner that in its disorder strikes some unoccupied corner of Wyn's senses as most becoming. Otherwise, all his powers are bent on picking a path through Pris's fury. *Truly*, he thinks, *truly, when she lets loose like this, it is like trying to find a way through a nettle-patch. Through a nettle-patch blindfolded, forsooth!* And did he not have an intention, a message of his own to impart, in coming here? 'But my dear,' he begins, 'what would you have me do?'

Put out your hand to me! Pris thinks. *Soothe me!* (With a *Woah*, perhaps?) *Show me my upset matters just as much to you!*

'Your – your *pipe-men*. You and all of them, you must – you must recall Parliament—'

'My *dear*,' says Wyn. He is almost chuckling. 'Would that I had such power – would that *any* of us did.' *My pipe-men.* How flattering! 'But we are far beyond that. The King has done great wrongs. He has flattered England's enemies. He has sought to corrupt her church. He has inflicted taxes on his people, with no mandate to do so. He has shown contempt for Parliament altogether. We must show strength till he has seen we are in earnest.' This is the wisdom of the day. Even if it means – yes, even if it means more blood must be shed. After that, both sides will come up to the negotiating table, that is how it will happen; Wyn has no doubt of it.

'*All* kings do great wrongs!' Pris shrieks. 'It is the business of kings to do great wrongs! It is only your *littleness* has kept you nice as you are.'

Littleness. Wyn feels his mood change foot. 'Little, am I?'

'Oh, Wyn, be wise! Old men should be wise!'

Little and old. A certain steeliness creeps over Wyn, despite the fact that Pris – bosom heaving, hair unkempt, face pink with passion – is exactly as he finds her most appealing. In fact, that may be why his mood contracts; he will not have her both insulting *and* arousing him, in one.

'Madame Oliphant was here.' (Pris shakes anew with fury at the memory: Madame Oliphant, here in Pris's parlour – 'Now it breaks my heart,' Madame Oliphant had said, 'but we are leaving for my sister's place, in Kent, till all this present nastiness is done. So much as it sorrows me, it is time to settle your account.' She had slapped a paper into Pris's hand. 'Fourteen pounds, eight shillings and ninepence. If you don't have such in readies, my nephew George here –' and she indicated the thick-necked boy beside her, already leering at Molly '– my nephew George will be pleased to take the same in movables.') 'She took my silver boxes, Wyn!'

'The graspy old bitch,' Molly puts in. 'To think of the money she has had from you!'

'From *me*, I think you will find,' says Wyn, unusually firmly. He picks up his hat. 'Pris, this brings me to the matter I wished to speak of. I too will be leaving London.' (He hears her gasp. Most satisfactory. He had thought he would request, but no; he will order.) 'In these troubled times I should be at Goodwins. I would have you accompany me.'

Another gasp, this one almost a yelp. 'Leave King Street?'

'There is no point in keeping these rooms if I will not be in London.' It is unlike Wyn to pull on the reins like this, but he must admit, it is something to see Pris stopped in her tracks. He continues: 'It is my intention to assist my neighbour Colonel Ancrum in raising a company for Parliament. I will have many claims upon my purse; this is one I can do without. We must all make sacrifices, my dear. You may perfectly well come with me; in which case you will be safer too. We will say you are my ward. Otherwise, your rent is paid to the next quarter—'

'*Wyn!*' Pris's thoughts are reeling, as if they had taken a blow to the jaw – *this*, she thinks, *this is how they manacle us to them, bloody money, every time.*

Wyn places the hat on his head. 'The next quarter. But beyond that, madam, I regret, you *and* your London debts, you would be on your own.'

A trip to Chelsea, one that is likely to be the last for some time. They sit in the garden of the Pightle, in amongst the greys and browns of autumn. Mary Frith smokes her pipe, Bess sits muffled in her Persian shawl. Abi, gripping Pris's hand, is in tears. 'But you will be so far away!' she wails, 'and no-one about you but strangers!'

'I was in the country once,' says Mary Frith, pleasantly. 'Out amongst the green. I was like to have died of it. God's blood, the lack of anything!'

'I am only going into Buckinghamshire, Mary, not out to Timbuctoo,' Pris answers, snappish. She folds Abi's fingers over hers. 'It will only be until Christmas, Abi. The King must come to terms by then, everyone says so.'

A snort of derision from Bess. Pris hears herself sigh. It is as if her spirits are giving up all on their own. 'Bess, whose side are we on in this? Are we for King, or Parliament?'

'We Hollands are on the same side as always,' says Bess, firmly. 'Our own.'

HERE WE ARE again, that chapel behind the deer park of the Coudenberg in Brussels. Words can scarce convey how delighted Carlo Fantom is to find himself summoned back here, amongst the gilded sunbursts, the pot-bellied seraphim, the sad-eyed inhabitant of that cross.

Don't you judge me, thinks Carlo, squinnying at it. *What have I done that you have not permitted worse?*

'Do you keep well, Captain?' Hooley asks, sitting down beside him.

Carlo shifts his focus, like a sharpshooter. He has never been one for small-talk, unless to lull some victim into a false sense of ease. And he has conceived a hatred of his present employer almost of a pitch as that he has for places such as this – he, who once had the ear of a cardinal, who once sold his services to kings.

'And did you restore your fortune?' Hooley asks next, then draws his head back, as if to take a proper scrutiny of Carlo – the boots down at heel, the torn coat, the yellowed linen – and answers himself. 'No, I see that you did not. So now here you are again. My old soldier.' He extends an arm and pats Carlo on the back.

Men have, literally, died for less. Carlo feels the anger grind within him like teeth. 'You summoned me,' he says.

'So I did.' Hooley leans forward. 'What do you know of England?'

'Grey and wet,' Fantom replies.

'Oh, but not always. There are seasons of the year when England is delightful.' Hooley taps a finger along the back of the pew. 'There was a time,' he says, reflectively, 'when England was Spain's ally. When Spanish ships might gather in safety off Dover, before they sailed against the Dutch. Do you remember that, Captain? It was but two short years ago. Why, there was a moment when King Charles was to wed the Infanta, and a fine thing that would have been for my country, Captain, a fine thing. With Spain behind us, all Ireland might have been regained for those who love her. Now England is at war with itself, and my masters are out of it entirely. That cannot stand. That cannot be. I need my own eyes over there.'

Carlo rubs at the tight skin on the one side of his jaw. 'England is not Germany,' he points out. 'I have no *netzwerk* there.'

'Ah, but *I* do,' Hooley tells him. 'There is a man by name of Ingram Skinner, a Londoner, in my employ. I propose to send you out to him without delay.'

Carlo rolls the word about his mouth. 'Skeener,' he says. 'London.' Another of those eerie smiles. 'Maybe I find Mercator for you.'

Hooley, unexpectedly, gives a laugh. 'The man who manages that, Captain, would indeed find his fortune burnished beyond his wildest dreams.' He stands. 'I think you will take to Ingram Skinner. He and his family are not on the side of the angels, but then again, Captain, neither are you.'

A WELCOMING COMMITTEE.

'Is that 'im, Mistah Tucker?' Bug wants to know.

'Bug, how the fuck could that be 'im?' Tucker hisses back. Tucker is an expert at reading the Skinner temper, and he has never seen Ingram as jittery as this. And while, where Bug points, a wherry has just landed her passengers, the man at whom Bug points is nothing but a jobbing porter, harness round his shoulders like a horse. Tucker grabs Bug by the ear, gives it a twist. Tucker as usual is hungover; also, it is cooler here on the Customs House stairs than a man might wish; the sun going down blood-red; the shadows deep. 'The man we're waiting for, he'll be wearing the badge of a silver wolf, on the front of his coat.'

'What's one of them, Mistah Tucker?' Bug asks, rubbing his ear.

'The mark of a hard man, that is. One of them, comes out of Germany, cain't be harmed by nothing made of lead, nor iron, nor steel. No sword will fell them. No bullet pierce their skin. They are impenetrable, Bug, and they have got that way –' (Tucker tilts his head down to Bug) '– they have got that way by *the selling of their souls*.'

'Tucker, by Christ,' says Ingram, without turning his head. 'Stow the blabber or I will *stitch* your mouth closed. There. That's our man.'

A second passenger has disembarked. Pushes back his hat to look along the quayside. The porter stands well clear. Now the man sees them; but no wave of the hand, no halloo. Instead, this chilly measuring up – Ingram, stood there with his oldest Ezra to one side and Asa to the other, and Tucker and Bug to the rear. The most presentable of the Skinners' wagtails, Dilly and Flo, are in attendance also; Dilly in carnation pink, and Flo in marigold orange.

The man walks up the quayside toward them, the line of his blade following slantwise behind. Dilly, like a reflex, swings her skirts, lowers her chin to her shoulder. The porter, forgotten, turns his own head and spits into the man's long shadow.

'Well now, Captain Fantom!' Ingram announces, going forward. 'Did you have a good journey, sir?'

The reply is too offhand for Tucker to make it out, but it sounds like *No such thing*. There's something – Tucker can't quite put it into words, but there's something awry about this one. It's maybe the man's eyes – so hot in colour. It's maybe the way he shows his teeth. It's maybe the teeth themselves.

It's maybe the way the porter spat.

'Mistah Tucker,' whispers Bug. 'What's wrong with the gentleman's face?'

'Well, sir,' Ingram is saying, 'we shall look after you, now you are here.' He gestures to the waiting coach. 'To Farringdon!'

They crowd into the coach – a hire, and too small for so many passengers. Tucker is squeezed between the two women; Bug is on the floor. Ezra and Asa on horseback outside, as escort. Ingram is not risking anything untoward occurring, not with this guest: he, Mr Hooley's chosen instrument; he, with that silver wolf upon his coat. 'Soon have you settled,' Ingram says. 'Rest after your travels, eh?' A roguish wink toward Dilly, who you would almost think their guest had failed to notice.

Flo, who has her nose stuck out of the window, is as skinny as a weasel, but Dilly is round as a pear. The warmth of her thigh is tangible to Tucker through her skirts; the image of it, plump as a bolster, so present in his imagination that he has to clear his throat. Now she glances at their guest and smiles. Licks her lips. *Good on you, girl*, thinks Tucker. *More'n with this one I'd sodding do.*

Captain Fantom pulls the glove from one hand, extends a finger in Dilly's direction. The finger is a match to the too-small, over-sharp teeth. 'Jan, Jan will eat no fat, and Jul doth love no lean,' he begins, in this weirdly high sing-song. All of a sudden, he leans forward, pulls Dilly toward him, and kisses her on the lips. Sits back. Wipes his mouth. 'A little too long in the window for my taste,' Carlo comments. The pointing finger roves sideways, past Tucker, comes to rest on Flo. 'What if I try her too?'

Flo considers herself Mr Skinner's, and the outrage now manifest in Flo's expression would tell you so even if you didn't know it already.

The smallest pause, then Ingram gives a shrug. 'Ah,' he says. It sounds like bonhomie. He leans across, pats Flo on the knee. 'What's mine is yours, Captain Fantom. What's mine is yours!'

THE DUNQERQER TAVERN: it sits – no, it doesn't sit, it does nothing so upright as sit, it *lowers*, then, on the bank of the River Lea, before the Lea floods out into the Thames. Nothing about you for miles but shocks of grey-leaved alder and waterlogged pastureland. Nothing till you get to the village of Poplar, and that's so far away you can only make it out from the vantage point of a path, which run high, hereabouts, raised up like seams, while the land itself puddles and floods with every breathing of the tide.

If you are on that path, keep walking. If the name isn't enough to put you off, the appearance of the place will do it. The Dunqerqer is so sunken, so broken-backed, that as you stand on the path you will be level with its attic. The patch of beaten-down grass before its door is a battlefield of rusting metal and broken bottles; on the other side of the building, where the river laps right underneath it at high tide, it seems to contemplate its fate as a drunken man might do, as if considering casting itself into the waters and ending this misery for good. God knows, in fact, what keeps the place from sliding into the river altogether. At low tide the props that support it reveal themselves as black with rot and sit in mud that must be deep as centuries. Pass by, pass by. Who on earth would spend their life out here?

Josh Arden, that's who. Josh Arden, that vile-tempered old bugger; that vile-tempered, rum-soaked, foul-mouthed, one-eyed old bugger (and this is his friend Walter Spikenard speaking), who lives here year in, year out, solitary as a heron.

He was not always thus, Old Josh. He had two eyes, once upon a time. Two eyes, as speedy a frigate as you could find amongst the Dunkirkers, and a reputation dark with blood – so dark, in fact, that in the end there was nothing for it but to scuttle his boat, and let it be assumed he had gone down with her. Even amongst the Dunkirkers, there are rules. What was it Old Josh did to so offend against them?

Well. Once upon time, Old Josh had a daughter. Sally. Sally Arden. Yellow hair in shiny curls; eyes dark as agates. Oh, how he loved her. One evil night, drunk as the devil, he tried to show her how much; Sally was gone by morning. Found herself a Frenchie, so Josh heard, a soldier, a captain of cavalry. Good luck to her. Josh even knew the man's name once – something alien, tough-sounding, but Old Josh, his brains are aged, they are addled with drink (see the bottle there, under his chair?), and struggle as he might he cannot bring it into mind.

What circles in his dreams instead is his famous brawl from years back, at the Pelican in Wapping, right by Execution Dock. Josh had gone there looking for trouble, and by God he found it. In his dream, Old Josh has reached that moment when he threw his assailant clear across the room, that moment where the man had staggered to his feet, a final weapon grabbed in desperation in his hand. Old Josh took a look and burst out laughing; unwisely as it turned out, for—

Something is swinging old Josh's knee like a gate. 'Josh!' comes Walter Spikenard's hiss. 'Josh, rouse yourself. There's summat happening outside!'

Old Josh struggles back to consciousness. Standing, he cocks an ear toward the world outside. 'The hell is that?' he snarls.

Both men know the sounds of the river as well as that of their own heartbeat. They know the nearness of its lapping as the tide comes in under the trapdoor in the Dunqerqer's kitchen floor; they know the gurgle as the waters ebb away and that bottomless mud is revealed. But what they hear now is neither of those. What they hear now is the sound of the mighty Thames rippling along the sides of something bigger than a rowboat by far, and that creaking is masts and rigging; that thunder is canvas sail.

Up they get, steadying each other; Walter with the low-built heft of every pikeman, Old Josh above him like a bear. Hobble to the window. There, above the Styx-like blackness of the river, the silhouette of something tall enough to overtop the alders with ease, and with a small, sharp-angled shape snug under her bowsprit, might put you in mind of a bat clinging to a wall.

'That's the *Guid Marie*,' says Walter, amazed. ''Tis that owd devil Mungo Sant,' and no sooner are the words out of his mouth than they hear the *Guid Marie* lower her gangplank. Then voices. A moment more and they hear hoof on timber, the sound of splashing; they see horses outlined in the moonlight, being gathered together on that raised-up path. Two men moving between them, men whose hair shines in the moonlight white as candle-flames. Now more, pulling each other up the bank, and the murmur of voices – 'Is that,' asks Walter the old soldier, in an astonished whisper, 'is that *Rotwelsch* I'm a-hearing?'

'What the fuck-a-doodle-doo—' Josh begins, and makes for the door.

Out they go, up the bank on swollen-knuckled hands and arthritic knees, but you wouldn't want to miss this: such a gathering of horsemen in the moonlight, such a lighting of torches to show the way, and such low-voiced camaraderie, all the jollity of men making landfall –

– and the unmistakable sound of a flintlock musket being readied behind them. Old Josh, slowly, stands. Walter does the same. Lifts his hands.

The man standing behind them on the path had come up without a sound. Stands now with hat pushed back to give himself a better view, revealing the fact that even in the moonlight, one eye is half the size of the other. 'Hello,' he says. 'Hello, *meine Engelska frind*.'

A shout from below. From amongst the mass of men and horses, two more stomp up the bank. One, a proper short-arse, carries a torch. He also has a pair of pistols stuck in his belt, like a buccaneer, a sword at his side and the hilt of a knife protruding from his boot. But the other, who is freckled as a giraffe, he seems an altogether friendlier type, in that he is waving at them. He holds a book. He gestures with it like a preacher. He summons the torchbearer to join him up on the path; the flame of the torch beating itself against the wind. There are still more horses being led to land, there are yet more men, splashing through the water, pulling themselves free of the mud. There is more low-toned laughter. Walter and Josh exchange glances. Josh's mouth moves about the words *What the fuck...*

The preacher is leafing through his book. He urges the torchbearer to bring the torch nearer: 'Luka! Luka, *kom hit*!' He finds his place. He holds it with his thumb. He addresses himself anew to Walter and Josh. '*Gott seive yoo*,' he begins. The words come out as something between the lowing of a cow and the hooting of an owl. 'Howdooyoudoo.' He cocks his head, as if listening to himself. Says it again, then, 'Ah!' All has come clear. '*Meine Herren*, how do you do! Gott geeve you good life!'

'Eh?' says Josh.

The preacher holds up a finger. '*Ein moment*,' he says. Tracks the finger down the page until he finds the phrase. 'My friend,' he begins, 'where is the right way from 'ence to your sittay of Otsford?'

CHAPTER TWO

When the Time Is Come

'Arise, and put on strength; for the time is come that thou put on strength, yea, the time is come.'

The Cavalier Soldier's Vade Mecum

TUCKER'S OWN MOTHER would tell you her son has no more brains than does a beetle, but even he knows persecution when he sees it. If Hag Place was unhappy before, now it is terrorized. Carlo Fantom has the whole house under his thumb, a feat he has achieved, so far as Tucker can make out, for no better reason than to pass the time. This one – Tucker shakes his head. *This Mr Grim. This toadstool of a man…* It's not just the damage been done the man's face, there is that glint in his eye as well, as if imagining what you might look like should he do his worst, and pondering whether today he will satisfy his curiosity. There is the fact that he is Hooley's man as well, of course, that adds to the shimmer of deadliness that surrounds him; there is the silver wolf on the front of his coat, but that ain't the half of it. Tucker has sinned, he knows he has, any number of times in the Skinners' service, but this one – this one might truly have sat down with the Devil himself. The Skinners' women won't go near him. Their dogs creep away. Asa Skinner, Ingram's youngest, that beef-witted blockhead, last week he had answered the door to Tucker sporting an eye swollen as a plum. 'What happened to you?' Tucker had asked, but Asa would not say. *He picks the weak spots*, Tucker tells Bug. *Mr Grim, he picks out the weak spots and he starts with them. You keep yourself outta his reach.*

Even Ingram Skinner seems unable to rule his guest, which is a thing unheard of in Hag Place; but Carlo Fantom regards Ingram Skinner with undisguised contempt, like Ingram was a thing he'd trod in, in some London gutter. Ingram brings him all the intelligence, all the news he can; all Carlo Fantom does is mock him. Waves a broadsheet in Ingram's face. 'You bring me nothing. You *know* nothing. *Wooooh*, your king has run away to Oxford. *Wooooh*, he makes an army. *Wooooh*, it fights with Parliament. Everyone knows this. It passes all through London and it ends up here because you are London's *shit*. You think Mr Hooley will pay you for this? You think he will pay *me*?' A glance at Bug, standing there behind Tucker. 'You like this? You like to work for these shit people?'

Something must be done. Hag Place must be freed of Carlo Fantom without delay. 'So, Captain,' Ingram says, as Fantom's unwelcome silhouette again fills the doorway to his chamber. He stands. 'We have a proposal for you.' He indicates the other man, who also rises to his feet – a man wearing the toggled waistcoat of a sailor. 'This is Mr Barlow,' Ingram says. 'He is captain of the *Sapphire*.'

Carlo Fantom crosses the room, pulls forward the chair in which Ingram himself had been sitting, places it facing Barlow, and sits. 'Speak,' he says.

Barlow's eyes rest for a moment on the small silver badge, there on the front of Carlo's coat. He swallows. If you were watching closely, you might spy a pinprick of satisfaction break through Carlo Fantom's otherwise indifferent gaze.

'Well, sir – sir and Mr Skinner,' Barlow begins. 'There is a carter, a man as I know well, Plumstead by name.' He glances at Ingram. His eagerness to tell his tale seems to waver. Ingram encourages him: *Go on.*

Barlow licks his lips. 'Plumstead and his boys, they run the routes north-west to Oxford, sir. Busy man, just at present.'

Carlo moves to cross one leg over the other. Flicks something carelessly in Ingram's direction from the knee of his breeches. 'And?' he says.

'And this,' says Ingram. He pulls across a chair. 'Plumstead says there is a Colonel Ancrum out Aylesbury way, recruiting. Putting together a company for Parliament.'

'The colonel is another such as yourself, sir, a soldier out of Germany,' Barlow puts in. Again he pauses, just as Ingram Skinner had told him to do, this being the sort of telling detail Ingram believes assures success.

Carlo puts his hands behind his head.

'Plumstead says this Ancrum – he's having trouble with his bills. He's cap in hand to a patron, and it's an expensive business, kitting out a company,' Barlow continues. 'I don't doubt as you would know, sir.' He darts a glance at Skinner.

'Our thinking,' says Ingram, taking over, 'is that perhaps the colonel might be willing to pass on a little fresher information.

For a consideration, if you get my meaning. A little of Mr Hooley's gold, some better intelligence for you, sir, and a few more saddles and helmets for Ancrum. What do you say?'

'Ancrum,' says Carlo, meditatively. A long pause. How does that name feel on the tongue – is it sour or sweet? 'I think I find this Ancrum,' Carlo announces, at last.

Ingram casts a terrible glance over to where Tucker stands beside the door: *Don't you dare let out your breath.* 'I did think you would,' he says.

'Yes,' says Carlo. He sounds ruminative. 'I think I shall have him recruit *me*.' A smirk. 'I have missed my time as a soldier. I think I will go back to war. I will cut you out of this, Herr Ingram. What do you say to that?'

Small price to pay, in Ingram's view. 'But Ancrum is Parliament's man. A country Puritan. What would Mr Hooley say?'

'Herr Ingram,' says Carlo. 'You think this is the first time I turn my coat to serve my purposes?' The shiny place where flame had licked his face wrinkles with amusement. 'Only—'

'Only what?' Ingram asks, only a little faster than he had intended.

'Only a captain, a veteran, he would not enlist on his own. He would have a servant to go with him.' He swings his head. 'You,' Carlo announces, pointing at Tucker. 'You will come with me. You.'

There is a walled yard behind Hag Place, before the ground sogs its way into the ditch that is the River Fleet. Everything in it is black with London soot, and the two crippled-looking trees have hardly a leaf between them. But here, this evening, stands Mr Barlow of the *Sapphire*, with Ingram Skinner. Barlow holds in his hand a dozen half-crowns. 'Two of those to Plumstead, remember?' Skinner is saying.

Barlow closes his hand nervously over the coins, as if to render them invisible. 'You didn't say as he was a hard man,' he mutters.

'Ach, those old tales!' Ingram replies. 'You got more sense than that!' He sweeps an arm toward the world beyond the wall. 'Barlow, out there, there is a *war*. And that war is enough to swallow even such a one as Carlo Fantom. You mark my words, we'll not be seeing him again.'

'But he will have Tucker with him,' Barlow points out.

Ingram shrugs. 'No great loss,' he says.

THE WAR ARRIVES in Varney pulling itself along the fence. On its forehead, its face is open to the bone, and one hand has blood dripping from it as from the cloth about a cheese. Its thoughts are mazy and disordered and doing constant battle with a pain within its eye socket that feels as big as its head. It only knows that it has reached the house when it hears Ocker and Todd run toward it, barking and growling, and then Topham's voice crying, 'Toby! Oh my lad!'

Toby sinks to his knees, holding his arm across his face. He feels Topham hoist him upright, then the captain is there too. Toby's legs are scooped up beneath him, and he hears the captain saying, 'Mind that hand,' and the hand is placed against his breast. The sound of gravel underfoot is replaced by that of stone flags, and Toby knows he is at last within Varney's walls. He thinks he may die now. He feels himself being laid on something flat and strong, and understands this is the kitchen table. The dogs are bounding round and round. He hears the captain order them away, then the captain saying, 'Topham, get into Oxford. Fast as you can. Bring us back a surgeon for his eye.'

He hears Mrs Mayhew's voice raised in horror; he feels her take his hand – the other hand, not that at his breast; his breast that is both warm and cold at once, and the hand in the centre of it, a single throb of agony. He hears the captain speak again, he hears the captain saying, 'We have to seal that. That is too much blood.' Then Mrs Mayhew's voice, and the captain replying, 'No, broader. It needs a wider blade.' An awful instinct has Toby turn his head, to blink at the captain bending over the kitchen fire, holding something in the flames. The same instinct has Toby try to call out 'No – no,' but everything that comes from his mouth is wordless. Now the captain is back at his side, is telling Mrs Mayhew, 'Hold his arm out, hold it steady as you can.' He cannot see what it is the captain brings toward the hand; the captain is using his body to shield Toby from the sight, but he can feel the heat from it. He hears the captain saying, 'I am so sorry, lad.'

Mrs Mayhew is there. She strokes his cheek. She is saying, 'Look at me, child, look at me.' As he drops into the pit Toby realizes he is weeping, but only from one eye.

When the world returns, it is still dark, but it is the world again. Toby is in bed, or in a bed, one that seems to have been made up for him in the scullery. There is a glow of candlelight; he tries to turn toward it, but his head won't move as it should. He lifts his good hand. There is a bandage round his head, covering one eye, covering that whole side of his face. The knot of a sling at his neck. The hand in the sling is grumbling with pain; the eye under the bandage aches so much it feels as if it will never cease, as if he will have to live with this for the rest of his life.

He hears a voice saying, 'I am so sorry for your hurt, Toby.'

Lily! He reaches out his good hand. For the rest of his life this is what Toby will have, the good hand, and the other, where all that is left is the thumb and two stumps. Just as, for the rest of his life, what he will have is the good eye, and the one that is rolled in its socket like a marble. For the next few months, the world will appear to Toby as if he is viewing it through an out-of-focus spyglass. Then, gradually, his brain will adapt, the edges of things will come back, and he will see the world almost as it is. But he will never be able to judge distance again. There will be no more crafting of cunning little traps with those clever hands of his from bullrush and twig, no more leading the reapers in tying and stacking the sheaves at harvest. He will walk into furniture and trip over anything left on the floor. And it will make him miserable.

'Lily! Is that you?'

Now he sees her, or at least under the edge of the bandage he sees a smudged form that speaks with her voice. 'I am so sorry,' she repeats. Her head is turned away. It makes her voice difficult to hear. He thinks he hears the suppression of a sob.

'Don't cry,' he says. 'Don't cry, Lily. I'm here.' He stretches the good hand toward her. He and Lily have an understanding; he wants to reassure her that they have it still. 'We'll be all right, Lily. We'll be all right, I promise.'

But she will not look at him. She will not take his hand. By the end of the week, Lily will have gone back to Banbury, to her own people.

There is a small room off the inner hall at Varney. Topham stands just inside its door. He says, 'They came from Aylesbury way, sir. Breaking heads and making trouble. They caught the boy as he walked back to us.'

The room is just big enough for a table and an old-fashioned solid-sided chair, been part of the house for as long as anyone can remember. The captain sitting in the chair has an ominous quality to his silence, one that has Topham addressing his remarks to the hat that he holds in his hands, turning it round and round. He says, 'There never was no love lost between the men of Aylesbury and those of Oxford, sir.'

A deep, deep sigh. 'They came a long way to make trouble.'

'Yes, sir.' The hat completes another quarter-turn. 'Colonel Ancrum, I hear he has a veteran from Germany with him. And all the young hotheads thereabouts, fired up against the King. 'Tis said he is putting together a company for Parliament.'

And now the captain lifts his head. *Oh*, thinks Topham, *oh, this is a different man now.*

'I hoped,' says Jack, 'I hoped we would be seen as being near enough to Oxford to keep the war from us. I hoped, perhaps, that it might work itself out somewhere else entirely.' He pushes himself up from the chair. 'But, by Christ, Topham, by Christ, if Ancrum wants a fight, he's going to get it.'

AMONGST THE OFFICERS in the army of His Majesty King Charles, there is one Joseph Cantley, captain of dragoons. He is a bit of a doodle, is Cantley. An uncle is Charles I's ambassador in Paris, no less, but the brains in the family have not come down on Cantley's side. You can tell that from the fact that he was schooled at Eton, whereas everyone knows the true wits and whipsters scratch their slates at Winchester. Anyway, here he is, easing his bladder against the wall of a many-cornered alleyway known as Hell Passage, which leads to yet another of Oxford's taverns, the Spotted Cow. Cantley is buttoning up when he hears a commotion in the street outside, and running out, finds himself confronted by a group of horsemen heading toward him at the speed of a charge, the beast in front ploughing to a halt not ten feet away; legs braced, head back, eyes rolling; its mane so luxuriant it spreads as if the animal were underwater. The rider slides from its back and strides up on Cantley, reins in his fist.

Cantley retreats a step. Such are the times, you do see men of this stamp in Oxford, but not often and not many – the battle-scarred buff-coat, the glare like an attack. And good God, the troop of bandits with him! The pistols and the blades!

'Good day to ye,' the man calls out. He pulls the horse after him; the beast responds by rearing upward, front legs swinging. The man hauls on the reins to bring it back to earth. 'Now *stay*!' he orders it, as one might a disobedient dog. 'I told you, no dancing about!' He turns back to Cantley. 'I am in search of your commander,' he says. 'Sir Jacob. Jacob Astley. I would speak with him.'

By contrast to Cantley, Sir Jacob Astley is sixty-four years old, a veteran of the Dutch Revolt, the army of King Christian of Denmark and the wars in Germany. In happier times, he was tutor to Rupert, Prince Palatine; by God, under the old Queen, he sailed with Walter Raleigh. His face is – let us call it grown-in-the-grain. The hairline shelves away; the cheeks are lined, the eyes are eagle-ish. He finds himself these days Major-General of the King's Foot, in which role he is already celebrated for the bluntness of his bearing on the field: coming face to face with the enemy at Edgehill, Astley dropped to one knee, raised a hand to the troops behind him and bellowed, 'O Lord, Thou knowest how busy I must be this day. If I forget Thee, do not thou forget me. March on, boys.' He is dining this evening at St John's, awaiting the hoped-for arrival of his one-time royal pupil. Instead, who comes bursting through the door (with an *extraordinary* lack of grace), but that clod-poll Cantley. 'Your patience, Sir Jacob,' Cantley begins. 'A hundred pardons, but there is a man outside the college, in the street, says he will speak with you tonight.'

Sir Jacob rises to his feet. He wipes with his napkin at his moustache, which is of that brushed-up sort so fashionable at present, accompanied by the dab of beard upon the chin. 'Does he, by God,' he replies.

'He does, sir. He says he is a discoverer, and is known to the Prince, and is here with his men from the wars in Germany, and that he knows we lack such of our own, and that he will deliver to us all the intelligence of Parliament's forces as you will ever need, and that he will do so only for the brief loan of a company of dragoons.'

'A company of dragoons?'

'Yes, sir.'

'And does this ruffian – this importuning ruffian – have a name?'

'He does, sir,' says Cantley. 'It is Fiskardo, sir. One Jack Fiskardo.'

CHAPTER THREE

Supper with Colonel Ancrum

'He who keeps company with the wolf will learn to howl.'

John Ray, *A Collection of English Proverbs*

D*earest Bess* (writes Pris)

My loving duty to you. Ho for the spring, and an end to the war.

A blot. The paper is rough; the pen Pris had to cut herself.

Till then, here I be, as Mary put it, out amongst the green. Oh Lord, Bess, I might as well have pricked my finger like that sorry princess, and be in her sleep of a hundred years.

There is nothing to do here, NOTHING, but play cards with Moll, and listen to the house creak in the wind. I am not allowed to venture beyond the gardens, for that the roads are all a-crawl with cavalier-ravishers and royalist malignants; I am not even meant to be writing to you, for that our posts are no doubt close-watched and reported on. By whom, I ask, and Wyn tells me those who wish to frustrate his plans with Colonel Ancrum. Meantime, his people all stare at Moll as if she had two noses on her face, and pretend her London way of speaking is beyond them, so you can imagine what frolics there are in the getting of hot water of a morning, or, indeed, the getting of anything. I languish in the worst bad odour here for having brought my maid with me in any case. Also, I must live this mad charade that I am Wyn's ward, which fools not a soul, but means Wyn's chamber is at one end of the house, and mine at the other, and unused for so long the cobwebs have cobwebs, and my bed so damp when we arrived, when I pulled back the sheets, I would not have wondered to see a flounder swim off between 'em.

We are so far out in the green here that the carrier comes but once a week for the mails, and I must put this in his hand myself or it will never reach you. And I must not tarry, for Wyn would have an interview with me this very afternoon. Give my loves to Abi and to Aaron, and to Greville too – there, that is a measure of how I pine for King Street, and for all of you.

Your gosling,
Pris

'Well now,' says Wyn. To Pris's amazement his smile is generous, his step is brisk. He is in a better humour than he has been for weeks. 'We have news, my dear.' He walks back and forth before the window, rubbing his hands together – a recent habit and one Pris finds intensely annoying, but Wyn is not to know that. Indeed, it would never occur to Wyn that his behaviour could be found annoying in this way, least of all by his mistress. Women do not judge men in such a wise. What would the world be coming to, if they did? 'We are to have a change of scene,' he announces.

'Back to London, Wyn?' Pris suggests. She had been engaged in dressing Molly's hair – yes, what *is* the world coming to? Wyn had pondered, on entering her room. Cards and titivation, cards and titivation, this is all they do, all day. Tut-tut. When he had walked in, there had been giggling too. And he regards poor Molly, who has skittered to the back of the room, with distaste, for leading her mistress astray, a thing that is hardly fair, as the hairdressing session had been entirely Pris's idea.

'Not back to London, no,' Wyn says. 'I have heard from Colonel Ancrum. He is setting up a muster.'

'A *muster*, Wyn?'

'Indeed yes. A final push, don't y'know – to bring our company up to strength. It will be brave doings, I am assured, and we shall be a part of them. We are going to stay with Colonel Ancrum at Upper Aston Hall. Now, Pris—'

He crosses the room to her, sits down. Molly, unregarded, pulls a face. This is the posture my Lord Wyncanton adopts with Molly's mistress when he wishes to admonish her.

'You must be aware, Colonel and Mrs Ancrum – they are plain people, Pris.'

'How sad for them,' says Pris, at once.

'I mean that they *live* very plain,' says Wyn. 'Plain and godly. There is no London frippery in Upper Aston. You will pack from the modest end of your wardrobe. You will dress dark, madam, an't please you.'

'Will I so?' comes the reply. It is plain to Molly that her mistress is beginning to bridle, but again, this is lost on Wyn.

'You will. Colonel Ancrum sees me as a proper man; I will have my ward leave an impression of propriety also. Thus there are some few items I would have you remove from your conversation while we are with them.' He produces a paper from his pocket. 'I have made a list.'

'A list,' Pris repeats.

'Indeed. As an aid to memory.'

He hands the list to her. 'Pox,' Pris begins, reading from it.

'You will not say pox, no.'

'Nor whoreson. Nor fuck. Nor variants thereof, I see you set down here.'

'Exactly,' says Wyn. He glances up. He has the strangest notion that Pris's nuisance of a maid, there in the corner, had been smirking.

'Nor shitten-cum-shite,' Pris continues, reading.

'Beg pardon, sir,' comes the voice from the back of the room (and is not this kind of insolence exactly why Wyn wanted the girl left in London in the first place?), 'but 'tis I says that. Not me lady.' She bobs a curtsey.

'And one thing more,' says Wyn. He rises to leave as he speaks. 'Colonel Ancrum will have maids aplenty of his own, and would no doubt be insulted if we should act as if he could not provide you with one. Your girl, therefore, will remain at Goodwins.'

'Leave Molly here?' Now Pris is on her feet as well. 'But Wyn! Who is to help me dress?'

'As I said, I have no doubt Dorothea Ancrum will furnish you with a maid of her own. Who will be better versed in the manners and the habits of the place.' He glances at Molly's uncapped head, the ringlets half-coaxed from her mop. 'Let that be an end to the matter.' A flap of the hand. 'To your packing, madam. We dine at Upper Aston tonight.'

'Oh, miss!' Molly wails, as the door closes behind him. 'Oh, mam'selle! Please don't leave me 'ere, with the scarecrows. They hate me!'

'They hate me too, Molly.' Pris scowls at the door, through which Wyn, oblivious, has passed, then goes to her clothes chest and opens it. There, on the top, is the cinnabar silk – yet unworn. Her fingers reach out longingly toward it. *Dress dark. Dark and modest.*

Pox!

IT IS A fine day on which to make a journey. Something softer and warmer is in the air. How blithe the world looks! thinks Wyn, as his carriage bowls along the road to Upper Aston. And how compliant his whore – cry your pardon, his *ward* – as she sits opposite in gown of grey, caped and hooded and hands hidden in a muff. 'You look most fitting,' says Wyn, kindly, leaning across to pat her knee. He ought to spend more time upon her, yes, he should! A woman's world is little enough; he will take more interest in her hereafter. Once the muster is done. Once his company is out there, Ancrum at its head, the Wyncanton martlet on its flag, proudly borne aloft. 'What is this cloth?' he enquires.

''Tis called paragon, Wyn,' Pris answers, wanly.

How perfect the opportunity! 'And so you are,' Wyn tells her, patting the knee once more. 'And so you are.'

A knocking on the roof of the carriage: Wyn's coachman is banging on it with the handle of his whip. He calls down to them, 'An't save us, my Lord, the Hall is straight ahead.'

Upper Aston Hall. It is not as ancient as Goodwins; nor, judging by its windows (Wyn is quietly pleased to note), does it have Goodwins' run of rooms. No noble gallery in which to exercise, should the weather be inclement, no little arbours in its garden – indeed, no garden. Handing Pris down from the coach, Wyn perceives there is nothing before them but a bare courtyard; and there looks to be nothing behind the house but untended country – but then, Wyn reflects, a garden is a vanity. His own borders and walks (so pretty in the spring!), truly they are no more than man's attempt to play Creator, and Ancrum, he is sure, would have none of that. As he hands Pris down he persuades himself therefore to overlook the extreme – the extreme *barrenness* of the house, and the way it sits, mis-founded, facing north, and the lack of anything – not even a creeper – to soften the lines of its walls. He also tells himself to ignore the noticeable smell.

'Wyn,' Pris hisses at him, 'Godsakes, what is that *stench*?'

Pig-shit, unmistakably. 'Stench?' says Wyn, bravely. 'I smell nothing out the ordinary.' From the corner of his eye he sees the door to Upper Aston Hall come open, he sees Colonel Ancrum approach. He attempts to fill his chest. The only result is a fit of coughing. My word yes, the odour, it is strong.

'My Lord!' Ancrum begins, coming up. He is exactly as Wyn remembers him: pink-faced, white-haired, full (as Wyn thinks of it) of command; a presence, indeed. 'My Lord Wyncanton, an honour, an honour. Are you well, sir? Are you well?'

Wyn, eyes watering, is still attempting to master the coughing fit, but Ancrum has turned to Pris, who has her muff held up before her face, and who extends one solitary finger from her hand, as a woman might to check the dust along a wainscot. 'You remember my ward,' Wyn manages at last. 'Miss Holland?'

Ancrum bobs his glossy white head. Pris, looking at him (the pink wattle, the dark coat), finds herself thinking at once, *Christmas turkey*. Now a woman and a gaggle of servants stream through the door. 'My wife,' Ancrum announces grandly. 'Dorothea, my Lord Wyncanton, and Miss Holland.'

Dorothea Ancrum bows her head. Pris, being the younger, drops a curtsey. Dorothea Ancrum puts out her hand. '*Delighted!*' she exclaims, a little more loudly than one might expect. 'Delighted, Miss Holland!'

Thinks Miss Holland, *I can see full well that you are NOT.* The hidden Dorothea Ancrum, you might call it, unscrolls before Pris like manuscript: *She speaks loud because secretly she fears she is of no account.*

'We have made a reception for you, my Lord,' says Dorothea Ancrum, revealing herself as the kind of woman who not only speaks rather too loud, but stands rather too close to you to do it, too. 'A *souper*, as you would say in London. Would you not, Miss Holland? Is that not what you would say? I have a sister, lives in Shoreditch,' she adds, by way of explanation.

Who is younger and fairer than you.

'She is wed to the master of the Cordwainers Company,' Dorothea continues, in a tone in which spite clings about the boast like ivy to a tree.

Ah – and made so much better a match of it than you.

'Do follow!' Dorothea Ancrum urges them. 'Do! Our other guests await! They are most anxious to know you, my Lord. Our guest of honour! Oh, and Miss Holland too, of *course*!'

Colonel Ancrum's dining-room. Some of the smell of pig has found its way in down the chimney. The guest of honour is conducted forward and presented to Upper Aston's rector, the Reverend Henry Gage – a man in clothes so very dark, and with jaw so very shadowed, he reminds Pris of a stick of charcoal. In fact, all those others in the room are in clothes sombre enough to make Pris's grey paragon seem positively gaudy. There is much looking askance at her hair, also. Mrs Gage, head held rigid by both collar and ruff, is in the saddest of browns (a colour Madame Oliphant would describe as Dying Monkey), Dorothea Ancrum upholstered in satiny black, relieved by a single mangey-looking strip of fur laid across the shoulder. Before seating herself, Dorothea Ancrum had gone to the window, opened it (fresh wafts of pig) and, removing the odd-looking fur, shaken it out of the window with a snap. Perhaps it is her imagination, but Pris seemed to see innumerable small items flying from it – *oh Jesus Christ*, thinks Pris, *it is a flea-fur!*

'London!' exclaims Mrs Gage, breaking into the horror of this revelation. 'And you *abide* there? In the city?'

Pris, mastering the need to scratch herself all over, replies, 'Near to Covent Garden Market.'

Mrs Gage, clearly attempting to square 'market' onto the mystery that is 'city', peers at Pris as if she were something from the menagerie at the Tower, and exchanges a glance with Mrs Ancrum. The men have sat at one end of the table, the women at the other; and now in that inimitable female way, as Dorothea Ancrum takes her seat, Pris feels herself and every detail of her appearance being slowly picked and pulled apart, like a dummy being stripped in Unthanks' window.

'In my girlhood,' says Dorothea Ancrum, 'I remember the crowds in London at the coronation. To think that it has come to this!'

'We strive,' Colonel Ancrum declares. Amongst the dishes on the table (a glistening brawn; a bowl of tripes in mustard; a fricassée of eels in curdled sauce), there is a pig's head, over which Ancrum stands, armed with carving knife and fork. It is the only fork in the room, as far as Pris can see – at her place she has a knife to one side of her plate, and nothing but a spoon the other. She looks longingly at her glass, willing it to fill. 'We strive to set the world to rights,' Ancrum says. He slices off one of the pig's ears, waves it on the end of the fork toward Wyn. 'With God's grace, all things may be done.' He pushes the ear down upon a serving plate, begins to slash about the animal's cheeks. 'And now my Lord Essex has taken Reading—'

'Yes, yes!' says Wyn, nodding his head, as if Essex was there, at the table, and would appreciate the encouragement. 'And will go on to Oxford? He must do so, for sure.' He smiles down the table toward Pris. 'You will see, my dear, we will have this sorry business over within weeks.'

Ancrum hesitates. 'Ah. Not quite at once, my Lord. It would not be wise. His men are yet unpaid. Perforce, Essex must wait for their salaries. And his London brigades are all gone home—' He drops his voice. The words *fever* can be heard. *Fever in the ranks.* 'He must make a pause in his plans.'

'Dear me!' says Wyn, nervously. He dabs at his mouth with his napkin, then stares at it, as if expecting to find contagion in its very folds.

'Aye, aye, a quartan ague. I saw the same in Germany. The scourge of every army. Most debilitating.' Ancrum continues hacking at the pig's head. 'This, my Lord, is why I would take our company to join William Waller's forces in the west. I know my Lord Essex waits in hopes that Waller will come to him, but surely he waits in vain.'

Says Pris, politely, 'I hear you served in Germany, Colonel.'

A pause, but only for an instant. 'I did, Miss Holland.' As he speaks, there is a motion to Ancrum's body, puts Pris in mind of juicy winkle meeting silver pin. *I wonder what went wrong for you there?*

Perhaps one might find out.

'So will your brothers-in-arms from Germany be coming to join you?'

Astonished silence round the table, that a woman (and the youngest here!) should pursue such a conversation. Wyn has raised his eyebrows at her. Go no further with this, madam, his expression says.

'It was some years ago,' Ancrum repeats. He shakes his head. 'A sorry country. A most misjudged war.'

I am amazed you lasted a day in it, thinks Pris. She has an image in her head again, of those men in Breda. The *man* in Breda; that long-jawed, dragonish profile.

'These are times of trial for all righteous men,' says Henry Gage. The serving plate begins its journey round the table, but the solitary bottle does not. The Reverend Gage has a flush to his cheeks. The pig's head, teeth exposed, is removed to the buffet. Reverend Gage watches it go with regret. 'Where there is war, there perforce one will find the Devil, and his minions.'

'Of the war,' says Wyn. 'Speaking of that, Colonel, our muster, on the morrow—'

'Indeed,' says Ancrum. He beckons to the manservant standing at the door: more feasting to come! 'You will not find us wanting, my Lord. And I do, in fact, have a veteran of the wars in Germany, has offered his service to me.' Ancrum tips his glass to Wyn. 'A gentleman renowned.'

The bottle at last approaches the distaff end of the table. Pris fills her glass, takes a sip, feels her tongue shudder, and knows at once she must somehow dispose of this without swallowing. She lifts her napkin. 'Ah!' Wyn is saying. 'A veteran. Shall I meet him?'

'You shall, my Lord. He is a magnet for recruits, I promise you.'

Out the corner of her eye, Pris sees a servant creep forward to set before Ancrum a great fish, a kraken, perhaps, something all scale and slime and bones. No, it is a sturgeon – the evil little snout, the ridged back. How many miles will that have travelled to get here? The marks of corruption are already livid on its skin. *I will be getting up from this table hungrier than when I sat down.* And her head is beginning to throb. Is it a megrim? That would be the final touch. 'And what of the enemy?' Mr Gage enquires nervously. 'Are they about? Our arrangements for the morrow—'

Ancrum wipes his carving knife upon the tablecloth and sets about the fish. 'Thanks be to God, we have none of the enemy to worry us for miles around, you may be sure of it. You do not eat, madam?' Ancrum enquires, holding out a slab of fish-flesh toward Pris.

'I do not, sir. I will keep my plate,' Pris replies.

'I hear there was a fish,' says Mrs Gage, inclining her head toward Pris, 'was took from the river in Oxford, and it had the seal of the Pope marked on one side of it. The Pope!'

'Witchery,' comments Mrs Ancrum. 'We had a side of beef at Christmas with a mark upon it, black as a crow. Had a witch spat upon it, do you think? For we ate it all!'

'Rabbits,' says Mrs Gage. 'They go about as rabbits. They suckle at the cows and sicken them.'

'Who does, madam?' Pris asks.

'Why, witches!' Mrs Gage drops her voice. 'I would never eat a rabbit,' she confides. 'Are you much troubled by them, at your market in London?'

'By rabbits?'

'No, by witches!'

The servant is back in the doorway. He goes to Colonel Ancrum, whispers in his ear. 'Ah!' says Ancrum, rising. 'My Lord, our veteran. Captain Carlo Fantom, he is here.'

There the man stands. He pushes his cloak, on its cord, from his shoulder. He walks forward. He removes his hat. When he speaks it is as if the words are being inspected, one by one, before they leave his mouth. 'My Col-on-el Ank-erum,' he says. He smiles. His teeth are like pips within his gums.

'Is that man of yours with you, Captain?' Ancrum asks, in genial tone. Obviously, a joke between them.

'My fat donkey? No. I send him to the stable, he sleeps there.' He looks about the room again. He bows. 'Such honour.' Fingertips to mouth, the sound of a kiss. *Well*, thinks Pris. *You're going to be an annoying little arse-fly, ain't you?* One side of the stranger's face bears the scar from a burn. And the skin so pale. And the eyes so hot in colour…

'My Lord Wyncanton,' Ancrum is saying. 'May I present Captain Carlo Fantom, late of the wars in Germany.'

Captain Fantom bends a leg to Wyn, sweeping the air with his hat. Some battered-looking silver badge on the front of his coat. As he lifts his head, his eyes land on Pris.

'My ward,' says Wyn, as Pris rises to offer her hand. 'May I present Miss Holland.'

'Such *pleasure*,' Fantom responds. He takes the hand in his.

Pris has as long as it takes this man to bow to her to master the screaming in her head. It comes at her like a bullet: one minute nothing; the next, she can hardly get her breath. It is all she can do not to stagger. *Oh God* –

Those hot little eyes meet hers, and (she is convinced) see what she sees, and are amused.

The moment ends. She understands they are to shift to some other room. Dorothea Ancrum is trilling, at an even louder volume than before, something about marrow tartlets. Carlo Fantom and Ancrum go through the door together, speaking again of joining Waller, of heading west, and Wyn, beside her, rubbing his hands, dips his head to Pris and says, 'Well now. Does this not all proceed most excellently well?'

She reaches for his arm. 'Wyn, we must go back to Goodwins. I am unwell.'

'How do you mean, you are unwell?' Wyn is astonished. Never was he more so. Also, the conversation must be conducted in the hallway, in whispers. Also, his ward will not meet his gaze. 'I must go,' is all she will say. 'We must leave here, Wyn.'

He bends his head to hers. 'Is it your monthly courses?' Such things can be a trouble for a woman, he knows, but are they not supposed to appear in predictable manner?

A flash of anger, a furious hiss. 'No, it is *not* my courses. Why is it, whenever a woman says she is unwell, a man thinks it must be because she has her flowers? I am – I have –' (a hand raised to her head) '– my head. I am fevered. It must have been the journey here. I have took a chill.'

'It is but the country air,' says Wyn. He means it kindly; he puts his own hand on her forehead. 'You are unused to so much of it.'

'It is *not* the country air.' She moves herself away. 'Ancrum's house is foul. His table worse. And as to his notion of a *soldier*—'

Her head is pounding. Her thoughts are like ants, streaming from their nest. It is as if she feels the touch of Carlo Fantom's hand again; hears those screams anew. She had lowered her eyes – the first defence a woman has, the first every woman reaches for, but looking down she had almost expected to find the hand on hers besmirched with blood. She had looked up –

– and seen of a sudden her own body, stretched, exposed. A female Prometheus. *This is what he would do to you.*

And all she can do now is repeat, 'We must leave. Wyn, we must.'

Wyn removes his hand from her forehead. She is dear to him, his Pris, and she has behaved better than he dared hope, but then so is the notion of taking the salute at the muster, of seeing the Wyncanton arms fly upon a flag. To leave now? And her forehead does not feel feverish at all. And she has slapped his hand away. 'Impossible,' says Wyn, with decision. He sees Ancrum approaching, a look of enquiry on the man's face. 'We leave *after* the muster, madam. Tomorrow. Not before. And you will attend.'

SHE WAKES. A dreadful night. In the hand-mirror in her trunk (of course, the room would not have a looking-glass) Pris examines the shadows under her eyes. She goes to the window. The day is bright, in fact sparkling; everywhere but in this miserable house. She lifts the grey paragon from the chair where it has spent the night. She rings the bell for a maid to come pin and lace her into it.

None appears. *Now what?* Pris asks herself. In London she might take two hours or more over her toilette – choosing her ribbons and jewels, making up her face, arranging her hair – but to put herself into a gown that laces at the back a lady cannot do. A gown as high-necked, as tight-sleeved as the paragon has the complexity of rigging. She is becoming angry now, to add to her aversion to being here. Why would Wyn not listen to her? Why would he not take her away?

I never want to see this place again. Or his Colonel Ancrum.

Or, worse—

No. Don't name that creature, even to yourself. Those dreams, all night: a bridge of bones that shattered and splintered under her feet with every step, the river beneath running thick and red with blood – oh, get these things out of her head!

She rings again, walloping the clapper in the bell up and down. Goes to her trunk to get out her box of paints, to deal with the shadows under her eyes at least. Lifts out the tray. Puts her hand across her mouth.

'Oh, *Molly*!' Pris breathes. 'You *angel*!'

CHAPTER FOUR

Small World

'It is an ordinary thing in war to study how to endamage an enemy, and to distract his forces, to which purpose all possible means must be used…'

John Cruso, *Militarie Instructions for the Cavallrie*

UPPER ASTON. IT has a single street – church at one end, courthouse the other, with a marketplace before it. To call this a town, thinks Tucker Turnbull the Londoner, is akin to calling a jakes a gentleman's residence. But today there is also a bank of seating set up against the courthouse wall, where Upper Aston's worthies are to be accommodated to view the muster. The Wyncanton martlet flutters above them on a banner.

Here they come. Tucker, deputed to hold the horse for the guest of honour, this old-toast Wyncanton, entertains himself watching Upper Aston's wives take their seats with their husbands, with much female fussing over the splintery edges of the planks and the sticky knots in the wood, not to mention for those on the lower tiers the indignity of sitting with another's knees at your shoulders, and their feet just where the pleats of one's skirt are most vulnerable. Ah, the ladies. Bless 'em, thinks Tucker, though to be honest, they're a dowdy lot, these country wives, their clothes the colours of pottage or ash-heap…

'Master Tucker, if you would be so good,' his charge requests, tapping the handle of his whip on the crown of Tucker's hat, 'take me again through the order of events.' Must be the tenth time the old futtock has asked this, thinks Tucker, resentfully, settling his hat back into place. Ain't you got summat else as I can do? he had asked Carlo Fantom, on being told his role in today's events.

'No, my donkey,' came the reply. 'You will play page to this old man. You will stand at his stirrup. You will help him mount up; you will help him get down. Or you are no use to me. And donkeys who are no use, what do we call them?'

Sausage. So once again, Tucker explains. 'Me Lord, the new recruits from Upper Aston will march down from the church with the lads in your company, and all muster here in the market square. Cap'n Fantom, he will pass command of 'em to the colonel, then the colonel leads 'em through the firing of their muskets, then you an' the colonel, you take their salute. Then the fresh meat—'

'The what? What was that you said?'

'Saving your reverence, me Lord – the new recruits will make their mark in the muster-roll, and be give their shilling, and then all march off back to Aylesbury and so done.'

'But the firing of their muskets?' Wyn asks, uncertainly.

'Yes, me Lord.'

'But this is a quiet animal?'

'She is so quiet, me Lord,' Tucker assures him, 'she will hardly twitch.' He looks longingly over at the door of the public house, where a crowd of loungers of the type who always gather to watch honest men do honest work have arranged themselves, tankards in hand. How Tucker would love to be amongst them! How good that ale would taste! But something else here has that easy gang's attention. Tucker peers over to see what it might be, and spies amongst all the dowdy plumage, all that black and white, a young woman taking her seat on the top row of seats who stands out like a drop of sealing wax upon a draughts-board. And not simply for her gown, either. *Fuck me*, thinks Tucker, open-mouthed. How's that fine-laced partridge found itself down here? Then he looks again. *Double-fuck me! That's Pris Holland!*

Does Pris recognize him? Perhaps for a moment she wonders who it is that he reminds her of, but after that, all her attention is taken up in settling her gown without mishap; in contemplating the spectacle Wyn makes on horseback (looking as he always does, as if expecting any minute the animal to detonate beneath him); in relishing the unmissable spectacle she is making of herself. Ah, the cinnabar silk. Oh, the kingdom of a splendid gown, how unassailable a woman feels within it. The tissue of the sleeves like puffs of breath; the acreage of tiny pleats and furrows governing the fullness of the skirts, and oh my heart, the colour! The colour like the rising sun, vivid as the hussy's hair! So bright, so vivid, so overpowering it positively leaves an after-image on the eye. There had been gasps from those around her on first catching sight of it, and it had been one half the reason for Wyn's *froideur* toward Pris upon her descending the stairs this morning. This is not the gown one wears to a military muster; it is scarce the gown one wears to a gaming-house, and its wearing, its choice, must be deliberate – Pris does not make errors with her clothes. 'What was I to do?' she had demanded, when he took her aside. 'I have no maid. I must be back-laced and pinned into the paragon, and none of Mrs Ancrum's girls attended me this morning. This one laces at the front. This one, I can get into meself.'

And such lacing. That had been the rest of his outrage. The bodice of the cinnabar silk displays almost as much of Pris as Wyn had been used to seeing in the bed in King Street. And its wearer has improved the uncompromising tightness of its tailoring with the insertion of a wooden busk beneath the front-lacing, so that Pris's breasts sit above the cinnabar silk like the cream atop a syllabub. 'Madam,' Wyn had said, 'this is not seemly.' He bent his mouth to her ear. *Sotto*, he added, 'And you are wearing *paint*.' (She was. And not a little, either.) 'You look – you present yourself as a whore.'

When he is in Westminster, sonorous and holding forth, Wyn makes an impressive figure, as his fellow MPs have often told him. But when he is angered, all his dignity runs away. He has not the vocabulary for it. He has not the bearing. His deepest rages come across as spluttering irritation; the deeper, the more spluttery.

Pris, however, is an adept at a tiff. 'But I *am* a whore,' she had informed him, fluttering her kohl-dark lashes at him. 'I am *your* whore. Is this news?' She had rattled out her fan. 'I told you, Wyn, I said I wished to leave. You would have none of it. So here we are.'

Now she takes the fan from her sleeve (their mighty volume has a use, as well as setting off so prettily the trimness of one's waist), and begins to waft it back and forth across her bosom in a manner that would make Bess Holland purr with pride. Together with the dress and the black lacquer fan (as stiff, as delicate, as glossy as a dragonfly), there is also a tip-tilted hat, of no practical purpose whatsoever other than to direct the gaze of an admirer toward Pris's eyes and set off the arch of her nose. In London, her ensemble would have had bows being swept her in the street.

From up by the church, a drum. Doors come open; those few windows not already crowded with heads are populated at once. There is a waving of little flags – a flock of Wyncanton martlets. Here is Carlo Fantom (Pris turns away at once), then the Aylesbury lads showing that they at least know how to do this, and behind them, the new recruits, marching six abreast. The crowd along the street gives a cheer. The recruits are so overcome at this, at finding themselves marching down this same street where they have run about all their lives, and so puffed with pride at the thought of doing so with mothers, sweethearts, baby brothers looking on, that the Aylesbury drummer must stop in the middle of the road and wait until they have caught up with him. Look at them – muskets and musket rests shouldered more like rakes than weapons; bandoliers of cartridges banging about their hips. They reach the market square, where they come to a halt like ripples on a pond, each man running into the one before. Another moment while they disengage themselves, then they shuffle into grinning rows. Carlo Fantom dances his horse to stand in front of Ancrum, and from horseback sweeps a bow. Pris, in the stands, yawns audibly.

Time for Ancrum to take centre-stage. He trots his horse forward.

'Unshoulder your musket!' Ancrum bellows.

The unshouldering is done, most unhandily. A musket rest clatters to the ground. Wyncanton's recruits look more like something you would put against a sunny wall to grow beans up than they do fighting men, and some of those muskets might last have seen service against the Armada. *Those poor lads*, thinks

Pris, *all hung about with the antique junk of someone else's war*, and horribly unexpectedly, she feels her eyes begin to fill. *We are at war. England is at war.*

'To the left hand,' Ancrum bellows. 'Muskets to the left!'

This takes longer. 'Your other left,' comes a helpful shout from the tavern door. A dog starts barking somewhere out of sight.

'Prepare your match!'

Much comedy blowing and coughing. The match – a length of twisted cord soaked in saltpetre – must be blown upon to make it flare into red-hot life, and when it does, it stinks.

Ancrum clears his throat. 'Cock your match!' Hilarity amongst the watchers at the tavern. Upper Aston's mothers are covering their children's ears.

'Hold your musket and present!'

The rests are lodged into position beneath the musket barrels.

'GIVE FIRE!'

My Lord Wyncanton's company disappears behind curls of musket smoke. Small children wail. Wyn's horse sidesteps wildly, almost putting its rider into the hedge. The smoke clears. There they are, this brave new company, badger-faced with smoke, wiping smuts from their eyes. 'Bravo!' Pris cries, astonishing herself. 'Bravo!' She is on her feet, she is encouraging those either side of her to stand and applaud as well, and yes, now the bells of the church are ringing too. Wyn is nudging his horse cautiously forward, ready to deliver words of thanks, encouragement, waiting only for the bells to cease – but they do not. They ring, if anything, even more frantically than before. Pris, shielding her eyes, sees a tiny figure appear at the top of the church tower. It is waving its arms above its head. Those beside her in the rows of seating are turning to each other – what is this?

'God in heaven!' comes the shout. 'It's the alarum!'

Many things now happen all at once. Upper Aston's mothers race their children back indoors; windows slam shut. Wyncanton's company are levelling their muskets at anything and everything in sight – the muskets that must now be rammed anew with shot, and primed with powder, before they are of any use at all. Not a few are taking aim at the church tower. Those in the rows of seating, with some sense of their exposed position, are scrambling to be out of them. The stand lurches one way, then the other. There is the crack of splintering timber. Mrs Henry Gage, on Pris's left, gives a squeal. Yet another crack, but not of timber this time, no – this one is a pistol shot. And behind it, the percussion of hooves, and no sooner have you had a chance to register this, than there they are, sweeping round the church from either side, whooping and hollering: row upon row, the horses with their heads going like pistons and their shining hooves lifting and falling like the jacks on a harpsichord. It is like Pris's awful vision as a child, only these horses are tricked out as if for a charivari – the flat fronts of those plunging horse-heads painted white, like skulls, their legs painted like barbers' poles, and ribbons streaming from their manes. Their riders are painted up too, as death's heads, with blackened eye sockets and triangles of black for noses, or faces quartered in some mad heraldry of red and white. There are screams and wails of terror all about her; the row of seats teeters so crazily Pris must grab the rail to keep her balance. But before she does so, she stores somewhere in her head the sight of Ancrum laying a hand to one side of Wyn's bridle, and Carlo Fantom grabbing the other, and the two of them pulling Wyn along between them. She shrieks his name – 'Wyn! *Wyn!*' – and thinks she sees him react, but no attempt to halt his rescuers, to turn back for her. Then the rail behind her gives way. Pris, with a scream, falls from the stand.

She lands on hands and knees. She feels the cinnabar silk rip across her shoulders. Through the rows of seating, yawing this way and that, she sees the horsemen have surrounded the square as fast and as exactly as the jaws on a pair of tongs. Now more men coming in behind them at a run. As Pris watches, they drop to one knee and fire. Horsemen, swords bared, charge through the smoke. She sees one of the Aylesbury men go down like he had slipped on something, only with this irregular red pennant erupting from the back of his head, separating from him entirely before he hits the ground. The new recruits, encircled, are rooted to the spot. She sees one horse, an enormous animal, rear up, dancing toward them on its hind legs, mane and tail streaming; she sees for a moment the rider in stark silhouette, then the stand of seating collapses altogether. Pris is away like a hare.

She doesn't slow until she finds herself in a lane behind the marketplace. Her hat is gone. Her fan is gone. Her shoe is loose on her foot. She cannot get her breath; she has to double over. No, she has to find somewhere to hide. She spies a hut, a narrow door – she almost misses it, in such a panic is she, but she throws herself through, pulling her skirts in after her, to find herself in soft and smelly darkness, and with something that flies straight at her, beating its wings about her face. Then just as suddenly it is gone, out through a hole in the roof. Two more survey her from on high. Her palms are caked with straw and chicken-shit, so is the silk across her knees. She's in a henhouse.

Pris subsides against the henhouse wall. She puts her hands to her eyes. 'Oh *God*,' she hears herself wail, 'oh Jesus, oh God!' She is gasping as a child does in a crying fit, almost choking herself. The swoop of those horsemen! The man being shot! She wants to give way, as you can only when you really are a tiny child. 'Wyn!' she wails. 'Oh, Wyn!' Her protector – he abandoned her! She can hardly believe it, but he did! Was he truly that angry with her? To let himself be hauled away with not even a backwards glance?

She fights to bring herself under control. *Think*, she tells herself. *Think. Wyn is gone, the only person you have to get you out of this is you—*

Oh no. There are footsteps outside. Right outside. Separated from her by only the henhouse door. They come to a halt. Pris's eyes are fixed on the latch – will it move? Will the door open? But then a shout from further off, in some language that she doesn't recognize; and the footsteps move away, grow fainter.

She counts to fifty. There are still noises coming from the square, but they sound like shouted orders, no longer panicked yells and screams. She counts again. Her heart ceases to wallop quite so painfully. She wipes her hands on her skirts. She ties her shoe.

I might… I might… Do what? Hide here till nightfall? But the engine of her thinking is itself a comfort. She waits a little longer, then she eases open the door, listens again and tips herself out.

At the far end of the alley stands a man with a shock of yellow-white hair like the head of a dandelion. He has his back to her, but she can tell from the angle of his arm, he has his sword in hand. Without a sound Pris turns about, walking on her toes –

– and walks straight into him. A scuffle of hands and feet – his hands, her feet, vainly kicking as he lifts her by her wrists. He shouts, '*Kamrad!*' and the first man comes running, that yellow-white hair like a flag. Two of them, as alike as looking in a mirror. Even their scalloped leather jackets match. Pris tries to pull herself loose; the only result is to have her captor place his free hand almost idly about her throat. He holds her so, against the wall, leaning away from her to keep his bollocks out of reach of her feet, and his twin, his reflection, saunters up the alleyway toward them.

The Gemini hail from Latvia; their native tongue is a mystery to everyone but themselves.

My brother, says Konstantin, Pris's captor, *what do we do with this?*

I do not know, Kazimir replies. *But it is very fierce. See it fight and kick.*

It has spirit. I think we should lock it away. For safety. He looks down at Pris. 'Ve lock you op,' he tells her, as if he is doing her a favour.

'No!' Pris shrieks. She stares from one man to the other. 'No! Don't you bloody dare!'

'*Jā*. Ve lock her op, we tell *Herr Kapitan*.'

IN THE BUSINESS of taking a town, especially when done with such a wildly enthusiastic youthful company, afterwards there is so very much demanding your attention. There are houses to be searched, there are folk to be allowed back into them; there are hysterical women (Mrs Gage) to be reunited with their husbands. There are sentries to be posted; there are horses to be fed, watered, rubbed down; congratulations to be exchanged, jokes to be made. There are interviews to conduct, intelligence to be gathered; as a result, there is the enemy's stash of muskets and armour to be removed from the crypt beneath the church and loaded onto carts to be taken back to Oxford, where King Charles is so short of the stuff that his wife is over in Holland, selling her jewels to buy more. There are recruits to be sworn in, from those amongst the lads of Upper Aston who have decided, as is so often the case, that the side you wish to sign up to is the one now victorious. Jens, leaning out from the courthouse window, watches as Per, down in the marketplace, shows the last of the newly recruited where to make their mark in the company ledger, and exchanges a wave with Cantley, now getting that same company ready to depart. The night has gone by; stretched itself into a thin dawn that (lest one imagines such an operation can be conducted without loss) also exposes the burial party in the churchyard, digging out a pit. It has been the busiest day Jens can remember for a good long while. All too easy for some small detail to be forgotten.

'Domini,' says Jens. He rubs a hand against his forehead – still a little of that red and white, up in his hairline. 'Domini, do we go after Ancrum now?'

'We do not,' says Jack. He stretches his arms above his head. 'Much as I would love to. No, we go back to Oxford. With his arsenal. Hah!'

'So what do we do about the prisoner?' Jens asks.

'What prisoner?'

Verdammt! 'Domini, did you not know this? There is a prisoner here, under your feet. The Gemini put her in a cell beneath us.'

'Wait,' says Jack. 'The prisoner is a woman?'

'Yes, Domini. The other woman, the one who wails and cries so much, she says this one is Wyncanton's mistress.'

'Wyncanton's *mistress* is our prisoner?'

'Yes, Domini.'

There is a splendid lantern clock on the courthouse wall. Its tick can be heard distinctly in the silence that follows.

'I don't suppose,' says Jack, at last, 'as you would know if she has red hair?'

*

The moment he steps onto the stairs to the cells he can hear her, pounding on the door. When Jens unlocks it, she is there at once, eyes aflame, before he has even stepped into the cell. 'What is the meaning of this?' She hitches her gown, which seems oddly loose, back onto her shoulders. She is so angry she does it without seeming even to notice. 'I have been left down here for hours, I have not been given a blanket, not so much as a God-damn piss-pot – who is in charge here? How *dare* you treat a Christian woman so—'

She sees him. She draws in a breath big enough to fill a bellows.

'Good day, Miss Holland,' says Jack. 'How small this great world can be.'

CHAPTER FIVE

Otsford

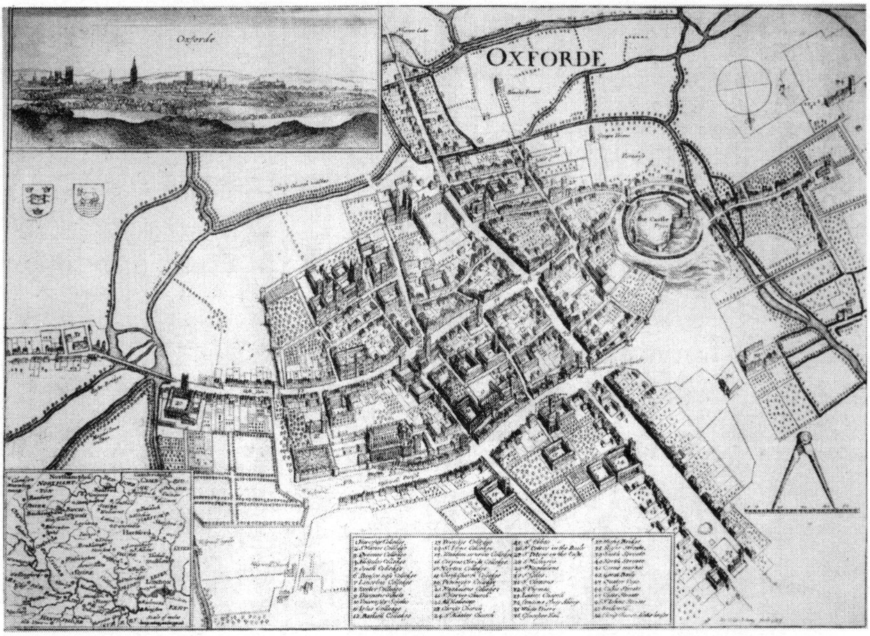

'She can love well… but she will try before she trust, and have some reason to like before she loves.'

Richard Brathwaite, *The English Gentleman and the English Gentlewoman*

EVERYTHING – SPEECH, thought, perhaps for a moment even her heart – comes to a stop. Pris is silenced, no less. Then she is not. '*You!*'

He is not at all as she remembers him. That rough-edged beard is gone. That hair, the colour of old rope, it has been barbered. The boots are not muddied, the linen is clean. What became of the *no rank at all*? This man is every inch the one in charge.

He is exactly as she remembers him. Those pale, pale eyes, the flint in them. That long-jawed smile. The battered leather of his coat, the tattooed hands. 'Believe me,' he says (he walks about her as he speaks), 'I am as amazed as you.'

She hitches up her dress again. *I swear to God*, she thinks, *whenever I am on my beam-ends, this BLOODY man is what the gods throw at me.* 'I have been mistreated grievously. I have been locked in here all sodding night, I have been left sans food, sans *anything*—'

'You present us with a dilemma,' her captor says, interrupting. 'We were not expecting prisoners.' Turn and turn about. 'You came here with this Wyncanton, yes?'

'Yes, damn his eyes,' says Pris, with renewed fury. 'He *abandoned* me—'

'Wyncanton and his Colonel Ancrum? It was their company we scattered to the winds, I think?'

'Ancrum, yes. Damn him too. Double-damn him!'

'And were you privy, by any chance,' this Fiskardo continues, 'to any passing conversation between the two of them?'

The thing to do here has to be to plead ignorance, surely. 'None of that was of interest to me. I paid no heed to any of it.'

'That's a pity. Although I doubt much of anything gets past you.'

'A pity? Why?'

'This is the dilemma, Miss Holland. I would be loath to leave you here, but…' A shrug. A shrug that both maddens and appals her. She is wondering, *Would tears work with this one?* when he speaks again. 'But, if you have intelligence, if you overheard anything that might be of use to us—'

She lifts her chin. '*If* I did?'

'What did you hear?'

She has to think. That abominable supper… 'They spoke of how the army of Lord Essex had took Reading, but that it must bide there—'

'Bide there? Why?'

What was it Ancrum said? Before that monstrous creature made his entrance. 'Because his men are unpaid. And there is some fever come amongst them.' Yes, and after that – 'Then Ancrum had this veteran from Germany join him, this Captain Fantom—'

'This *what?*'

She stops. It is extraordinary, the change in him, it is like a shark scenting blood. 'Captain Fantom,' Pris repeats.

'*Carlo* Fantom?'

'Yes. *Yes.* Do you know him?'

'I know him.' The steel in his voice. 'Go on, Miss Holland. Tell me what it was he and Ancrum said.'

'They said—' So alarming is the change in the man before her that Pris has to stop, draw breath. Marshal her thoughts. She remembers how he had been in the fight with the Spaniard in Breda, how he had circled his prey, teeth bared, his whole face a-snarl.

'They spoke of how Essex cannot come on, how all his London troops have marched away, and of how Essex hopes for Waller's men to join him, but Waller will not do it—'

'Miss Holland, you are coming with me,' he says. 'With me, to Oxford. As our prisoner.'

Pris is no admirer of the horse. She mistrusts their back halves, and the way they lift their tails and piss like rain-spouts; she's not keen on their front halves either, always stamping those huge feet of theirs about; and she has never understood why a creature that lives on grass need have so much in the way of *teeth*. Yet here she is, perched nose-bleed high on a beast whose back is as wide as the keel of Miguel Domingo's rowboat, and every bit as comfortable to straddle, and on her way to Oxford.

They have tied a string from her to the man in front. The man in front of her is Per. Beside her, there rides Jens ('Miss 'Olland! Do you remember me?'). Yes, she does. Also, Luka, the little one. Ulrik, the giant. The other, Thor. But they have added to their number. Dozens of men ride with them, and now the recruits from Upper Aston too, marching along behind. The two with the white-blond hair, they ride rearguard (she has a suspicion they take much amusement in the state of her gown), while the handsome one with the moustaches, Zoltan, he is up there at the front with Fiskardo. Satellite groups peel from the edges of the file, go cantering off, return, are replaced by others, a motion like migrating birds in flight.

On they go. The clip-clop of hooves, the jingle of harness, the dust from the road – settling onto her hair, drying on her lips, working itself into her palms. There are flies. There is the bump, bump, bump of her arse against the saddle. Her shoes slip from the stirrups, no matter how hard her toes try to grip. She has a cramp up one calf, then the other, and it feels as if her skirts are being rubbed away to nothing.

They cross one river, green as glass; another brown as beer. Rabbits go fleeing across the fields at their approach. There is a wood. The echoes of the horses' hooves knock from the trees, and set the wood-doves croodling: *Who, whoo, whooo goes through, who, whoo, whooo*—

Pris's head jerks up off her breast. Freckled Jens, beside her, is offering her his flask. Gun-metal-flavour water, at blood-heat, goes swilling round her teeth. 'When do we halt?' she asks, handing the flask back.

'When we are in Otsford,' he replies.

'When will that be?'

'Oh, we are there by tonight,' Jens tells her, confidently.

'We don't stop till then?'

Progress continues, in a miasma of dust and the hay-like odour of warm horse that gives Pris a sneezing fit so violent she must wipe her nose on her sleeve. The flies seem not to know which smells the more appealing, her horse, or her. One of them buzzes straight into her hair, and she does consider, at that point (wildly batting her arms about her head), hurling herself from her mount altogether – would they halt then? *No wonder*, she thinks, *no wonder they are all such heartless whoreson bastards, if this is what they must endure every day*, but when she looks about her, they are all going along perfectly happily. Indeed, Fiskardo and Zoltan, side by side, are in low and easy conversation; while at every bump, every rise and fall of the horse beneath her, the bones of Pris's spine feel as if they are being shuffled like cards.

At last, the sun starts dropping in the sky. They ride into its rays. A wafer of moon comes creeping out, and with moonrise comes the rain. You feel the damp in the air, the first drops released, and then the smell of the earth rolls up to meet you in a wave. The horses raise their heads, snorting and blowing. The men take off their hats, tilt their faces to the sky. Per lets out a long, long sigh and knuckles his back, like a woman heavy with child, but Pris is too miserable to care. She is almost willing herself to faint, to fall from the saddle, or perhaps it would be better to die outright. There are specific pains in every portion of her body – cramp in her elbows, nerve-fire running down her legs, agony across her hips. She is nothing but one long ache, encased in whalebone. She has to bite the inside of her cheeks to stop herself from crying, not that in this rain anyone would notice – this rain that runs off her shoulders, and down inside her dress, and chills her legs and frizzes her hair. The country drops away from them, laid out for miles and miles, unprotected, unsuspecting. How many other armies are there, moving across England in the dark? *Nights like this Queen Mab goes riding, Puck dances on the village green…* Her thoughts are getting slower and slower. *There should be goblins peeking out from under those hedges…* Instead, an owl flaps off from one hedge to the other; sits on a gatepost, picking at its toes. Jens touches her arm. There is a spatter of lights in the darkness ahead. 'Otsford,' Jens says.

The lights take on the shapes of windows. Then there are house gables overhead. Pris finds herself gazing up at them as if she never saw such things before. A fine wide street, in which a seemingly endless crowd mills round them; Oxford at night is as crowded as London Bridge at noon. The men kick the horses up, to force a way through. Convoys of carts and wagons pass by. Here's a cobbled alley. Here's another, narrower, scraped along either wall at the level of a rider's boots. Human noise fills the space ahead; and now at last the men in front of her are dismounting. Stable-boys dart between the horses. She has a sense that they are known here, Fiskardo and his men.

Fiskardo is at her stirrup, looking up. 'You plan to stay up there?'

She is so weary, she can barely form the words. 'You want me to come down, you will have to help me.'

He lifts his arms. 'Hands on my shoulders,' he says.

She slides from the saddle with all the grace of laundry. Her feet find the ground, her legs buckle. His arm tightens round her. 'What's up with your legs?'

'They are *benumbed*,' Pris replies, with a sob, into his shirt-front. 'I may never walk again.'

He lifts her; she feels his thumbs against her waist and then her feet are off the ground and she is over his shoulder, legs adangle, with his arm most familiarly under her rump. There are faces peering into hers, there is a man who might be the landlord, clearing a path before them. Now a door, lights; many voices, even louder than before. At the door Fiskardo pauses to throw a handful of coins into the air. The stable-boys go scrabbling after them like pigeons after grain.

Now she is carried inside. A room so very crowded, the many jugs of ale criss-crossing it must do so held aloft, at the same level as Pris herself. A flagstoned floor passes beneath her. A timbered ceiling is over her head. A staircase. Up, up… her ride hitches her more securely into place. Doors open off the staircase, many rooms, all of them occupied – a card game in one; in the next, a woman shushing a bed full of children. The landlord's voice. 'Up atop, Captain. We're full as an egg.' She watches the staircase elongate behind them. They pass through another door. A room pitched under the eaves, with miniature window, maybe a foot square. A bed. Oh, joy – a bed.

He half tips, half spills her onto it. Pris rolls sideways, face hidden in the tangle of her hair. She hears more stitches snap in the cinnabar silk, but she is too defeated to care. Through the lattice of her ringlets (oh, misery! Her hair *smells*!) she sees Fiskardo with the landlord, at the door. A blink of time – did she fall asleep? – then there is a serving girl in the doorway, and Fiskardo is coming back into the room with pitcher and basin in his hands.

He puts the basin on the floor beside the bed. 'Sit up,' he says. Pris levers herself to sit. He fills it with water hot enough to steam, wets a cloth and holds it out to her. The woman she was but a day ago would have told him to go to hell; the woman she is, meek with misery, takes the cloth, and rubs it over her face and round her shoulders, and yes, does feel a little better, for all that her paint is gone, but then so is the grime and the dust. Now he is kneeling before her, easing off her shoes. The heel of one shoe detaches as soon as he touches it; one stocking flops to her ankle. Now he is most familiarly pushing her skirts to her knees. 'Hold these,' he says, and over their ruin she watches as he undoes the ribbon of her remaining garter and eases the stocking away. Now he is lifting her feet into the water, her raw and bloodied feet, and this hurts so much and her toes look so pitiful it makes her wail out loud.

'Oh, come now,' he says. 'You are braver than this, I know you are.' He wrings out the cloth. She unclenches her fingers, rubs a hand under her nose. He moves her feet into his lap and starts to dry them. *Oh*, thinks Pris, or the woman she was but yesterday, *oh for the strength for one good kick now.* Instead, she lets her head drop to his shoulder.

'Oh,' she says, with low and loving reverence for the words, 'oh, you misbegot blasted God-damned bastard *hell-hound*, Jack.'

A huff of laughter in reply. 'It was a long ride,' he says. 'Proper pair of boots, you'd have done well enough.' His head is at a tilt, his eyes on a level with hers; it feels as if this is the first time their eyes have met since the cell below the courthouse, and it is a surprise to her how it is his that are the first to look away, and how clear the image of them left with her – the transparent blue, the darker halo, the feather of his lashes, the wrinkle of that triplet of scars, the lines that come and go. It is – it is – it is most confusing. It is as if the lineaments of his face sink into her, somehow. And his name. She spoke his name.

More scratching at the door. There is the maid again, bearing what smells like – yes, it is, a plate of cutlets. Food! Pris grabs one in each hand as the plate goes past her, tears the meat from them. Fiskardo sits, offers her another; she grabs that from him too. A rummer of wine; he holds it out to her, she drinks, like a cat from a bowl, then takes the glass and empties it as if it had been water. The wine goes straight up into her head. She hinges forward, like a puppet, knuckles on the floor between her toes, and feels her shoulders pop from her gown altogether. Laughter drifts up from the yard below. Her head is buzzing. Fiskardo is on his feet again. He sits her upright, then he crouches down. Their heads are once more on a level and this time there is a distinct feel to their proximity.

She glares at him. 'Surely,' says Pris, 'you jest.'

He raps his knuckles on her busk, like a man testing the plaster of a wall. 'You sleep in this, do you?'

Sleep... 'No,' she says. She bats the hand away, glaring at him. 'But *I'll* do it.'

She undoes the lacing and he shucks her out of her bodice, lifting it over her head. Then her stays. She shakes herself loose from them. Then the remains of her skirts. She must lie down to kick them from her, but now she is horizontal nothing matters beyond that. Oh, bed... oh, at long last. In her shift, she rolls to her side and closes her eyes.

The creak of a chair, a quiet oath. 'What are you *doing*?' Pris demands, sitting up, and sees it is his boots, he is trying to take his boots off. 'Oh, for the Lord's *sake*,' she says, reaching out. A tug of war; she hurls one boot one way, the other the other. 'Why do you wear the bloody things if you can't even get out of them on your own?' She flops backwards. Sleep...

The next moment it is as if a tidal wave has travelled through the mattress. He has thrown himself down full-length beside her. The wave subsides. It has washed her next to him.

She lies rigid, holding herself away. She feels him stretch out one arm beneath the bolster, working it this way and that, and then a chuckle, as if for no other reason but the pleasure of finding himself prone. 'Oh, *yes*,' he says. All her senses had flared alert; now, as fast, they subside. It had never occurred to her that he might be as weary as she.

His oxter is under her nose. 'You smell like a goat,' she says.

'You're none so sweet yourself,' comes the reply.

'I'll sweeten myself up in the morning,' she tells him.

'You do that. Sleep well, Miss Holland.'

But she does not. The bed keeps up a stealthy motion all night long, as if she were still on horseback, and there is a clock above the tavern roof, chiming the hours. At one point, Pris could swear she is awake, the door is open, there is a light beyond it, and in the doorway, in the light, there stands a pair of children, hand in hand, both boys, one very much smaller than the other, and both looking in on her with expressions of absolute amazement. The sense of their being there is so strong she lifts her head, but as soon as she does the door is closed, the room is dark, and nothing is looking in on her but the stars.

There's too many people under this roof, she decides, *and I got someone else's dreams inside my head, that's all that's wrong with me.*

She listens to Fiskardo's breathing. Deep and steady, like the sea.

Then nothing. Not until she hears a serving girl outside the door, a stable-boy's whistle from the yard, and the whinny of a horse in response to the whistling. The man beside her moves slightly in his sleep. Was the horse that whinnied his? She lifts her head, then props herself up on one elbow and gazes down at him.

He is as stern-faced in his sleep as if giving orders in his dreams. The long angle of his eyebrows – surprisingly well marked, for a man. That bony nose – did he break it, to put that bump in it? The stubble poking through his jaw; the bump of a pulse in his throat. The set to his mouth. Yes, stern-faced, but looser-limbed, a great star-fished sprawl of him. His shirt has fallen open; there are the muscles of his chest, squared off, like Roman armour. And one arm has fallen round her, like an earthwork, as she slept. She turns her attention to the arm, to the hair on it, darker, finer, as if combed. Ten straight scars, evenly placed, scored into the skin beneath.

Learning his markings.

Oh, what nonsense! she tells herself – or rather, Bess's voice does so. *Girl, what nonsense you do think!*

Pris lies herself back down. She thinks of Wyn, she remembers Felipe. *This is some other order of man I have lying here with me.*

HE WAKES. LIES there a moment or two, blinking, letting the world gather itself. Yes, Oxford, and ah, yes, the woman. He has to ease himself out from around her, but she hardly stirs. The curls of her hair are all over the pillow, like driblets of paint. What a colour.

He gathers his boots and jacket, comes back to the bed. Good God, she looks so clean. She looks as if fresh-popped from the pod. Her gown, though, on the floor – her gown looks as if it had been run over by the mob. He rolls the day forward in his head. No, that gown will never do.

The last time he stood like this, looking down, he had been on his way to Yosha Silbergeld in Amsterdam, and the woman lying asleep in the bed had been Mirelle. It is a complicated moment, not helped by the memory of that rush of feeling, once he realized who Wyncanton's mistress might be. *Yes, and all this*, Jack thinks, rubbing his jaw, *all this when a man ain't even visited a barber yet.*

He tiptoes from the room.

The serving girl is sweeping the stairs. She squeezes herself against the wall when she sees him, which strikes him as a tad unfair, however roughened and unshaven he may be. He finds a tuppence in his pocket, holds it out to her. 'Tell me,' he says, 'if I needed a gown, a woman's gown, a fine one – where would I look for it?'

'Unthanks,' the girl says at once. Nods her head for emphasis. 'Unthanks, from London. On the Cornmarket.' She adds, wistfully, 'It's lovely, what they have there.'

Then Unthanks it is.

The Cornmarket is as crowded as every place in Oxford these days, and Unthanks, when he finds it, is as crowded as the street outside, although in a manner wholly its own. Jack opens its door to a tinkling chime and a finger of lace at once caresses his cheek. Wheels of cord and ribbon hang above him, more face him, plus plump bales of cloth. When the man – an actual Unthank? – appears, he does so from between the gowns floating on a rack on the back wall: a man with waistcoat to his knees and a pin-cushion on his wrist the way a woman wears a nosegay. The man is as thin, as gracile, as a deer. Jack, by contrast, feels as clumsy as a rhinoceros. Talk about being lost in the enemy's camp.

The man evens out the ends of his tape about his neck, as if adjusting a chain of office. 'You desire, sir?'

To be out of here as speedily as possible. Instead, Jack takes a step forward, as if to inspect the ghostly ballroom hanging from the rack. As he does so, a woman's face appears between the hanging folds of silk, and a second Unthank steps out to join the first. There is a sharpness to the woman's scrutiny; she whispers something to the man. 'Ah,' says he. 'Would I have the honour – is it Fiskardo, sir? Of Varney?'

Jack is amazed. 'Do we know each other?'

'We do not, sir. But Miss Suzanne here is a friend of Mrs Endicott. How may we assist?'

Jack looks again at the rack of gowns. He feels wholly outnumbered. The silks and satins seem to rustle closer.

'A costume for a lady?' Miss Suzanne suggests.

'Yes,' he says, gratefully.

'Of what type, sir? What style?' asks Unthank, and he finds he has no idea.

'For what occasion? Will it be –' Miss Suzanne chooses the word with care. 'Will it be *courtly*?'

As can be, thinks Jack. 'It will be at Christ Church, yes.' Christ Church, where Charles Stuart lives and breathes and from which he and his counsellors run his war.

'And the lady, sir,' says Unthank. 'What type is she?'

Type? He casts about for the words, for any words, to describe her. *She looks as if she is made of mother-of-pearl. She swears like a quartermaster. She is unafraid of anything. She has the merriest laugh I ever heard.*

'The lady's height, sir,' says Miss Suzanne, taking pity.

He puts the edge of his hand to his breastbone. He finds he remembers exactly where she came up to against him; as an aide-memoire there is the notorious scar from where he was shot. Although on that occasion (comes the thought, unbidden), Cupid missed. *What is wrong with me?*

'And her colouring?' Unthank is asking. 'Her eyes, sir? Her skin, her hair?'

'Her hair is red,' says Jack, with decision. 'Fiery red.' He can be sure of that, at least.

'Ah!' says Unthank. 'A redhead! In that case, we must clothe her with the greatest care. Miss Suzanne,' he continues, 'would you fetch out the Japanese yellow?'

Miss Suzanne disappears between the gowns. That errant end of lace is again tickling Jack's cheek. Unthank, smiling, rocks on his toes. 'A moment.'

Miss Suzanne returns bearing something in a colour so strong it seems to fill the shop as if it were noise. She holds it up before herself: bodice, skirts – a tiny bodice, but sleeves so huge they seem almost unmade, skirts full enough to carry on a whispering conversation between themselves. It is like looking at a field of crocuses. Like daffodils. Like gold. He touches it. The cloth feels thick as felt. There is embroidery across the bodice and within the sleeves – pads of blossom, the twirl of a tendril, some bright-eyed bird, little creatures delicate as damselflies.

'The cloth is from Hirado, in Japan,' Unthank is saying. 'It was in our last consignment. Before –' (with a sniff) '– we had to shift ourselves here.'

'It adjusts,' says Miss Suzanne, brightly, showing him eyelets, a placket, and he nods, as if all this makes perfect sense to him and is exactly what he would expect. 'There is ribbon too. To go about the waist. I would suggest this, Captain, a nettle brown. A bow tied here – it soothes the yellow, do you see? And will you need lace, sir? A collar? We have some fine lace. And petticoats and such, to go beneath?'

He thinks of Pris, lying as he left her, her naked shoulder between those dark red curls. 'We will need everything,' he says.

NOW PRIS, TOO, opening her eyes. She finds she has rolled over into the space left by the man. The smell of his skin – leather-ish, like the backroom at a saddler's, not goaty at all – is in her nose; but the man himself is gone. There is a vexatious childish inward *muh* of disappointment, and now who is it outside the door?

''Tis Cicely, miss, the maid. May I come in?'

'You may,' says Pris, lifting herself onto her elbows.

Cicely enters, carrying a bundle, on top of which reposes a pair of shoes. She places the shoes on the floor. Bronzed kid, with pink pom-pom rosettes as big as cabbage roses. Pris, eyeing them, approves. She is still less than half awake.

Cicely puts the bundle on the bed. 'An' I am to tell you, the captain sends his compliments, an' when you are ready, he awaits you at The Bear, by Christ Church, an' there is one of his men downstairs to take you there. An' there is water a-coming too. Hot,' Cicely adds.

Pris moves her foot beneath the bundle. Its contents slither upon themselves. She knows that slither. She seizes the bundle, pulls it open, and yards of satin spill across the bed. She reaches into it, into its folds and folds; feels the pointed hardness of a waist, a curve of bone so stiff it rises up to meet her hand; the soft drop of a sleeve; ribbon the colour of seaweed. 'Oh!' she exclaims. '*Oh!*'

THE BEAR, TUCKED down off the high street, but a step from Christ Church, so now finding itself co-opted as a sort of antechamber to King Charles's court, a waiting-room, if you like. Movement inward requires all those near the door to lift themselves onto their toes; just as in the waiting-room to an audience chamber, in fact, thinks Jack, who has experience of such as would astound his companion, Cantley. But this is Oxford: everywhere a crowd. The streets teem; it is a wonder how soldiers can be marched so often through them. The riverbanks, where students wandered, whittling sonnets in their heads, are now set up for target practice; what were their rooms in college home baffled children, transplanted here with their bewildered mothers – gentlewomen who once walked state rooms and long galleries, and who find themselves here crammed in one atop the other like bees in a hive, with husbands and brothers God knows where, fighting for the King. Whole buildings have been requisitioned; Oxford's residents told to open up their attics and welcome common soldiers to their table. The city has its own mint; it even has its own newspaper, the *Mercurius Aulicus*, sold with particular gusto from Endicott's Bookshop in Broad Street, where the owner, it is understood, has experience of such matters, and smuggled at a premium into London amongst the barrels on Plumstead's carts. (Not to be outdone, Parliament has the *Mercurius Civicus*. So there!)

'The boldest stroke,' Cantley is saying. 'I never knew an encircling brought off better. And you were entirely right, sir, about the painting of the horses and the tricking out – give the enemy something to gawp at, they wholly forget to shoot!' An elbow brushes his head. 'Cry you mercy,' says the elbow's owner at once. 'Nay, nay,' Cantley replies. ''Twas all my doing. I shall remove my hat.' The hat is placed on Cantley's knee. 'But then, who is it we are fighting? The sons of shopkeepers. Ploughboys, I don't doubt. What would they know of war? 'Tis almost sin to put them on the field.'

Oh, these English gentlemen. These same English gentlemen who tally-ho off the field after the enemy as after a fox. 'They will learn, Cantley. You may be sure of that.'

'And what is more,' says Cantley, blithely unconcerned, 'now you bring fresh intelligence, sir!'

'So it seems.' Jack takes a sip of ale – young, green, mild as water, but such is demand for everything in Oxford now, who complains?

'But will it be believed, Captain, that is the question,' says Cantley, with worried frown. 'There are so many opinions of what Essex might do – and it must be admitted, there are those amongst the King's advisors do not… do not always have a soldier's understanding of what's what out there.' Cantley, too, applies himself to his tankard in a mighty great gulp, as if in relief at having aired such sentiments.

'Cantley, I am well aware, I could not be more suspect if I tried. I am no English gentleman, and my reputation is –'

Dark as can be, and full of the shadows of the dead. There was a term the Scribbler used, one of his favourites, to describe the Dead Men as they were in Germany.

'– my reputation is *Cimmerian*, to say the least,' says Jack, and has the wicked pleasure of seeing Cantley sit back, blinking in surprise. 'But my witness's credentials are impeccable. I defy any man not to believe intelligence from such a source.'

'I hope you are right, sir. The King has a shockin' lack of intelligence,' says Cantley. *Don't he just*, thinks Jack. Also, ports, foundries, money, most of the south-east of England, and the entirety of the English navy, which has declared for Parliament.

'But 'tis all new to us, this business,' Cantley continues. 'When was the last war in England? Not since Lancaster and York!'

A brightening of tone in the noise from the street. Cantley has twisted about in his seat. 'Ah,' he comments, as if he were a connoisseur of such, 'some fine lady of the court passes by us, no doubt.'

But the fine lady does not pass by. The fine lady would have ingress. Jack feels his heartbeat pick up from a trot to a canter. The crowd about the door of The Bear presses itself backwards to clear a path in a manner that a moment ago you would have thought impossible, and as it does so, delivers itself of this particular male noise, a sort of muted roar, and there she is, jaunting across the room toward him, holding her skirts from the ground as if inviting admiration and laughing at the show she makes all at once. She makes him think of music – the yellow, the bronze, the copper of her hair. When she sees him, she outright sweeps him a bow. What can he do but return it?

Cantley is goggle-eyed. The landlord of The Bear, deep within the crowd, is bellowing, 'Seat! *Seat!*' because of course that is what you do with a woman like this: drop everything until she has all she might need. She waits, smiling, brilliant of eye, everything about her gleaming. Here comes Per in her wake. Here comes a chair for her over their heads. Cantley seizes the chair, placing it as reverently as if for an archbishop. Miss Holland settles herself. Jack takes a moment to murmur to Per, 'All go smoothly?'

'No, Domini, it did *not*,' says Per. He is sweating. 'I thought I would have to draw my sword. There were bravos applauding her in the street!'

Now she is settled. Now she extends her hand, the lace of the sleeve falling back. Oh, the curve of that wrist – this has to be why women put so much lace on their clothes, Jack thinks: where it parts, it's like the drawing-back of curtains on a bed. He puts his fingers under hers, lifts them to his lips, and somewhere close by, he could swear, some invisible harp supplies a glissando. It is as if something runs between them, claps its hands and shouts *Begin!*

'Hello, Captain,' she says.

'Miss Holland.' All that noise and riot in The Bear, it has all drifted away. Ah, no, not quite, it hasn't. Cantley clears his throat.

'Miss Holland, may I introduce Mr Cantley.'

'Miss Holland,' says Cantley, reverently. He makes a bow. 'I am sure we know each other. I am sure that we have met.'

'Oh, I am certain *not*, sir, though thank'ee,' she replies. Her eyes are still on Jack. 'Do you ride with our captain here?'

'I do, madam, yes,' says Cantley, 'yes indeed, I have, and shall,' and is clearly preparing to launch into the lengthiest of accounts of how and why, only Miss Holland, without shifting her gaze from Jack by even a degree, gives Cantley's hand a pat, and says, 'And one day you shall tell me all about it.' All there is in the room for her –

– *is me*, Jack realizes.

Cantley retrieves his hat from the table. 'Miss Holland. An honour. Until we meet again.'

Another waft of her hand. Cantley leaves.

And still her eyes hold his. 'Captain,' she says, as if testing the word. 'Do sit. May we order food? I am *famished*.'

He sits. It feels as if his legs have somehow added an extra knee. Was he always this much of a gangle?

Now she has him at her mercy. 'You told me in Breda,' she begins, 'that you were a nothing.'

'War is a great changer-upper, Miss Holland,' Jack replies.

'Ain't it so.' She smooths the satin across her lap. 'This is a very beautiful gown,' she says next, then, 'Thank you.'

The whirl of possible responses moves through his head at such speed, all Jack can do is grab at one and hope. 'Well,' he hears himself say, 'it is now.'

Her head goes back, one eyebrow lifts. Plainly, she never thought he had it in him to pay a compliment. 'And yet,' she says, 'I have a sense there is some reason why I wear it.'

Ah. Indeed.

'There is to be a gathering this evening,' Jack begins, 'in Christ Church. It is a small matter, merely the presentation of reports –'

It is not. But a tongue-tied intelligencer would be of no use at all.

'– but it would be mighty useful if you could relate to those attending what you heard at Upper Aston.'

Again she tilts her head. 'And for that I have this gown?'

'You do.'

'And I may keep it?'

'It's yours,' he says.

A wriggle in her seat. A grin – ah, there's the little punk that he remembers. 'And tuppence, for to buy a pot of rouge?'

CHAPTER SIX

Scaresome Men

'It was quickly discerned that he meant to make himself as considerable as he could.'

Clarendon, *Four Portraits: George, Lord Digby*

THE MEETING-ROOM CHOSEN for the evening's business is close enough to Christ Church's cathedral for the sound of evensong to drift toward them as they approach. No doubt, thinks Jack, in happier times the room would have been the abode of some earnest candle-waster such as Rafe Endicott, scribbling away. Or even Andrew Frye, dramatist for the company of actors in Prague, now plying that quill of his under the olive trees of Italy. How people can amaze you. What wonders they perform.

Here's hoping for another miracle this evening, eh?

Christ Church itself; the quad wide as a field, big as a village green, three sides ponderously enclosed, the fourth still open. 'Modest lodgings,' he hears Miss Holland comment as they go in.

It is the prettiest evening. There is the scent of blossom on the air. Not for the first time, Jack finds himself thinking, *This town is wasted on the bloody scholars.* Two such had passed them, turning in their tracks as Pris Holland went by, as if they have never seen such a thing as a woman before, or never such a thing as this woman, at any rate, and it had surprised him, the heat of his annoyance on her behalf. Do all women go through this? he wonders. Surely Mirelle was never stared at so – or did he simply never notice?

A figure capers past them. Its clothes are bedecked with gauzy scarves, in pinks and blues. As it twirls past, it is strumming on a lute. Two more follow, two girls, adorned in silver spangles and with plumes of feather on their heads. He sees Miss Holland's nose rise a little higher in the air as she passes them; he sees the women pause to scrutinize the yellow gown as it ripples by. A fourth figure appears, this one in a suit festooned with cut-out leaves of green. It stops dead in front of Jack, mimes apparent terror, then skitters away. The girls laugh, tittering behind their hands the way girls do.

Miss Holland waits for him. The quartet of oddities has taken up position in front of a cloth painted with sun and moon, before a small audience reposed upon the grass. The girls in the silver spangles hold up a garland, the green man gambols between them.

'I am glad that it is as inexplicable to you as to me,' says Jack, as he comes up to her.

'Not inexplicable,' says Miss Holland. 'It is a masque, and they rehearse. Because what else would you do when England is at war?' Her voice is just loud enough for the masquers to hear. The girls stare at her, stonily; Miss Holland ignores them. 'No, not inexplicable, but just as ridiculous.' Next moment, she has put her arm through his.

They walk together across the grass. They reach a doorway. Once inside, again she waits for him. They walk together up the stairs, she with one hand holding up her skirts, the other laid upon his forearm. There is a knot of courtiers waiting on the landing, who tip their hats, and Jack is damn sure, not to him. Had he truly worried his companion would be overawed? She is as at home as if she had been born to this.

The warmth of that hand on his arm…

Outside the meeting-room, the strains of evensong are drowned by those of furious dispute. Even as they reach the landing, he hears the Prince: *It ist imperatif—*

'Miss Holland!' Zoltan exclaims. 'May I say—' He surveys her. 'No,' Zoltan concludes (the treacle-tongued knave!), 'there are no words.'

'He makes a fine couturier, your captain, do he not?' says Miss Holland, with that same grin as before.

Enough of this. 'How goes it?' the couturier enquires.

Zoltan pulls a face. 'As predicted.' Through the door, a voice declaring loudly, 'This rogue. This common ruffian. Why should we listen to what he has to say?'

There you go. Cross the sea, reclaim your rank, kit out a troop of the finest discoverers any man could ask for, there will still be some soapy-necked eater-of-swans denouncing you as a rogue. He sees Pris cock an ear. 'Who is that?'

'My Lord Digby.'

'A *Digby*.' All mock-respect. 'Bess had a Digby at the Leaguer.'

'This one's father, I suspect.'

'He had a most peculiar member, apparently,' Miss Holland continues. 'Thick at the root, but short. And pointy. And he was *most* niggardly with the douceurs. So the story was, one time as he lay sleeping, the girls dyed his parsley green and painted his goodfellow orange. Like a Dutch carrot, d'you see? Supposedly he had to forswear Mrs Digby two whole months till the green had grown out and the orange worn off.' A happy smile. 'Why do they argue?'

Jack looks over at Zoltan, but Zoltan is beyond speech, clearly, shoulders heaving, waving a hand – *no, no, leave me be.* Says Jack, 'There are those who see the Earl of Essex as a mighty threat, and would have the King quit Oxford on the instant, and then there are those who do not.'

'And which are we?'

We. 'We think the King should remain where he is. But a discoverer's opinion is not worth much.'

Now she meets his eye again, holding his gaze with hers. 'I don't agree with that,' she says. 'I don't think that at all.'

There is a school of thought that when lovers' eyes meet, or even more so, lovers-to-be, their eye-beams tangle, and it is all up from that moment on. It is the first time Jack finds himself daring to wonder whether that is so. Well, no, not the first time. But it is the first time he dares admit as much.

A clock in the quad grinds its way up to six. Zoltan has recovered his voice. 'Jacques, it is almost time.'

Miss Holland glances toward the door. 'All you need do,' Jack tells her, 'is repeat to those within what you told me.'

'Seeking only to assist my king, in any way I can.' Her hands are knit before her. Female fortitude. There is even, he notes, a tremble to her lip. 'Too much?' she asks, brightly.

'No. Perfection.' *You are perfection.* The door to the meeting-room is opening, Zoltan holding it aside; the voices within even louder. He sees Pris set herself. 'Wish me luck,' she whispers. 'Toi, toi, toi. As they would say at the Red Bull.'

Of a sudden, he finds he has his hands round hers. It's as if they put themselves there on their own: his the outer, hers the bud. 'You don't need it.'

In they go. The light of candles, the glint of crystal. The shine, Jack notes, of foreheads; and yet another of those woolly little dogs, this one even more sheep-like, in that its coat is white. And as always, at the back of the room, the one door, standing open by an inch or two. Sir Jacob calls out his name. 'Ah! Fiskardo!'

He bows his head. 'Highness,' he begins, to the Prince, as one must. 'My Lord. Gentlemen.' He bows again, steps back. 'Our new intelligencer. Miss Holland.'

WELL NOW.

Ain't it extraordinary, how many threads the mind can separate itself into, like the brain was a lace-maker's cushion, positively rayed with separate strands of thought. So, one, how polished was that introduction, who would have thought Fiskardo had such courtly manners in him? Two, for just a moment: *Oh, Bess, if you could only see me now.* Three: the Prince Palatine, how beau is he? And four, the size of that map, spread across the table, big as a bedsheet, and Lord, the temper to which it bears witness, scrawled with plumbago, scribblings crossed out, written in again, scrawled over anew. One great black cross: 'OXFORDE,' she reads, and THE KING. Others, smaller: REDDINGE. HENLEE. THAMES. 'THAMES' is in blue. The roads are marked in red. There are hills; there are single sorry little trees, standing in for woodland. She sees Fiskardo move around the table, as if to orient himself; to be honest, Pris can make no sense of the map either – why is REDDINGE so far to what seems to be the north?

The Prince is on his feet. 'Highness,' Pris murmurs, dropping a curtsey like a bird shot through the breast, and plunging into a lake of yellow satin.

The Palatine hand extended. The Palatine hand assists her up. Otherwise, all this is oddly reminiscent of those evenings in King Street when Wyn brought round his pipe-men.

'Miss Holland,' she hears Jack saying, 'was in Upper Aston and was witness to our skirmish there. She has information on the disposition of my Lord Essex. And his force.'

Keep your eyes down, she tells herself. *Be modest, be overawed.* All the same, one must see who one has as an audience. So: to one side of the table the Prince, who has an older man leaned in toward him, like a consul (an older man she rather takes to; there is an unvarnished quality to him very akin to Fiskardo), and on the other side, the Digby, with a supporter on either side. She was given their names, she knows she was, but their names matter not: she knows what these men are, human spandrels to the diamond, as my Lord Digby so clearly fancies himself to be. Is this truly how such weighty matters are decided? A roomful of men, shouting at each other?

It seems it is. She can imagine Aaron's cackle: *Oh, sis. Susanna and the elders. Only ever a matter of time.*

'Lord Essex –' (this from the Digby) '– has outmanouvered you, even as we sit here!' A furious finger, wobbling in the air above the map. 'Look at the map, gentlemen, look at the map! *Periculum in mora!*' And he glares at Fiskardo as he says it, as if such outmanoeuvring was Fiskardo's own fault. 'Do you not agree, Captain? *Periculum in mora!*'

There is danger in delay. A man who scatters Latin across his speech, Bess was wont to say, is like a cook who strews a dish with anchovies, to hide the bad meat underneath. Pris takes a prospect of Lord Digby, sat there with his fluff of artfully disordered hair and the twiddle of his moustaches, as if he had gone to his barber and said 'Make me martial'. Also that outrage – that is all assumed. *You remind me of Greville*, she thinks. *And I do not care for you.* She glances at Fiskardo, whose face remains exactly as before, grave and steady – so grave and steady, in fact, that you would have to look very deep indeed to see the simmer of contempt beneath.

'But we haf no reason to think this!' the Prince replies, just as incensed. 'We haf no reason at *all*.'

'It is here in front of you!' Digby declares. 'Essex has outflanked you, you and your discoverers.' (This word held up, as if between tweezers.) 'Will you believe it when he arrives at the doorstep? All the man need do is retrace his steps!'

'If I may,' says Fiskardo, leaning forward. 'By your leave, my Lord.' He turns the map. OXFORDE is now at the top; REDDINGE beneath, to the south, and nearest to the Digby.

A guffaw of laughter from the Prince. The little dog, as if in agreement, gives a bark.

'If Essex retraces his steps,' Fiskardo is saying, 'they would take him only unto London. Which we might desire, my Lord, true enough, but that would not outflank us, either.' And into the furious silence that follows, 'Miss Holland. Would you tell again what it was you heard at Upper Aston?'

'Most happily.' Pris folds her hands at her breast, like a child about to recite its catechism. 'It was that my Lord Essex would not come up to Oxford, not at all. That he cannot. He has sickness in his ranks, and his men of the Trained Bands have all turned back to London for fear of it, so for now, here –' (she presses at the *R* of REDDINGE) '– here he will stay. His men that are fit are unpaid, and will not fight without their salaries. So he must wait, in hopes that Waller's army will come up from the west to join his. But word was, Waller will not do so, either. My Lords.'

The turning of heads, one to the other. 'Waller!' exclaims the Prince.

'Highness,' says Fiskardo, 'my thinking is that Essex keeps our eyes on him, while it is Waller, and Waller's army, is the true danger. The King must be safer in Oxford than he would be outside it. Waller knows his business.'

'Because he is a veteran of Germany, as you?' the Digby snaps. 'You *professionals*, Captain, you forget war is a place of honour—'

The plain old soul holds up a hand, as if for peace. 'Miss Holland, would you tell us how it was you came to hear this?'

'To *over*hear it,' says Pris. 'I was at Upper Aston with my – with my guardian. He was in conversation. I was in the room.' She looks up. 'My guardian, Lord Wyncanton.'

More turning of heads, even of Lord Digby's spandrels, and a murmur to go with it. *Oh, these men*, she thinks, *these high-born men, even in the middle of a war, they still all doff their hats at mention of each other's names.*

At the back of the room, the door has opened by another inch.

'But Wyncanton is Parliament's man!' exclaims Digby, like this must throw everything before into doubt.

Pris draws herself up into the moment. 'But I, sir, as you can see full well, am not.'

She hears the old soul laugh. He and the Prince Palatine exchange a glance, then the Prince is once more on his feet. 'Madam,' he says. Extends the hand again. 'We thank you. Heartily.' There, one more swooping curtsey and her moment on stage, it is done.

She finds herself again outside that door, Zoltan waiting as before, and Jack exiting the room behind her.

'Did we carry the day?' Zoltan asks.

'Not we,' says Jack. 'But Miss Holland did.'

This same Miss Holland who still has nowhere to lay her head tonight other than that room at the Spotted Cow.

He has Zoltan escort her back. Coward, coward, coward, but he does. He makes the excuse that he must wait for Astley, must post-mortem with the Prince, even though he suspects not a word of the conversation will stay with him. He contemplates saddling M'sieu and riding back to Varney, then and there. *Coward.*

He contemplates the image of her, as she was, lying asleep in that bed, one single ringlet stirring as she breathed. He contemplates her at the Spotted Cow without him. Then, with.

THE MAIDS AT the Spotted Cow have views every bit as trenchant as those of Charles Stuart's advisors – in particular, that even the least of them is superior to a woman who paints. Yet so confusing is the world, such women always seem to come in train with the men who are most generous with the douceurs. Cicely's mien, as she attends on Pris, is therefore a carefully judged mix, both condescending *and* accommodating all at once.

'Fiskardo,' Pris begins. She finds she is under a strange compulsion to say his name.

'Yes, miss?' asks Cicely. Not only is it impossible for a fine lady to dress herself, it is almost impossible for her to undress herself either, so Cicely finds herself again in that topmost room with her arms full of yellow satin.

'Do you know him? Fiskardo?'

'Know *of* him,' says Cicely.

'What do you know?'

'I know as he seems a scaresome sort of man at first,' says Cicely, cautiously. 'Then, he don't.' She folds the yellow, lays it on a chair. 'Will there be more for you tonight, miss?'

'No, thank'ee,' says Pris. In the darkening yard below, one of the new recruits has climbed on a table and is leading his fellows in a song:

'We'll laugh and make good sport,
And cry not a fig for care,
What though our means grow short
The world has enough to spare –'

The 'fig' might possibly be misheard as something else, so many of them shout it out at once.

'They do love that song, don't they?' says Pris.

''Tis the noise they can make with it they love,' Cicely answers, scornfully. She waits. Like all maids, she has a pointed way of waiting.

'I am put to the blush,' says Pris. 'I have these fine feathers, yet not a penny to my name.'

'Don't you fret, miss,' says Cicely, the realist, relenting. 'The captain will be good for it.'

So nothing to do now but wait. In her shift, Pris moves the chair to the tiny window.

She has goose-skin, although the evening is warm. She pulls the coverlet from the bed.

But he may not come back here.

You know damn well that he will.

But he may have no interest in me.

You know damn well that he does.

She sees again that smile of his; the way it starts at the corner of his mouth and travels, as if along a fuse. She rubs her arms. It is as if every grain of her skin is somehow separately alert for him, as if it can sense what might happen next. It is as if every single thing in the room is part of this, as if there was some extra nervous life in the matter of the universe. Pris puts his face before hers, his face that looks like it was chopped out with an axe, and is astonished at the effect it has – that squeeze of excitement, and then this inward kick, like a convulsion. As if she stood upon a well and the cover gave way. A plunge, a vertiginous plunge into pure desire.

No, this is absurd, she tells herself. Be sensible. What would Bess say?

Be damned to Bess. I want to know how he kisses. I want to know how he feels. I want to know how he sounds. I want—

Someone has entered the yard downstairs. She hears cheering.

Him. I want him.

She waits. Now noise from within the house, more voices, then boots ascending the stairs. Up, up, up… at every footstep her heartbeat gets louder, till she is all but deaf with it.

And there he is. He takes her in, she in her shift, with the bedcover gathered under her breasts. He asks, 'Where is your gown?'

She points a finger. 'There,' she says. She had not expected his presence to be so heady. She is almost wobbling where she stands.

The fuse is lit. 'Why so?'

'I did not wish it to get crumpled.'

The fuse travels. 'Is crumpling – likely?'

'Inescapable, I would say.' She lets the bedcover drop. She goes – she does not walk, she's sure of it, because she thinks her legs could hardly carry her, but somehow she crosses the floor between them. She puts herself up on tiptoe. She puts her arms about his neck. He is still too tall. So she puts her naked toes on the great square ends of his boots and lifts herself up that way. Stood on his feet she puts the front of her body against the front of his, and looks deep into his face, as only lovers do.

Oh, the confusion! This man who took Upper Aston from Ancrum before Ancrum could draw breath, this man who is greeted with cheering, this man who has the ear of princes, yet here he is, stood before her, dark-eyed with need but so uncertain, so unsure, and drawing back his head like his bloody horse offered something it don't understand. *This is what I want*, Pris thinks. Not the warrior, not the hero the rest of the world gawps at, but this.

'Oh, for the love of God, man,' says Pris, laughing, '*kiss* me!'

CHAPTER SEVEN

Well Now, Sir. Well Now, Madam.

'Love requires boldness.'

Giovanni Torriano, *Select Italian Proverbs… newly made to speak English*

DAWN AMBLES INTO Oxford over the water meadows. It reaches the shops of Broad Street, still shuttered at this early hour; it crosses the unhappy corner where not a century before, Bloody Mary burned bishops Latimer and Ridley at the stake (and is not that fire in men's hearts burning even now?), and only then is it high enough in the sky to light Hell Passage and the attic window of the Spotted Cow, and the man stood there, watching the woman as she sleeps.

No, the sun has reached her face, and she is waking. One arm lifts from the sheets, shielding her eyes. A groan. Says Pris, 'I might have known you'd be one of those up with the lark.' She pushes herself onto her elbow. For a moment all they do is gaze at each other.

'I was watching for the sunrise,' he says.

'Was it a pretty one?'

'The prettiest.'

Think of those eye-beams as not merely tangling but performing pirouettes. Jetés. Arabesques.

'Well now, sir,' says Pris, softly. When she stretches her limbs, it feels as if they too have sunrises within them.

'Well now, madam.'

And another long moment of looking. At length, Pris sets an index finger to her temple. 'Think she to herself,' she says, 'where do we go from here?'

'I was wondering that.' He moves from the window. 'I have a house near to here. We might go there. If it would please you.'

The coach was waiting for her when they came downstairs. She has no idea how he managed to bespeak one so early, but there it was. He had led her across the yard – the yard where his men now slumbered, heads pillowed on their arms. That giant Ulrik flat on his back on a table, legs dangling to the ground, and the titch, Luka, curled beneath Ulrik's enormous booted feet, like the dog on a tomb at the feet of his knight. The maid, Cicely, came out the kitchen as they went by, and Fiskardo laid a finger to his lips and put a shilling piece into the girl's hand. A whole shilling. Miss Holland notes it, but says nothing. She finds she is in somewhat pensive mood.

Oho, says Bess, with a cackle, up in her head. *It worked, did it? Always the ones you least expect.*

That kiss. You would have thought their mouths had found each other a hundred times before, so familiar did it feel, so easy, yet like no kiss ever before.

He had laid his face against hers, closed his eyes. He said, 'Pris, it has been so long a time.'

'What,' she'd said, laughing still, 'you think you'll have forgotten how?'

She remembers tugging at his shirt-front. 'Too many *clothes*,' she had said. She remembers hooking her fingers into the waistband of his breeches and pulling him to the bed. Throwing the shift over her head even as he was kneeling there unbuttoning himself, all of a fumble, all thumbs – 'Oh, come *here*,' she had said, sitting up, and put her hand in at the vent, and there it was, arching its back beneath her hand like some big cat.

Above her, the coachman is singing. 'Ho, the dames of France are fair and free, and Flemish lips are wi-i-lling...'

Yes, because the world of men is public, while that of women is private and solitary, and that within their heads most secret of all. Pris leans back against the seat, and memory passes through her like something physical, like the flutter of feathers.

It had felt as if the mattress had become a magic carpet, lifting beneath her. It had felt as if she was the keystone in a bridge, both falling and suspended, all at once. The gasp of her breathing. The gasp of his. His groan as he went into her – it was the most intoxicating sound she'd ever heard.

And this morning he had been her lady's maid. Had stood there, holding out her stays for her, had laced her in, the snap of the tapes being pulled as no woman would do it, ever. Had held the bodice out for her, to slip her arms into. Had waited as she pulled the dentilles of lace out around her elbows; held the tortoiseshell pins as she put up her hair; watched as she rouged her lips. 'Because?' he had asked.

'To me, to go out without paint would be the same as for you to go out into the world without a sword on your hip.' One hairpin slipped a little out of true, and he caught it, tucked it back in place for her. It was only then she found herself a-blush.

There is his voice now, in conversation with the coachman. The coach is pulled to a halt. Fiskardo is opening the door. He bows to her. 'There is a view,' he says. 'It would be a pity to miss it.'

Down she steps, on his hand. 'Close your eyes,' he tells her.

She closes them. She feels him put one hand over her eyes, then with the other, lead her forward. All her nervousness seems to have gone down into her toes, which hardly dare creep. 'I have you,' he says, softly. 'Trust me.' One step, two – 'There,' he says, and takes his hand away.

Over the trees, there is a chimney. *That's ridiculously high*, is her first thought. And then she sees there is another. And—

'Oh my good God! *Jack!*'

The huff of his laughter. 'And you thought I'd live in a den in the woods.'

NO-ONE REMEMBERS, BUT Harriet Mayhew had a husband once – dead before he was thirty, poor soul, for what at first had seemed no more than a toothache. *For an aching tooth: take ragwort and bruise it, and mix it well with oil of cloves and saffron…* It was God's will, one does not question; instead, one keeps a cupboard full of every cure, every potion that one can. Which is why Mrs Mayhew sits here at one end of the kitchen table with a pile of coltsfoot leaves in front of her, harvested while they had the dew still on them. *Take leaves of the coltsfoot, pick and wash them clean, and boil them… an excellent cooling draught…* At the other end of the table, James and his brother are picking over an equal pile of flowers of the primrose, which may not be the most manly of occupations, true, but small fingers are excellently suited to the task, and a spoonful of primrose wine, sweet and flowery, makes a fitting reward for a brave boy who must endure the miseries of these squalls of fever and mysterious aches in his bones.

Beneath the table, Ocker lifts his head from Mrs Mayhew's slipper and gives a whuff, as if brought some news of which he is doubtful. Todd, not to be outdone, immediately scrambles to his paws; the dogs are of such a size now that if the kitchen table were any less solid, when they stand, they must bear it away on their backs. As it is, the table bumps and scrapes; Mrs Mayhew has to throw her arms around her harvest, and now here is Toby running in from the front of the house, one hand as ever hid beneath his coat and calling out, 'Mrs Mayhew! Mrs Mayhew! The captain's here!'

'Well?' She smooths her apron, sets her cap. The boys are gone at once, James's cry of 'Wait for *mmme*, wait for *mmme*!' echoing behind him. 'Go to meet him, lad! What are you waiting for?'

'But Mrs Mayhew,' says Toby, 'he ain't on his own.'

Here is the carriage, crunching over the gravel, there go the dogs, there stand the boys, and there is the captain himself, sliding from the saddle and then, with Fiskardo handing her down from the carriage, a woman with flabbergasted face within the riot of her hair. The dogs charge up to her, circle her, sniffing her hands; before anyone can stop him, Todd gets up on his hind legs with his paws on the woman's shoulders. Mrs Mayhew waits for the scream.

Scream there is not. Instead, the woman pushes Todd away with a hoot of laughter. 'Lord, your dogs are as giant as your horse!' Her gaze travels the length of the façade, window to window. It comes down to the doorway. 'The household,' the captain is saying. 'Toby Dearlove, who is in charge of our fields and woods, and Abram who tends the garden…'

The woman nods her head to each of them in turn, takes off her glove, puts out her hand. From behind the house, the peacocks shriek. 'Mrs Mayhew, where is Topham?'

'He is gone out to Woodstock, sir, collecting the news,' Mrs Mayhew replies. She cannot take her eyes off the woman's gown.

'Then Peter Topham you will meet anon, no doubt. This is our goodwife Henty.'

Old Henty's eyes are moving up and down the woman as the woman's had the house. There is muttering. Mrs Mayhew steps speedily in front of her.

'And here, Mrs Mayhew who keeps all things exactly as they should be.'

'I am *very* pleased to know you,' the woman says.

Now Ned, who throws a bow, stiff as a hinge, and James, who is immobile and wide-eyed, until at a nudge from his brother he hinges forward too. Mrs Mayhew can see the small brain pondering: *What is that stuff round her eyes? Why is her mouth so red?* 'Why—' James begins.

'And these are mine,' says Fiskardo. 'My sons.'

You might almost think the woman knew them, so amused is she. 'Of course they are!'

Into the house. Mrs Mayhew follows, the dogs ticky-tack in rearguard.

Here is the great hall, the virgin in her garden. The woman exclaims at it. Then the dining-room. The woman puts her fingertips against the panels of gilt leather in a way that tells Mrs Mayhew at once that she knows how costly they are. The inner hall, the staircase. 'And this,' the master says, 'we call the solar.'

The drench of sunlight, the hardstone table. 'That is an orchis,' James says, pointing. 'You *m*mmustn't water it too *m*mmuch.'

Ned has yet to say a word.

'You have a tongue that trips,' the woman tells James, bending down. 'Like the King. When I was in London, all the men at court would try to sound like you.'

James's eyes are round as marbles. Bless the boy, thinks Mrs Mayhew, because he looks over to her, as if for confirmation.

Fiskardo beckons Ned forward. 'This is your favourite, ain't it, Ned?' he says. He points to the tapestry. Ned, Mrs Mayhew notes, is keeping his distance.

'What is it?' the woman asks, encouragingly. 'What's it show?'

Slowly, slowly, Ned comes nearer. 'Breitenfeld,' he replies. 'A battle. In Germany.' His tone is frosty. 'That is Gustavus Adolphus. He won it. He knew Dada.'

'So he did, chick. To my honour, so he did.' Now the captain opens the door beside the solar. 'Come see our garden,' he says.

Mrs Mayhew and Henty return to the kitchen, and to the picking over of the leaves. James's treble floats in toward them: he is explaining to the woman something about Varney's river: where it comes from, where it goes.

Old Henty is incensed. 'What sort of hussy is this? What is she doing here?'

'I think you will need to come to peace with this, goodwife,' Mrs Mayhew tells her. She is thinking of how the woman laid her hand on the gilded leather, how she had touched the heavy silver of the punchbowl, but she thinks too of the expression on the captain's face as he held the door from the solar open for her. Mrs Mayhew remembers her own man looking at her like that, how her own husband's face had softened in that self-same way. 'I think Miss Holland may not be a passing thing.'

There is a terrace beyond the solar, a terrace overlooking a fountain and an arbour, a-drip with yellow tassels, a terrace where they sit, she and Fiskardo, and the housekeeper (Mrs Mayhew, Pris tells herself, Mrs Mayhew, I must learn these names, I must not make mistakes with them) she brings them wine and thumbs of pastry filled with curd-cheese and raisins, and Jack puts a newly opened rose in Pris's glass, so when she drinks, it is with the rose's gold coronet under her nose, and its scent filling the glass. 'You are a man full of surprises, Jack Fiskardo.'

He tips his head. 'Do me best.'

'Tell me about your boys.'

'What of them?'

'Little James.'

A pause. 'Born before his time.'

'And thus you lost your wife.'

'Thus. Yes.'

'And brought them here. And made a home. Is this why you want the King to stay in Oxford? With his garrison?'

She watches as he puts the answer together. 'Soldiers ain't great thinkers, Pris. They have to see the thing they're fighting for. If the King goes further from London than this, he will be nigh-on invisible. Added to which, a lad with a catapult could put Essex's army to flight. Abandoning Oxford on account of it is the silliest notion Digby and his cronies ever put their name to, and that, by all accounts, is saying *much*.'

She lifts an eyebrow. He, in his battle-scarred coat; he, just as battle-scarred himself. 'You know a deal of such men as he, do you?'

'We discoverers, lady, we know everything.'

'Do you indeed?' says Pris. 'So who was it, listening at that door?'

He whose tongue also trips, thinks Jack. A man who would sooner listen to twenty opinions than come up with one of his own. But out loud, all he says is, 'It's a court, Pris. There is always someone listening at the door.'

She laughs, shakes her head. 'Full of surprises,' she repeats.

They sit. They watch the sun go down. Pris thinks that she can feel contentment spread out from the man beside her like a cloak across the ground. 'It is very lovely here,' she says, at last.

'Yes,' he says. 'It is.'

She gives a sigh. She looks up at the house again. 'Where do you sleep?'

He points to the topmost great curved window, outlined against the dusk. 'Up there.'

'And where do I sleep?'

He points to the same place.

'So there is to be none of this putting me elsewhere and tiptoeing about?'

'There is not,' he says. 'Why would there be?'

She smiles. 'It ain't unknown.'

'It is here. I am not one for pretending, Pris.'

'No,' she says, 'I see that.'

Jack Fiskardo's bed is such a size it had to come up Varney's stairs in pieces, like a puzzle, but damnation, said its owner, for once in my life I will have a bed long enough that my feet don't hang out the end. Its posts are so strong-looking, so solid in the round, they might almost still be trees. Its curtains admit not the sharpest draught. It is a room within a room, an adult's den, and in it, here in the small hours of the night, sits Pris Holland, cross-legged, holding Jack's hand in hers, and by the light of their candle, examining his tattoos. 'What are these?'

So he explains them.

'And this?' she asks, tracing the scars on his palm – so old now, they are almost a part of the lines of life, of fortune, what you will. She twists his hand this way and that to make them out. 'G.F.R.N.,' she says. He had forgotten how lovers do this, how they play with bits of each other, like toys.

'*Gefroren*,' he tells her. They talk in whispers, like children, awake when they know the rest of the house will be sleeping. 'Swedish. It means you are proof against any weapon made of iron or lead or steel.' A wry smile. 'My ABC was up to that.'

'You did this to yourself?' She leans back, away from him, as if to get perspective on such baffling behaviour. '*Why?*'

'Why do men always do such things?' He reaches up, he wants to pull her back down to where she lay before. 'I was young and drunk and stupid. Why else?'

She is so matter of fact, sat there in her nakedness. You'd think that Eve had never touched that apple. While he, lying back against the bolster, has never felt so biffed and battered, so irregular. 'And these?' she asks.

The tally of lines on his forearm. Ten of them, all told.

'An aide-mémoire,' he says. 'One for each of those I've lost.'

She sits back. 'You take everything out on yourself, do you?'

He's never thought of it that way before. Yes, probably he does.

She taps the dip between her collarbones. 'And what is this you wear here?'

He lifts the silver wolf on its cord and holds it up for her to see. 'A memento. A foolish superstition, nothing more.'

But her face has changed. Her face and voice, both. 'How did you come by it?'

I took it from my mother's hand, after I found her dead. She took it from the man who killed her. The same man who took all the rest from him. No, that would assuredly not be the right answer to give here. 'It's a long story,' he says.

'Tell it to me.'

'Why?'

'Because I've seen one of those before. Carlo Fantom. He wears one.'

How much to say here, and how much more not? 'This once was his,' says Jack, at last. 'He and I, we have a history.'

'A bad history?'

'That man has nothing but bad history.' But he does not get to spread his poison here. Here in my house. My *bed*.

He sees how she has narrowed her eyes. It must be said, the silver wolf was ugly enough before, and the bullet flattened into it has not improved its looks one jot. 'It is vile,' she says. 'It is the vilest thing I ever saw. Keep it from me.'

He wants to explain, in Germany that was the point. That might be what kept you alive, being more terrifying than your enemy. But that was his world, not hers. He closes the silver wolf in his hand. 'There,' he says. 'Now it's gone. Carlo Fantom is my ghost, not yours.'

She is still studying him, head to one side, ringlets a-flop on her shoulder. 'Tell me of your wife,' she says.

Who saw that coming? 'My *wife*?'

'Yes. How was she? What sort of woman gave you those boys?'

What sort? 'She was gentle,' he begins. 'Kind. Calm.' There was never a rush, never a panic with Mirelle – until of course there was. 'She was *une formidable ménagère*, that's what the French would call her. A splendid housewife. And – brave.'

She shakes her head. 'I am none of those things,' she says,

almost as if in warning. 'I am selfish and indolent. I hate housewifery. And my temper, it could wake the dead.' That impish grin. 'But then you have been drunk and stupid.'

'And young,' he reminds her.

'And young. And *proof*.'

Gefroren. Frozen, is what it means, if he were being honest. Impenetrable. A man without feeling. She still has her thumb across the scars on his palm, almost as if she were taking their pulse; now she cantilevers herself forward, puts her other hand to his breastbone, the dint, still there. 'Hmmm,' she says – the hum of a woman giving some matter deep consideration. 'Yes, I see how well that has worked for you.'

He puts his arm behind his head. He imagines her lolling on cushions satiny as her skin, a dish of sweetmeats to hand, dainties and delicacies to him unknown. Moonlight washes her with blue, the way it might a statue – the gleam of her thighs, the sway of her breasts, the eye of her belly, and even in the moonlight her hair is still red. He is so distracted by her, he hardly knows what he says. 'Woman, there is not one straight line on you.'

The gurgle of her laugh. 'I know,' she says. 'Ain't you *lucky*?' Leans forward again, and kisses him. Then sits back, still laughing. Puts a finger to his mouth. 'Oh,' she says. '*Me*.'

ANOTHER SUNRISE, ONLY this time the rays of the sun slide not across rooftops, but the crowns of trees. Climb up the outside of the solar and wake the woman in the bed with a warmth like a blanket being drawn across her. She yawns, she stretches, she sits up – and again, the place where the man had been is empty.

We most emphatically do not keep the same clock, thinks Pris.

Some noise outside, of horses being moved about. A man's voice, urging them along. Not Jack's.

Her shift is hiding down amongst the sheets at the bottom of the bed. She pulls it on, then goes looking for some other thing to add to it. It feels delightful, to be free of stays and petticoats, but even in the Leaguer, if you went wandering, you wandered in more than this.

There is an antechamber off the bedroom, a dressing-room no doubt, a place for some trusted manservant to lay his head when the house was in its heyday. It holds now a broken pair of boots in the corner, a cupboard with a couple of shirts on the hooks on its back board – *What a monk this man is, truly!* – and thrown across a stool, a long velvet robe, wide-sleeved and heavily braided. That will do.

Down the stairs she goes, out to the terrace, which is already warming in the sun. Grit under her toes. Between the stones, the faintest lines of green. Everything putting forth, everything new… She thinks of Bess's garden in the Pightle as she had seen it last, full of stalks and browning leaves. She hears the tinkling of the fountain, she smells the scent of pinks, of honeysuckle. A peacock hops onto the wall behind her, flourishing its tail, and the two halves of Pris's heart feel as if they are trying to press the moment between them, like prayerful hands.

Here is the gardener. *Abram*, she thinks, remembering. He sees her, taps his forehead, but it is clear she is of a deal less interest than whatever he, with his bucket and syphon, is set to squirt from the gatherings of rosebuds. 'Good day to ye, lady. How bist?'

'I bist very well, Master Abram,' Pris replies. The fountain lies ahead: a trio of Neptune's horses, fierce and unbiddable-looking as M'sieu. In the pool beneath, twists and darts of silver. She sits herself on the edge of the pool, dusts off her toes. A fish jumps, falls back into the water; the peacock lifts its head and stalks away, and from across the lawn, a child's high shriek, merry with delight.

She follows the sound to the bridge. She spies Ned first, running along the edge of the bank, arms out, stick-limbed with excitement, then his little brother, running the way he does it, one leg hail and strong, the other hopping along behind. A wooden jetty pokes out through the rushes and the boys run onto it, slap-footed; they don't so much enter the water as run out of anything solid to run on, plunging in, arms and legs windmilling through the air; and then she sees their father dive between them from the bridge, shoulders shining as if he had scales. It seems impossible that anything as small and neat and roundly made as his children could grow into a form like his. Now the boys are doggy-paddling in circles, heads held up and stiffly back, as children do, and now the agate-coloured water bursts between them, sends them squealing for the bank. Their father catches them easily, one beneath each arm, still furiously trying to swim away even as he stands upright with them and splashes to the bank; bound about with little fingers, arms and legs.

He sees her. He sets them down. 'Go,' he says. 'Go, get some clothes on you,' and off they run, across the grass, back to the house, babbling, joyous.

Here he is, scribbled with water weed. 'I didn't mean to spoil the game,' says Pris. She feels peculiarly modest; good God once again, she is blushing.

'You spoiled nothing.'

His arm is round her waist. His kiss is coaxing her backwards, she feels herself falling, falling, the sky moving further and further away. Ho-hum, thinks Pris abandoning herself. This must be why those endless nymphs was forever wandering about the Grecian meadows: for the chance that some great river-god 'ud come out of the rushes and swive 'em.

RAFE ENDICOTT, BOOKSELLER, also up and about betimes this morning. He has kissed his sleeping wife, has had his horse saddled and brought round, and was on his way to Varney before the sun has even reached the doorway of his shop. Rafe's is a good steed, he had the most excellent advice in buying it, but Rafe is a poor horseman; when he dismounts outside Varney's front door, he has to walk about kicking his legs out beneath him until they feel they will once again work in the usual way. There is a clutch of horses ranged at the fence; he sees Topham inspecting one, a portly little thing who holds an ear at an angle and has a blueish cast to one eye. Is King Charles truly as short of mounts as that?

From far off, under the trees, he spies more horses, seemingly being led through their paces, and with them, unmistakably, Ulrik, who lifts an arm in friendly greeting. The game must be, once more, afoot.

Mrs Mayhew is at the door, hands folded beneath her apron. 'Mrs Mayhew. Is our mighty Alexander at home, by any chance?' Rafe has news.

'He is, sir, if you mean the master.' Rafe is already heading past her into the hall when a naked elf half runs and half hops by him, followed by Henty, holding out a miniature shirt and calling, 'You do come here! Master James! You *hellion*!' Ah, the heedlessness of youth. Rafe finds he is much occupied by memories of his own more carefree days at present, in particular the year he calls 'my late adventures', out in Germany. He sees the man with whom he shared those late adventures has set up yet another purchase, a pier-glass, in his hall, the type made in two halves and butted together with gilt-metal. He examines his reflection. Rafe too has been fostering a dab of beard under his lower lip and carefully brushed-up moustaches above; it is the kind of adornment in fashion amongst the men of Oxford, as opposed to those clean-shaven Puritans, all braying for Parliament, and even worse, the close-cropped Roundheads. Let a man be shaggy! thinks Rafe, at the same time pondering would this make an essay, for *Mercurius*?

'Rafe!'

It is the man himself. Tall as ever, striding forward, one of those rare great smiles upon his face, even if he is somewhat eccentrically dressed this morning, Rafe sees, in what appears to be the velvet coat of a Turkish dragoman. 'Rafe, the devil brings you here?'

'Neighbourliness,' Rafe answers. 'Not that you would know anything of that. Here you are, back again, and not so much as a word – great saints.'

'Good day to you,' the woman says, as she steps forward.

He doesn't recognize her, not at first, she looks so – so *innocent*, bare-footed, in her shift, hair a-tumble and her face a little pink, and Jack with his hand at the small of her back; and then he thinks that hair, those eyes, great saints, great *God*. Pris Holland.

'Pris,' he hears Jack say. The shockable portion of Rafe's wits rush to inform him that Jack, too, appears to be naked under his robe. 'This is Rafe Endicott. A friend of many years standing. Even as far back as my time in Germany.'

'Mr Endicott? Mr Endicott the bookseller?' She comes forward, she is offering him her hand. Rafe bends across it; never before did he appreciate how such courtesy gives a man a chance to recover his poise. 'Madam!'

What pretty manners, thinks Pris. *Like grass-stained shifts is what every woman of fashion is wearing this year.* 'Why, I know you,' she says, as Rafe comes back to the vertical. 'In London

I was your customer many a time.' A smile. 'At least, on account I was.'

'Ah,' says Rafe. His eyes circle round toward Jack.

'Miss Holland is my guest,' says Jack, as if that explains all.

'Ah! Indeed!' Rafe rocks backwards and forwards on his heels. Inspiration! 'In that case you must, you must – you must be our customer again, Miss Holland. My business is one of those many has moved itself here, and my wife would delight to meet you, I am sure.'

'It would be my honour,' Miss Holland answers. The prettiest confusion. 'But you find me unfit for visitors. If you will excuse me, gentlemen.' The grass stain, as she walks away, is like a green blush over the cheeks of her arse.

They watch her go. Rafe turns to Jack.

'Not one word,' says Jack, warningly.

'Not one, but thousands! How – how –' (Rafe is waving his hat about as if to beat the answers from the air) '– how has this come about?'

'Miss Holland and I met some few years ago,' says Jack. 'We met again more recently. Now she is my guest here. That is all.'

'It is? But how did you – figs and bones, Jack,' says Rafe, moderating his language from the soldierly to the salon, 'you saw her at the Red Bull, and said not a thing of knowing her!'

'I know,' comes the answer. An even broader smile. 'Deep, ain't I?'

'I need a chair,' says Rafe. Already he sees himself taking this back to Belle – *Sweetheart, sweetheart, I have such a tale for you! No, you will never guess!* 'And to think I imagined I was the one with the news this morning. So, does Miss Holland stay here? Is that how it is to be?'

'To be honest,' says Jack, 'we ain't so far discussed it.'

'I would most heartily recommend that you do. Discuss it, I mean. Women do not care to be left uncertain in such matters.' Rafe brings the paper from his pocket. 'And it has already been announced in *Mercurius* that you and your discoverers, you are to ride with Cantley and his dragoons. Also…'

'Also what?'

'The old Cardinal,' says Rafe. 'Richelieu. He is dead at last.'

DAMN THAT SCRIBBLER, but the man is right.

Very well then. Draw up your forces, choose your ground.

He chooses the terrace. So here they are; the hem of the yellow satin swish, swish, swish.

Detail your campaign.

'Pris, I will not be here, at least a while. We have Essex to discourage, and then we must deal with Waller. So there are matters you and I should settle.'

'Oh,' she says. 'Yes.'

Make the first move. 'It would not be an easy or a simple thing to get you back to London. But I would find a way to do it. If that is what you want.'

The swish of her skirts ceases. She looks astonished. 'Why would I want that?'

'Because that is your home. Your family—'

She pulls a face. '*Family*,' she says. 'Well, I will write to them. But trust me, they will survive my absence.'

Another yard or so. The roses bob; the birds in the hedges begin another sort of evensong. 'Your life here would be very different,' he begins.

She has her arm looped in his, just as she had done crossing the quad at Christ Church. Now she uses it to bring him to a halt. 'My life is already very different. And I took myself back to London once, remember? The gods still threw me in your path.'

So they did. 'You believe in such, do you? Providence? Destiny?'

Now she is smiling. 'When I was found, in Crossbones graveyard, the grave I had been left on was that of a moon-girl, a Roma. Moon-girls believe in everything – heaven above us, hell below, Mother Earth who holds us here and now. And since she is the closest I am ever like to have to a mother, so do I. Fate, Providence, the gods – I believe it all.'

'Money,' he says.

'Ah,' she replies. 'I believe in that too.'

'I have a man of business in London. Cornelius Vanderhoof.'

Her head makes that tilt. 'Vanderhoof? In Green Dragon Court? I know him. Or I know of him, any rate. My brother Aaron, he does business with a Mr Vanderhoof, I'm sure of it. And Felipe, too. Gad, my peacock silk was bought through Mr Vanderhoof.'

Mild-mannered affable Cornelius, who would think it? 'That man,' says Jack, laughing. 'He never ceases to amaze.' Yes, but to it. The matter in hand. 'I could have instruction sent him, to arrange a line of credit for you, with anyone. Unthanks. Endicott's – it would be as if you had money of your own.'

'Of my *own*?'

She sounds so took aback by this, it makes him hesitate as well. 'Would that be the way to manage it? Pris, I am all at sea here. Tell me if this is how the thing is done, or no.'

He hears her let out her breath. Now what is that? Has he misstepped? Misspoken?

'Yes,' she says. 'Yes, this is how it is done. It is.'

'Then you would stay here? You would be happy to?'

'Oh, I suppose so,' says Pris. 'If I must.'

CHAPTER EIGHT

What Would St Paul Say?

'... if the trumpet give an uncertain sound, who shall prepare himself to the battle?'

St Paul, *Letter to the Corinthians*

THE KING'S ARMY outside Oxford – specifically its vanguard, specifically the company of one Arthur Cantley, in the King's forward camp at Shotover, to Oxford's east. To narrow it down for you even further, the tent of one Jack Fiskardo, discoverer, seconded to Cantley's company, waking under canvas and to the sound of rain. He had been dreaming of his mistress – a dream so vivid he almost expects, on waking, to find her there in the tent with him: she as she was in the bedroom of the Spotted Cow, dropping her shift from her shoulder. He wakes just as he had been about to touch his hand to her breast, to the nipple, red as a cherry, hard as its stone. Instead, outside, all the disorder of a camp at daybreak – the tending of fires, the chatter of men coming in off the night-time pickets; the Gemini, their incomprehensible patois, then a burst of laughter; and unmistakably, further off, his own horse, M'sieu, yelling for attention. He wakes with a groan. Sweet Jesus, here we go again.

He clambers outside. The first he sees are Per and Jens, so helpless with laughter they must hold each other up. 'What's the joke?'

Jens points across to one of Cantley's men, who is strangely humped, like a camel, and fighting with his straps. 'He puts the – he puts the backplate on the front, and the – and the—' says Jens, but can get no further. Per is doubled up, wiping his eyes.

Backplate on the front and breastplate on the back. Good grief.

'As one calls into the forest,' Kazimir informs him, going past, 'the forest echoes back.'

And stupid begets stupid. I see.

'English gentlemen,' says Konstantin, just in case he should not.

DAYBREAK AT VARNEY. The hounds of hell come whuffing out of the kitchen, thunder up the stairs and barge into the master's bedroom. Ocker stuffs his nose into the bed, sniffs at the warm body lying there, but finds it is not his master, so of no interest at all, despite the way it shrieks and beats the air with its hands. Todd gives it an inspection of his own, just to be sure, arriving on the bed in a maelstrom of muzzle and dog-feet, and then as suddenly as they arrived, the dogs are gone. Their place is taken by some mighty rumpus out in the corridor. When Pris pulls open the door of the bedchamber herself (her hair all everywhere, and dog-slobber on her nightgown), this turns out to be Old Henty and James, in a scuffle of their own. 'The devil is this?' Pris demands.

''E will not be drest!' Henty tells her. She is panting with fury.

'I *www*ill!' James shouts. He is naked from the waist down, holding himself at that characteristic angle: one leg turned toward its fellow. 'But *I* will do it!'

'But 'e do not do it right!' Old Henty says. She holds up a padded square of linen on two straps. ''E do not wear 'is little vest!'

'What difference does that make to you? If he doesn't want you fussing him, he doesn't want it. Let him dress himself, Henty. Leave him be.'

James snatches his breeches from Henty and one-twos it back to his room, slamming the door. Old Henty goes down the stairs, muttering.

Pris returns to the bedroom and sits down heavily on the bed. Outside a peacock screeches like it had been trod on; then Topham's voice, at a shout, from the stables, and Toby Dearlove, also at a shout, in reply. She puts the heels of her hands to her temples. The master of Varney left the day before; this is her first here on her own. 'Different?' she asks herself. 'God above!'

Somewhat later, down she goes, in a morning-robe the pink of apple blossom. Miss Holland is losing no time in making herself one of Unthanks' best customers. Her hair is brushed and pinned, she has a little paint on her cheeks, and here is Mrs Mayhew, waiting for her at the bottom of the stairs. 'Yes, Mrs Mayhew,' says Miss Holland, brightly. 'Do we have business, so early?'

It seems they have.

'To begin,' Mrs Mayhew says.

An immense bunch of keys is lying before her on the kitchen table, of a size that might jangle from the belt of a Yeoman of the Tower. 'This,' Mrs Mayhew says, 'is for the first wine cellar, this for the second, and this for where we keep the coals and the wood for the fires inside the house.'

'Very good,' says Pris.

'This is the key for the bake-house. This one for the wash-house, the laundry. This with the ribbon on it, is for the game larder. This for the store for dry goods. This for the cold store.'

'We have a cold store?' Pris asks, faintly.

'Yes, Miss Holland. For the butter and dairy stuff.'

Key by key, the tour continues. The dining-room. The large closet. The small closet. The bedrooms for the boys. The master's room—

'Mrs Mayhew,' Pris asks, 'what is all this for?'

'Why,' says Mrs Mayhew, looking baffled. 'In case you should wish to take charge of them.'

'Lord, no!' says Pris. 'Keep 'em, please!'

The morning-robe of apple-blossom pink takes itself off to the solar. Old Henty enters, armed with a feather-duster. It is extraordinary how aggressively one can wield a feather-duster; Miss Pris exits the solar moments before it seems Old Henty would dust her from it for good. She considers returning upstairs and restoring her equilibrium in re-dressing her hair, but pox upon it, why should she be chased away? Has she not their master's blessing on her presence here? Yes, by God, she has. So instead, she takes herself out to the garden.

On the terrace, the boys are playing skittles in the sun. 'Good day to ye!' Pris calls out. James makes as if to reply, but his brother stops him: 'Demi-Cuit, it's your turn!'

She waits until the turn is complete. 'May I try?' she asks.

Ned stands there, tossing the ball from one hand to the other. 'It's not a game for three,' he says.

'Oh. I see. Very well.'

As she turns to go, she hears the patter of feet behind her. There is James. 'I like your hair,' he says, then his brother calls him back, and he is gone. 'Wait for *mmmee*!'

In the end she removes herself to sit by the fountain, and even here there is to be no peace. The squeaking of a wheel announces Abram, with a stick of something in his barrow, its roots all wrapped in sacking. Abram taps his hand to his head (Pris finds herself so discommoded, she almost taps hers in reply), then she hears the 'How bist?'

I have bist better, she thinks. 'What have you there?'

'She will be a tulip tree,' comes the reply. 'When she is grown.' He surveys the tulip tree, rubs an errant something from its trunk. 'We have waited a long whiles for her. I doubt there will be another like.'

The leaves of the tulip tree look far too big for it. The whole thing appears to be trembling with apprehension. Abram regards it with pride. 'She will go there,' he says, pointing to a spot at the edge of the grass beyond. 'She has come far on 'er travels, so we will leave 'er to accommodate herself a while. She will do well.'

'Do you think so, Abram?' says Pris, with a sigh.

'Yes, Miss Holland. I do believe she will.'

From the terrace, the sound of the boys in dispute. Then Mrs Mayhew attempting to adjudicate. The echo of the dogs.

Behind her, the squeak of the barrow being wheeled away.

Miss Holland squares her shoulders and marches back into the house.

SHILLY-SHALLY. ESSEX IS on the move – an attempt to leave the fever in his ranks behind him. He sets up headquarters at Thame, fifteen miles to the east, in a week of foul weather that ends in a hailstorm fierce enough to put holes in your tent, and waits for his troops to come up as best they can, but to what purpose? Still a mystery. Thor spies a couple of wagons, lost and lumbering in the lanes out from Reading, and Cantley launches a troop of his dragoons at them. The escort flees, and they dine that evening off a porridge of mutton – some poor woolly wanderer, baa'ed its last – and Parliamentary barley. Jack eats leaning against a tree, wondering how the flocks do in the fields round Varney. Or, without him, his sons. Or his mistress. He puts a hand to his breast, where it feels as if there is something tight. Behind him, Cantley's men, or some of them, are having a sing-along to end the day, the cheery little bastards. And here is Cantley. 'A good day's work, Captain!' Cantley calls out, as he picks his way to the edge of their vantage point.

'Your men are in fine voice this evening,' comments Jack.

'They are indeed!' Cantley too admires the view. 'They have been waiting for this, to be out in the field.'

'A shame that a plague of deafness has so afflicted Essex's troops,' says Jack. 'I'm sure they'd love to know as we were here.'

'Ah,' says Cantley, and goes back the way that he had come. A moment more, and the singing is silenced.

Will Essex regroup? Will he attack? Is he waiting for that convoy, carrying his pay? It is rumoured to be carrying as much as £20,000. 'Twenty thousand!' says Cantley. 'Why, gentlemen, that must match your loot from Prague!'

Zoltan and Jack exchange glances. 'For sure, Cantley,' says Zoltan, 'for sure.'

The talk amongst the pickets (who must pass the watch somehow) is that all Essex is waiting for is the chance to retreat to London. Where does this wisdom come from? Jack enquires.

Oxford, comes the answer. My Lord Digby. He has changed his tune.

'You made an enemy there, I think,' says Zoltan, as they ride along together in the rear of Cantley's men. M'sieu is chuntering bad-temperedly to himself about something or other – the indignity of riding rearguard, the offensive blue of the sky, the singing of the birds, who knows, but his rider would love to be able to do the same.

'And my Lord Digby,' Zoltan continues, 'is not by repute one to give up a grudge.'

'My Lord Digby,' says Jack, 'can buy a ticket and get in line.'

He has them keep to the high ground, which means they must go single file, which Cantley's men, being convivial sorts, seem not to care for. Also, Cantley's men are gentry – have they not been born knowing how to do this? What need they take instruction from this surly oddity, with the death's head on his coat? Then one of them spots a deer, and lets off a shot, and seems astonished that when he returns with the carcass behind his saddle, it is not to heartier congratulations from the scouts.

On they go. The deer-hunter's horse, it transpires, lost a shoe in the gallop. The Dead Men roll their eyes. Then he can walk, in Jack's view.

Cantley objects. They have other horses. That would be hardly fair.

Technically, these are Cantley's men, and Cantley the officer in charge. 'Cantley, if he were mine,' says Jack, 'I'd have him *carry* the fucking deer.'

Cantley departs. ''Tis a sad and sorry thing,' Zoltan comments, 'what became of Jack Fiskardo. How the man lost all his mirth.'

'I am outliving my enemies,' comes the reply. 'It makes a man sore-headed.'

'Sore-hearted, did you say?' Zoltan enquires, sweetly. 'Oh, I could have so much sport with this. My poor friend.'

'Go to hell,' says Jack.

They do not see Cantley again until evening. Then he jogs his way back to them. 'Gentlemen!' he announces. He is wildly excited. 'I believe we have something for you!'

Below them and beyond, a field, and at one edge of it, a line of reddish lights. The wind brings up to them the smell of smoke.

'There!' Cantley exclaims. He points with his sword. 'Essex's men!'

Luka is on Ulrik's shoulders, spyglass to his eye. They can all make out some small erratic movement in the field. '*Kaninen*,' Luka comments.

'What did he say?' Cantley asks. His men wait behind him, holding their horses, expectant, ready to go.

'He said, rabbits,' says Jack.

'What of it?'

'Cantley, ask yourself. If you were a rabbit, would you choose to make your supper in a field full of Essex's men?' He leads Cantley forward. 'See there. See how the lights don't move. What you are seeing, Cantley, are lengths of match, left burning, lodged between the stones of a wall to fool us.'

Murmurings of outrage behind them. What duplicity!

'Which suggests,' says Jack, 'that those who left the match will be gone the other way entirely. So let's go take a squinny that way, eh?'

*

Jack and Zoltan, once more on their bellies, Cantley beside them, smoking his pipe. If there were a triangle pointing south out of Oxford, this would be its apex, and there's something about the trackway now beneath them, hidden under its tent of summer leaves, has woken the whatever-it-is in Jack's head. He hears its low hum, like a tuning fork. If you were Essex, if you were to make a final lunge at Oxford, is not this hidden way exactly what you might make use of?

'I know these fields,' says Cantley. 'I used to play here as a boy.' He points again, this time with his pipe. 'That is Chalgrove village over there.'

The sun sets. Chalgrove's bats emerge and flit about their heads.

'Well,' says Cantley, pleasantly, 'I see nothing.'

'Give it a while, Cantley. Strange as it seems, sometimes you see more in the dark.'

'No,' says Cantley, 'gentlemen, I promise you. Lord Digby has the right of it. Essex has given up.' He gets to his feet, brushes off his breeches. 'I leave you to it.'

Wait and watch. 'At least,' says Zoltan, 'they no longer try to end the day with a sing-song.'

'I have been thinking,' says Jack, 'that I foresee no more gifts of orchid-plants. How Ava must curse my name.'

'Daily. I am here on the understanding that I will be restored to her, and lack of orchids will be the least of your worries if I am not.' A pause. 'I imagine,' Zoltan continues, 'that your Miss Holland will have made the same bargain in her head.'

A sigh. 'Does it get easier?'

'Not that I've noticed,' says Zoltan. 'We are men without women. Even St Paul thought that a poor idea. And he had never so much as met Pris Holland.'

There is a spider crawling over Jack's hand – a tiny thing, like a knot in a thread. He waits for it to complete its journey. 'Don't noise this abroad, Zoltan, but if Pris has it right, there is an old enemy of mine over here even now.'

It takes a moment. 'You don't mean it,' Zoltan says.

'You know what a war is, Zoltan, it draws in everything. Even better, apparently, he's serving with Ancrum.'

'God above,' says Zoltan. A pause. 'Why would I bother making sport, I have nothing to vie with that.' Then, 'Brother, are there fireflies here in England?'

There where the track lies beneath them, little bobbing trails of light, clear as Ariadne's thread.

'That is a great many men,' Zoltan comments as they watch the musketeers pass by, lit match looped over their shoulders. He cocks an ear. 'And that is the sound of harness. And that, a gun carriage, I believe.'

'Damnation,' says Jack. 'I suppose we have to do something about this.'

He finds Cantley sat outside his tent, downing a nightcap. 'Cantley,' says Jack, 'I am about to make you a hero.'

Cantley blinks at him. 'You are?'

'You are to ride back into Oxford, hell for leather, and fetch out the Prince Palatine and all the horse you can, and tell him Essex is ranging himself south of Oxford, and if the Prince gets himself here fast enough, he will catch our man on the hop and can force battle on him. We'll be waiting. Go!'

CHAPTER NINE

The Return of Molly Tubb

'There is witchcraft in fair words...'

Francis Marbury, *A Contract of Marriage between Wit and Wisdom*

'MRS ENDICOTT,' SAYS Pris. 'I am very glad to know you.'

'And I you, Miss Holland.'

'You must forgive me,' Pris continues, stepping carefully between the unbound books piled across the bookshop's floor, 'for not making a visit sooner, but Topham would not venture forth until it was known Essex had been dealt with, and it seems a woman can go nowhere these days without an escort, so I must wait –'

And must wait again. A company of infantry is crashing its way down Broad Street. A sergeant bellows out an order, those folk pressed back to let the solders pass break out in dutiful applause.

'– must wait on him,' Pris concludes. She looks about her. 'Mr Endicott is not here?'

'No,' says Belle. 'No, all the men of Broad Street are to give of their labour today, digging out fortifications. So it is us wives keep shop.' So it is in this new world. There are times when Belle wonders if all England wakes itself with the words *Pinch me. Is this real?* 'And you must forgive us that we are in such disorder.' Although to be honest, when is the bookshop not? 'We brought all our stock with us from London and have no place for storing anything. Although if we were not already such a squash, very like we would have men billeted upon us too.'

'No!' says Pris, opening her eyes up wide.

No woman would say that she was beautiful, thinks Belle. She is note-taking, for her next letter to her mother. *But in a very little while she does convince you that she is.*

'And the rooms upstairs so tiny, without we push the bed aside, you cannot open the door.' Belle nods toward her dog who, now Miss Holland has sat herself on one of those same piles of books, is resting her muzzle on Miss Holland's knee. 'I tell Dash, we must begin to charge her rent.'

Pris lays a gloved finger on Dash's nose. Dash's eyebrows rise. The glove is grey chammy, newly purchased, the knee, moss-green armazine, also on its first outing. 'We must all do our part,' Pris tells the dog.

'And the captain?'

'We had him back with us a week, he and his men. The stables full, the house likewise. Great maps all over the dining table. Ocker and Todd met a *pudel*, and were prevailed upon not to eat it; Ned got to fire a musket. He was in his seventh heaven. And then they were gone. Jack is grown so famed as a discoverer, he and his have all been sent down to the west to join Sir Ralph Hopton, I'm told, in hunting –'

Outside a bugle call, and then the racket of passing horsemen, the riders banging fist to breastplate. Clear the road!

'– hunting Waller's army.'

'He is most celebrated. After the battle at Chalgrove Field, particularly so,' Belle responds, politely.

'If you can call it that,' Miss Holland replies. 'Jack said one charge, and Essex's men were but dots on the horizon. All over in half of an hour. I, meanwhile, have a letter to go to London.' The letter is produced from within a matching green reticule. 'I'm told the Roebuck is where I must take it, for the mails.'

'It is your family you write to, I suppose, Miss Holland,' says Belle.

'My old nurse,' Pris replies. 'She is the only one who will be fretting for me. Oh, it is not a difference of politics,' she adds, seeing Belle's look of shock. 'My family have none. Although I dare say my uncle is doing splendid business kitting out the men of London's Trained Bands for Parliament, even as I sit here. No, what will have offended them is my – well, my directing of myself, you might say.' *And my ignoring of everything they would have me be.* 'And yours, Mrs Endicott? How do they do?'

'They are gone down to Sussex,' says Belle. 'My father is – he is – calmer there. The last months in London disordered him dreadfully. Nothing any of us said or did was right.'

'Families,' Pris says, with feeling.

'And how do the captain's boys?' Belle asks.

'They circle round me. Much like the captain's dogs. I think they are bemused. Supposedly James asked his father if he planned to grow a crest.'

'They are not—' Now it is Belle who is uncertain where to go from here. Not accustomed to their father keeping a mistress in his house? *I know you will say it is not fitting to receive her, Mother, but times have changed so.* 'I suppose they have only ever known Mrs Mayhew. Or Old Henty.'

'They are unlike to mistake me for either,' says Miss Holland, coolly. 'Do you have children? You and Mr Endicott?'

'Oh, no,' says Belle, at once, shaking her head. 'We did suppose – but with the world as it is – no, we do not.' Unconsciously her head droops. Miss Holland, watching, takes silent note. There is yet more bugling from the street. Something out there wishes to be acknowledged.

'But I am quite settled in my new routine,' Miss Holland says. 'Shall I tell you of it?'

Belle's head comes up. 'Indeed,' she responds, politely.

'So, I have my own bugle call, which is when Ocker and Todd are let out the kitchen, which gives me all of a minute to prepare to receive them. Now you,' says Pris, addressing Dash, 'I am sure you never jump upon a bed, do you? No, I can see you would not dream of it. Then it is downstairs, where Topham leads the house in prayers, and where it seems my presence is a must, so there I go. Then we breakfast, all of us, the boys and dogs as well – not at the same trough, you understand, but for the mess we make, it might be. Then Mrs Mayhew takes me to inspect the stores and larders, which is most kind of her, as she does it exactly as if she thinks I know anything of such at all. I believe she plans on teaching me to cook. Do you cook, Mrs Endicott?'

In the one room upstairs that does not have the bed in it, and in the one pot and pan the King's demand for iron has left her with. 'I do,' says Belle.

'It has been a revelation. Pastry, now. It goes in as wet leather – it comes out, it is flan!' Miss Holland throws her head back.

And she is the most carefree company you could ask for.

'Ah, when I think of my days in London – up at noon, an hour at least to dress – but you laugh, Mrs Endicott. That is unkind.'

'I do, Miss Holland. I think you intend it. An hour? Surely not.'

'An hour,' says Pris, holding up a finger for emphasis. 'And that would be for an undress day. Then perhaps a promenade, or a turn about the shops of Covent Garden—'

'Oh, I remember them!' Belle puts in. *And I take to her, Mother, I do indeed.*

'And then mayhap a play. I was most fond of plays. And to end, a hand of cards. Or two, if I am winning. Or three, if I am losing.'

'What do you play?' asks Belle.

'Oh, everything. All Fours, Lanterloo, Cul-bas, Bon Ace, Wit and Reason – do you play, Mrs Endicott?'

'We do. Rafe and I play many an evening here.'

'But then you must come and play cards at Varney! The boys speak of you so often, and I would relish the company, and if we can prevail upon Topham, we might make a four.'

'Miss Holland, I would be delighted,' says Belle. 'That would be most wonderfully kind.'

'And,' says Miss Holland, 'you must call me Pris.'

Is that yet more noise outside? Yes, it is, but now with *huzzahs* mixed in. Dash is whining at the door. 'What *is* happening out there?' Pris asks.

What is happening is the passage of a body of horses of the very grandest sort, high-stepping, harnesses a-jingle, and their riders all kitted out in yellow and scarlet. 'Oh,' says Belle, on tiptoe at the door, 'oh, it is the King's guard!' Next a row of halberdiers. The cheering is riotous. And now a man on a great while palfrey, red and gold cloth under his saddle, a sash of blue across his breast, and so upright that you hardly notice his smallness, or the sag beneath his eyes, or his melancholy air.

'Oh, that is brave!' says Belle. 'To let us see him! To show that all is well! Do you not think so?'

Brave, ponders Pris. She takes a prospect of the bodyguard, she takes a prospect of the halberdiers, she takes a prospect of the man on horseback. 'Yes,' she says, at last. There we are, that is our king. Both brave and – utterly ridiculous.

PRIS, RIDING UNDER Topham's careful eye, is returned to Varney. Her mount she has christened Annie – she of the wall-eye, she of the ear out of true; she who Topham would have sent to the knackers weeks ago, had Miss Holland not took such a shine to the beast. 'Good *girl*,' says Miss Holland, as Annie mumbles a carrot from her hand. 'You see, Topham? Never a jog, never a jig – I swear, one could fall asleep atop of Annie.' She re-enters the house, and the first person she sees is Old Henty, polishing the pier-glass. 'Where is everyone?' Pris asks.

'Master Ned is gone out with Toby,' comes the grudging reply. 'Fishing or shooting or some such, I'm sure as I don't know.'

'And the rest, goodwife?' Pris enquires.

'Mrs Mayhew, she is in the laundry. And Master James, he be in there.' There being the library. 'With the books.'

'Thank'ee,' says Pris, drawing off her gloves. She feels

pleasantly buoyant. There, the letter to Abi is on its way, Miss Pris's survival and her new situation declared; she has made herself a friend; she has been but yards away from royalty. And royalty not listening at doors this time, either. She walks up behind Old Henty and puts her arms round Henty's waist. 'Old woman, you will learn to love me one day, you know you will.'

In the library, James is sat upon the floor, an enormous book open before him. Pris fears for its binding, but of course, the floor is one place always available to James when so many others are not.

He looks a little wan.

'So this is where you hide yourself, is it?' Pris asks. 'What is your book?'

James turns to the title page. The book is such a size, it takes the fullest extent of his left arm to do so, right hand as ever nestled under his chin. Pris reads:

The History of the World.
Commonly called
The Natural History of C. Plinius Secundus

'Pliny?' She smiles. 'You're reading Pliny?'

The left hand points to a bottom shelf, where stands another volume, twin to this. They are almost as tall as James himself. 'I can *p*ppull,' James tells her, miming how he extracted it. He indicates the shelves of other books, row upon row of them, brown leather, red Morocco, vellum white. 'I can't reach those, so I read this.'

Well now. 'Go on then,' says Pris, sitting down beside him. 'Read to me.'

The pages are turned just as carefully as before. 'Of Peacocks,' James announces, and continues, 'The *p*ppeacock far sup – surpasses – all the rest in this kind—'

He stops. He sees how Pris is staring at him. 'No, go on,' she says.

'For beauty, but prin – prin—'

'Principally,' Pris tells him. 'It means of the mostest.'

'*Principally* for the glory he taketh in himself.' A pause. 'Ours do that,' he tells her, seriously as before. 'I like this book because it's true.'

'*James.*' She is astounded. 'Who taught you to read?'

He looks puzzled. 'Your father can scarce scratch out his name,' Pris says. 'And you had no mama to help you. So who taught you?'

He makes a little face. It's as if he's unsure whether he has done wrong here, or whether this is something to glory in, like the peacock. 'Mrs Mayhew showed me my *n*nname,' he says. 'And some of the letters say themselves.' He rounds his mouth like a fish. 'Oh,' he says. 'Oh, oh, oh. Ssssss.' A finger snaked down the page. 'The rest I worked out.'

'Well,' says Pris, sitting back. 'When your father returns, we will show him. He will be very proud, I'm sure.'

Another page turned. James still seems a little flat in his spirits, despite her praise. 'My *m*ama died,' he says.

'I know,' says Pris.

'I was only just born and she died.' A sigh.

Pris is unused to children taking her into their confidence. A novel sensation in her breast. 'So did mine,' she tells him.

His small smile. The two of us, is what the smile says. Both singled out. 'I miss Dada.'

'So do I,' says Pris.

He peeks up at her. Those pale and candid eyes; they might *be* his father's. Then he leans toward her, and his head makes contact with her sleeve. It's what Helen of Troy used to do; it's like being bumped by a cat. An indulgent surge of fondness possesses her.

It comes to her that the forehead against her arm is rather warm. She puts her hand to it. Says James, mournfully, 'My *legs* hurt.'

Here he lies, curled up in bed; Pris looking down at him from one side and Mrs Mayhew from the other. There is a special helplessness in the speed with which illness can reduce a child. Mrs Mayhew is wringing her hands. 'I have been so in dread of this,' she says.

'This has happened before?'

'Too many times. In another child you would say it was growing pains, but with Master James—' Mrs Mayhew makes to tuck the cover more closely round James's shoulders. A plaintive little bleat: 'Stop *fussing* me.' Those pale blue eyes so hectically bright, they sparkle like gems.

'What do you do?'

'His father would consult with a physician in London. He sent powders down to us, for Master James –'

That is hardly available to us, is it? thinks Pris.

'– and I would make a draught of coltsfoot. And French balsam. Or a purge—'

'I think most definitely *not* a purge,' says Pris. 'But a draught, by all means. Let me sit with him.'

Mrs Mayhew departs. Pris waits, to be sure Mrs Mayhew is gone all the way downstairs, then she nudges herself onto the bed. Lifts up James's hot little body to sit cradled against her. 'Master James,' Pris says, softly.

His eyelids flutter. She lays her hand on his forehead, as gently as she can.

It's like putting your hand to the lid of a pot on the fire. Everything seething. Everything in James, pushing against everything else. A human London Bridge. 'Oh, little one,' says Pris.

'I think quite enough of this, eh?' She lays her cheek to his hair. 'You tell me what goes on in there, and we will make it better.'

If you were to ask James what goes on in there, he would say it feels as if there are rough ropes within his legs, all pulling in different directions. He would say it feels as if he is creaking inside. That his head is full of bad dreams, of some sharp-beaked bird pecking at him. He would say it makes him hate himself when he is like this. He would say he dreams there is a window that he cannot open, because his hand doesn't work, but strangely this time he can, and the bird flies out of it and away, and the ropes go slack, and Pris has brought his favourite book from the library, and he is leaning against her as they read it together, and here is Ned at his bedroom door, and all the pains and the pecking and the pulling have gone away. 'Hello,' James says, brightly. 'Was it good fishing, Ned?'

It was – roach, and a single brown trout – but his splendid catch is no longer uppermost in Ned's mind. He steps cautiously into the room. 'Mrs Mayhew said you had a fever.' He is baffled to see his brother sitting so in bed, with Pris beside him, and with the book from the library on his brother's lap.

'I did,' James agrees. 'I *think* I did.' He rubs his hand across his head. 'It's gone now.'

'But they never pass off as fast as that.' Ned comes a little closer. A glance at Pris, as if for explanation. 'Last time, he was in bed a week and more.'

'I have no doubt it was the excellence of Mrs Mayhew's draught,' says Pris, confidently. 'Or, if these are growing pains, mayhap James is outgrowing them. Wouldn't that be a happy thing?'

You would not say Ned looks convinced. But when they sit at supper, and Mrs Mayhew makes to put the brown trout on his plate, Ned stops her. 'No,' he says. 'That one for Pris.'

*

When she looks in on James again, he seems to be asleep. But when she goes to move the book from the bed, a hand emerges from under the covers, and holds her fingers, and a small voice asks, 'Will you stay?'

Very well, Pris tells herself, *a moment.* She tucks herself back in against him, and now James does sleep, the way small children do, into some other world entirely and at once. How extraordinary to be so trusted. Another new sensation for Miss Holland. Then the door creaks open and there is Henty.

Who comes up to the bed, just as if Pris were not there at all, and inspects its sleeping occupant.

'I know you love him,' Pris says, quietly.

Old Henty mumps at her, as if chewing on a thought. 'I had a little 'un, once,' Henty says. 'He did not last long.' A nod down at James. 'Is he better, then?'

'Let us hope,' says Pris.

Henty lifts her eyes to look at Pris directly. 'I know what you are,' she says.

'That so?' Pris answers. Those of us who know Pris might be surprised at the calmness of her tone, but perhaps this is not the first time she has heard such a claim.

'They –' (one knotted old hand, the veins like roots, lifted in dismissal of the rest of the house) '– they's too young to remember, but I know what you are. Used to come through here in the old Queen's time, your people. They with their ponies and their ways.'

'If that's so, old lady,' says Pris, in the same even tone as before, 'you will know women such as I are not to be trifled with.'

'No,' says Henty. 'But I know what you are, and you remember that, missy, you remember that I do.' And she goes out, pulling the door closed behind her.

A stirring in the bed, like an animal making its way from its burrow. There is James, blinking up at her. 'Why did she say that?' he asks.

'Because people are very foolish,' says Pris, smoothly. 'Because if you have one thing different about you, they think every other thing must be different too.'

'Like your hair,' James offers.

'Like my hair.'

'They do that with me too,' says James, with a sigh. 'They see my arm and my leg, and they think my head must not work either, and that all of me is only half-cooked.'

'Children used to call me names as well,' Pris tells him.

His eyes are wide. 'What did they call you?'

She leans toward him, smiling, finger to her lips. 'They used to call me a witch.'

ABEL PLUMSTEAD THE First won the route from Oxford to London in a card game, so the story goes, back in those same glorious years under the old Queen, and Plumsteads the Second, Third and Fourth have been rolling carts and wagons up and down it ever since. Plumstead the Fourth knows the route so well he could drive it in his sleep – the muddy bottoms where you stick, the lonely heaths you do not want to cross at night, the inns where they change the horses the speediest, those that accommodate an honest man in other ways. The roadside kitchens should you need a bite to keep you going, the blacksmiths, the saddlers, the wheelwrights should you (God forbid) come a cropper that way. But at least a man no longer has to fret about running into Essex's troops, may God be thanked. 'Here we are, lass, here you be!' Plumstead announces to his passenger, pulling his cart to a stop. 'Varney.'

'This 'ere?' she says. His passenger sounds amazed.

'This here.'

His passenger gets herself down from her seat, ignoring Plumstead's wince as she uses the spokes of his wheel as a ladder. Dusts off her palms, smooths her hands down her skirt, tucks her back hair up into her cap. Reties the neckerchief over her breast. Looks at the house again, hands on her hips.

'Well, shitten-cum-shite!' Molly declares.

Toby Dearlove is outside the kitchen door with the dogs when the girl comes striding toward him. Ocker and Todd back up, ears flat, growling. 'Shurrup!' the girl yells at them, and when Ocker edges closer, follows this up with a 'Gerroutofit!' Her voice has all the shrill aggression of a wren. She sees Toby and calls out, 'You! I'm in search of my mistress.' She rebalances the mighty bundle in her arms. 'This is hers.'

Toby is too astounded to move.

'I 'ave been in search of her for days,' the girl declares, 'an' she will be mighty glad to have me back I kin tell *you*. So is she here?' What Molly will do if Miss Pris is not here she cannot think – sit down and weep, she imagines, and perhaps there is some likelihood of tears already in the shrillness of her voice for now the lad comes forward, one hand hidden in his weskit. 'Me name is Tubb,' Molly says. 'Molly Tubb, an' I am Mam'selle 'Ollands's maid.'

'Do you follow me then,' the lad says, and ushers Molly before him, in a manner that makes Molly think at once the hidden hand has summat wrong with it, and it seems one of the lad's eyes is not seeing her properly either. 'Shall I help with that?' he asks, indicating the bundle. The hidden hand must be produced to take it. Molly looks at the hand askance – that's all Miss Holland's pretties in there, that is – but she has carried the bundle so very far, and her arms are so very tired. 'Thank'ee,' says Moll, handing it over. 'Go on, then. Lead the way.'

Oh, it's a big house. It is *such* a big house. The passage twists and turns. They pass some old tabby in a pantry, inspecting a rack of game, and she gives Moll a sideways look as Moll and the lad go by the door, so Moll gives her the same right back. Now the kitchen proper, and two boys in there at table, and a woman standing over them as they eat, as if they have had to be summoned in to their nuncheon. The boys – one big, one small (something a bit skew-whiff about him too, if Molly is any judge) – stare at her open-mouthed. 'Eat up!' Moll tells them. Another door, backed with green baize. The lad must grapple the bundle to him to open it. He sees her peering at the hand – the thick scarred edge, the finger-stumps. 'What 'appened to you?' Molly asks.

Toby is so astonished even his bad eye reacts. 'Troopers,' he says. 'Parliament's men.'

'Gerraway.' Molly is impressed. 'You're a brave one, int'cha?'

A light blush creeps up Toby's neck. ''Tis an ugly thing,' he says, 'I know it.'

'Oh, I've seen worse,' Molly assures him. 'I saw Lord Strafford get 'is 'ed cut off on Tower Hill. After 'e buggered it all up with the Scots. An' you know what? His blood weren't blue at all!'

'It weren't?' Toby is pushing the door wide with his shoulders.

'Not a drop of it,' says Molly, cheerily, then looking into the black and white tiled space beyond gives a cry. 'Oh, miss!' Molly squeals, running forward. There is her mistress at last, and an old man in gaiters with a great pot full of lilies, pushing it forward on rollers across the floor, and a man and woman, stood off to the side, who are a smart-enough couple, for sure, but nothing compared to her mistress, who stands there like a queen – the gleam of her gown! The froth of her lace! 'Oh, miss, I've found you!'

Oh, this is better. This is so much better. Now it is Molly sat on a chair, and everyone is standing about her and marvelling. 'Molly, this is a miracle!' her mistress is saying. 'How did you ever find me?'

'Ho, that was easy,' Molly declares. 'I get me into Oxford, and first thing I see is Unthanks. So I go in there, even though the hoity bitch behind the counter tried to rush me out –'

Moll has a glass of perry in her hand. She takes a good big sip, at the memory.

'– an' I arst 'em, did they have any clients as was flame-haired wonders, and they said what was it to me, and I said, if you 'ave, that lady is my mistress and we was split apart by the war an' I have come miles in search of 'er and where is she if you please an' you will be well rewarded, an' they said *Varney*.' Moll knocks back the rest of her glass. 'Varney, they said, out on the Woodstock road.' She looks round, beaming. 'An' they was right!'

The housekeeper, this Mrs Mayhew, refills the glass. 'But Moll,' her mistress is saying. 'Goodwins to Oxford! How did you do it?'

'Oh *that*,' says Molly. 'So my Lord Wyncanton, he comes back to the house in a proper lather, saying as how Ancrum was all sorts of an ass and how could 'e not have known the King's men was about, and I said, but where is my mistress? And he said as you was lost in the tussle, and he did not know if you were living or dead.' And Moll sees the young woman grip her husband's arm at that. 'He was so shook, miss, he was weepy! And next day Colonel Ancrum came by, and said how you had been carried away into Oxford by the cavaliers, and my Lord Wyncanton told him not to show his face again, and how there would be no more coming from him for Ancrum, who was a knave and a picaroon. And all my Lord Wyncanton's people wailing how King Charles's men would be sure to come and burn down the house about our ears.'

'Oh, what a thing to say!' the young woman exclaims. Which is kindly of her, Molly thinks – bit soft, for everyone knows what soldiers are and what they do, but kindly of her, all the same.

'And then we had news of the battle, and how Essex was gone running back to London, and my Lord Wyncanton said as he would close the house and do the same, and I must suit myself if I go back with him or no, as he had more than me to worry about, and I was to hell with that.' Here Molly puts an expression of furious outrage on her face. 'What, leave? With not a notion how you might be faring? Not I!'

'Well said!' declares the husband. Moll feels herself warming to the pair of them.

'So I packed up me bundle, and I waited till it was early-early, and I snuck to the gatehouse at Goodwins, and begged the man, would he put me on his nag and take me as far as he could, and I would give him the red gloves in payment. Them with the gold lace. I'm sorry, Miss Pris, but I had to give him something. And he got me to Thame, but he would go no closer, he said, so then I had to walk. Oh, miss, you should see my blisters!' says Molly, leaning forward to ease a shoe. 'But that got me to Oxford. And then outside Unthanks, there was Plumstead, and I asked him did he know a Varney, and he did, and he said he would take me there for no more'n a kiss, the randy old bugger, so here I am.' She sits back. Her glass is empty.

'Good God,' says the husband. 'Belle, what do you say? Why, it is like the wanderings of the tribes of Egypt!'

'Molly,' says Miss Pris, 'I swear, there is not another girl in all of London would have attempted that. Let alone brought it off.'

Molly is beaming. 'I was not about to leave your dresses and your doings with the scarecrows. But can I stay here, miss? Can I stay with you?'

They make up a bed for Molly in the dressing-room, and Moll sits down on it and kicks off her shoes, and looks around at the gowns hung off the wall, and the petticoats spilling out of the cupboard so's you might hardly close its door, and the table of knick-knacks and ribbons beside the looking-glass, and says, 'Lord, Miss Pris! Did you ever land on your feet!'

'Oh, life here has its moments, Moll, trust me on that.' Pris sits herself down beside her maid. 'Moll, when Ancrum came to Goodwins, did he have any other with him?'

'Any other?'

'A Captain Fantom. Another out of Germany. A man with a burned face.'

'No, miss,' says Moll. 'No, there was no-one.'

Thinks Pris, *I wonder why.*

THIS IS WHY.

In the uncertain light of early dawn, a party of horsemen has arrived in a lane outside the town of Thame, and halted at what looks as if it is, or was, a pound for stray animals. It is now a lock-up for stray soldiery, and to prove it, it has a sergeant waiting with his keys at the door. There are four horsemen in the party, one of whom is in that awkward, bent-over shape of a man with his hands tied to the pommel of his saddle. The horseman in the lead dismounts and marches up to the sergeant. The two others pull the prisoner unceremoniously from his saddle. A glum-faced servant follows on foot.

A conversation now takes place outside the door of the lock-up. 'Ancrum,' the lead horseman declares, holding out his hand. 'Colonel Ancrum. Sir William Waller's Horse.' It is immediately apparent that he is in a fume of fury. Were the morning even a little less clement, he would be steaming with it, just as the fields do all about, shedding their blanket of dew.

'I have been ill-served before,' says Ancrum, all a-blaze. 'I have had men who proved themselves unworthy, but never such a one as this. He is of the devil. Ravishment, sergeant, rapine. He will not escape his punishment, for all he claims invulnerability. There will be no mercy, I swear it.'

The sergeant looks over to the prisoner, who is an ill-favoured fellow, for sure – the damage to his face of an ancient burn, by the looks of it, and of course much roughed-up during his captivity, but what can you expect? 'Hell is empty, all the devils here,' the sergeant comments unexpectedly, in a world-weary tone. If you can read and write, there are roles the army of Parliament will slot you into at once; sergeant on the staff of the provost-major, the keeper of military discipline, that is one.

Ancrum gives the speaker a suspicious glance. 'He will be taken to Aylesbury,' Ancrum says. 'I would have the man hung here and now, if I could, but I must hie me to the west. Give me your name, sir. You will see me again.'

'Lodowick,' says the weary sergeant. 'Lodowick Alembert.'

CHAPTER TEN

Runaway Down

'And so they marched, with scouts out before…'

Sir Ralph Hopton's Narrative of his Campaign in the West

'WILLIAM WALLER,' SAYS Sir Jacob. 'He and Ralph Hopton both served Prince Rupert's mother, once upon a time. Now Sir William fights for Parliament, and is our enemy.' He has to raise his voice; a summer squall is sweeping overhead and the rain drums on the canvas of his tent like the fingers of impatient men. Men eager to do battle, perhaps. In which case the rain must also be a supporter of Parliament, as the news of Sir

Ralph Hopton's forces is not good. Bested outside Bath. More than a thousand of his cavalry fled, some of them as far as Oxford. And Sir Ralph himself, blown from his horse by the detonation of a powder wagon, and carried into Devizes with his hair melted on his head and with his buttocks cooked like meat. 'This war,' says Sir Jacob, 'this war delights in mischief, does it not?'

Sir Jacob's tent is such as one might hold conferences in. The table set up within it could seat twenty, but all it seats at present are Sir Jacob, and that esteemed discoverer Jack Fiskardo. The Dead Men wait outside, hats pulled low against the rain. Somewhere further off, M'sieu can be heard shouting his displeasure at this halt. Luka is his hapless groom; Jack calculates they have maybe five minutes more before M'sieu also arrives in Sir Jacob's tent, dragging Luka with him.

Sir Jacob is on his way to Gloucester. 'And I would take you with me if I could, Fiskardo, but Hopton's need of discoverers is greater even than mine.'

'I understand Waller has a fine eye in choosing ground,' says Jack.

'He does. Could not be less like to Essex if he tried.'

'And five thousand men with him.'

Behind the curtain dividing Sir Jacob's living quarters from his conference room, his servant can be heard preparing Sir Jacob's breakfast. There is a smell of butter, the sizzle of frying meat.

'So it is said. Our intelligence has failed us there. Waller is coming out from Bath, we know that much, so must assume he intends finishing the job. Where, how and when – discovering that, that is yours. At the Prince's particular request, may I say. His brother, young Maurice, is with Hopton.'

'He does me honour,' says Jack.

'Ye-e-es,' says Sir Jacob. 'His Highness also requested I enquire as to the health of Miss Holland. "How does the lady?" were his words. "I would be remembered to her in particular."'

HE'S A LIKING for high ground, has Waller. There's an immense great hill above Devizes, and there Waller ranges himself, looking down on Hopton's troops immured within the town – they, with their stores of ammunition reduced to almost naught, with Hopton still blinded, still having to be carried about. Rupert's younger brother, Maurice, has an idea that he will race back to Oxford overnight, and return with reinforcements. Forty-four miles one way, forty-four miles back. 'You vill guide us out, Fiskardo,' he says to Jack. 'Guide us 'ence, and vait for us, for our signal, on our return.'

He has the look of a second stamping, does Maurice. Not quite so tall as his brother, nor quite so beau, and an accent like a hand smacking a tabletop. Softer in the face, pouchier about the eye – you can see the Stuart in him. But plainly, every bit as much the hothead.

There are skirmishers from Waller's troops continually about Devizes' walls. Possibly the only thing stopping Waller from overrunning the town right now is the fact that Hopton is his one-time brother-in-arms, from their years serving Rupert and Maurice's mother, Bohemia's unhappy queen. *God save us*, thinks Jack. The war in Germany, stretching its fingers out to reach us here.

Waller delivers terms for the town's surrender. Hopton, scalp covered in blackened stumps of hair, like stooks in a burned cornfield, begs for time to consider them. His men go round the town knocking on doors, demanding the strings of bed-curtains

– they may be down to two barrels of black powder, but they have no match-cord whatsoever. Curtain-string, boiled up in resin, will have to do in its place. *This*, thinks Jack, *is as desperate as men can get.* Sweeping a bow to Maurice, he says, 'Highness, we must wait till midnight. We'll take you out then.'

Midnight? Why can they not go now?

'Because you will need that time at the blacksmith's. Hind legs of every horse, get 'em reshod with the shoes facing backwards. And anything and everything on their harness as might make a sound – bind it up, or get rid of it.'

Midnight. Maurice's company of horse depart the town in eerie silence, leaving a trail so cunningly contradictory it would fool Argus himself. One quarter mile out, their guide brings them to a stop, while his men scout forward. 'Why do we halt?' Maurice demands.

'We need to find a sheep.'

A *sheep*?

'Highness, we need to get you and your men around that hill, and up, to put you on the road to Oxford. Waller will have his scouts on every path and every lane out of here. If we try to make our own way up that slope, the horses will slide, they will stumble, and they will be heard. We need a sheep-track, and for that we need a sheep.'

The hoot of an owl from up ahead, long, steady, strident: *Hoo, hoo, hoo.* Great grey owls are rare in England, but in the high north of Sweden, you hear them all the time. 'There,' says Jack. 'We have one.'

Roused from her slumbers, a Wiltshire ewe. There she goes, around the flank of Devizes' mighty hill, the Gemini encouraging her along, and an entire company of horse following as quietly as they can in her wake. They breast the hill. They find the road. The lights of Waller's camp diminish behind them.

Says Jack to Kazimir, 'I'm loaning you two to the Prince. Oxford has to furnish us another army.'

'An army, Domini? When the owl's tail blooms, it will.'

You have to ask yourself, do they spend their nights dreaming these up?

'Then he brings us back whatever he can. And you bring us word.'

Sunrise. Maurice and his men disappear toward Oxford at a gallop; Jack leads his back around the far side of the hill.

What is this hill even called? Roundway, say some; Bagdon, say others. Fringed with trees and dotted with tumuli across its windblown top. The Dead Men use one such as forward cover. 'Who made these?' Jack hears Per ask, wonderingly.

'Soldiers,' Jens tells him, 'soldiers like to us, you can be sure of that.' Jens is atop the barrow with the spyglass, belly flat to the turf. With his free arm, he points – the far horizon, the fields and woods, and Devizes itself, small as a toy. 'Look at the range you'd get from here!'

They are high enough for it to feel as if they have all England laid out beneath them, while Waller's lines are close enough, through the spyglass, to watch the doings of individual figures, catch tags of conversation. Dislodging Waller from up here will be like picking out a tick.

M'sieu, back amongst the trees, has his lips flexed, teeth bared. Plainly, they are close enough for him to smell Waller's horse as well. 'Don't you dare,' Jack tells him, seeing how M'sieu is readying himself to shout a challenge.

'Should'a loaned him to Maurice for the gallop to Oxford,' says Luka, pointedly.

'His brother would already take my mistress. Be damned if they will have my horse as well.'

As the day progresses, a group of Waller's men can be seen manoeuvring a gun out from camp and along the rise overlooking the town. The piece looks to be a culverin, an artillery elephant – as heavy, as disobliging, but long barrelled and that barrel reinforced. It takes the gun crew all day to heave and drag it into position. Their target would seem to be St John's Church, a good two miles beyond and below them, in Devizes itself, storage for Hopton's precious remaining powder and his new-made match. A culverin can throw a ball two miles with ease; three, if its crew is skilled enough; but not today. Now they have their mighty gun in place, ready for the morrow, this crew is interested only in lighting their pipes and settling down to whatever Waller provides his men with in the way of supper. Which creates an opportunity, let us say. And what do you do with opportunity?

Grab it by the balls.

The culverin has sandbags under its barrel and chocks under its wheels. The Dead Men wait till night has fallen, strip off their linen shirts, blacken themselves with mud and crawl along the skirt of the hill. They hear the gun crew talking, they see them light their pipes; with infinite care they ease the chocks sideways until they are almost out from under the wheels, stab the bottom two sandbags, let the sand trickle down the slope. Then they crawl back to their hiding place behind that same barrow, housing at least one of those warriors from centuries ago.

Come dawn, the gun crew stretches and yawns, and feeds its fire, and can be seen peering out over the early morning mist, so prettily tinted by the sunrise. Devizes is hidden from their sight, but the tower of St John's rises from the mist, its weathercock a-shine. The gun crew load their gun. They touch their match to its firing-hole. The culverin fires, rocks back, rocks forward, the sandbags topple, the chocks give way, and the piece goes rolling forward down the slope.

And keeps rolling, the cries of dismay of the gun crew echoing above it. It gathers speed. It bowls end over end. It disappears into the mist. They can still hear it falling, the noise of the wheels as they fly into pieces, the bell-like tolling of the barrel as it turns and rolls and somersaults down the slope, on and on and on. Who knew that it would fall so far?

'This hill,' says Zoltan, thoughtfully, 'must be a damn sight steeper at the bottom than it would appear from the top.'

'Perhaps,' Jack suggests, 'we should investigate?'

The day wears on. They eke out water, food; they watch and wait. They play at spying creatures in the clouds: a dragon, a galleon, a cat. Some paunchy Hercules, wearing a three-cornered hat. That's you, they tell Ulrik. They hear the complaints of cattle being driven off by Waller's men. The sun is at its zenith, yet there is that grey owl again.

Kazimir and Konstantin join them behind the barrow. They are breathless, their horses a-foam with sweat. Where is Maurice?

'Ten miles behind us, Domini. Coming on fast.'

And with him?

'Three brigades. All horse.' Konstantin lifts his palms. 'It is all Oxford had.'

So, two thousand against five. Christ all-bloody mighty.

All battles are the same, more or less. The cavalry come on at a smart trot (hopefully not at the gallop of a tally-ho), get within range, fire their pistols, draw swords, close with steel. The foot come on at a steady march, close up their ranks if their fellows fall, break into a run only if their nerve cracks. Go to it hand to hand.

Not at Roundway Down. They have no foot, to begin with. Hopton's infantry sits tight down in Devizes, despite Maurice firing a cannon to announce his return, and despite that being loud enough to have Waller send all his troops swarming into position on the hill – his horse, his foot, his guns; every man he has. This is the point where all of it feels impossible, as it always does before every battle, watching the other side come into order, into shape, the ranks filling, staring into the lines of those men staring back at you. What a ridiculous way to spend your days, Jack finds himself thinking. What an even more ridiculous way to end them.

A nudge from Thor, at his side. 'Lobsters, Domini.'

Waller's heavy cavalry, armoured top to toe, coming into ponderous position on the right, blocking Waller's artillery and, come to that, his foot. That can't be wise, surely?

Skirmishers dart across the open space between the two armies, like insects over a pond. A herald riding hell for leather across the front of Maurice's lines. The rattle of shot. The man stands up in his stirrups, he waves his hat. His reedy cry reaches them. 'Fiskardo!'

Here we go. 'Were you ever in a cavalry charge?' Jack asks, and the Dead Men, behind him, look one to another and shake their heads.

'I think this will be your chance.' He puts his hand around the silver wolf. *If I forget thee, do not thou forget me…* 'Keep close. Like fish. In a shoal.'

The herald turns his horse about. The Dead Men thunder out from behind the barrow, in his wake. There is an unlikely cheer from the royalist lines as they emerge – our discoverers, there all along! They come up to Maurice, encircled by his bodyguard, and his horse paddling about like it would go all ways at once. *They know, these creatures*, thinks Jack. Cavalry horses, they smell the action, they know when it is coming. 'Fiskardo,' Maurice shouts. 'How is our ground?'

'Not as it appears.' He hands Maurice the spyglass. 'Do you see the rise, on the right, behind Waller's lines?'

'I see it!' Maurice exclaims, spyglass to his eye.

'It looks as if it slopes down gently, after. It does not. We spied it out. It shelves away to nothing, like a cliff.'

'And Waller does not know this?'

'I think that he cannot. He may have twice our numbers, but he has no way to move.'

'*Ach tzo*...' Maurice closes the spyglass. 'Your men. Into line, you ride with me.'

Knew it.

All the accounts of Roundway Down (and there will be many) will speak of the charge across the plateau. Some will speak of how Waller's foot stood there, baffled, unable to fire for fear of hitting his cavalry. How four of his guns fell into Maurice's hands almost at once. How there was a second charge. How Hopton's foot finally came out of Devizes, and watched in amazement as the action of the fight swept across the top of the hill from east to west, and carried on up that gentle rise and then how Waller's horse and his foot cascaded over those great slopes and gullies down the hill's western side, only that would be absurd, for what man could run himself or his horse down that?

No man ever gives the same account of a battle as the next. Jack's own would start with the heat building in the air, the heat and the nerves too. Then seemingly from nowhere, just as they had all begun to wonder why nothing was happening, a drumbeat, and the flourish of sword-blades ahead. And then the surge forward, one solid line, rising like a swell, and after that, nothing but instinct, instinct and noise: the crack of shot, the deeper noise of carbines, deeper yet, of cannon. Everything else – the sound of hooves, of horses, of men – filtered away. Even on horseback, somehow it was still hand to hand; you were as like to push a man from the saddle as fight him out of it; although by God he knew he must have done that too, because he felt the warmth, the spatter of blood across his face and neck and knew it was not his. The world divided – this, up here, in the saddle; that, down there, below them, ground level, like the damned in hell. The Gemini were not ten foot from him at one point and Jack could hardly see them for the press of men, of rearing horses, all about. It was as if the cavalry was a swinging scythe, and the carnage they left behind them, a harvest. He was using his pistol like a club, his sword like an axe; in his memory this lasted only moments but it must have been longer, far longer, they had to fight the whole length of the spine of the hill – surge forward, take the ground, surge forward again. He remembers the taste of M'sieu's reins between his teeth; he remembers M'sieu rearing up, dancing on his hind legs, overtopping everything about him; he remembers his horse screaming into the face of one of Waller's men and the man falling from his saddle, going down among the damned, as if the scream itself had been enough to do it, and then the movement of the field seemed somehow to tilt, to twist, and there were the Gemini again, Kazimir standing in his stirrups, Konstantin pointing, 'Domini! Ancrum!'

He presses in with his heels, M'sieu leaps forward. Ancrum has lost his hat, or his helmet, there is that white head of hair. He spies Jens and Per, battling toward him; is it Luka behind them? Too short in the saddle to see. He hauls M'sieu up, has him rear, for no-one can miss M'sieu. He shouts, 'To me! To me!' and sends M'sieu forward again, full tilt. Ancrum has thirty yards on him. Twenty. Less. Ancrum wheels about, pistol in his hand, shoots wildly – the only thing that will have brought down is a bird in the sky. He sees Per levelling his own shot, a good shot, sees it strike and *nothing*. Ancrum is wearing mail over his arms as well as back and breastplate, Ancrum is become a bloody lobster. 'Take him,' he tells M'sieu. Hunkers down. 'Take him, that one there.' M'sieu bounds forward like a ball exiting a cannon.

And Ancrum hears them. Ancrum turns about, gawps, begins beating his own horse over the head with his gloves. There are men and horses in headlong flight all about him. Closer, closer – Jack hears himself yell, 'Ancrum, take quarter!' Ancrum puts his head down.

'Take quarter, man!' They are almost neck and neck. Ancrum, sword in hand, makes a stab at M'sieu; Jack pulls M'sieu back, and it is probably the one thing that saves his life, for as he does so he hears Luka's earthquake bellow, 'Domini! *Sluta! Sluta!*' Stop!

There is a sort of tumbling going on ahead. There is a break in the line of men. Of horses too. The outline of the hill comes back into his head, the rise and then the drop to that western slope, the edge, the depth of those gullies beneath —

He hauls M'sieu's head around. A horse thunders past behind them, straight over. A man runs past – the same. M'sieu is rotating on his hind legs, but as he circles that edge is coming closer and closer, and there are more and more going over, some in silent disbelief, some screaming as the ground disappears before them. All he can think is to throw himself from M'sieu's saddle and become his horse's brakes, so he does, and his leg gives way instantly, and he is on his back, skidding across the ground, M'sieu's reins tangled round his wrist, his horse's hooves in and out across his vision. There is a cacophony of shouting behind him and then he sees the corner of the rock sticking up out of the turf, feels it scrape across under his shoulder, the inevitable bang into the back of his skull, and then—

A tapping at his cheek. 'Domini!' He feels himself being pulled from the ground by his shirt. '*Domini!*' An almighty slap across the face. 'DOMINI!'

They are crouched around him. There are fireworks going off in his head. Where is M'sieu, where is M'sieu—

'I have him, Domini,' says Ulrik, kneeling down, and then his horse is nuzzling him like an enthusiastic dog.

'You stopped him?' Jesus, every word, another firework. 'How did you stop him?'

'Same as you, Domini, only I am meat, not string like you. I weigh enough for that to work.'

They sit him up. The world swirls about him. There is noise – he had thought it was inside his head, but it's not. It's like a man – men – articulating fury, outrage, horror, only far, far off, made somehow even more horrible by being so small, for what can it sound like close to, and what is it? What is it?

'Down there, Domini,' says Jens, pointing, over the lip of the hill. His face is blenched of all colour, here in the bright summer sun. 'It is all from down there.'

They make their way down the hill along the sheep tracks. Their descent is punctuated by those screams – on, on, on, and then a shot, and a moment's peace, and then there is more screaming and another shot, endlessly so. They come down to the bottom of the hill and the first thing Jack sees is a woman, a matron, must have come out from Devizes, a well-dressed woman, yet sat upon the ground like a beggar, speechless, and with her hands to her cheeks. Now a trooper, sword yet drawn, but with his other arm across his eyes, so as not to see more than he has already seen. They are coming closer to the foot of the hill. More townsfolk, gripping at each other, like folk do when watching a conflagration. The shots are loud enough to have you flinch, you cannot help it. Zoltan's mouth falls open, then Zoltan murmurs, 'Oh, sweet Christ. Oh, gentle God.'

They are opposite the first of the gullies at the base of the hill. Jack cannot put a name to what he is looking at. He closes his eyes, but the images stay. White and red. Bone and meat. A horse that cannot move, a shot, the last slow thankful dipping of its head. Men crawling out from the gullies like maggots, pulling their bodyweight behind them; movement, ghastly movement everywhere you look, the piles shift, a horse gets its head up; a man rolls from the top of one pile to its base. What happens to a man when he falls three hundred feet, and scores of men and horses land on top of him? Look there, before you, that is what. Back and breastplate hold what is between them together. A flattened helmet, flattened, but not empty. Everything else, is gone.

At the side of one of the gullies, Jack sees a man throw his own pistol away, seize another from a hand poking out of the heap, take aim and fire. Was that at the pistol's owner? Yes, there will be living men being given the coup de grâce as well.

Luka is on his knees, hands raised in prayer.

'Domini!'

The Gemini stand with a boy between them, a boy trembling from head to toe, and holding an arm in the unmistakable fashion of one who has had it put out of its socket.

'Domini, this one. He says he was with Ancrum.'

'You may be the luckiest man on the field,' Jack tells the boy. He looks up to the edge of the slope, those hundreds of feet above, and the boy follows his gaze, then turns aside and vomits.

Jack holds out his flask. 'Take a drink, get your wind.' He waits. 'You were with Ancrum?'

'Yes, sir. Seconded. He had not enough of his own.'

'You saw him fall? You know where he lies?'

The boy points to where cloaks have been laid across the grass, over a series of misshapes, more or less the size of men. Jack thinks of those barrows up there on the hilltop – no, no such grave for these. Protruding from one, the top of Ancrum's head, his white hair. Then a dip beneath the cloak, then the rise of a breastplate, but there seems to be nothing after that. No feet are visible. He looks until he feels his mind has grasped this, dealt with it, wrestled it down. He says to the boy, 'Do you know where Ancrum lived? His house?'

'Yes, sir.'

Jack digs in his pocket, finds a coin. 'Ancrum had a wife,' he says. 'She deserves to know what became of him.'

'Yes, sir.'

'And there was a captain, a veteran from Germany, rode with him. He had a burn on his face.' Jack turns his own face to show where the scar would be, but there's no need.

'Yes, sir,' says the boy. 'Captain Fantom. But he was with us no longer by the time we came here. Colonel Ancrum had him arrested, in Thame.'

'Thame? You're sure of that?'

'Yes, sir. He was to hang.'

CHAPTER ELEVEN

Shoot!

'The words of his mouth are iniquitie and deceit: he hath left off to be wise, and to do good.'

Psalms, 36:3

'YOU ARE, BY some degree,' Alembert begins, 'a fortunate man.'

The prisoner rolls his shoulders. 'I do not feel it,' he says. He is a commissioned officer, this one, apparently, hence the lack of chains, and the fact that the man's hang-dog servant stands here with them, sharing this miserable space.

'But you are. Your Colonel Ancrum, he who laid the charge against you – it seems he fell at Roundway Down.'

'God have mercy,' says the prisoner, solemnly.

'Even so, the charge has been brought, and must be answered. Now, your name.' Alembert scans the details of the charge. 'I have here –' (he peers again, the name is unusual, to say the least) '– Carlo Fantom.'

'Kapitan,' the prisoner replies. He is seated on the planks of the bed here in his cell, and now extends a hand over each kneecap. The smallness, sharpness of the fingers gives the hands a claw-like look, like a bird of prey. 'Kapitan Carlo Fantom.'

Alembert glances up. 'You are a Deutscher? I too have been in Germany.'

The prisoner eyes him. 'Indeed?'

'In my other life. I was amongst a troupe of actors.' A modest clearing of the throat. 'We played in Regensburg, in Schwansdorf…'

Then over the border into Bohemia, and on to Prague. No, second thoughts, best not to mention Prague. And he already has his audience's full attention. The captain has released his grip upon his kneecaps. 'I would not expect to meet such here,' he says. 'You are most unusual, I think.'

Alembert gives a laugh. 'You won't find many men out here have played *The Spanish Tragedy*.'

'Forgive me that I do not know it,' says the prisoner.

'Oh, 'tis bloody,' Alembert tells him. 'One death after another, all full in the audience's eye.'

'That would be the Spanish for you,' comes the wry comment.

'Aha! Well said!' Alembert is warming up. What on earth can such a man have done to fall foul of the provost? He glances at the charge again. Oh. Not what he had expected.

'It says you forced a woman.'

'Ach,' says Fantom. 'Ach, she lies.'

'It says here, a grocer's daughter,' Alembert reads out. 'Fourteen,' he adds.

The sorry-looking servant shifts from foot to foot.

'A whore. I lay with her, I give her coin, then this. Women. They are all duplicity. From the time of Eve.'

Are they not, Alembert finds himself thinking. Illusions fade, dreams come to naught. His own life in the army has hardly been what he hoped for, either. Where is the chance to play the hero? Where the renown?

The prisoner – a man of similar bitter experience, clearly – is shaking his head. 'I am traduced, I promise you.' Another smile, even franker than before. 'It is good to speak with a man of education.' He gestures to the walls, the barred window. 'Even like this.'

The fellow seems so truly grateful. 'I will see if I can uncover more details of your case, Captain Fantom,' says Alembert. 'If I can, there may be more that I can do.'

The prisoner rocks back upon his stool. 'Why, my honour! My service!' he declares. He stands, he reaches out his hand.

Alembert takes it. 'Alembert,' he says. 'Lodowick Alembert.'

'Ah!' says the prisoner. 'And you almost have a German name!'

Alembert returns at sundown. He brings with him a jug, and two clay pipes, and a plug of tobacco.

'An actor,' this Captain Fantom says, as if this was the most amazing thing that he had ever heard. He fills their beakers as he speaks – horn beakers (since drinking vessels, like everything else out in the field, must be reduced to the rudest necessity) – but he does so with what strikes Alembert as much deftness. Those small fingers, there is precision to them.

'And what was your life before?' Alembert enquires. How long has it been since he had a conversation such as this?

'I am a soldier. Always,' says Fantom, raising his beaker. '*Dobro zdravlje!*'

'Your health,' Alembert reciprocates. The beakers are refilled, the pipes are lit. They puff away in silence. The servant stands off to the side, looking every bit as miserable as before. 'Your servant,' Alembert asks. 'Does he not drink?'

'Oh, my fat donkey? No, he does not, not with me.'

The servant stares at his feet. Belly on him like Falstaff. 'Looks like he hardly needs it, any case,' Alembert murmurs, and Carlo Fantom rocks backwards again as he laughs away.

'We make merry,' he says, with a wink. 'For tomorrow, we die.'

'Let us hope *not*,' says Alembert, although to be honest, the case against the man looks watertight. The girl will swear, there are other witnesses. And rape is a capital offence. A shame. Alembert sits with left foot over right knee; now he sees Fantom has done the same. Truly, they are not so unalike, in fact they are positively *like*, in height, in build… But Parliament's troops in Thame are making ready to quit, to shift; the news from the west could not be worse, and all will be up with this fellow soon as they reach Aylesbury. No wonder the man welcomes distraction.

They drink again. The beer is gut-warmingly strong. 'Tell me,' says Carlo Fantom. 'On stage, when an actor must die – if he must be shot, like a soldier – how is this done?'

'Oh, a flourish of a pistol, a bang on a drum.' Alembert nods his head toward the noise outside. A changing of the watch is imminent, a thing that also happens to a drumbeat. 'A bladder of pig-blood within the clothes. The actor strikes with his hand, where the shot would hit, with a pin between his fingers, d'ye see?' Alembert demonstrates with the stem of his pipe. 'The bladder explodes, the man falls. But 'tis a tricksy thing to make convincing, all the same.'

'You do not load the pistol?' his companion asks.

'Why, no,' says Alembert, puzzled. A sudden uncomfortable

movement of the wretched servant. Alembert does his best to ignore it, as his audience is speaking again.

'The drum makes the noise? That would not convince me.'

'Ah, but you see,' says Alembert, 'the audience, the actors – we are in a pact. We all agree, what we present on stage is real.'

'Ah.' This audience seems disappointed. 'You do not know then in this country, the trick of how to take a shot?'

'The trick?' Alembert is nonplussed.

'Indeed. It is useful thing. *Especially* for a soldier. You do not know it?'

'I do not,' says Alembert. He waits. 'Captain, if you please – what trick?'

'Oh, I think perhaps I speak too far. You will think me a mountebank.'

'I? Never. No, sir, please. Tell all.'

Captain Fantom frowns; a man deep in thought. At last he says, 'You have a pistol?'

'Aye, I do!' Alembert pulls the pistol from the back of his belt, and a paper cartridge with the round lead bullet twisted in its end. The servant, the donkey, is staring at him. It seems to Alembert that the man is shaking his head.

Carlo picks up the penknife with which Alembert had shredded their baccy, holds it out to him. 'Please, if you would – put your initial on the bullet.'

Alembert does so, carving into the lead. *LA.*

'Now you will charge your pistol, if you please. As you would do in battle.'

Alembert obeys. *Pick a card*, he is thinking, *any card.* Still, he is intrigued. And it could be a worthy trick, once he is again on stage – whenever that might be.

'Now my friend,' Carlo is saying. He moves to the wall. 'You shoot.'

'I shoot?'

'Shoot me.'

I shoot him? 'But the pistol is loaded, sir. I shoot you, at the least you will be wounded, maybe grievously.'

'No, no,' says Carlo, calmly. 'I will take the shot. It will not harm me. Then, I will show you how to do so too.' He ignores his servant, who at these words has made another convulsive movement. 'Shoot. Now. Shoot!' A glance at the window, head cocked to the noise of the drum. 'No-one will hear. Shoot!'

'But—' Alembert begins. No, he cannot. Still, he is most intrigued. No, he cannot. But his man is in earnest. See how he pulls straight his coat, spreads his arms, as if to make the biggest target that he can. That little silver badge upon the coat, how it shines!

'Shoot! *Shoot!*' For a moment a flash of something in the other's eyes, like a window let into the door of a furnace. *Hot as the flames of hell*, thinks Alembert, surprising himself. He fires.

The flash, the bang, the stink of cordite. Alembert thinks he fires almost with his eyes closed, but his man staggers, and the servant too reacts, jerking away. For one horrible moment of sobriety, Alembert is thinking, *Ah, Christ, I have killed him!* Then Carlo Fantom straightens up. He is searching under his coat, in which, at the shoulder, there is a round black hole, the size of a guinea. Now he seems to find what he is looking for. He holds something out to Alembert. 'You want it?' he asks.

By God. The bullet, complete with scratched *LA*; still almost too hot to touch.

Carlo casts the bullet into his beaker. The liquid, briefly, seethes. Fishes it out and gives it back. 'Now that,' says Alembert, tipsy with relief, casting the bullet up into the air and catching it again, 'that is as neat a trick as I have seen since my own time on the stage. You must show me how you brought it off!' Of course he has heard of men who claim invulnerability; of course there are such things as misfires, and Alembert would be the first to admit, he is a dreadful shot, he might have missed his man altogether. Did the bullet merely pierce the leather coat, and not the flesh beneath… no, no, he can't imagine how this was done. Some sleight of hand? Something to do with the scratching of the initials? 'Sir, I implore you. I must know!'

'Very well,' Carlo says. 'Load your pistol again. Load it for me. I will show you how it is done.'

The servant, the donkey, has turned his head away. Outside the drum still beats – *bang, patta-bang!* 'Same bullet?' Alembert asks, jocularly, ignoring the man, and Carlo replies, mock-serious, 'Of course.'

The pistol is reloaded. 'Stand as I stood,' Carlo says. 'That is most important.'

Alembert takes up position. Opens his arms. 'Now, a brave smile!' he hears Carlo Fantom say.

He puts back his head. Of a sudden, he doubts, as before, but to the power of ten. *No, no, a man cannot take a bullet so…* But to cry off? Not to go through with it? Does he doubt the evidence of his own eyes?

With his own eyes he sees the flash, and that is all.

Silence. The drum outside has ceased. The smoke inside the lock-up clears. 'Pick it up,' Carlo orders Tucker, pointing.

Tucker crosses to the heap that had been Alembert, puts his arms under what were Alembert's (and Caesar's and Hamlet's and Tamburlaine the Great's), and turns him over. The bullet caught Alembert in the right cheek, took the other side of his face with it. The curve of bone round the left eye remains, like the half-arch above a ruined doorway.

'Put it on the bed. Put the pistol in its hand.' Carlo is already stripping off his coat. 'Put it in my coat. Give its coat to me. Take its keys.'

A snuffling noise. Tucker, as he works, is sobbing. '*Tchoh*,' says Carlo. 'You think I let them stretch my neck upon the gallows, for some piece of quim? My gods preserve me still, my donkey. It will take more than that to finish *me*.' He is shrugging his way into Alembert's coat. 'I will have my war. We will go north, my donkey, I will have my war, I will mend my fortunes.' He pulls the sleeves down to his wrists. 'Lodowick Alembert,' he says. 'Do you care for it, my donkey? My new name?'

THE MOST OVERWORKED man in Thame is its gravedigger. Who takes not kindly at all to being hoiked out the tavern where he has been drinking loyal toasts to the King ever since news of Runaway Down, as the wits are now calling it, reached the town, and brought to stand out here, surrounded by this group of ruffians. 'Yeah, I remember 'im,' the man says. 'Provost took 'im in charge. Burn on his face.' He rubs a finger under his nose. 'Worr 'appened to 'im, I wonder?' he muses.

'Made the wrong man wait for an answer, maybe?' comes the growl. 'Could be.'

The gravedigger gives the speaker an offended glare. Christ in 'eaven, look at 'em. Look at all of 'em. The dirt on 'em. At least, he hopes those darkish splatters are dirt. 'Awright, Captain, awright. I 'ave ter think.'

One – who seems a little more civilized than the others, with his bright eye and wide moustaches – digs in his pocket and holds out a coin.

'Ah! That was it!' the gravedigger says. He pockets the coin.

'Provost put his sergeant under orders to have the fellow took to Aylesbury. Only it all got a bit busy thereafter. Bit hot, as they say, what with the news of your victory, sirs, and the man went unwatched and somehow 'e contrived to shoot 'imself.' A mime: cocking a pistol, holding it to the cheek. 'Blew his face off. Couldn't endure the tree and the 'emp and the jig.'

'Shot himself,' Jack repeats.

'That's it.'

'Then where's the body?'

The man opens his arms in a circle to take in the ground all about them. 'Under 'ere. Him, and every other corpse the fever and the fighting left us with. Unless they was officers. They're turning black in the church. But a villain such as that, he went in here.' He grinds the heel of his shoe down into the hard-packed earth, to make the point. 'Can I go now, gentlemen?'

They watch the man weave his way back whence he came. Says Zoltan, 'Do we dig?'

'No.' Jack crouches down, touches the earth with his fingertips. He has to force himself to stand back up. Every muscle in his body is whining with fatigue. 'It won't be him. Whoever it was, it won't be Carlo Fantom. If he had been hung, I might have believed it, but shoot himself? He'd never do that. He truly believes he's proof. No, he's out there still.'

Back they go to the road. Jack has just hauled himself back into the saddle when there is a shout behind him. Here is Maurice, deserting his bodyguards, jogging up alongside. 'Fiskardo. Your eye, sharp as efer,' he declares. This green boy, with his pretty horse, trotting along so merrily. 'Your eye and instincts, both.'

'You do me honour, sir,' says Jack, wearily.

'You are vaisted, you are *vaisted* as scouts, you and your men. I tell my brother, he vill gif you a regiment.' Then in the same buoyant tone, 'And you gif his salutation to Miss Holland, yes?'

They watch him go, he and his escort, taking congratulation here, congratulation there. 'This was a victory, Jacques,' says Zoltan, quietly.

'No,' says Jack. He shakes his head. 'No, it was not.'

Zoltan looks behind them, to where the Dead Men are waiting. 'I will take them into Oxford,' he says. 'Strong drink and impudent women, that's what they need.' He lowers his voice. 'Chase the devils from our heads.'

'You do that. All I need waits for me at Varney.'

At least, he hopes it does.

Everything I love...

This time, he sees the lights of the house even before its chimneys. Every window is aglow. She must have worked it out, that victory would bring him home.

He leads M'sieu round to the stables, puts a bucket of water under his horse's nose, takes his knife to a sack of hay and fills the manger in the stall. 'Well done,' he tells M'sieu. 'Well done, my beautiful.' On the way out of the stables, he finds he has to prop himself for a moment against the door. *Don't close your eyes...* Don't see those sights again.

As he walks up to the house he hears singing, laughter, a fiddle playing. Pulls at the door with what for sure must be the last of his strength; walks – no, staggers – in.

The first thing to hit him is the fragrance in the air. Two great pots of lilies, one either side of the door. And someone has moved the lacquer cabinet from the inner hall to here. It looks very well in its new place. *Of course*, he thinks, *I have a woman in the house. If I weren't so weary, I would smile.* And then the sound of the two voices, duetting, one of which is unmistakably Pris, and at that he wants to weep, that this world can hold both the beauty of a woman's voice and the bloody shambles that still swims across his vision every time he closes his eyes.

And then the girl, coming to a halt in her bustle across the hall, holding her laden tray. 'Who are you?' she asks. She peers at him. The horror in her expression grows. He looks down at himself. Oh.

His hands are black with smoke, smeared with rusty-brown. He still has the taste of cordite on his teeth. His breeches are ripped at the side, the bucket-top of one boot flapping. The splatter across his shirt. The mud from Runaway Down still wiped across his skin beneath it. The tug of dried blood on his neck, in his hair. He tries to smile, and the girl's reaction makes him think all he did was make matters worse.

'You do stay there,' she orders him. 'Don't you move. I'll fetch Mr Topham.'

It has been such a celebration. Mr and Mrs Endicott with all their troubles forgotten for once, and she and Mrs Mayhew titivated too, and even Toby tapping his foot and daring to return Moll's grin; and everyone saying after such a triumph, the war must now end, surely; Parliament be brought to terms and all this nonsense over, and Ned and James all smiles and best behaviour, and oh how they had feasted too. A turkey, gilded, and studded with *quelquechose* of almond paste, and little quail, and sweetbreads and a dish of cherries and the redcurrants she and Master James had picked together, and Miss Pris and Mrs Endicott duetting so beautifully, and Mr Topham on his fiddle, and even Old Henty with some pink in her cheeks, and it was Molly's part to bring in the *pièce de résistance* of candied pudding and now *this*. 'Oh, Moll, that looks splendid,' her mistress says, as Moll puts the pudding on the table. 'Yeah, but,' says Molly. 'There's some big old scruff outside.' She holds three fingers up against her cheek. 'Some big old scruff, got these scars on his face, and he's *filthy*. I said as I'd get Mr Topham.'

Her mistress is already running to the hall. She is beaten only by the boys, who run straight to the man standing there, Ned throwing his arms about the man's waist, and little James around one booted leg. The dogs go whuffing and bounding round him too.

'Oh, my dear good *God*!' Miss Holland cries, on seeing him. 'Take off every single thing you wear and drop it all, right there. Mrs Mayhew, water. Hot!'

She puts him in a tub in the laundry, has it filled to the brim, strews him with lavender. Wash-balls like grapeshot. Even so, he falls asleep in it, wakes to find her rubbing round his ears. 'Lean forward,' she says, and goes to work on his back while he rests his forehead on his knees. She is diligent to a fault; the lace at her wrists unpinned, sleeves rolled up, sponge wrung out, applied again and again. 'What happened here?' she asks, her fingers exploring the back of his head.

'Fell from my horse,' he murmurs. 'Where are our guests?'

'Gone to their beds. The boys too. I keep telling Rafe and Belle, they should come here to live. Who buys books in Oxford now? Nobody.'

Another wash-ball. Now his face, his neck. He makes to swing the silver wolf out of her way and out of her sight, but she forestalls him. 'No,' she says. 'Let it stay. I think it has proved itself.'

'The last time anyone did this for me,' he tells her, 'I was ten.'

'You have bathed since, I hope?'

She is working up his arm, between his fingers. She lifts the hand. His knuckles are skinned. 'How did this happen?'

He has no idea.

'And this?' A raw red runnel across his arm. That has to have been a bullet. Did Ancrum get off a shot after all?

She feeds him. A plate of bits of this and that, a glass of wine. Another. There are candles all about the tub. She lifts his fingers to her lips. She says, 'Did you know James has taught himself to read?'

He did not. 'He surely don't get that from me.'

She rests her forehead against his, her hand around his head, on his wet hair. There is that pale mark, like a crescent, on her neck. 'You keep this up,' he says, 'I'll start to think you're growing fond on me.'

'Oh, I might come to it, at that.'

He hears himself heave a sigh. 'I thought perhaps I might find you were gone.'

'Gone?' She sits back on her heels. 'Why would I be gone?'

'You caught Rupert's eye,' he says. 'Or so it seems.'

'What of it?'

'I thought –' What did he think? '– I thought he might have made an offer. While I was gone. It is the way these things are done. A promotion for me, a change of quarters for you.'

Her eyes flatten, like a cat's. 'Surely,' she says, 'in such circumstance, it should be the woman gets promotion, not the man.'

'Well. A prince of the blood.'

'Do you not have blood?' She is trailing her fingers in the water. 'Truly, a bauble on the arm of a princeling. Does that sound like me?'

'He is – he is a sight nearer your age than I am.'

'I hate to be the one to break it to you,' says she, and now her eyes are merry again, 'but there is an army of men out there younger than you.'

'And less knocked about.'

Now she laughs. 'Whatever holds me here, Jack, it is surely not your looks.'

'Why are you here?' he asks. To his amazement it takes almost more boldness than it did to get into line in Maurice's cavalry, to ask it.

'Oh, good *God*.' Has he made her angry? No, her eyes are smiling still. 'If I had but a shilling for the number of times I've asked myself that since you went off a-soldiering.' She sets her hands on the side of the bath, puts her chin on top of them, tilts her face. 'I like my life here. It is the life I chose. I like the man I have chosen too.' Now it is not only her eyes that smile. 'Even if he is the greatest fool I ever met.'

He lies his head back. It is as if he can feel everything wash from him. 'Lady,' he says, 'will you take this fool to his bed?'

AND SHE WAKES in the middle of the night, and there he is, in his nightshirt, at the window, elbows on the sill. It's like having one of his dogs stood there: just as lean, just as bony. And what man ever looked the hero in a nightshirt?

She ducks under his arm, puts hers about his waist. For a moment he is quiet, then she hears him say into her hair, 'Those gods of yours are not giving us much time together, are they?'

She wants to tell him how it feels, to be stood with him again; she wants to tell him the peerless value of his ribs, the incalculable worth of his great feet; the prizes that are his forearms, the knops of his wrists; and how he must, *must*, always bring this back to her, but you can't say that to a man who will be returning to the war. Not possible. Instead she says, 'Jack, why are you doing this? You're not like Cantley and the rest, you ain't no cavalier. And you're sure as hell no Digby.'

'Good question,' says he.

'Then give me a good answer.'

A sigh. She feels it rise right through him. 'Because the King can win this war faster than he will ever consent to lose it, and I want the damned thing done. Pris, I have been thinking. We need a signal.' He has his hand about the silver wolf. 'If this comes back to you, you and the boys, I want you to go straight to Cornelius Vanderhoof, in Green Dragon Court. He will get you safe to Amsterdam, and I will find you there.'

'Leave Varney?' She is shocked. She feels chilled even to say the words. 'But Jack—'

'It's a common thing, with soldiers and their families. To have a signal.'

Now she has drawn her head away from him. 'But what of Mrs Mayhew, Topham—'

'I spoke with Topham long ago. He understands. It's a precaution, only.'

'Do you truly mean this?'

Yes, he thinks. *Yes. Because our enemy will never forgive us. Six hundred men fell to their deaths at Runaway Down; Maurice turned Waller's own cannon on the survivors. Waller himself is rumoured to have fled to Bristol. It was a victory out of all proportion to sense, to logic, to anything.*

The night wind moves through Varney's trees, the moon rides on the clouds. At last she asks, 'What will happen now?'

'Now?' He lets his head rest on hers. 'Now we must take Bristol, which will give the King a port, so we can bring in arms, as long as the King can pay for them. And as long as he can be dissuaded from using it to bring in troops from Ireland, for if he does that, there will be no treaty with the Scots to keep them out of the north, and we cannot march on London if we must march north, and if we don't retake London we have all wasted our time. Every field on which we meet 'em, Parliament's troops are going to learn more and more how this thing is done, for if they don't, they die, and there is no better tutor than that. So there will come a tipping point. So we must get close enough to victory before then, to make Parliament in London tremble, and when we do, they sue for terms, and the King, if he has the sense God gives a cabbage, rides down Pall Mall on a great white palfrey, throwing out pardons like manna.' His arms are round her. 'And we cover ourselves in glory. And I come home.'

'That last part,' says Pris, leaning against him. 'I like that.'

None of this is what will happen.

PART III

London 1645

CHAPTER ONE

Brotherhood

'This twenty-fifth day of June, 1645. Lord's Day.

... of matters here in England, I can report only as Providence has willed it: the King has made his final play, and the dice have all fallen against him. Naseby has destroyed him. Of his army, he has but the ruins. England is like a man who has received a mortal blow, yet still stands, tottering. Not a soul knows what will come after.'

Mercator

COMES BROTHER JENKIN, from Amsterdam – merry as a jester, fat as Friar Tuck. Brother Jenkin with his bills of lading and his manifests, and his small shrewd eyes, like the ends of sharpened pencils, only no-one ever seems to notice this, amongst the chubbiness and the chins. There he goes along the quay at Blackwall, greeting and hallooing and pressing douceurs into palms; and only when all that has been taken care of does Jenkin seat himself with the greatest of care in Miguel Domingo's rowboat, to be taken round the Isle of Dogs to Rotherhithe. 'And who's this?' Jenkin asks, spying the naked-kneed, coxcomb-headed scraplet, sat at the rowboat's prow.

'This is Master Barnaby,' Miguel answers, as he pulls on the oars. 'When I am lucky, he keeps lookout for me.' For a wherryman rows with his back to his prow. 'He is also known as Bug.'

Jenkin settles himself more comfortably. 'And what, my friend, is all the news?'

'The news?' They are nearing Deptford Creek; shoals of craft contesting this way and that. 'Move off, you Deptford sluggard!' hollers the child, as an unwary flat-bottomed dory drifts too close.

'The news of the war,' says Jenkin, as a prompt. 'Some mighty big fight, I hear. It was all the talk in Amsterdam.'

'Naseby Field,' says Miguel. 'Yes, it is all the talk here too.' Another pull on the oars, another swirl of blue-brown Thames. 'The news of the war is that it is done.'

There is a jetty at the back of Greville's house in Rotherhithe, with Walter Spikenard standing guard upon it, in honour of their visitor. Miguel Domingo ties up, and holds his craft as steady as he can while Jenkin heaves himself onto dry land, assisted by Walter and Aaron, hauling on his arms. 'Thank'ee, Walt,' says Jenkin, brushing himself down. 'And how goes it with you, nephew, in these strange new times?'

'Bad as you might imagine,' comes Aaron's reply. 'Theatres are all closed up, and poor old Sullivan's has pamphlets poked under its door every morning, saying sotweed is a sin. Them Puritans. No dicing, no dancing, no flirting, no fuckery – I swear, they'd take the yellow out of the sun if they could, for that he looks too happy in the sky.'

'Yet *you* look cheerful,' Jenkin points out.

'Oh, well,' says Aaron, 'goes better for us than it does for King Mullypuff, that's for sure.'

In Jenkin goes. Walter, shouldering his battered halberd, follows in his wake. The door to Greville's office is thrown open. Impatient as ever, there stands the man himself.

To business. 'Ah,' says Jenkin, selecting the widest-seated of Greville's chairs, 'we've come a long, sad way from one good battle and all this will be over, that's for sure. 'Tis a strange, strange time to be an Englishman.' He sets a paper on the table, smoothing it with both hands. 'There you go, capo. One manifest. Nags, powder, bullets… you must be a popular man.'

'Me and the Trained Bands,' says Greville, holding up a hand as he reads, with one finger leaned into the next. 'Like *that*. And I tell you, brother mine, we all mind our manners these days where they're concerned. Still, 'tis an ill wind, eh? Every cloud, a silver lining.'

'Make hay, capo. Make hay while the sun shines. What I hear, this will all be coming to its end right soon.' Jenkin leans back. 'What do you do, when your own people have defeated you?'

'Fuck off to France,' says Greville, with a growl. 'And the sooner the better.'

All this manly wit and wisdom. Bess, also at the table (her dress as midnight black as Helen of Troy these days, but her lace still creamy as spindrift), might at this point be observed raising her eyes to the plasterwork upon the ceiling.

Jenkin settles himself. 'Good day to ye, sis.' He looks about. 'And where's my pretty niece? Where's Pris? She grown too grand to wait upon us, has she?'

Bess points her gaze toward Greville.

'Pris,' says Greville, magnificently, taking his place at the table's head, 'is no longer mentioned in this house.'

'She ain't?' Brother Jenkin pauses in his filling of his glass. 'Why so? What's the girl been and done?'

'She deserted us,' Greville says. 'Us, and what is more, her protector too. Threw in her lot with some Oxfordshire soldier, like a common trull.'

'She did?' Jenkin is astonished. 'That don't sound like her. That don't sound like Pris one bit. Who's the fellow, do we know?'

'Some nothing and no-one out the wars in Germany,' answers Greville, unhelpfully.

'One Fiskardo, by all reports,' his sister puts in. She sounds weary. 'She sent Abi word to say as she was under this man's roof now, and that Abi was not to fret. Greville,' she adds, 'forbade us to reply.'

'Exactly so,' says Greville. 'The girl is dead to us—'

He stops. Jenkin's trio of chins has become one single roly-poly, so agape is he. '*Jack* Fiskardo? You don't mean *Jack* Fiskardo?'

'Why?' Bess asks. There is a note to Jenkin's astonishment that seems to hold promise of much more.

Jenkin sits forward. 'You ever hear tell of the Dead Men?' he begins.

'Of course we have,' says Greville, with irritation. 'A tale to frighten little German kiddoes up to bed.'

'No, they ain't, capo,' says Jenkin, shaking his head. 'Not they, nor the fortune they robbed off the Prince-Bishop of Prague. That's real as real too, by God. I've seen it.'

'Seen it? Seen it where?' Greville demands.

'In the strong room of the Wisselbank, in Amsterdam. Leastways, a corner of it. Unconscionable proud they are of having it there too. 'Tis a good part of how they come to be so well founded.'

Greville, as we know, does not care to be contradicted. 'And what would you be doing in the strong room of the Wisselbank?' he asks. His tone is indulgent; the words *little brother* drift unspoken in the air.

'Yosha Silbergeld,' Jenkin answers. 'Thought as I might care to take a tour.'

'Yosha Silbergeld?' Greville repeats. Yosha Silbergeld: a veritable senator amongst the merchants of Amsterdam, a man whose dealings stretch from St Petersburg to the shores of New England. An emperor of trade. His little brother is cultivating Yosha Silbergeld?

'Aye, him,' says Jenkin. He refills his glass. 'And Jack Fiskardo, brother, lived in Yosha Silbergeld's house when he was a boy, and was the Dead Men's captain when they stole that gold.' He tilts his glass toward Bess. 'Your health!'

Aaron, meanwhile, has retired to that wooden jetty, sits upon it dangling his boots toward the Thames. The river sings its song below his feet; the breeze dances about his head; Aaron finds himself much affected by both. For the first time in his life, Aaron understands the content to be found when the outer world mirrors the mood of the inner. Aaron is in love.

Yes, he is. Mock him not; this is as much of a surprise to him as it is to you. Love has crept over Aaron with the gentleness of sunlight, so softly he never even heard its approach. How unguessable its choice for him, yet how flawless – and how it has changed him! Aaron finds himself reflective, he finds himself unselfish, he finds himself *strong*, even in the face of the frankly incalculable difficulties this situation presents him with. *Love conquers all*, he tells himself, a dozen times a day. And right at present all he wishes to do is marvel at its glow and bask in its warmth.

His uncle's voice fills the garden. '*Aaron!*'

Aaron scrambles to his feet. There stands Greville at the window to his chamber, and from the expression on his face, that was not his first such bellowing of Aaron's name.

'What is it, Unc?'

'Where the devil is your head these days? Get yourself ready. You're going to Oxford.' And the window is banged shut, even before Aaron can respond with an astonished 'An' how in hell am I meant to do that?'

Plumstead is how, apparently. Plumstead, and a wallet's worth of bribes and douceurs, and in return a sheaf of permits and passes. For the two sides of England must still connect somehow, and Plumstead's wagons still go back and forth between them, at least as far as High Wycombe, which is a place that was barely a blink before, yet now finds itself a sort of lych-gate between that part of England controlled by Parliament, and that small portion still ruled by the King.

'Think of it,' Aaron says. He puts his arms behind his head, lies back upon the bed in Green Dragon Court. His face is flushed, his breast salty with sweat. 'Think of it. Your Fiskardo, and our little Pris. Why, that almost makes us family, you and me.'

Says Cornelius, lying beside him, 'I would be proud to be your family.'

Aaron shakes his head. 'Nah,' he says. 'Nah, you would not. My family are whoreson bastards, top to toe.'

'I am sure they have their virtues,' says Cornelius.

'You see?' says Aaron. He points a finger. '*That's* why folk tell you their secrets, a'cause you make 'em feel good about 'emselves. All I do is make 'em check I ain't lifted their purse.'

But Cornelius has gone quiet. 'You will be going where the war is,' he says at last.

'The war is bloody everywhere,' Aaron answers, swinging his legs out from under the sheet. Look at him, as he walks across the room. Aaron, at eight and twenty, has the bounce of a street-fighter, built for sudden violence, while Cornelius, by contrast, is a man made of peeled willow, his limbs as smooth, as straight. 'And I cain't believe as you never told me who your father is, neither,' Aaron continues. 'Who has Yosha Silbergeld as his pa, and don't noise it out abroad?'

'One who wishes to do business in England,' says Cornelius. 'Your King Edward, he threw out my father's people long ago, so here in London, my name is Vanderhoof. I am a Dutchman, Aaron, and always will be. Top to toe.' He watches as Aaron pulls a shirt over his head, draws its tail up between his legs.

Aaron, seeing him watching, gives his rump a shake, the way a duck shakes its tail. 'What 'ud your paymasters say if they could see you now?' he asks, grinning.

'If my service to my country is good enough,' says Cornelius, 'I hope they might not care.'

'There ain't nowhere they wouldn't care,' says Aaron, reaching to pull up his breeches, to tuck all tidily away. 'You might sing the King's tune, or Parliament's, they'd all see you an' me dead and damned. You remember that.' For who is to watch over Cornelius, if Aaron is not here to do it? 'Every single thing you do, Cornelius, every single thing might be the end of you. Parliament has more men out there on the hunt for intelligencers than there is intelligencers 'emselves. I heard there was this old biddy up on Holborn, she had some bully from the Trained Bands searching through her petticoats the other day. She was like to have had a fit of it. Poor old granny.' He starts doing up his buttons. 'And I won't be here to keep an eye on you. Not for a while. You have to promise me, Cornelius, you'll keep your wits about you, you hear?'

'I promise,' says Cornelius, calmly. 'But they are not looking for me. This pale Dutchman, with his comical name? This man who is a friend to everyone, and who listens to all their troubles with his face so solemn, like so?' And he pulls that face for Aaron, as evidence – the eyes full of seriousness, the mien full of sympathy. 'No, they are looking for this Mercator. This human octopus, who pulls their secrets from the air. That is who they are looking for. Not me.' He reaches across, takes Aaron's hand in his. 'And I will weep if Aaron Holland, on his travels, comes to harm.'

Aaron puts his hand over Cornelius's. 'And *I* will weep if Mercator is discovered.'

There's a bakeshop in Rotherhithe, does a pasty of cod-cheeks and oysters, fatty and fishy, melting on the tongue. It's Walter Spikenard's habit, when he does duty at Greville's door, to buy a half-dozen and bear them back downriver to the Dunqerqer for supper. It makes a pleasing change from whatever mangled creature Josh Arden has retrieved from his traps.

'And,' says Walter, as they watch the pasties sizzle in the Dunqerqer's frying pan, 'I've some news of young Pris, after so long.'

Josh Arden's teazle eyebrows lift, even that over his empty socket. 'You do? What become of her?' he asks.

'Found herself some man-of-war out Oxford way,' Walter tells him. 'Shook herself free of that old Puritan, and got herself some right land pirate, by the sound of him, some fellow made of gold.' He chuckles. 'Greville Holland, when he heard, I thought he'd fall clean off his chair.'

'So who's the lucky man?' Josh asks, jiggling the pan.

'No-one I'd heard of, but seems there's plenty have. Name of Jack Fiskardo.'

A beat, a pause. 'Say that name again?' Old Josh asks.

'Fiskardo. Jack Fiskardo. Here, Josh!' Walter exclaims, jumping up. 'Watch what you're at, man! You'll have our supper on the coals!'

CHAPTER TWO

Not One Loss, But Another

'… he never had any design that did not miscarry, either by bad play or bad luck.'

The History of the Kings Majesties Affairs in Scotland

PRIS HOLLAND, OXFORD edition. Rises earlier. Is noticeably less fussed about the state of her ringlets. Has been known to don an apron. Melts and remakes candles; understands how laundry is accomplished; insists Ned does his lessons; sits herself down opposite him to do her own accounts. Passes by the looking-glass in her bedchamber with a shrug. Thinks of the woman she was as a creature she knew once, somewhere else, whose acquaintance she may remake when there's time, but at present, there is none. All there is, is the constant list of wants rolling through her head: coal (coal, coal, always coal, and there never is any); white soap (hah, ditto); nutmeg, raisins, isinglass for brewing, and saffron because they have no flour, but they have rice. No-one ever has flour. But this is what it is to be at war – you always lack something; you are always planning your way around that lack. Never before has Pris felt herself living in so many different directions at once. She feels as if she is the lacquer cabinet downstairs, with all its little drawers pulled open. Nutmeg, raisins, isinglass, Pris is thinking, as she twists up her hair. The Endicotts dine with them tomorrow – what will she feed them? Plain rice and stewed pigeon. It is becoming a staple. She leans in toward the mirror, examining her face. Yes indeed, that is the moss-green armazine Miss Holland wears, cut short to the ankle and hemmed by the wearer herself, so that one may walk across the grass in it to fetch the eggs, while the bodice has been converted to a doublet, does up without assistance at the front with hook and eye. And yes, you have seen that mighty bunch of keys at her waist before, too.

She sucks in her cheeks. Pushes back the hair on her forehead, scrutinizing it for wrinkles. *Oh God*, she thinks, *we are all so sick and tired of this, Oxford is so weary of this war.*

It is sick of the taxes, it is sick of the stinting of itself; it is sick of the men billeted upon it and the muck in its streets and the rats that come with the muck; and the terrifying outbreaks of fever that come with the rats, and the men, and the billeting. It is sick of artillery parks on its riverbanks, and never knowing, was that thunder or was it cannon-fire? It is sick of the panics, the alarums; it is sick of living scared and joyless; in a few dark private corners, it may even be it is sick of the King. There is only one thing anyone in Oxford wants, that anyone in England wants, and that is *peace*.

From outside the boys' rooms, the eruption of dispute. Pris goes to the bedroom door. 'Those men who cannot march along peaceably together,' she bellows, 'will be set to shovel out the stables, do you hear?' Not that this is much of a threat, as the stables at Varney are home to but two horses these days: Topham's ancient gelding and little Annie, who is so accommodating she would muck herself out, if you could but show her how to hold a shovel. Now she hears Topham himself outside, returning from Oxford, but she cannot make out if he brings more news or no. One way or the other, no doubt she will be told. They long for news; they live in dread of it.

The King took Bristol; he did not take Gloucester. He did not regain the south-east. London thumbed its nose at him. Egged on by Digby, he did indeed make peace with the Irish; egged on by his wife, he sought to bring in aid from Catholic France. ('You cannot fault Her Majesty's loyalty,' said Belle, stoutly. 'No,' said Pris, 'but you can fault her bloody *sense*.') Outraged on both counts, the Scots allied themselves with Parliament, and together, beat Prince Rupert at Marston Moor, and so the King lost the north. Now, at Naseby, in the grey-green Midlands, it seems he has lost everything else. 'All the old guard, such as Essex, all the old way of doing things? They are gone. A new model army,' Topham had said, spreading the broadsheet out across the kitchen table for all of them to see. 'That is what Parliament is calling its soldiers.'

'And what do we call ours?' Pris had demanded. 'The Done For?'

One last thing to do. She goes to the bed, and from under the pillow, pulls out a man's nightshirt. Lifts it to her face, breathes in. Yes, very foolish. Laugh. Like she would care. Varney's master has not been home in months; there is no scent of him in his nightshirt any longer; all this does is help her bring him into mind.

I know you will come back to us, Pris tells Jack, in her head. *Bad as everything is, I know you will.*

Bring on the day.

'WE MUST BE resolute,' says Cantley. 'We must be men of iron. We must summon up the blood. Henry Fifth,' he explains. 'Shakespeare.' Then, seemingly, an appeal. 'Fiskardo, there are worse places than this.' This being Hereford, its ancient market-place: last place ever beheld by so many of Herefordshire's cattle, and truly, is this, the remains of the army of King Charles, so very different?

In headlong flight from that grey-green battlefield in the Midlands, you can make it to Hereford in three days. Even if, like Cantley, part of your scalp is on a flap, held in place by a filthy bandage. Even if, like Luka, you took such a tumble that your shoulder is split, and you blench with pain at so much as a nearby footstep; or like Ulrik, have a broken elbow and a hand swelled like that of a corpse; or like Per, have your nose broke and two great black eyes, from which you stare out at the world like a bear. It's the small hurts cause so much anguish in defeat, as Jack knows full well; not the drill-hole through the flesh with a bullet at the end of it, not the chasm of a sword-slash, but these – *We were utterly, utterly defeated, and some bastard broke my nose.* The men of the garrison at Hereford, watching the remnants of the army of King Charles come in through its gates, had but one question: *Where are all the rest?*

The King believes he can raise another ten thousand foot from here.

'The Welsh Marches,' Cantley declares. 'They were ever loyal.'

'Cantley,' says Jack, 'there ain't ten thousand men left in the whole of England loyal to the King.'

Says Cantley, 'There are worse plights than ours.'

Name one, thinks Jack.

They were defeated, on that grey-green battlefield, when the King's cavalry again tally-ho'd off the field in pursuit of the foe, and came back to find the foe victorious. It seems one does not, after all, have to be a gentleman to know how to fight. It seems yeoman farmers can learn how to do so perfectly well. Parliament's victorious general in chief is a farmer, apparently. 'Great-great-grandnephew to Thomas Cromwell, that rogue and traitor,' Cantley had said. 'By Christ, if ever a family was made to be the scourge of England's kings!'

On that same field, Parliament's troops found some hundred or so wives of the men of Wales hiding in the baggage train. They took the women for Irish, supposedly, and on that pretext, slaughtered them all.

The King believes it matters not that his private papers were captured, and have been printed, and gleefully sent all over England, to reveal his plans to bring over troops from Ireland. The advice of my Lord Digby is mentioned many times in them.

The King believes he will retake the north, and this despite the destruction of his infantry, the deaths of a thousand men, the capture of four thousand more and the carrying-off of all the royal artillery.

'Montrose, that Scottish Hector, he will bring his army down to us,' Cantley informs them. Cantley's skin has the yellowed look of old paper; from time to time he pokes a finger into the bandage round his head, wincing when he does so. 'Or the King will go north, and lead Montrose's troops himself.'

It is almost wilful. It is like arguing with a child.

'Prince Rupert will go to Bristol. He will hold Bristol for the King and there receive the men the Queen will send over from France.'

A bark of laughter from Zoltan, so flat, so humourless, it's like the dropping of a plank of wood. 'Hold it with what?'

The King is confident that he and his wife will soon be reunited, despite the fact that his commanders flee, and his soldiers tiptoe away into the night. Indeed, the King's choice of commanders is so reduced that even my Lord Digby takes to the field. He is a disaster, and seems proud of it.

The King believes that all he has to do to be victorious is be the King. They will rest here, rest, recuperate, regroup, raise more men—

For the first time that Jack can remember, even Zoltan's face is wholly without hope. 'The King would start another war?'

Cantley is still speaking. 'I am to go to Paris. I am to return to Oxford, then I am being sent out to my uncle. I am to turn diplomat. I am to aid the King in his negotiations.'

There used to be a manor house near Hereford, in the village of Canon Frome. The Earl of Leven – another Scot, but on Parliament's side, and another who learned his craft in the Swedish army – fell upon it a month ago, killed its commander and half its defenders, dug a pit in a field and higgled them all in; and every time Jack hears mention of the fate of Canon Frome, what he sees in his mind's eye is Varney. And now they are meant to go to war anew? Be defeated all over again? Lose, down to the very last man?

Don't despair, he tells Pris, in his thoughts, a hundred times a day; but would she, ever? *No*, he thinks, *no. The one despairing is me.*

BRISTOL FALLS, TO Parliament's New Model Army.

Says Sir Jacob, 'We go to Worcester.'

'Worcester,' Jack repeats. In Astley's tent, the wind beats against the canvas like a warning no-one heeds.

'Indeed. The very first skirmish in the war took place in Worcester, at Powick Bridge. And now we circle round to it again. Winter there. Recruit, renew.' A shuffling of the papers on his knee.

Sir Jacob, thinks Jack. *Of all men, to shuffle paper.*

'I recommended that you and your discoverers should come with me,' Sir Jacob continues. 'I recommended it most strongly. But my Lord Digby was of the contrary view. In his opinion, it is intelligence of the enemy's movements that we lack. He would have you scout back toward Bristol.' He looks up. 'Lord Digby's views. They carry weight.'

Don't they just, as Digby is almost the final counsellor the King still has. Since the fall of Bristol, Digby is said to have even the Princes Rupert and Maurice in his sights. As for that notorious discoverer Jack Fiskardo and his men, what are they? 'Bristol,' says Jack, heavily. It would be tantamount to execution to go back to Bristol. 'Into the mouth of the wolf, as we would say in Germany. I suppose I should be flattered my Lord Digby yet remembers me.'

'Indeed. Although there is a small service you might first perform for me,' Sir Jacob adds. 'Take your men, and scout forward.'

'Forward to where, Sir Jacob?'

'Forward,' Sir Jacob tells him. 'To whatever you find in front of you. I do not need to explain your business to you, Captain, I think.'

'Forward to whatever is in front,' Jack repeats.

'You understand my meaning, Captain? Forward to whatever is in front.'

Even so, he might not have done it. Only as he limps back through Astley's camp he sees Zoltan, propping himself against a sapling, spewing watery phlegm and shaking like the tree itself. Jack sits him down, mops him up. 'How long have you had the judders?'

'A while. It comes and goes.' Zoltan rubs a hand across his mouth. 'I'm pissing pink as a rose as well,' he adds, with a horrid attempt at a smile.

Tertian fever. In his head Jack takes a roll-call of his men – Per, with his nose as if it had been kneaded like dough; Ulrik, one-handed; Luka, one-winged; and the prospect of more and more of this, until there is nothing of them left.

Says Zoltan, 'Jacques, if I must break Ava's bargain, will you be the one to go to her and tell her how it was?'

That's what decides him. *The fuck with this. I'm done. It's time.*

He finds Cantley. 'Cantley, would you take a letter to a friend in Paris for me?'

'I would, of course. Most willingly.'

'And would you deliver a message for me in Oxford too?'

'Another letter?' Cantley asks.

'No,' says Jack. His hand goes to the cord about his neck. 'This.'

IT'LL TAKE CAREFUL handling, this, Aaron knows that full well. Plenty of rehearsal. Sis, old Greville sent me, he will say, aiming for the perfect mix of resignation and concern. Yes, old

Greville. Oh, same as ever. How does he trim that beard of his eh? Compass and set-square, d'you think? And he and she, they will make secret mock of Greville, as they always did. And how are all the rest, she will ask. (It must be said, the Pris in his head is a deal more tractable than the real thing is likely to be. Two years of the brush-off, Aaron is thinking; she's not about to forgive that in a hurry.) But how is Abi, this Pris will quiz him, and how does Bess?

That'll be his cue. They miss you, Aaron will say. He will turn serious: *It is a bitter thing, Pris, when a family tears itself in two. It is a sad and bitter thing. Look at me – I'm the paper. I'm the tear. I am heartsick over this.* (In rehearsal, here in Plumstead's jolting wagon, Aaron shakes his head in sorrow. Although now he thinks of it, that's true. Ripped down the middle, that is exactly how he feels.) *But the war is coming to its end, and everyone knows it. We too, we would be reconciled.* He thinks how he will not mention the role of brother Jenkin in this. Nor his meeting with her captain, and how the man had loped across the stage of the Red Bull, ready to deliver that handshake. Astonishing. The Pris Aaron knew went for pretty boys, lads of the same good looks as she; not some great flinty-jawed growler, but there, he tells himself, who knows where or how Cupid's arrow will strike? Might he even be so brave as to hint that for him too there is someone… of course, he cannot go too far with that. But he could drop a hint. It would be fun to tease her, like he used to do—

'Here!' Aaron demands, sticking his head out from the canvas. 'Where are we? Why are we stopped?'

'High Wycombe, Mr 'Olland,' Plumstead informs him. Wycombe of the many mills: a place of endless delays; a place where every load must be unpacked and examined; every pass, every document, read through; every satchel shaken out. Plumstead knows it well. And the men deputed by Parliament to carry out these tasks are such as you find deputed to 'em wherever: an unholy stew-up of the bully and the bureaucrat. 'Here we go,' he tells Aaron, long-sufferingly. 'Look'ee there.'

Ahead, a living wall of armoured troopers, blocking all traffic from the west, just as in front of them a sergeant of the London Trained Bands has his men block all that coming the other way. High Wycombe's high street has become a no man's land. And the inevitable line of travellers, waiting.

'Mr 'Olland, I'm thinking as we might be here a while. Why don't you take yourself off to the Wheatsheaf?' Plumstead suggests, naming the most civilized of Wycombe's twenty-odd inns. 'I'll see if I can find out what's doing here. And watch yourself. There's tricksters and deserters and every sort of hedge-creeping villain you could shake a stick at, round here. Right fucken rookery, Wycombe is.'

'As you wish,' says Aaron, mildly, hopping down.

Plumstead watches him go, then joins the waiting line.

Bless old Plumstead, Aaron thinks, *reckoning as I can't look out for meself* – and here of all places, a tavern so decorous it greets its patrons with a notice reading:

NO KNIFES

NO BLADES

& NO PISTOLES

You'd not get that in Southwark – or not for more'n two minutes after it was put up, any rate.

'I'll take that,' says the bangster on the door, laying his hand on Aaron's sword. It's a handsome thing, is Aaron's sword, the blade inlaid with the maker's name in gold, and with the Holland's motto: *NON TIMEO – I fear none.*

'Ho yes? You and whose army?' Aaron asks, then hands the sword over with a smile. I am grown so gentled, he'll tell sis, I scarce know meself. Also, his rejoinder strikes him as one of the wittiest things he's said in weeks. He finds himself a seat, snaps his fingers for a pot-boy, and with a tankard of ale, settles himself to watch the room. What a mixing and milling of men. Aaron hears accents from the north, he hears those of the flatlands of the east; there's buff-coats, new and pale and darkly weathered; hats sporting the emblem of this regiment or that – you can understand why the Wheatsheaf might seek to separate its patrons from their weapons, you can indeed.

Lord, you can feel the wallop of those mills right through the wall. The Wheatsheaf must be nearer to Wycombe's river than he'd thought.

A man sits down heavily in front of him. Aaron is about to make objection when he sees the man wears a sling on his arm.

'You permit?' the man asks. 'I grow weary.'

He looks it too. Walking wounded. When he removes his greyish felt hat, there is the shine of an old burn on the man's face. Well now, thinks Aaron. News – true, fresh, reliable – is so precious an article it has almost become coin, and if you want to know what is truly happening out there in the fields of English mud, you talk with the men who've been out in 'em. 'How'd you come by that?' Aaron asks, nodding his head toward the sling.

The other settles himself before he replies. 'My horse. It is shot beneath me.'

'Better the arm than the neck,' Aaron suggests, and the man responds with a long, slow '*Jah...*'. *A Deutscher, is he?* Aaron wonders. There's many such, come over from Germany, the sensibilities of Lutheranism being pretty much side by side with those of Parliament. 'What do you reckon to this notion of King Charles, to bring men over here from Ireland?' Aaron begins. It's an old trick: start a conversation with a stranger with some remark guaranteed to show you and they are on the same side.

The man directs a sort of cold curiosity at Aaron, as one might some oddity worthy of investigation. 'You English,' he begins. 'You are great haters, no?'

'No, we ain't,' says Aaron, stoutly.

'You hate the Irish.'

'No, we don't,' Aaron declares. ''Tis they hate us.'

'Oh, this I know,' the other says, nodding his head. 'This I know full well. Myself, I hate no-one.'

Find that hard to believe, thinks Aaron. 'So, going home now, eh?' he tries next.

The man lifts his chin in a pout of contempt. 'Home… no. Your Parliament, it does not pay its soldiers. I am not paid, I do not fight.' A snap of the fingers. Odd little fingers. Pointy. 'I must mend my fortune some other way than this. I take me back to London. I have friends there.' An eerie show of tiny teeth. 'I surprise them, I think.'

Bet they will be delighted, mate. 'Ho yes?' Aaron asks, as Londoners will. 'Whereabouts?'

The other waits a moment before replying; when he does, he seems to have some peculiar relationship of his own to the answer, as if it amuses him, a wry and private joke, perhaps. *If you ain't the oddest little beetle I ever met*, Aaron is thinking, then the man speaks. 'The Green Lizard.'

Aaron takes a gulp of beer. This is out of rhythm with the conversation, unmistakably so, but Aaron needs a moment to steady the alarum ringing in his head. 'Green Lizard,' he repeats.

'You know it?' asks the other.

'Not me,' says Aaron. 'Can't say as I do.' Every nerve within him, flared into life. No beetle this one, no. More like a fucken scorpion. Who is this fellow? One of Parliament's searchers-out of spies?

'No?' the man asks. He has Aaron under close examination. 'You look for a little minute as if it means something to you.'

'Not I, friend.' Aaron puts out his hand. 'We oughter introduce.' *Find out more*, he's thinking. *Get the bastard's name*. 'Aaron Holland.'

The other answers, 'Lodowick Alembert.'

Out here in the street, the grinding of the mills is loud enough for a man to have to lift his voice. Abel Plumstead watches as the sergeant of the Trained Bands runs Abel's papers past the end of his nose, line by line. He takes his snuff box from his pocket. 'Pinch?' Plumstead asks, offering it over. 'Sullivan's. Number three mix.' It's his experience that if a man will open up his nose-holes to a pinch of snuff, he may open up conversationally too. 'Something up, is there?'

The sergeant eyes Abel as if assessing whether he is to be trusted with such information. The men of London's Trained Bands are what London's apprentices grew up to be; power is precious to them. 'Priznurs,' he says at last. His accent is pure Billingsgate. 'Priznurs from Naseby Field. The Eastern 'orse bringing 'em to London. 'Unnerds of 'em, poor bastards.'

'God's will be done,' says Plumstead – a phrase that has become as handy as the offer of a pinch of snuff.

'He has smote our enemies,' the sergeant declares, magnificently. 'Well – he and General Cromwell.' And then, in a more everyday tone, 'Don't expect to move on from 'ere a while. They'll be bringing 'em through once it's dark.' The voice drops again. 'Less upset that way,' he adds.

'Upset?' Plumstead queries.

The sergeant drops his head into his sleeve, delivers himself of an almighty sneeze. Rubs the sleeve under his nose. 'They walk 'em,' he says. 'Church to church, all day long. Great gangs of 'em. There's some have been on their feet for weeks. 'Unnerds of miles. There's a camp set up in London, down in Tothill Fields, but God have mercy on 'em, I should not think there is one man in three amongst 'em will live to see it.'

Lodowick Alembert. Aaron is in shock. He'd almost be laughing, did the man opposite not have such an unsettling effect. *What the – what fresh fuckery is this?*

'*Jah*,' says the man, this – this – whatever he is. His face is as expressionless as Aaron hopes his own to be. He takes another gulp of ale, under cover of which to order his thoughts. There's bugles blowing their alarums from one side of Aaron's skull to the other; his face feels stiff with the effort of denial, and this man calling himself by Alembert's name, who watches Aaron as if he could hear every blare of those bugles, yet is no more than entertained by them. 'Aaron Holland of London,' the stranger repeats. He rubs at his unshaven chops. 'But you do not know the Green Lizard. I think it is a tavern, maybe. A place like this?'

'I told you, I don't know it, if it is,' Aaron replies. The bugles have been joined by a drum, louder even than the pounding from the mills outside. Aaron realizes it is his heartbeat.

'Or perhaps it is a street,' the stranger continues, musingly. 'One of your little London streets. They have such stupid names, do they not? Your little London streets.' At least the voice is musing. The eyes, so strangely hot in colour, they are gleeful. Aaron feels as if he were being nipped at, baited, a dog at his heels. '*Jah*, a little street,' the stranger is saying. 'I think so.' He smiles, nods toward the window. 'My servant, I see him outside.' He rises, a little off-balance, to his feet. '*Auf Wiedersehen*, Herr Holland. Maybe in London we meet again.'

Aaron, for a moment more, sits, stupefied. Then he shakes his head. Then, he realizes the man is gone. He leaps up, begins to force his own way through the crowd in the stranger's wake.

There is a lane runs down beside the Wheatsheaf to the river, and as he steps out into it, Aaron, sword in hand, is rolling his shoulders, ready to go. He can smell the water, that cleanness in the air. The thump from the fulling mill is deafening out here, drowning even the water's rush.

Where's his quarry? Gone out into the street? No, there's that greyish hat, moving away down the lane. The light is fading, but there's enough to make it out, silhouetted against the scraggly foliage. Where's the man going? To take a piss? Aaron's fingers flex about the hilt of his sword; he walks on his toes. Generations of thuggery have gone into creating Aaron, and in any case where anything that might touch upon Cornelius is concerned, Aaron would walk through fire. And a man with one arm in a sling – this will be easy. *I'll have you, you stoat-eyed masquerader*, Aaron vows. *I'll find you out.* He pads forward. Another yard. *Thud* go the mallets in the mill. He shoots a hand forward, spins his man around, and finds himself facing –

A punctured Falstaff, is what he is facing. Bowlegged, hunched, in doublet now vastly too big for him and wearing the stranger's hat. But a familiar Falstaff all the same, Aaron knows him at once. Tucker Turnbull.

'You!' Aaron exclaims. 'The *fuck*—' Tucker, the Skinners' man. In which case, the stranger, the Skinners' man. 'You!' And in that moment, feels a hot belch of pain spread upward from his back to fill his chest.

He cannot get his breath. He feels himself rise up, as if to get away from the pain, and then he hears the stranger's voice behind him.

'This is my panzerstecher,' the voice says. 'She hides within my sling, you see? I do not like to be without a blade. And then she bites.'

Aaron feels sweat pushing out upon his forehead. 'She runs in cleanly,' the voice continues. 'I withdraw now, you heal. But if you move, or if she does—' The pain is now so great, it feels to Aaron as if it is bulging into his throat. 'Now you tell me,' the stranger says. 'This Green Lizard. What, and where?'

He must not speak. He must keep his mouth clamped shut. He must not say a word.

'What and where?' the stranger asks again. Aaron, on his toes, feels his whole body throb. He thinks he feels the blade move inside him. A hiss of pain escapes between his teeth. 'Where?' the stranger demands again, and then as if he loses patience, Aaron hears him say, '*Zehr gut*,' and for Aaron the whole world starts to slide away, as if everything about him was no more than wet paint being wiped from its canvas. The panzerstecher; so sharp, so keen; with it you may reach the entire inner landscape of a man: the cushions of the kidneys, the upland pastures of the lungs; even the echoing chambers of the heart. Aaron can hear nothing but the thud of mallets. But already the pain is being pushed from its place, something even greater is replacing it. It occurs to Aaron that he knows what this is, because it is bigger than everything –

What should happen now is that Plumstead comes into the lane in search of Aaron, and see the one man sagging between the two, and gives a shout, and raises the hue and cry; but it does not. Plumstead has only just walked into the Wheatsheaf. His description of his man elicits no more from the bully on the door than the information that Aaron is gone outside. Gone where? The jakes?

Aaron at this moment is being dragged through the scrubby plants at the river's edge, although he doesn't see them, only greenish light. His consciousness is scrabbling for a grip at the edges of what is happening to him; trying, in some instinctive way, to reach toward Cornelius, because Cornelius matters, even now, even here, and he would so dearly love to see Cornelius again. But all there is before him is the black surface of the river and its rotting lily pads, and the dreadful thumping of the mills. He tries to ride the noise. He tries to mirror each thump with another heartbeat, he tries to reach to reach to reach to anything to anyone he can—

There is a falling away. There is detachment. Aaron understands what he must do, and closes his eyes. The water meets over his head and floods the inner devastation left by Carlo Fantom's blade, and he is gone.

'Aaron Holland,' Tucker wails. He stands on the riverbank, presses his hands across his mouth. 'That is Aaron Holland.'

Carlo gives a chuckle. '*Was*,' he says.

'But you—' Tucker is almost bereft of speech. 'You can't. He's a *Holland*. They will – they will—'

'They will what? Listen to me, my donkey. I will tell you who this man was. This was a man who knew I lied, and who said nothing. This was a man who knew this Green Lizard. I see it in his face, I see it in every grain of him. The gods smile on me, my donkey. We go back to Ingram Skinner, you and I. We search out every place this Holland knew. We find this Green Lizard. And I think we find something else there too.'

Plumstead, growing more troubled by the second, has gone back to the high street. One Londoner, he hopes, will always favour another. 'Mislaid me passenger,' he tells the sergeant.

'What's that to me?' the sergeant replies, distracted. At the far end of the street, the unmistakable up-and-down of approaching horsemen.

'But it's Aaron Holland,' Plumstead says.

'An *'Olland?*'

The Wheatsheaf? No, Plumstead has already looked.

The lane? Empty. No, wait –

The sergeant bends down to whatever it is, lying there amongst the tangled grasses at the side of the lane. He straightens up. He is holding Aaron's sword.

The thud of the mallets in the fulling mill, it is as if it draws them to the bank. 'There,' says the sergeant, pointing. 'There, under them lily leaves. What's that?'

Plumstead drops to his knees. 'Oh, fuck me,' he groans. 'Oh, hell's bloody bells!'

They run back to the street. They will need grappling hooks, ropes, more hands. They shout for attention, but the street has none to give. On either side, the street is lined with horsemen, and between them, filling the street itself, carrying their wounded, dragging themselves along, the prisoners – ragged, bloody-footed, walking till they drop.

IT'S BECOME THE custom for meals at Varney to be taken in the kitchen, everyone eating together and the heat from the cooking serving to keep the diners warm as well, since firewood is yet another thing that one must hoard. It still gives Toby an oddish feeling to eat at a table that (however well scrubbed since) had so much of his blood upon it, but as Molly says, the world as it is, what's a few more drops, one way or the other? Besides, says Moll, it is his, Toby's, blood, 'so I don't mind it, anyways.' It is Moll's habit to sit opposite him, on the women's side of the long kitchen table, and this evening, as Mr Endicott holds forth on how the King's so-called letters, taken at Naseby, are Parliament's arrant fakery, the toe of Molly's foot, secretly unshod, is on Toby's kneecap. She is a terrible forward lass, is Moll, Toby knows it. She makes his head spin.

'Armies from Ireland,' Mr Endicott declares, contemptuously, 'armies from France, forsooth! Why, I could write better impostures myself.' He reaches over and takes his wife's hand. (How Toby would love to be able to reach over and take Moll's hand in that way.) 'By God, I shall. When this war is done, Belle, I will write it. I will write its history.'

'And I know you will do it better than any other,' says little Mrs Endicott, loyally.

Mr Topham clears his throat. Topham likes to keep order at mealtimes. Conversation should wait till after they have said their prayers, not occupy the table before. 'God give us grace,' Topham intones, as they bow their heads. 'God give us peace.' And waits (since she is the closest they have here to a master) for Miss Holland to say the Amen.

But she does not. Instead she stands. It is as if she is about to make a toast, but she does not do that either; instead she wavers, she seems unsteady on her feet. 'Miss!' Molly cries out in alarm. Miss Holland seems not to hear her. Instead she utters a single word, she says, 'Aaron?' – then spins about, knocking her glass, her plate from the table, and runs from the room. By the time they have caught up with her, Miss Holland has Varney's front door thrown open. They can all see the rider who has come to a halt outside. The rider dismounts. He comes up the steps, the tops of his boots slapping together. 'Miss Holland,' he says.

'What is it?' Pris demands. 'You bring news, you have word—'

'No,' says Cantley. 'I bring this.' And into her hands he presses the silver wolf.

CHAPTER THREE

Bad as Bad Can Be

'When any person departeth this life, let the dead body, upon the day of burial, be decently attended from the house to the place appointed for publick burial, and there immediately interred, without any ceremony.'

The Directory of Publick Worship

IN THIS NEW London, this new England, death holds your hand and black is everywhere. Are you in mourning, or simply devout? Greville goes unshaven, adopts a strip of black tied round his arm, but against the severity of his wardrobe nowadays, it is barely noticeable. Bess is cased in black, from head to toe – lace, veil, jewellery, gloves; Mary likewise. And

Abi? Abi simply weeps. Morning, noon and night, until her cheeks are raw and her eyelids purple. Greville can hardly stand to look at her.

Mary asks, 'Will you weep your life away, Abi?'

Abi draws her hand under her glistening nose. 'God has forsaken us. What else is there to do?'

'Come with me,' Mary says. 'Come with me to Tothill Fields, to do what we can for those imprisoned there.'

The men in Tothill Fields die in their dozens, for all the good Samaritans with their baskets of food and gifts of old blankets can do. Every so often a Puritan divine will come and preach over 'em, seeking to convert such a useful reservoir of soldiery to Parliament's cause, but Parliament, finding itself so suddenly victorious, has more recruits than it knows what to do with, and London more prisoners than it can count, or lodge, or feed. There is a suggestion that Whitehall Palace (its state rooms emptied, leaves blowing along its corridors) might be converted to house them – them, and all those now being marched up from Somerset (another defeat), or down from Cheshire (another there, as well). Truly, the strongholds of the King – they fall one after the other, like beads off a broken thread. The life of man is as grass. The wind passes over it, and it is gone.

In Rotherhithe, there is to be a funeral.

They bury Aaron at night, as is the custom. Greville hires a phalanx of young toughs to escort the coffin to St Saviour's, and is astonished how many come forward offering their services for free. He had no idea Aaron was so popular – the lads of Southwark, the pot-boys at the old Red Bull, the assistants at Sullivan's; even some young Dutchman who writes from Green Dragon Court, praising Aaron's spirit, his generosity. Greville distributes funeral cards that are grisly with skeletons and skulls, and Abi, weeping still, is put to snipping so many locks of

Aaron's hair that the back of his head is rendered as bare as when he was a tiny infant in his cot. Greville will have them made into mourning rings. Meanwhile, what was Aaron lies on his layer of bran in Greville's front parlour; but the weather, thank God, is cooling, and the undertaker, shaking in his shoes at the thought of botching a Holland, did a more than decent job of stitching him closed. The cart carrying the coffin, when it finally sets off, is followed by torches in their dozens. Wise to show proper respect. It is noised all up and down: the Hollands have sworn bloody vengeance for Aaron's death, and God help those responsible, for in this world there will be no escape for them, that's sure.

Then Greville locks himself in his chamber, with Aaron's sword laid across his knees.

It is a handsome weapon, the handsomest. Greville presented it to Aaron when he turned twenty-one. The hilt has the elegant curves of a seed-pod, made to hold the hand safely within. And there on the blade that famous motto: I fear none.

Nor did you, thinks Greville, *you bloody young idiot.* His hand strokes the grip that his nephew's fingers might have held. Aaron never quite grew into this sword, any more than he ever quite grew into solid manhood – always the hothead, always the roarer. Now, of course, he never will.

The window of Greville's chamber overlooks the Thames, and it is the first of those days when you feel the year coming to its end; the sky so silver-white it's hardly there, the river sunk. Greville looks out, seeing without seeing. Aaron is gone. His niece has deserted them. What is the point of anything? Man is a creature without sense or hope, he's thinking, and all our striving, all is doomed.

The sun sets. The smoke of London's many chimneys appears like smears of chalk against the darkening sky.

Comes a scritching at his door.

'Greville? May I come in?' It's his sister.

'No.' He may never know peace again, but he will at least have quiet for his thoughts.

Bess is not to be dissuaded. She is even more no-nonsense since her nephew's death. 'Greville, we have a visitor. You will not want to miss him.'

'Why? Who is it?' Greville demands.

'It is the Skinners' man. Tucker Turnbull.'

'I have to do this, Mr 'Olland,' says Tucker. A glass of brandy sits before him, but it is untouched. Courage is liberation. 'I was there when your boy met his end. I know who did it, Mr 'Olland, I know who took his life.' Tucker's hands are squeezed between his knees. 'Forgive me, Mr 'Olland, but this is very 'ard for me. The Skinners 'ave been bread and board to me for years.'

'The Skinners did this?' Greville exclaims, disbelieving. 'As far away as Wycombe, and it was the Skinners' hand?'

'No, Mr 'Olland. But the man who did – he is here in London with them now. He is a Deutscher, Mr 'Olland. I've served him these two years and more, I had no choice, but oh, he is a brother to the Devil, this one. You would not believe—' Tucker has to make another stop. There is an image in his head – the rear of a wagon in the baggage train at Naseby. The women, huddled there, hands to their faces, the blood running down the backs of their hands, their moaning. Their eyes. 'You would not believe what I have seen him do. Sins the weight of which would drive another man to madness, to him they are no more than meat.' He shakes his head. 'Even the Skinners go in fear of 'im. And I cannot tarry, Mr 'Olland, I must get back to Hag Place.'

'A Deutscher,' Greville echoes. 'What, some freebooter, is he?'

'Not so. He is the agent of one Francis Hooley. And Hooley is in the service of Spain.' To utter such treachery is almost as bad as to be it. 'Mr 'Olland, this is all as bad as bad can be.'

In the silence that follows, it is as if you can hear Greville's blood begin to roil. 'Give me his name,' says Greville, at last. 'Give me his name, Tucker, and you will never need anything from the Skinners again.'

'Carlo Fantom,' says Tucker. 'Carlo Fantom. But I want nothing for this, Mr 'Olland. All I want is free of 'im. Can you do that for me, Mr 'Olland? Can you?'

It's a long walk from Rotherhithe to Hag Place, and all in this newly silent city – no carousers outside the taverns, no beery salutations as Tucker passes by; yet Tucker never felt so light of heart. Terrified, yes, but a terror that is almost joyous. *I've done it. I have freed meself. I made me plan, and I saw it through, like a – well*, Tucker thinks, *like a warrior!* Here he is, already at Holborn, and there he goes, toward Turn Again Lane, as brimful of triumph as an overflowing cup, and on the last such night he will ever know.

Ezra Skinner opens the door to him. 'Where you been, Tucker?' Ezra hisses. 'Captain Fantom, he's been asking after you.'

Not going to have to worry about him much longer, Tucker comforts himself. Oh, he feels invincible! Now here is Carlo Fantom's voice, oily with menace as ever, drifting down the stairs. 'Mr Tucker. Where have you been, as late as this?'

'Went searching for Bug,' Tucker calls up, into the darkness. 'Searching for Bug, up on London Bridge.'

There is the man himself, leaning over the banister, candle in hand. 'You walk about almost as late as me, Mr Tucker! Come up, come up. Let us end this day with a drink.'

*

At about the same time that Tucker, feeling a deal less bold than he had been on his walk back to Hag Place, is being encouraged up its stairs by Carlo Fantom, Greville Holland walks in on brother Jenkin.

'Hey up, brother,' says Jenkin. Jenkin's floor is deep in papers, sorted into careful piles. His boots await a final polish, his coat, hung on the door, a final brush. Jenkin is making ready to return to Amsterdam. He peers at his brother. 'Capo, something on your mind?'

He is a cautious man, is Greville. For all the bursts of temper, he never made a plan yet without walking round it first one way, then the other. Revenge, on Greville's buffet, is used to spending most of its time good and cold. But now –

Now it is time to breathe upon it once again.

'You have paper spare?' Greville asks.

'I do,' Jenkin answers. 'Why, am I about to need it?'

'Yes, you are. You are going to write out a note for me. I need it to be untraceable and your hand is unknown. I've information for the Trained Bands. We are going to start a fire, brother, and by God, such that will burn down the house of Ingram Skinner once and for all.'

'Mr Tucker,' says Carlo. 'Sit, sit.'

Tucker, movements staccato with apprehension, lowers himself to sit. This is the chamber where Ingram Skinner used to interview him, yet tonight of Ingram there is no sign at all. Instead, it seems Carlo has made the room his own. Here he is, coming back to the table with a bottle in one hand and two glasses in the other. Proper glasses too, not the beakers Tucker is used to being provided with.

'Mr Tucker,' says Carlo Fantom, 'you trouble me.'

I do? thinks Tucker. He feels his bowels loosen. Also, since when did he become a mister?

'I feel we get off on the wrong boot.' A glance across the table. 'You say this, yes? The wrong boot?' Carlo picks up a glass, holds it against the candlelight.

'Wrong foot,' says Tucker, as apprehensive as before. He watches as Carlo pulls the bung from the bottle, fills two glasses.

'Ah, yes,' Carlo says. 'That is it. The wrong foot.' He turns his face, to expose the shine of the burn, the melted ear. 'You are uneasy to drink with me, Mr Tucker. I see that you are.'

It comes to Tucker that his host is waiting for him to choose a glass. Fears of swift and subtle poisons possess him – but surely not, if he chooses himself?

'But then, I should be used to this,' Carlo is saying, with a melancholy shake of the head. 'I am a man accursed.' He waits for this to register. 'Oh yes,' Carlo says. 'Did you not know this? As a young man, I am cursed. I am cursed by a Roma.' A glance at his audience. 'You have them here? The Roma?'

'Might have a few tinkers,' Tucker offers. Ingram Skinner's wine is excellent, Tucker's head feels fumey on one mouthful. 'But Roma, no. Hang 'em.'

'In my country we have many. And they are a haughty people, troublesome and proud. There is no respect for us amongst them. And my family, Mister Tucker, they are noble. I am from the wrong side of the blanket, as you say, but my father, he has a name, and this Roma tribe, they take his name, and they traduce it. They spread lies. There was one – a young man, a teller of fortunes, so troublesome – my father had to have him locked away. But even then, there is no end to their nuisance. Wherever my father is, there they are, pleading, importuning, saying we must set him free. So I go to the mother, I say, you have a daughter. Give her to me, and I will have my father give you back your son, while there is still something left of him.' Carlo lets his face grow dreamy. 'The daughter, she was a beauty. She would have been a prize.' Watched by Tucker, he takes a sip of wine. 'But the mother, this old woman, she says no. She spirits the daughter away. We keep the son locked up for many years thereafter. So long that – oh, what irony! He has been for so long in the darkness of his cell, that he goes blind!'

And Carlo laughs. It is a sound with a lot of wet in it; it makes one think of some long-nosed, sharp-toothed creature, rootling. Tucker makes an attempt at joining in, which seems to satisfy his host. 'You comprehend the joke,' Carlo is saying. He sounds delighted. 'This one who says he sees into the future, who dared foretell my father's death – now he sees nothing at all! But Mr Tucker – you spill your wine.' A napkin is flourished from across the table.

'Kindly of you,' Tucker says, 'but there's no need.' He can't see that he has spilled any.

'No, I insist.' Carlo mimes, *There, on your chin.*

So Tucker takes the napkin, and dabs at mouth and chin. He makes to hand the napkin back.

'And so they curse me,' Carlo continues, not taking it. 'This old Roma woman, she and her sisters, they curse – do you hear something, Mr Tucker?'

A moment ago, Tucker could have sworn he heard movement outside, on the stairs, but right now it is taking all his concentration to follow Carlo as he speaks. The words keep elongating in the strangest manner, sliding past. He feels a coolness at his back. He tries to see where the draught is coming from, but it is extraordinarily difficult to move his head. His hands too – his hands are clenching, uncontrollably. He cannot stop them. The wine glass stem fragments. Blood wells up between his fingers. Tucker thinks of the women at Naseby, he tries to lift his eyes to Carlo's, because he has the sense of something most horribly awry here, but his eyes will not go where he wants them either. All they will do is stare at his fingers as they drip.

Because this is how it works, this favourite amongst Carlo's methods of disposal. Rigor before you are dead. It is an irony Carlo finds amusing. He sits back, to enjoy its creep.

'They curse me, Mr Tucker. They say I will walk through the world like Cain. I will be damned, in life and then in death. And do you know who they say will bring about my destruction? They say it will be a woman. A woman!' Another laugh, fiercer this time. 'Do you not think, Mr Tucker, of all the jokes, that is the best of all? A *woman*.'

He leans across the table, peering. 'Mr Tucker? My donkey?'

The door comes open. There stands Ingram Skinner. He steps forward. Pushes, with one bony finger, at the back of Tucker's head. Tucker's body slumps from his seat to the floor.

'Fuck me, that stuff works fast,' Ingram comments.

'Yes,' says Carlo. 'I remember it so. Of course he will be alive inside a little longer.'

'Fucking *traitor*,' Ingram comments. 'Fucking *Judas*. Sat there at my table, all these years.' And he makes as if to pick up the napkin.

'No. Leave that,' Carlo tells him, sharply. He picks up the napkin himself, on the stem of the broken glass, and throws both into the fire. The fire for a moment burns with a greenish flame. 'It is when it is breathed in that it starts to work. I used it first in France, many years ago. There was a soldier, a cavalryman. A noted warrior. A Titan, in fact. And I was young. Sometimes one does not wish to risk the fight. It took a long, long time with him.' He stands over Tucker; he spits. 'With this one, it took no time at all.'

*

Londoners have been choking the River Fleet with their rubbish for centuries. 'He will not sink here,' Carlo says, meaning Tucker, or what was Tucker, but which now lies wrapped in a blanket and with Ezra locking a chain about its ankles. He points toward the crowded surface of the water. 'This is no good to us. This is no more than a ditch. He will be found.'

'Patience, Captain,' Skinner tells him, nodding to where Asa is drawing out, on dripping rope, a rowboat. 'We take him out to the river proper. Sink him there.' He contemplates the blanket, which has moulded itself somewhat to Tucker's shape. 'You fucker,' says Skinner, aiming a kick. 'You turd-breathing doubler. Take yourself off to meet with Greville Holland, would you?'

'Calm yourself,' Carlo tells him, with a glance to the darkened windows of Hag Place's neighbours on the other side of the Fleet. 'This piece of dreck, it is nothing. The sooner we are rid of it, the sooner we can begin to look again for our green lizard.'

Ezra gives a groan. He has no time for more of this. 'But we've looked for your green lizard,' he snarls. 'We've hunted high and low. There ain't a tavern nor a street nor a nothing of that name, not anywhere in London.'

'There's a green dragon,' says Asa, as he pulls the boat toward the bank. He likes to be helpful, does Asa, no matter how many times it has backfired on him.

'There's a what?'

'A green dragon. Green Dragon Court. Up by St Paul's. Where all the bookshops is. I go up there, nar'n again,' says Asa, a little shamefacedly, as if proximity to St Paul's or to bookshops is something of which a man should be ashamed. He looks from his brother to his father. 'What?'

'Green Dragon?' Ingram repeats.

'That's it. The Hollands' agent, Vanderhoof, he's a bureau

there,' says Asa, pleasantly. 'Used to spy Aaron Holland up there all the time. That any use?'

'You witless fucking blockhead—' Ingram begins, then, 'Hi, Ezra! There behind you! Get him, quick!'

A shadow has moved inside the yard. A small shadow, but movement nonetheless. Ezra bounds back into the yard. For one of such muscle-bound heft, Ezra can move with the speed of a charging bull. There is a scuffle, and a high-pitched cry, and Ezra emerges holding Bug by the shirt. 'Gorra intelligencer, pater,' Ezra announces. He gives Bug a shake. 'What shall we do with 'im? String 'im up?'

Ezra is joking, but Carlo is not. 'Ingram…' he begins. 'A witness. A spy.'

'Throw him in,' says Skinner without hesitation, and Bug is hurled into the rowboat on top of Tucker's body. Down the Fleet they go. Asa uses an oar to punt them round the worst of the obstructions – a cart, tumbled in; a horse with its belly ballooning out of the water. Ezra keeps a grip on Bug, who is shivering with terror. Bug's gaze keeps sliding over to the form folded in the blanket; at one point it is as if he makes to reach toward Tucker's forehead. 'Oh no, Mistah Skinner,' he keeps saying. 'Oh no.' Ezra finally cuffs him into silence.

Skinner keeps his eyes on the bow. 'Go at the speed of the river, Asa,' he growls. The Thames is dotted with craft, all with lanterns swinging – late-night fishermen, late-night travellers. 'We don't want no-one asking themselves why we're in a hurry.' He cocks an ear – did he hear another oar just then? He points ahead to a stretch of water of uninterrupted darkness. 'Take us over there.'

Asa aims the prow where his father is pointing, then pulls ahead anew. The bank is very far from them now. Asa ships the oars. They glance about, but any other craft are too far away to see, or for them to be seen. Asa reaches forward, gets hold of

Tucker by the shoulders, Ezra lifts his legs. The boat rocks. Carlo, unused to this watery business, grabs the gunwales on either side. Skinner grins at him. 'And there goes problem number one,' he says, and over the side goes Tucker, feet first, with barely a splash. As he hits the water, the blanket unfurls about him like a spathe, and for the briefest moment Tucker, revealed, is looking up at them, eyes open still. Ezra, pointing, gives a snort of laughter. 'Pater, he don't look happy!' Then Tucker sinks. In the silence, Bug can be heard, crying quietly to himself.

'And while we're at it,' says Skinner, 'let's rid ourselves of problem number two.' He makes a grab for Bug, picks him up and holds him by his shirt over the side of the boat.

Bug's legs windmill, as if seeking to race away. The river slides beneath him, one smooth black fascia of water overlaying the next. It looks horribly swift, the tide racing to be gone. 'Don't do this, Mistah Skinner!' he pleads. 'Don't do this to me, I beg of you!'

'You, you shit-stain,' says Skinner, holding him out. Skinner's arms may look like those of a corpse, but they are strong as wire. 'I'd a daughter, like to you. Always creeping about where she'd no call to be. Shuffling about on her knees. Turning those eyes of hers on me. Trailing my name in her prayers, begging me to change me ways. You, you miserable scut. You've been a pain in my arse ever since that piss-pot Tucker brought you to my door. I have done this to my own flesh and blood. I won't even *remember* doing it to you.'

He opens his hand. Bug drops.

Bug surfaces with the taste of the river in his throat and the chill of it forced up into his brain. The Skinners' boat is already yards away, turned back toward the bank; he can see Asa pulling at the oars, and Skinner, still standing, as if to be sure Bug has gone. He can swim, can Bug, after a fashion, but the river has caught him as it would a leaf, is turning him round and around, and it is so cold, it stings every pore of his skin. He goes down again, fights his way back up to the surface. Fury engulfs him, rage at the relentless hardship his life has been up to this point, at the fact that neither his living nor his dying will make a difference to a single soul but him. The tide is making the river choppy, waves hit him in the face and blind him, but not before he has seen that there is an obstruction ahead of him, large and without a lantern, and that he is being swept toward it, and that this is going to be the end of him.

Instead, he is pulled from the water, legs still kicking, swimming for a moment in the air, and then there is timber beneath him, and Miguel Domingo's face before his own. 'I have you, Barnaby,' Miguel is saying. 'I have you.' A fisherman's knitted jerkin is placed over his shoulders.

'Miguel!' Bug's teeth are chattering so violently he can hardly speak. 'Miguel, we gotta get to Mistah Vander'oof!'

'And we will, Bug, we will.' The usual long, slow pull at the oars.

'But we have to make haste, Miguel! You don' un'erstand! The Skinners know who he is! They'll be coming for 'im!'

'But I do understand, Master Barnaby,' says Miguel. 'You think you are the only one to work for this man?'

Cornelius Vanderhoof, the man of the hour. Here he comes, back into Green Dragon Court, his step perhaps a little slower, a little more measured than usual, but even so, you would never guess from anything about him the heaviness in his heart. But then if you are Cornelius, you learned dissembling very early on.

He glances at the modest frontage of his bureau. Time and again, coming back here, it would be to find Aaron lounging against its door. Now, never again. The relentlessness of the fact, its inescapability; it is like a prison sentence. *My love is gone*, Cornelius thinks. No escort when he goes about the town. No more that arm, placed over him at night. *My love is gone, and I am on my own. My friends are scattered, God knows where, and all things are in ruins.* His pace falls away, he comes to a stop. He lifts his face to the sky. One solitary greenish star up there, over the Hampstead hills, otherwise nothing but clouds and moon, spiked with church towers in silhouette. Here where he stands within the modest rooflines of Green Dragon Court, Cornelius can make out three of them – St Margaret Moses, St John Evangelist, St Mary-le-Bow… He turns about and as he turns, he listens, and as he listens, he hears –

– nothing. Not his neighbours in their own emporia; not even the screech of one of the many cats that usually patrol the court like watchmen. Cornelius enjoys the cats, has been known to feed them; when they hear his step they come running, tails held up in greeting, but this time there are none. He hears the passing of pedestrians in Wood Street, he hears the roll of a carriage, but within Green Dragon Court itself, not a sound.

Cornelius looks over at the darkened windows of his office. *You keep your wits about you, do you hear?* Faced with such unusual quiet, Aaron would have his hand to his sword by now. Cornelius, however, wears no sword, and has no-one to issue warnings to other than himself, and he, it seems, has no need of them: at the back of his neck every hair has righted itself, like a hackle.

'Mistah Vander'oof!'

The voice comes from under the steps of the yard behind him. 'Mistah Vander'oof, sir! Come away!' A face, a whitish smudge, is visible. Bug creeps into view. 'Mistah Vander'oof, you can't go 'ome, sir! They know about you, sir, they're coming for you!'

'Who, Bug?' Cornelius whispers, as Bug creeps closer.

'The Skinners, Mistah Vander'oof! The Skinners!' A grimy hand, extended from whatever it is the boy is wearing. 'Come away, sir, come away!'

CHAPTER FOUR

Never Ever

'Be stronge, and let us be valiant for our people…'

The Souldiers Pocket Bible

ANNIE, MISS HOLLAND'S mount: to be honest with you, were horses any the less scarce than in these times they are, Annie would have been glue long ago. Hardly bigger than a pony, Annie is, and then there's the ear, and the eye, and her constant nudging for food. But she has her virtues. She is endlessly accommodating, to begin with, and with no-one but Topham's morose old gelding to share her days, pathetically welcoming of company. 'Poor girl,' Molly says, while Annie mumbles a windfallen apple from her hand. 'I think she's lonely.'

Toby is fond enough of Annie, but he can't help feel she is not the one truly hard-done-by here. Miss Holland is taking the boys to London and Moll is to go with her. I must be with my mistress, is all Moll says. 'It won't be for always, Toby. One day everything will be as it was, you'll see.'

'But London,' Toby begins. London, in Toby's imagination, is full of wickedness, a place of monsters. He is almost wordless at the thought of it. 'London, Moll!'

'We ain't to stay there,' Moll tells him. She pats his hand. 'We're going on to Amsterdam, with this Mr Vander'oof.' She says it boldly, but a deal more boldly than she feels, truth be told. What does Moll know of Amsterdam? That those who live there can't abide a cobweb, and eat fish without cooking it. She is not at all sure how she will get on in Amsterdam. But if that is where her mistress must go, Moll must go too, because whereas being a man is all about looking after yourself, being a woman is all about looking after each other. 'You didn't know?' she asks, seeing Toby's face.

No, Toby did not. *Amsterdam?* For a moment he truly is wordless. 'Moll, nothing is going to be as it was.' He hears how his voice cracks, like a child's. But why would Moll ever think of staying here with him? Half-blind, and with his ruined hand, why would she care anyway? 'None of it. *Ever.*'

Moll's mistress is up in the great bedchamber with Belle, and with every gown she owns thrown across that mighty bed. 'Take them, Belle,' Pris had said. 'Wear them or sell them, or anything you wish. Take them all. I can hardly wear such in London, and we cannot go with luggage, in any case. We cannot have it look as if we mean to flee. It must all be a subterfuge.'

Carnation, Lincoln green. Murray red and purpurine. Couleur du Roy. Gingerline, pearl. Belle has never seen such a paintbox of gowns, such a carnival of ribbons, such a tumble of lace. 'You will write to us,' Belle begins. 'You will write to us, to tell us you are safe, and we will write to you. We will not leave you not knowing, Pris, we promise—'

She addresses her comments to the dressing-room. From within the dressing-room, the sound of drawers being hauled open, possibly even being pulled in a fury to the floor.

'You will have every bit of news there is, so you will know when to – when to—' When to come back, Belle had been going to say, but at that point, her head droops, her heart misgives. No-one can say when that might be.

'Belle,' Pris calls, 'come here.'

Belle enters the dressing-room. There stands Pris, with yet another gown in her arms, this one so bright a golden yellow it is as if it had been dyed in liquid sunlight. She turns Belle around to face the looking-glass. 'This one,' Pris says. 'This one is lucky. This one, you must keep.'

Belle puts one hand to her heart, holding the bodice against her, the other, holding the skirts, to her waist. She stares at her reflection. The yellow of the satin lights her face like a buttercup. 'I will be so lonely with you gone,' Belle says, quietly.

Pris lays her head against Belle's shoulder, so that she too is watching Belle's reflection in the looking-glass. 'Oh, Belle, I will miss you too.' She sees Belle's eyes grow wet, the tears begin to spill. She puts her arms around Belle, over Belle's own, her hands crossed on Belle's stomach. She holds them there, eyes closed. For a moment Belle thinks Pris will speak to her, that something of great significance will pass between them; later she will almost think it did, that she heard some word, some whispered thing, but no. Belle is released, and Pris turns away. 'Plumstead will be here so soon. I have to speak with Topham.'

*

'You must remember, Topham, Ocker likes his mush in the morning to be warm.'

Ocker has his nose pushed into Miss Holland's palm.

'And the old grey mat in the kitchen, that is Todd's, though Ocker always tries to steal it from him.'

'Miss Holland, I will see fair play.'

'And Annie, Topham – don't send her to the knackers, promise me.'

From behind them in the solar, the sounds of Mrs Mayhew and Old Henty drawing dust-sheets over the furniture. Miss Holland presses her fingers to her mouth. When she speaks again it is in a voice where Topham can hear the wail behind it as if held behind a dam. 'We are letting all of you down!'

'Miss Holland,' Topham says, 'will you be so good as to come with me.'

He leads her to the kitchen, and down into the cellar, and along in the darkness to where Varney used to keep its coals. Of course the space is empty now, save for the piles of coal-dust in its corners. Topham stoops and, in the light from the cellar window, lifts a canvas from the floor, a canvas so black that until he lifted it, it was invisible. And there beneath, snug in a hole in the cellar floor, a strongbox. Topham lifts it out, inserts a key; raises the lid and at once the cellar ceiling is aglow. Light as bright and yellow-gold as when Pris was in her dressing-room with Belle.

'This is our war-chest,' Topham is saying. 'It is for me to make use of however it is needed, so the captain said. I may use it to pay off any as might come here and be troublesome, or it is to meet our needs, or both.'

She is astounded. 'How long has this been here?'

'It came here with the captain's men, right at the beginning of the war. We are to shutter the upstairs of the house, and make ourselves look of as little account as possible, he says. We are to keep our heads down and bide. There is only one of us has been in such times as these before, Miss Holland, and what he says to do is what we must.'

Pris reaches out her hand toward the chest of coin, then lets it fall. 'He never thought the King would prove victorious, did he?'

'No, Miss Holland,' says Topham, slowly, sadly. 'I do not believe he did.'

'Yet he still went to fight.'

'Miss Holland, I think it was the surest way he had to try to keep us safe.'

THE ROAD TO London, and not via Wycombe this time, Plumstead is not risking that again. 'Miss Holland, your brother. I was so stricken. It is the evil of the times.'

'It is. There is nothing but.' The voice that answers his is thin and hard and cold. Then as if remembering her manners, his passenger adds, 'Thank you.'

And not a word out of her since. There she sits, hair bound away under her cap, dressed dark as a mole and the boys behind her like a pair of little preachers. Given the younger boy's afflictions, Plumstead had made a nest of sacks in the back of the wagon, but the youngster had been too entranced by all this as some great adventure to settle within it. The older boy, he'd seemed to have more idea of what was at stake here. He'd been gudding down the sobs, the poor lad, as Varney moved off into the distance. Farewell, farewell, and be you safe and lucky.

That maid of Miss Holland's, though, she's as much of a cricket as ever. 'Oooh, it's nippish. Ned, you tuck your brother in. Mr Plumstead, where's this?'

'Wallingford,' Plumstead replies, but it's not, not no more. The farmhouse that had been there for as long as Plumstead could remember, that's gone. Raked in its own ashes, as they say. They come up to Goring, and the barn that was such a handy place to shelter – there it stands, roofless. He's heard the soldiers took its thatch as fodder for their horses. Whose horses? What soldiers? Nobody knows, and what difference would it make even if you did? Whose ever they were, pray you don't run into 'em, is all. The Trained Bands is one thing (as a Londoner, Plumstead feels almost warmly toward the Trained Bands), but these others, these Ironsides… supposedly the name began as a joke, but who's laughing now? Plumstead wonders, remembering Wycombe. Remembering the prisoners stumbling toward London. And poor bloody Aaron Holland, to boot. Nowhere's safe. Nowhere is the world as it was, and all negotiation through it, a thing of sharp passage and unease. 'An' I hate to say it, madam,' Plumstead tells his passenger, 'but when we come into Uxbridge, keep your eyes down. You and the boys and yer maid.'

'We will, Abel. We know.'

They reach Uxbridge, and no point trying to find beds for the night, Plumstead had seen that at once; there were folk lying out in the marketplace, under the stars. 'Never thought there'd be as many on the move as this,' he'd said, muttering. 'Never thought.' He'd handed Ned the reins. ''Ere, young shaver. You do take these, I'll go see what I can see.'

'An' *I'll* go see what I can find for supper,' announced the maid. Still with a bit of bounce to her, that one. She'd spied the fires in the marketplace at once, the lines waiting, the turning spits. 'Purse,' the girl had demanded, holding out her hand, and Miss Holland had handed it over without demur. 'You do stay here,' the girl had told her.

'I have my orders, do I?' Miss Holland said. Bit of a twist to her smile.

'Yes, miss. You do.'

When Plumstead returned, the vapour of spirits all about him, his face had been grim. Yet he had hauled himself up gamely enough onto the driving seat, even managed a joke or two to the boys. 'What d'you think of your hostelry then? Nice feather beds?' Only when the boys were asleep in the back of the wagon did he whisper to his passenger, 'There was a list of names.'

'Where? What list?'

'Up on the gates of the Crown. And the old Red Lion. And the Corn Market. "Notorious Malignants," it was headed.' He glanced over his shoulder at the boys. 'Their father's was upon it. Miss Holland, we need to get you safe to Mr Vanderhoof. Soon as we have some light, we must be on our way. We should not tarry here.'

He sees her take this in, all it may mean, set herself anew. 'No, Abel. We should not.'

THEY CHANGED HORSES at Hillingdon, bought breakfast from a woman frying eggs at the side of the road, for which she'd charged thruppence apiece. Thruppence! For an egg! Plumstead had been incensed, but as she paid, Pris heard herself wishing the woman good luck. Outside Hayes they passed a windmill, and she found herself pondering how curious it was to see its sails still turning, just as ever, and all this happening around it. She had told herself how they were coming to the end of it, Green Dragon Court and then shipboard, yes; all this would be over before they knew it, then she had glanced at Molly, and seen the same trepidation on Molly's face as she felt on her own.

Now they are at Ealing, and the line of traffic on the road is never-ending, as far forward as one can see.

'Miss Pris,' Molly whispers.

'I know. Patience, Molly. There's nothing we can do.'

A fingerpost to Hammersmith. Off to the right, a place where the earth seems to have been pulled away as you might pull the crumb from a loaf. 'Kensington,' Molly breathes. 'The gravel pits.' Plumstead is munching his pipe. The boys have come up behind them, James with his hand on Pris's shoulder to steady himself. All they can see ahead of them are more wagons, more carts, more travellers. The sky is darkening, then ahead it lightens too. 'What's that?' Ned asks, pointing.

Oh, thank God. The lights of Westminster. Where Ned points is the abbey. Nearly there.

On they – no, not go, but crawl. At one point Ned looks down over the side of the wagon and comments, 'There's a dog with three legs down there, and it's moving faster than we.' Now there are stars peeking out above them. But here, between the houses, the river, and a stretch of moonlit sand. They have reached the Strand. Moll shakes the boys awake. 'There, do you see? St Paul's!'

It is so strange, to be amongst these roofs again. Pris finds herself looking for the places she used to know as you might search for some feature you would recognize on the face of a long-lost friend, but everywhere that she and Aaron used to dally have their shutters up, and many have chains across their doors. So few folk about, and all of them hurrying, hurrying, heads bowed. They go on. Now there is rain needling her face, but say this for dressing dark: your clothes are a sight less likely to spoil.

Says Plumstead, 'Miss 'Olland, I will take you as far as I can, but I don't know as I can get you into the city.' He points ahead. 'Look there.'

Ahead, between them and St Paul's, is Ludgate, and where Plumstead is pointing with his pipe, a company of infantrymen standing before it. There are even men up on the old gate's roof, and more working their way down the street on either side. They are armed, they are armoured, they have muskets slung across their shoulders. There is one man with boots so tall they are up to the edge of his buff-coat, and a sash about his waist. Under his helmet, even his face is behind bars.

'*Fuck*,' says Plumstead, under his breath.

'Bribe 'im,' says Molly, at once. She pushes the purse into Pris's hand.

'Don't be a blockhead, girl,' Plumstead hisses. 'Ironsides. There is no bribing *them*.'

The man is working his way toward them. It's plain what he is about. *Your business, your papers*, at every pause. There is a knife-grinder ahead of them, his wheel atop his barrow; see how he raises his hands in objection, see him pointing like the aggrieved local that he is: *But I live here, who are you—*

They see how the soldiers haul him to the ground, how they stand above him, the butts of their muskets poised. They see how the man is half led, half dragged away.

The Ironside officer looks down the line toward them. Pris pulls her cap forward, closes her cloak over her skirts.

Plumstead is munching the stem of his pipe again. 'I didn't know there would be this.'

'Say she's your sister,' Molly hisses. 'Your widowed sister, and her boys. Say her man fought at Naseby under Waller, and he's gone.'

Plumstead stares straight ahead, his expression that of a man facing a firing squad. The Ironside spies Plumstead's wagon, easily the biggest in line. He strides toward them. The bells of St Bride's ring off nine of the clock. James is pushing himself forward. Pris tries to push him back. 'Not now, James. This is not a game.'

James is having none of it. 'But I know what to do!'

The Ironside approaches. The folk on the pavement edge back, out of his way; then as Londoners do, make a little crowd behind him.

James gains the seat. He poses himself, up at one shoulder, down at one hip, right hand under his chin. A woman points: *Look there. See the little cripple-boy.*

The echo of the bells dies away. 'The Lord is my shepherd, I shall not want,' James begins, in silvery treble. 'He maketh me to lie down in green pastures: he leadeth me beside the still waters. He restoreth my soul: he leadeth me in the paths of righteousness for his name's sake.'

Not one trip. James's voice is pure as water. The knot of onlookers on the pavement is growing. The woman at the front is wiping her eyes. The Ironside has come to a stop.

'Yea,' James continues, in his psalmist's sing-song, 'yea, though I walk through the valley of the shadow of death, I will fear no evil.'

A sob from the woman. An answering ripple of emotion from the rest.

'For thou art with me; thy rod and thy staff, they comfort me. Thou preparest a table before me in the presence of mine enemies: thou anointest my head with oil; my cup runneth over.' James lifts his face toward the starry sky.

'Oh,' cries the tearful woman, 'bless his sweet soul!'

'Surely goodness and mercy shall follow me all the days of my life: and I will dwell in the house of the Lord for ever,' sings James, and for good measure, puts his palms together at his breast. There is applause. There is a ripple of *Amens*. There is a cry: 'The days of wonder! The Lord is here!' Plumstead's pipe has dropped from his mouth. The Ironside calls out, 'Where are you headed?' and Molly hisses in Plumstead's ear, 'Tell 'im St Paul's!'

'St Paul's,' Plumstead calls back.

'God be with you,' the Ironside says. The line of infantrymen across the road is already opening to let them through. 'On you go.'

At the back of the wagon, hid behind its canvas, the boys throw two fingers at the Ironside until he is out of sight. 'Canny little bastard,' Plumstead is muttering. '*Canny* little bastard.' Moll has her arms about Pris's neck. 'There,' she says. 'I told you. I knew as we would be all right.'

They pass St Paul's, Plumstead woah-ing as the horses brace themselves on the downhill. Friday Street. And now an alley almost too narrow for the wagon to pass into it, the entrance to a courtyard visible beyond. Pris feels her shoulders drop by maybe an inch or so from her ears. 'Plumstead, that must be it. Let us down. We're here.'

And then the moment they enter the courtyard, Plumstead clip-clopping away, she feels her pulse start to rise.

The courtyard is dark. The bureaux are shuttered. This is not right.

Molly marches straight to the door marked 'Vanderhoof', raises her hand to hammer upon it.

'No, Molly, wait!'

There is something – there is –

What would you call it? Like someone was stood behind her, their breath upon her neck. Like she had snagged her skirt. It is as if she heard her name called, but with no-one there to call it. She looks about. She sees a cat trot along a roofline; she sees the boys, waiting, Ned with his brother leaning into him, Ned's arm around him, she sees how tired they are, how cold they are, how far they have come through this world of baffling adult strife, and how they need to be inside, they need a fire to warm themselves by, they need food, sleep, and she thinks, *Ah, pox upon it, these bloody little voices*, and she strides forward and bangs upon the door herself. 'Cornelius! Mr Vanderhoof!'

The door comes open. She steps in. 'Mr Vanderhoof?' The room before her, so far as she can make it out, is empty. She sees a table, a rack of shelves. A paper rustles under her shoe. 'Mr Vanderhoof?' She makes out the twist of a stair in the corner of the room, moves toward it. More paper underfoot. A chair, on its back – she walks into it, it scrapes across the floor. At once, some answering sound from the room above – the creak of a bedframe, the drop of not one but two pairs of feet being swung to the floor. *No, go back, no, go back now!*

Molly enters, with the boys. The door slams shut behind them.

Pris will realize later that the man who slammed it shut must have been waiting there, waiting for Mr Vanderhoof to come home, waiting in solitary delectation of the mayhem to come, had sent his lunkhead boys to loll about upstairs. She sees his shape behind her, then he opens the port of his dark lantern. In the light, the room jumps forward – the papers all across the floor, pulled from the shelves; the chairs on their backs; the whole place ransacked; and leering through the light toward her, horribly shadowed about the eyes and nose, the death-mask visage that is Ingram Skinner.

He seems nonplussed. Then he reaches forward, snatches her cap away. Her hair cascades about her face. 'Well, now, Pris Holland,' Skinner says. 'As I live and breathe.'

CHAPTER FIVE

Green Dragon Court

'Our enemies shall come out against us one way, but they shall fly before us seven ways…'

The Cavalier Soldier's Vade Mecum

HE HAS A very spartan bedroom, does Mr Vanderhoof. Well, Pris supposes, *had*. A chair and a bed, albeit one with a feather mattress, deep enough to hide Ned and James within it as completely as the babes in the wood. 'And who are these?' Ingram had demanded.

'Hers,' said Pris at once, pointing at Molly, and Molly, God bless her, uttered not a word, just gripped the boys' hands the tighter.

She heard Ingram's snort of contempt. 'Get 'em upstairs,' he had ordered Ezra. 'Lock 'em in. All of 'em.'

So now here they are, here in Mr Vanderhoof's bedchamber – she, the boys, and Molly dozing in the chair, with Pris's cloak tucked round her.

She can hear the men downstairs, Ingram and his sons. Low-voiced conversation. She gets down on her knees, puts an ear to the floor. She hears Ezra's thick-witted laugh. Then the door downstairs opening, and when she goes to the window, there in the moonlight is Ingram Skinner, crossing the courtyard like a scarecrow come to life.

Oh, little sis, says Aaron's voice, of a sudden, in her head. He sounds amused. *How are you getting out of this one, eh?*

She glances at the bed. All you can see of the boys is the silk of the hair. Looks back at the window. Yes, it even has a mullion. *You wait, Aaron, I'll show you how.*

She hears Asa and Ezra settle down, she hears a bottle roll across the floor; she waits some more, she hears the sound of snoring.

She hears the watch pass by on Friday Street. 'Three of the clock! Three of the clock and all well!'

'Molly!'

Molly wakes, rubbing her eyes.

'Molly, quick now, up. Those blockheads downstairs are asleep. We're getting out of here.'

Molly, blinking, and clearly not trusting her ears. 'What?' She scrubs at her forehead, as if this will wake her brains up. 'But how?'

Pris is already bending over the boys, whispering in Ned's ear, 'Ned, Ned, wake up.'

Ned, waking. Even less comprehension than Molly. 'What is it? Wos' happening?'

'Wake your brother. But quietly, Ned. Like *mice*.' Pris turns back to Molly. 'Get the window open. But quiet, Moll, no squeaks. Spit on the hinge.'

The window comes open. Pris pulls the sheet from the bed, bites it to start the tear, rips it into two. The boys, both awake now, watch her, bemused. Pris gives one half to Ned, takes the other herself. 'Twist, then knot it, Ned, do you see? Twist, then knot.'

'Twist and knot,' Ned repeats, sounding baffled.

Pris dips her head to his. 'It was your father taught me how to do this,' she tells him. 'In a town called Breda. It was how he rescued me.'

'He did?' Ned's eyes are wide.

'We made a rope from a knotted sheet, like this.' At mention of his father, Ned's hands start making sense of the instruction. 'He went down first, and he caught me. Which is what you will do with James.'

'We're going out the window?' Molly sounds aghast.

'Yes, we are. Moll, it's a nothing – ten feet to the ground, if that. Ingram's gone. His blasted boys are sleeping. We have to do this now.'

Ned is done with his half of the sheet. He hands it to her, she knots it to hers. 'Now,' Pris says, 'we tie this to the mullion, then we drop the rest outside.'

The knotted sheet drops with a whisper. Pris holds up a finger – *wait*.

No sound from below.

'Now you go first.' Because this is how you lead Ned – put him in front. 'Get up here, onto the sill.'

So he does.

'Wrap your legs about the rope, and sit on the knots. Think of it – think of it like climbing down out of a tree.'

He takes the sheet, ducks his head, gets his shoulders through the window. 'And mind your feet don't touch the shutters,' Pris warns him.

Down he goes. He makes it look easy.

'James, now you.' She lifts James up onto the sill. His weight is nothing, half that of his brother, and when he twists his head around to see the drop beneath him, his face shows no more than the same curiosity James evinces about everything. She squeezes herself up against the mullion to make room. 'Moll, come here. You take one arm, I'll take the other.'

They lean out as far as they can to lower him. James grips with his good arm and wraps his good leg round the sheet, canted back at an angle. 'There we go, Master James,' Molly whispers. 'Easy does it.' Ned, beneath his brother, has his hands raised as high as they will go. The sheet twists as James begins his descent. A slide, a stop, another slide. His small face turned to look up at them, then down at Ned, and then James judges himself near enough and lets go of the sheet altogether.

His brother catches him with ease.

'Molly – now you,' says Pris, patting the sill in encouragement.

Molly has just settled herself into position when they hear the noise downstairs. The creak of a stretch, a yawn. They freeze. Ned, below them on the ground, points in silent panic at the shuttered lower window. There must be light behind the shutters; it's cast in a line across the cobbles of the courtyard. A voice. 'Asa! Gerrup!'

Ned has hauled his brother back against the wall, out of sight.

It sounds as if Ezra has kicked his brother's chair. 'Gerrup! We're meant to be keeping watch!'

'Moll,' Pris says, under her breath. 'Molly, you've got to go.' She pushes the first knot into Molly's grasp. 'Take the boys. Get out of here.'

'But miss –' (Molly's expression is fearful) '– but what of you?'

'There isn't time for me.' Just to prove it, an answering grunt of complaint from downstairs: Asa is waking. 'Ingram's got no interest in you, it's me he wants. Moll, you have to take them, go!'

Moll turns her head to gauge the drop to the cobbles. 'But take them *where*, miss?'

'Anywhere. Anywhere safe. You'll think of somewhere. Molly, please—'

More noise downstairs; the sound of another kick. All of a sudden Molly's face has brightened. 'I have it, miss! I know where to take 'em—'

'Don't say it. If I don't know, I can't be made to tell.'

Molly's eyes meet hers. 'Oh, shitting shite, miss,' says Molly, miserably.

'Oh, Ingram isn't going to hurt me. He'll try to scare me as much as he can, but I'm worth money to him, he knows that.' From below them, they hear Ezra again. 'Moll, *now*.'

Molly starts easing herself through the window. 'Gentle on the wall!' Pris cautions her. Molly's head and shoulders pass out of sight. The sheet twists anew against the sill, the knot about the mullion creaks. The sheet goes slack. When Pris peers out the window, there is Molly, hustling the boys ahead of her. Ned has his brother on his shoulders in a piggy-back. An even louder noise from the room downstairs – the sound of a thump about the head, if Pris is any judge, followed by Asa's bleat of pain. The three look back, for just an instant, then they are gone, across the courtyard and away. Pris is pulling in the tail of the sheet just as Asa emerges from the door below.

Oh, little sis, says Aaron, in her head. *Ain't you the whipster, eh?* But he doesn't sound as if he means it.

Ingram poxing Skinner and his dunderheaded boys, thinks Pris. *He'll put me up for ransom.*

Yes, but I ain't no little tot no more. He thinks he'll have an easy time of it with me, I'll soon teach him different. He'll be paying Greville to take me off his hands before I'm done.

She hears the door downstairs opening again. By God, Ingram has those boys of his under his thumb. Every other minute, one of them comes out to look about.

But this time a greeting. A halloo. Footsteps in the courtyard. Conversation. Is that Ingram's voice? Pris had been roosting on the bed, now she sits up.

The sound of a man climbing the stairs. Pris gets off the bed. She hears a key being tried in the lock. She pulls her skirt straight, stands up. The lock clicks, the door opens.

Carlo Fantom stands there in the doorway.

'*Tzo*,' he says. The shiny skin to one side of his face stretches into what on any other man would be a smile. 'Miss Holland. The gods bring us together once again. You are surprised to see me, I think.'

She can smell something rising off him – mealy, fly-blown. And he has aged. All the suavity has gone. There is grey in the bristle on his chin, and when he removes his hat, his hair as well. There is a belly under his coat. He says, 'You were expecting Ingram, I think.' He makes a show of looking round the room. 'Where are they?' he asks.

'Where are who?'

'Ingram tells me there were children with you. Where are they?'

'I don't know. I woke, and they were gone.'

'And your maid too.'

'She too.' There is nothing within reach to use against him. Could she reach the piss-pot? Could she grab a pillow from the bed?

What good would it do her, even if she could?

He makes a run at her, a ploy, no more than a lunge, but it is enough to send her back into the corner. He smiles. She sees again those tiny teeth, the hot, dead eyes above. 'Miss Pris,' he says. 'Who were those boys?'

'I don't know. It was my maid found them. They were nothing to do with me.'

He clicks his tongue. Such an untruth, tut-tut. 'Do you remember where I saw you last? It was Upper Aston. Do you remember what happened there?'

'Your arse was kicked,' says Pris.

That checks him. 'I was most curious to discover the name of the man who led that raid, Miss Holland. The discoverer who found Essex's army. Who led Prince Maurice out from under Waller's nose.'

She feels how he watches her. It is as if he has his hands on her already. Her own are pressed against the wall. *Don't let him grab you, don't let him get a hold—*

'You see, I know. I know everything about him. I know him better than you do. I have always known him. He is my one loose end. And he and me, we find each other, always.'

Another step closer. She feels his eyes roam over her.

'I was at Naseby,' he says. 'There were women, in the baggage train. I tell the men with me, they must be Irish. When we are finished with them, you know what we do?' He lifts a hand, he puts those sharp-looking fingers of his round his nose, then with the other hand, mimes slicing with a knife.

She feels herself jump.

'It is a mercy, really,' Carlo Fantom says. 'No other man would want them after that. Miss Holland –'

He is easing his way toward her.

'Those like me – it is not lust. It is not that we desire you. It is to show your men how weak they are.'

He unbuckles his strange-looking sword, draws it from its narrow hilt, places it on the bed. 'Your hair,' he says. 'You have the look of an Irish to you. Or a Roma,' he adds, more thoughtfully.' He gestures to the weapon. 'You choose, Miss Holland. My knife, or – me.'

She can get no further from him than she is. There is no more space behind her. She sees her reflection in the window at Carlo's back. Her red-haired reflection.

Her reflection raises a hand, and points at Carlo Fantom. Her reflection opens its mouth, baring its teeth, as if making ready to lunge at its prey. An enormous calm possesses her. This is who they have been waiting for. This is who they want. This is why everything. This is why me.

'You touch me,' says Pris, 'it will be the greatest mistake you ever make. The greatest and the last.'

'No,' says Carlo. 'No, I do not think so.' He lifts one hand again, pressing together index and thumb. 'You know, in Germany, in Magdeburg, I broke a woman's belly once. I felt it – *snap*.'

From above, the slide of feet. The sound of Carlo Fantom's voice, idling, at play. 'Ezra,' says Asa. 'Ezra, this ain't right.'

'Shut your mouth.' Ezra is moving back and forth, fretful, discomfited.

'But that's Pris Holland,' Asa says. He watches his brother pacing to and fro. 'You know what he'll do to her. You know what he did with Dilly. And with Flo.'

Dilly's name strikes at some place in Ezra that yet has feeling.

Being Ezra, this means he must say or do something to prove that it does not. 'I *said*, shut it. You don't want any of her, it's my turn after.'

But Asa will not shut it. 'Ezra, this'll be war,' he says. 'Us and the Hollands, it'll be war. And they have the Trained Bands in their pocket. This'll finish us, it will—'

'Now you listen to me,' Ezra begins, rounding on him as their father might have done, and it is as if the gods were waiting for exactly that, because suddenly there is something to listen to. Bouncing now from one side of the court to the other, there is the tromp of marching feet. The roll of carriage wheels. The bellow of commands.

There is a man with the wasp-like yellow and black of the Farringdon Trained Bands on his hat, bursting in shoulder-first through the door. He levels his pistol and fires. Asa jumps to his feet and the shot catches him full in the breast. Ezra has just time to see his brother fall before a second trooper forces his way in, then a third, then a fourth. They fill the room, these men with their coats and their armour, but through and between them, before one raises his musket and knocks him to the floor, Ezra sees the carriage outside coming to a halt, its door opening. Now he is being manhandled outside, forced face-down to the ground. Surrounded by legs and feet, roaring his brother's name, Ezra sees a man get down from the carriage and walk past, into Vanderhoof's office. He has the look of a lawyer to him: the square flat collar, the half-length coat. More noise from within the office. Ezra's face is pressed against the cobblestones; there is a boot upon his cheek, holding him there, but now he sees Carlo Fantom being led past, then the lawyer escorting Pris Holland, his coat about her shoulders.

'Well now, mard-arse,' says the voice above his head. The boot presses down. ''Tis all up with you!'

Sudden disorder. A scuffle, a shot. The noise of men in sharp pursuit. A yell: 'Mr Franklin, sir! The prisoner, sir, the Spanish agent, Fantom! He's piked it! He's away!'

'Then stop him, stop him!' the lawyer shouts back. He is assisting the Holland bitch up into the carriage. 'We want that man taken! Don't waste your time on me!'

Ezra is being pulled to his feet. His brother's body is dragged past him. 'Asa!' he cries. 'Asa!'

'You want to join him, do you?' his captor suggests. The man has his pistol under Ezra's jaw. 'You traitorous Papist *fuck*. Do business with Spain, would you? We got you now.'

Ezra's eyes bulge. 'But I'm a Skinner! I ain't no Papist! You must be joking!'

'Feels like I'm joking, does it?' the man asks. Ezra hears the clunk of the mechanism as the pistol is cocked. 'How's *this*?'

'Miss Holland? Miss Holland?'

She comes back to herself little by little, or sense by sense, perhaps. She can see, but she seems unable to feel anything of her surroundings. Then she can feel – yes, a seat beneath her, she is sitting in a carriage, but now she cannot hear. She sees this stranger's mouth open and close, but she cannot hear him. Then she can: 'Miss Holland? Do you remember me?'

Does she? There is something about him – the scrub of his hair, the droop to his chops, the pouches under his eyes.

'I am my Lord Wyncanton's man of law, Miss Holland. His trampler, as the vulgar have it. I was there when he signed the lease for the rooms in King Street. Will Franklin. Do you remember me now?'

'Wyn?' she repeats.

'That's it, Miss Holland. You do remember. Splendid.'

Where are they going? West, along Cheapside. Now Holborn

Bridge. Her heart is in a riot. It feels as if it must be nursed back into life. 'Where are we?' she asks.

'Lincoln's Inn, Miss Holland. You will see.'

Yes, it is – here they go, across the green, across the Fields. The coachman brings the horses to a halt.

'Allow me, Miss Holland. Let me assist.'

A flagstoned path, with bushes off to either side. A house, with diapered brickwork. Mr Franklin opens the door. A black and white floor, and for a moment she thinks she is in Varney once again, but no, of course, she can't be, for the staircase in front of her is mahogany. She realizes she is still wearing Mr Franklin's coat, and hands it back.

'To the left, Miss Holland. That's the way.'

The door stands open. She goes in.

A panelled room, all polished shine, a pair of windows open to the green beyond. A tester bed, the covers pulled back to its foot, but with that air to it of its inhabitant having left it but lately, and there before her, this must be him, this old man, wispy-headed, his legs thick with dropsy, sat upon a high-backed chair, and he rises from it, all unsteady, holding out his hands and saying, 'Oh, my dear! My dear!' And stood beside him, Molly and the boys.

'Miss Pris!' Molly exclaims. 'Oh, Miss Pris, did I do right? It was the only place I could think of here in London. My Lord Wyncanton's!'

CHAPTER SIX

A Proposition

'In the pains of old age, the finger of God nippeth and pincheth men, to make them think of this call and prepare for death.'

John Paget, *Meditations of Death*

FAR FROM THE most mobile of characters, Sir Theodore de Mayerne. Leaving his piano nobile in St Martin's Lane requires descending that impressive staircase (even worse, returning, when it must be ascended), then he must struggle into his carriage, which has recently had to have its straps reinforced and its greyhound-like carriage horses replaced by a pair of sturdy

Clevelands. A man's bulk, in his own home, may be a source of pride, but away, it is nothing but one inconvenience after another. Also, let us look at the politics of this. Sir Theodore has his friends amongst those newly come to power, indeed he does, but he is also well known for having attended Queen Henrietta-Maria's many lyings-in, for being physician to the King, even (many years ago) treating that old Papist Cardinal Richelieu for the clap. All in all, in such times as these, far better for him to bide quietly at home.

Nonetheless.

Nonetheless, here is his carriage, coming into Lincoln's Inn Fields, which is still field, on three of its sides at least, and up to the row of houses at its south-east corner, with their diapered brickwork and flagstoned paths and one of them with a Wyncanton martlet stuccoed in above its door. Sir Theodore, with much pushing and heaving, gets himself down to the pavement. Two boys, with what might be their nursemaid, are sporting about on the grass before the house, playing at skittles in the last of the afternoon's light. The days have shortened; the year of 1645 is coming to its end, and after this one, who would dare forecast what might come next? Even to contemplate such makes a man dizzy. And that pair of boys, so cheerily noisy, so oblivious. What sort of world is this, that we will leave to them?

One of the children, Sir Theodore realizes, has stirred in him a ripple of recognition. Where do I know you from? Sir Theodore ponders. He is unevenly balanced, this smaller child, one good side and one less so, but doesn't let that stop him; his competitiveness against his taller, abler brother cheers Sir Theodore, who is an admirer of spirit, for where in these times would any of us be without it? He contemplates the house. Yes, spirit is definitely what is needed here. There is an unmistakable stillness gathering within these walls. Sir Theodore's patient here is dying, and knows it, and that knowledge charges even the air.

The front door is opened. Standing in the hall is his patient's lawyer, Will Franklin – God's-Will-Be-Done Franklin, if you wanted to use his full name, and be a proper crop-head about it, but Franklin, whatever the sensibilities of those who named him, is as much of a moderate as his employer, so does not. Such men, such moderates, have been few and far between in these recent parlous times. My Lord Wyncanton will be missed, he will indeed.

'How does he?' Sir Theodore asks. It is a little while since he was last summoned here.

'Frailer, but livelier,' Franklin answers. 'You will see why.'

His patient's bedchamber, now the sickroom, faces the Fields, and here my Lord Wyncanton spends his days propped up in bed, quilted and enrobed. As Sir Theodore enters, his patient raises a hand in greeting. Surprisingly, his patient appears very much more kempt than he had been on Sir Theodore's last attendance on him; his hair has been cut, his eyebrows edged, the few white bristles sprouting from his nose ruthlessly done away with. The bedchamber has been made more cheery too – it has been tidied, the windows opened to let some air into the room; there is a bowl of small, late, tight-budded roses from those bushes by the path. Sir Theodore had represented to his patient's household the desirability of making his patient's room a pleasanter place to be; he is relieved to see that his words are at last having some effect. 'My Lord Wyncanton,' says Sir Theodore, going forward.

'Ah!' says his patient, ''tis the Swiss!' That characteristic fussy little readying of himself. 'Did you see the boys? As you came in?'

'I did indeed, Sir Antony,' Sir Theodore replies.

'Did you see young James? He reads to me. A most uncommon child. I find my old ears follow his voice with no difficulty at all.'

'I saw two young men, and a set of skittles that are like never to be the same again.' Again, Sir Theodore wonders, who are they? Distant cousins, come to hover?

'They are fine lads,' says his patient. 'Fine lads. Are they not, my dear?'

There is a woman sitting by the window. Now Sir Theodore sees her. Good Lord, how unexpected. And now she lifts her head – her uncoiffed head, the hair bound back, all of a piece with the reserve of her pose, her sober dress. Even so, there is no hiding the colour of the hair, nor (in Sir Theodore's memory) mistaking that face.

She stands. 'You are very good to come, Sir Theodore.'

He is quite knocked back on his heels. 'By no means. My duty to my patient, madam.'

'He complained he could not get his breath. There was dizziness. A cold sweat and pallor.' ('Oh, fuss, fuss,' says the patient.) She nods toward a flask of cloudy liquid on the table. 'I saved his water for you.' She lifts her voice. 'Wyn, I will be here. Do you see? By the door.'

Sir Theodore proceeds with his examination, bending his ear (not without difficulty) to his patient's skinny back, examining the flask of urine, then the texture of his patient's skin, the whites of the eyes, the state of the belly, the breathing. The woman waiting by the door watches it all. She cannot hear, as Sir Theodore does, the desperate lollop of my Lord Wyncanton's heart, the way it stumbles as it goes, nor read the myriad other signs that its race is almost done; but from the way her eyes follow his movements, Sir Theodore is sure she understands what awaits them here. His patient has suffered a series of such episodes – breathlessness, vertigo, one attack after the other, plus (more recently) waking to the squeeze of pain in the dead of night. Like being closed in a fist, so his patient had described it. 'The hand of God, Sir Antony, I am sure,' Sir Theodore had said.

If that is so, his patient had replied, he has firm grip of me.

The boys come in from outside, their noise filling the hall. The woman goes to them, and the two men hear her bid them *Shush*, hears the nursemaid clack down the stairs to the kitchen. It is not grand, this house, it is bachelor-sized – the kitchen in the cellar, the one room here as you go in, two smaller rooms above. Sir Theodore, counting his patient's pulses, holds his wrist. His gaze goes to the two flower-pieces on the wall – the ragged-edged striped tulips, the irises, the roses big as cabbage-heads, the pinks, the lilies, snails and butterflies – even, if Sir Theodore does not mistake it, the long green calyx, the hanging white trumpet, the vestal self-possession of his very own Floripondio, his Angel-flower. Very fine, and yet how mournful. In life, the petals will wither, the bright-winged insects die; this will be all that is left.

'I will leave them to you in my will,' his patient says, with a chuckle, seeing where Sir Theodore's gaze has gone, and then it is his patient has Sir Theodore's wrist in his grasp, rather than the other way about. 'Tell me. How much breath have I left in me? How much time?'

'Sir,' says Sir Theodore, shocked, 'that is known to none but God.'

'I have matters yet outstanding,' his patient says. 'Unexpected business to resolve.'

Sir Theodore lowers his voice. 'Then I would advise, sir, to attend to it without delay.'

'Without delay?'

'None.'

The door to the sickroom opens, there she is. 'Wyn, I will take the boys downstairs to eat, then I will bring your supper to you.'

The patient's hands, which seem so overlarge compared to what is left of the rest of the man, compose themselves upon the quilt. 'Would you send in Mr Franklin, first?'

Sir Theodore finds that he and my Lord Wyncanton's nurse exit the room together.

'Forgive me,' says Sir Theodore, 'but it is – it is Miss Holland, is it not?'

An amused but seemly smile. 'It is, Sir Theodore.'

'So I thought. I did not know of your connection to Sir Antony.'

'No,' says Pris. 'Very few do, I imagine.'

Here is Mr Franklin. 'Ah, Sir Theodore – a moment, if I may.'

Women absent themselves from such conversations. Pris goes down to the kitchen, ushering the boys before her, James, in the lead, one-*two*-ing it down the twist of stairs; Pris and Ned, bringing up the rear. 'Who won the game?' Pris asks.

'He did,' says Ned, resignedly. 'It's too bumpy to play out there in any case. It's not like Varney.'

'I know,' says Pris. As he descends the steps before her, she gives Ned's shoulder a consoling pat. 'Nothing is.'

Meantime, in the hall above. Says Sir Theodore, 'Extraordinary. I had no idea.'

'It is an association of long-standing, I believe,' says Mr Franklin.

'And the boys?'

'It is my understanding Miss Holland acts as a sort of guardian to them. She has told me that their mother is dead, and their father –' Mr Franklin lifts his shoulders. 'One of those many, no-one knows where.'

'Sir Antony seems very taken with them,' says Sir Theodore. 'Especially the youngest.'

'Master James. Yes, I had noticed that.'

'James, did you say?' Sir Theodore consults his memory. 'Good Lord. Mr Franklin, indulge my curiosity. How on earth is it Miss Holland and those boys find themselves here?'

'Oh, *great* drama,' says Mr Franklin, clearly more than ready to do so. 'Events more at home upon the stage of the old Red Bull, you would think, than here in Lincoln's Inn. First, out of nowhere, the boys, and with them Miss Holland's maid – a young woman with great powers of *insistence*, let us say – with an account of Miss Holland herself being held prisoner by one Ingram Skinner and his sons. Have you come across the Skinner name, Sir Theodore? It is one to shudder at. Sir Antony bade me go at once to the Trained Bands, only to find they had an action already in preparation. Apparently, they had been informed the Skinners were harbouring a freebooter, an agent in the pay of Spain, forsooth. Indeed, we had the man briefly in our custody. I confess, I never was about so many blades and bullets in my life. It is extraordinary how it quickens the blood.'

'I am happy to take your word for it, Mr Franklin,' says Sir Theodore. 'But rescue was made?'

'Indeed it was. My Lord Wyncanton's servants were dispatched back to Goodwins, and Miss Holland and her maid and the children are become his household. And the unlovely tribe of Skinner is no more. Much as one mourns the death of any man, I cannot imagine either of the younger Skinners was a great loss to the world, while Ingram Skinner himself is fled with a price on his head. He *and* this freebooter, this Captain Fantom. They will be taken. This new London has no place for such.' Mr Franklin permits himself an unlawyerly grin. 'An amusing coda, Sir Theodore. When the men of the Farringdon Trained Bands arrived at Skinner's stronghold – his hive, one might call it – with their barrels of black powder to destroy the place, they found within it a pair of drabs, who, upon learning the reign of Skinner was no more, promptly disinterred his strongbox from the wall and walked out the house with it, bidding the Trained Bands leave not one brick upon another.'

'The workings-out of fate,' offers Sir Theodore. 'They constantly amaze.'

'The workings-out of something, certainly,' says Mr Franklin. 'I imagine the men of the Trained Bands were far from being the Skinners' only foe.'

Posset is what one gives an invalid: warm milk, rendered into curds with sweet wine, and spiced. It is supposed to help one sleep. Wyn detests it – this half-digested slop, he calls it – but this evening he allows Pris to spoon a bowlful into him. He is talkative too. 'Did the boys enjoy their game? I fear life here must be dull indeed for them.'

'They did. James in particular, since Ned let him win.'

'My dear, remind me,' says Wyn. 'I know you had mentioned, but tell me again. How old is little James?'

'How old? He is near nine years old now, Wyn. Small body, mighty mind,' Pris adds, smiling.

'Ah!' says Wyn. 'These days, how like to me!' There is a twinkle to his eye. 'Nine years,' he repeats. His hands compose themselves upon the bedcover. 'Do you ever think of this world as it was, nine years ago?'

'I do. I was in Breda. Although that is not a place I care to return to, even in my head.'

'And so you were. Poor child. Sent away.'

'Something like that,' says Pris, who finds the uttering of an untruth rather less comfortable than she did. She settles Wyn's nightcap into place, strokes his cheek. The skin of his face is so smooth now, no bristle to it at all. 'You were too long speaking with Mr Franklin,' she tells him. 'You have tired yourself out.'

Up she goes to bed. Pauses for a moment at the door of the room shared by the boys, but she can hear them both, breathing as you do when you are fast asleep, and in her own room, on the truckle bed, Molly is snoring too.

Miss Holland undresses herself – a lady can do that, with these new modest fashions. The world may be far dowdier than it was, but it does at least require less in the way of assistance. She puts on her nightdress, kneels by her bed, knits her hands and says her prayers. Who does she say them to? Who is named in them? And in what order?

Blows out her candle. All secrets are safe in the dark.

COME THE MORNING, and Mr Franklin is there again, down in the hall, Mr Franklin and an immense leather portfolio held to his chest. He rises from the settle as he sees her. 'Madam,' he says.

'Mr Franklin, it is somewhat early for the doing of business,' says Miss Holland, as sweetly as she can bring herself to do. The boy from the baker in Temple Bar has only just gone past with his tray, the bells of Clement Danes are striking a mere seven of the clock.

'Oh,' says Mr Franklin. 'You misunderstand. My Lord Wyncanton and I – our business is concluded.'

'Already?'

'Indeed, madam. He waits now for you.'

Pris has a routine when she first goes in to Wyn. To begin with, does he clearly know her (it is not always the case that he does), then how did he sleep, then are there pains of any sort; then does he need the close stool; but this morning those can wait. 'Wyn, what would Sir Theodore say if I should tell of you transacting business with your lawyer at this hour?' One jollies Wyn into the day, and Pris is opening the curtains as she speaks, rattling the fire. It is a greyish sort of morning. It is a greyish season. The year seems to have halted in its course.

'Pris,' says Wyn, 'come here to me.'

So she does. She sits, where she has sat before, here on his bed, with his hand in hers – warm, dry, but so much less substance to it than there was. She waits. Sometimes it takes Wyn a moment to mesh the gears of conversation into place. But today he surprises her. 'How does my miss?' he asks.

'She does very well,' Pris tells him. A smile, with just a little of that old impishness to it. 'All thanks to you.'

He pats her hand. 'Pris,' he says, 'I think we know each other well enough for me to speak my mind.'

'I hope we do, Wyn. I would speak mine to you.' She waits. 'What is it? What do you wish to say?'

'Mr Franklin and I,' he says, 'are settling my affairs.'

This she does not care to speak of. 'I don't know why you feel you have to do so, Wyn. There is no need—'

He surprises her again. He lifts her hand and kisses it. 'We both know that is not the case. I would not say I was resigned to it, but I am ready enough – oh, now, my dear,' as he sees her turn her face away. 'It must come, this thing. I am as at peace with it as any man can be. There is only one matter remaining upon which I am unquiet – well, one, and another that comes with it. But you can put my mind at ease on both.'

There is something brighter about Wyn this morning. It is as if a homunculus version of the old Wyncanton, the man so determined to have all as he wished, is watching her from within his eyes. 'Then tell me,' says Pris. 'What can I do? Whatever it is, I will do it.'

More patting of her hand. 'Pris, I wish to make James and Ned my wards.'

She feels as if she has been struck on the breast. His words go through her like the reverberation of a blow. 'Your *wards*?'

'Exactly so. Franklin has drawn up the papers; they are there upon the table, ready for you to sign.' He sees how she draws back. 'You are their guardian, are you not? Or as close as they have to one? You did say anything,' he reminds her, with that old man's pouting-out to his lower lip.

'Yes, but – Wyn, they have a father.' *And this would be like saying to them that he is dead.*

Wyn shields his eyes and makes a sort of show of looking round the room. 'Then where is he? Those boys stand without place, without protection in this world. I would remedy this. That is all.'

'I will think on it. I will, I promise you.' Now she takes his hand in hers. 'It is – it is kindness itself of you to propose this, Wyn. What was the other thing?'

'Ah,' says Wyn. 'That. That is even simpler. I wish for you and I to wed.'

There are very few places in this house for a woman to be alone with her thoughts. Pris has retired to her bed; sits upon it, head in her hands.

She had told him, 'Wyn, that is impossible.'

Wyn, within the stronghold of his own bed, had been imperturbable. 'Why so?'

'Because – because—' A whole jury-box of reasons, is how it had felt to Pris, all there staring at her. And all, now, followed her up here. *Because it would be false of me. It would be false to you. It would be false to James and Ned.*

It would be false to him.

'If we are wed, you have my name. You and the boys, Pris. Think of that. Think of them. Recollect the peril that you stood in on your own.'

Recollect it? Is she ever likely to forget? That laugh, like something sticking itself to you; the glee there had been in Carlo Fantom's eyes, once he saw that she was going to make a fight of it.

'I want to know that you and they will still be safe, Pris, when I am here no more. That you will not be left to the mercy of this most uncertain world.'

Beneath her, she hears Molly in the hall. No doubt Mr Franklin waits there too, waiting for Miss Holland to commit this act of apostasy.

'When I am gone, you would be on your own –'

But we are NOT, Pris wails, inside her head. Then in another voice, smaller, hesitant: *But are we?*

We are NOT!

'– but my name will protect you. Madam, I will not be gainsaid in this,' he had said, reminding her again of the old Wyn; as he was when he took her away from London in the first place. 'I will give you an hour to compose yourself. To examine your thoughts. Then you will give me your answer.'

'And if I say no?'

'I think that you will not.'

Oh God, what to do, what to do? She goes to the window, stands looking out at the muddy paths dividing Lincoln's Inn Fields; the figures going back and forth across them – a lawyer like Franklin, clutching papers, a pair of the Inn's many watchmen, endlessly patrolling here, a half-dozen of its militia company, who use the Fields to practise their drill; then, just to underline the bleakness of the view, a pest-doctor, in gown and hat and that hideous beaked mask, making his way past the Hall of Lincoln's Inn. Are there cases of the plague hereabouts? Surely not.

She had taken the boys to see the Hall. Ned had been unimpressed, but James, gazing up at the timbers of the ceiling, like the upturned keel of some great galleon, yards and yards above their heads, had been entranced. 'It is full of *thinking*,' he had said, waving his hand into the space of air, and then, 'I too will be a man of law.' But then he has also declared he will explore the Americas, and be a natural philosopher, to boot.

The boys... who will grow, who will need futures, livelihoods; and how is she, Bess Holland's foundling, supposed to help them to that?

Oh, memory, memory, what a traitor it is. How it slinks its way back in: there she is, once again on the terrace at Varney, the sun on her skin, the velvet sound of the bees in the roses, and there he is, at the corner of her inner eye, his shape at the edge of her memory, his shadow – the long legs bending, the arm folding, as if in doing so it was having to learn some new sort of movement entirely, and there is Jack himself putting the rose in her glass.

Yes, that in my head, but in front of my eyes –

So different a world. Sooty grass and puddles, and the great black elms of Lincoln's Inn, their branches bare; and the houses opposite, no sign of life in them at all. But then there are blank-windowed houses all over England; the families that lived in them gone into exile; the men who owned them fined or imprisoned or in their graves, or simply never heard from again, no-one knowing what their end was. Even the pest-doctor, even he has passed from sight. Here we be.

There is not much to this room. There is the bed, a chest, and by the bed a table for her candlestick, a table on which there is also a letter from Rafe:

Varney has its first visitation from Parliament's men, but we did as told, forswearing ourselves most horribly that Varney's owners were fled we knew not where, and we were all that was left. They were tattered fellows, but their escort, who waited outside, were armed cap-a-pied. They made a point of speaking most tellingly of Basing House, and how that fell; and how Oxford must be besieged if the garrison did not yield. Topham and I sat with them drinking toasts to General Fairfax and to General Cromwell, and never knowing that we had such courage in our marrow until so called upon to show it. They went around the house making lists, and it was a most uncomfortable thing to see Varney so recorded for the Parliamentary commissioners; when they were gone, I regret, but we discovered that the silver ladle did abide with us no more…

And her own attempt at reply:

Dearest Rafe, dearest Belle, my love to all of you –

And that was as far as she had got. There is a mirror, a small one, on a nail above the table. Pris glares at it, but it remains obstinately smooth and silver, undisturbed.

You persecute me with visions and portents, you cloud mirrors with your breath, you declare yourself to me, yet when I positively want a sign from you, there is nothing, nothing at all.

She turns her forehead against the cold glass. 'Oh, Jack, where *are* you? What am I to do?'

CHAPTER SEVEN

A Change of Plan

'In desperate times, the headlong way is best.'

Thomas Hughes, *Certain Devices and Shows presented to Her Majestie…*

THEY WENT SOUTH to begin with, then that inner compass in Jack's head began to swing, so they turned south-west. Up into the first low hills, the river curving left to right beneath them. Taking it slowly, nursing his men along. Zoltan says his fevers are fewer and less; Ulrik, working the swollen, puppet-like hand with the fingers of the other, declares that the feeling is returning. Jack has no idea if either is speaking the truth.

'And what of you, Domini?' Kazimir asks.

What about him?

'You are limping all the time now.'

He is?

'If you were a horse,' Konstantin adds, 'we would shoot you.'

Thanks for that.

He steers them by dead reckoning or starlight, like a mariner. They eat what they hunt, or forage, or steal. The bounty of an unattended wagon, hid within a barn and either forgotten or the men who hid it are no more, and the canvas of the wagon stencilled with the blazon of Waller's infantry, that's a pleasing extra. 'We are outlaws, Domini,' says Per. 'What is his name, they call him here in England – Robin the Hood!'

Thor says it is like their ride down the Elbe. Or when they wintered in the mountains outside Prague. 'Take that as a good omen,' Jack replies.

'What, you think another fortune, at the end of it?'

'I'll settle for the *Guid Marie*.'

How many days for the embassy to reach Paris? For Cantley to find Achille? Then how long for Achille to get word to Amsterdam? For that word to reach Sant? For Sant to bring his ship over here?

The horses' coats are growing thick. There is frost on the ground when they wake, then the frost is a powdering of snow. He puts his sons' faces before him as he rides. When he rolls himself into his cloak at night, there on the bare ground, he rolls Pris into its folds with him.

'What will you do when we are out of this, Domini?'

Sleep. Hold all three of them in my arms and sleep and sleep and sleep.

'I will do as Sergeant Ilya did,' Luka tells them. 'I will find me a Rosa, and we will make babies forever.'

'Your Rosa will have to be a little one,' says Thor, with a smirk.

'I do not mind if she is little, or if she is not,' Luka replies, with dignity. 'But I will have her be clever. That is what you need for happiness in coupling. One who is clever and one who is strong. As it is with you and Miss Holland, Domini. Not so?'

All coming out now, ain't it?

Into the uplands, into the forests. He and his men, between the trees like rays of winter sunlight. Disappear.

MR BARLOW OF the *Sapphire*. Not a happy man. 'I cannot do it, Mr Skinner,' Barlow says. Lord knows, it's not like him to dig his heels in, but for even the meekest of men, there is a thus-far-and-no-further. 'The Lord knows if I could, I would, but it cannot be done. The Trained Bands go aboard every vessel setting out. They search 'em crow's-nest to keel. If they ain't looking for intelligencers, they are looking for those trying to escape the fines and the impoundings, and if they ain't looking for them, they are looking for *you*. There's notices put up at every quayside, Mr Skinner. There's a price upon your head.'

'I will match it,' says Skinner. 'I will double it!'

The bold vow is worthless. The men of the Farringdon Trained Bands blew Hag Place to smithereens; Ingram Skinner has been left without a pot to piss in, literally. 'God damn your eyes, Barlow,' Skinner now protests, 'you cannot expect me to stay longer here!' Here being the *Sapphire*'s lighter, moored off Tilbury Ness, where Barlow and Skinner huddle, in her windowless cabin. 'Am I a sea-worm,' her new lodger complains, 'to live with my feet in the wet, in constant darkness?'

'You may lift the hatch, Mr Skinner,' Barlow tells him, mildly. 'You may lift the hatch, but if you do so in daylight, you will be seen.'

'But winter is upon us! I will perish, Mr Barlow! I will freeze to death!'

'I can have you put ashore, Mr Skinner,' says Barlow. 'In Essex there are many little places you might hide and I am happy to help you where I may, sir, for the sake of our long association. But to take you aboard the *Sapphire*, that I cannot do.'

Another barge is passing by outside. The lighter rises on its wake, the water on the floor of the cabin shifts in sympathy with that outside. The light of Barlow's lantern moves from one side of the cabin to the other. Ingram, his skull-like features made yet ghastlier by the swing of shadow, glares at the *Sapphire*'s captain. 'And that fucker Fantom,' Ingram says. 'What news of him?'

'None, Mr Skinner. Not a single sighting. And believe me, there's as many hunting for him as for you. Greville Holland, he has put a bounty of a hundred pound on that man's head, for his murdering of Aaron, and with that face on him, he would not be hard to find. If the man had any sense at all, he has run, sir. He has run as far and as fast as he could.'

'My boys, Mr Barlow,' says Ingram, mournfully. It is as if mention of Aaron has reminded him. 'My boys.'

'Yes, Mr Skinner. Grief and mourning. Untimely doings. It is become our meat and drink.' Barlow shakes his head. Why, there was even a pest-doctor, murthered in Blackfriars not so long ago. Pierced through and through and tipped into the river, robbed of his mask, his cloak, his purse, his cane. Who robs a pest-doctor, for the Lord's sake?

The pensive mood does not last long with Skinner. 'That Holland bitch,' he growls.

'Mr Skinner, she is gone far beyond your reach. She is with her old protector, Wyncanton. In fact, Mr Skinner, there are whispers they are to wed.' Barlow gives a smile. 'First that tiger of hers out Oxford way, then this. You have to hand it to the lady, Mr Skinner. Her timing is impeccable!'

London has had its first snowfall, out of a sky now yellow-white as the dirty snow itself, and against which those one-time chalk-smudges of smoke show up as dark as lines of ink. It's hardly the season or the times for getting wed; yet nonetheless, marriages are taking place. There is one happening right now, in the chapel of Lincoln's Inn, albeit very spare and unadorned – the bride attended only by her maid, the groom by his lawyer.

Ned, lying on his bed, watches the crumbs of snow fall into the world outside. He feels every bit as insignificant himself.

He hears his brother say his name. James is sat on his own bed, legs dangling, but even so their relative positions seem wrong. It is as if it is he, Ned, who is the younger here.

'*N*ed. *N*ed. *N*ed.' James can keep this up with the relentlessness of a ticking clock.

'*What?*' Ned demands.

'She's *d*oing it because he wants it. Wyncanton. *N*ot because *she* does. *N*ot Pris. She doesn't *m*ean it, it's *him*.'

Ned sits up. 'How can you get *wed* to someone and not *mean* it?'

THIS PLACE, THIS dewdrop of land, where the waters of one river push out into the flow of another, and from there flow on, on, on, out to the Bristol Channel and the sea. 'Does this even have a name?' Zoltan had wondered.

'I would hope not,' Jack replied.

Land flat as the water. A track, down to the water's edge. The weeks they have spent nudging their way here. Parliament's troopers down in the valleys below them every time they drew out the spyglass to check. *While my men*, Jack thinks, *they look like woodwose.* Haystack-hair, beards down past their collars. Breeches patched across the knees, thin as herons, and the horses, shaggy as bears.

Something about the river, the width of it maybe, its placid unconcern, has them all speaking low. 'You ever think, Domini,' Ulrik muses, 'if we, in England, we might be the last?'

The last of what?

'Of his army, Domini. Of the army of King Charles.'

Christ. Ain't that a cheery thought.

Dawn is approaching up the river's wide mouth. Here it comes, the first breath of the day. *Be there. Be there.*

Zoltan has lowered himself to the ground; now he blows out a breath, a huff of pure exhaustion.

The horizon is one bright line, the channel, dark. Watch and wait.

All Saints', is what he had put in his message. All Saints' Day, Achille. Tell Mungo Sant, I will have us there by All Saints' Day. We will be waiting. Fail me not. Be our sheet down the wall.

'Domini,' Ulrik says now, as if consolingly, 'to make this rendezvous – it would be like trying to thread a needle in the dark.' Holds up the puppet-hand. 'With *this*, what is more.'

'He'll make it, Ulrik. You don't know Sant as I do.'

Or at least as I hope I do.

The edge of the chop and swell in the channel, catching the light. *Be there. Be there!*

And then Thor, with the spyglass, pointing at the place where the channel meets the sky. 'Domini, there is a ship out there! I see her masts! She has a boat in the water!'

They watch as the rowboat pulls toward them, the tide bearing it in; at first no more than a flake of darkness on the swell; then they can make out the oars. Then a figure standing at the bow, recklessly waving his hat, and another, beseeching him to sit down.

'Useful things,' Achille carols out, as he splashes ashore, 'the diplomatic mails!'

'Useful fellow,' counters Zoltan, limping forward, 'Joseph Cantley.'

'Ah yes! Nothing like an uncle as ambassador to France!' Achille cries, and then, '*Que Dieu ait pitié*, look at all of you! Veritable wild men, every one!'

He had forgotten quite how much Achille loves an adventure. 'How goes it with your new employer?' Jack calls out.

'Mazarin? Ah well, you know – one cardinal much like another. You serve one, you've served them all.' Achille holds out his arms. 'My friend, you cannot think what joy it is to see you again!'

All up and down the narrow beach, with the weed-stained mudflats before them and the weed-waved water after that, nothing but jubilation. Hats aloft, shouts and halloos, Per and Jens doing a lopsided jig of delight. Ah, God, the *relief* of it. 'Cornelius!' Jack calls, to the figure picking its way over the mud. 'Cornelius, where are they?'

The answer is blown back to him, like a seabird's cry: 'Where are who?'

'Pris and the boys! Where do you have them?'

The figure comes to a halt. 'But I don't have them. What do you mean?'

No more jubilation now. His men watch on in silence. Did he truly believe the gods would grant him this? Has he forgotten who he is?

Everything I love, I lose.

'They were to come to you. Pris and I, we agreed, we had a sign—'

'They never did, Jack. When was this?'

'After Naseby. I sent word to them. Close up the house, go to Cornelius, I told Pris, you would see her safe to Amsterdam—'

'After *Naseby*?' There is some horrid putting-together of two and two in Cornelius's expression. Some further horrid putting-together, on top of that already revealed. 'Jack, I wasn't there. I had to flee.'

'To flee?' His thoughts are in a landslide, tumbling into disaster. Runaway Down.

'I had to leave London. I had to do it on the instant. I was warned—'

'Warned? Warned of what?'

The stench of the mud. The oily shimmer on the water, the iridescent blues and greens. Like silk.

The silk of her gown.

Cornelius is see-sawing his head left and right. 'Jack, I am sick to my soul at this—' His eyes flick up toward Jack, then they wheel away.

The orrery spins, and spins, and comes to rest. 'Felipe,' says Jack. 'Felipe Ortez.'

For a moment there is no reaction at all. Then Cornelius raises his eyes again, and this time, holds them steady.

'You knew him, didn't you? And he knew you.'

He takes Cornelius by the elbow, leads him out of earshot, here on this land that is half water, this place where everything is something else. In the grip of his fingers, even Cornelius's elbow seems to know what's coming next.

'It's you, ain't it,' says Jack, low-voiced. 'Mercator. It's you.'

Says Cornelius, softly, 'Your men are watching us, Jack.'

Indeed they are. Indeed they might. Jack is remembering Cornelius as a child – his timidity, yet his dauntlessness, all the same. 'You know, I always wondered how you did it. I was suspect in France for that I had an English mother, over here I was suspect for everything else, but you – everyone accepted you. And you did it by being something no-one suspected at all. I can't believe I never worked it out.'

'We were as brothers, Jack,' says Cornelius, soft as before. 'It is always hard to see what is closest to you.'

'Does Achille know?'

'Good God, no.' Cornelius casts a glance over his shoulder. 'There was only ever one who knew, and he is gone.'

Work it through, Jack tells himself. One step, then the next. 'You take my men,' he says. 'You take them, and you get them away from here. Give me the peace of mind that they are safe at least.'

'Of course. Jack, if I had known—' The eyes cast about again, then are raised up once more. 'If I had known Pris was coming to me, I would have waited, no matter what.'

'I know you would.' All the same, for a moment Jack finds he has to spread his fingers, shed the urge within them. 'If I thought otherwise, I'd break your neck.'

That same steady gaze as before; the stillness of the holder of secrets, the man who never lays down his cards. 'What will you do?' Cornelius asks.

What indeed. Jack glances over to where his men stand waiting – his men, his discoverers, his Dead Men. *Not this time.* This time, he is losing no-one. 'I will go back. I will find them.'

'What, on your own?'

'Cornelius, the only way to do this is on my own. You know that.'

CHAPTER EIGHT

The Tiger

'The tiger is of most swift foot, and of all beasts, most fierce.'

John Maples, *A green Forest, or a natural Historie*

MOVE BY NIGHT, lie up by day. Drink rain from your hat. M'sieu's meat is grass; his own must be rationed. But then are they not used to their bellies being hollow, horse and man alike?

Tell me where you are, Pris. Tell me where.

One day of such, then another. If he could gallop M'sieu non-stop, cross-country, they might be outside London in three. The thought is maddening; he pushes it away. M'sieu has no such gallop left in him, and in any case, where Parliament's men were down in the valleys, now they range higher. He and M'sieu wait, hidden, he with his hands around M'sieu's muzzle, like a gag, while those hunting the last of the army of King Charles tromp past.

'*Na vilku, Domini*,' the Gemini had said, when he bade them farewell. He hates farewells. (Domini, Thor had replied, we all hate this one.)

'What is that?'

'It means no wolves. God keep them from you.'

Good to see how well that has worked.

He tries not to think of Zoltan, lifting a hand as if in final exhausted blessing. 'This is, we meet again,' Zoltan had said. 'Not farewell.'

By God, it is, Jack had replied. You think I want Ava on my tail, as well as Parliament's men?

He and M'sieu, they must go north. Ford the river, turn south, head for the Wessex Downs. His horse is limping, he too favours one leg. 'Oh, brave lad,' says Jack, having the suspect hoof rest in his lap, examining the crack in it, creeping up from the shoe. 'I know, I know, it hurts you. We will both walk.' They go so slowly that from the top of the hill they reach by evening, he thinks he could look back and see where in the morning they had started out. M'sieu needs oats, he needs hay, he needs something.

The moon rises, and shows him the roof of the farm beneath them and the darkness of a pond.

He circles round it, waits and watches. There is smoke from the chimney, and a light at one window. Then there is not.

The ground is damp and soft. He can get M'sieu right up to the fence without a sound. Ties his horse, then creeps to the barn behind the house. The door is held shut with rope, that's all, and inside everything speaks of how hard life has been for these people – empty stalls, and the cobwebbed collar for a plough horse. A scythe with a broken handle, a hay rake sans half of its teeth. But there are sacks, and there is old straw, and for a hungry horse with another hundred miles ahead of it, that's a banquet.

He is gathering it up, stuffing it into a sack when he hears the first honk from the field. Geese. Geese, sleeping around the pond. *Damnation* –

He is out of the barn and across the yard before the farmhouse door comes open. Hurls the sack over the fence, vaults it himself, geese running ahead of him in all directions, necks stretched, wings a-flap, in terror at M'sieu's stallion roar. M'sieu has torn himself loose from the fence, is cantering across the field with a rail from the fence bouncing across the ground behind him. Jack hears the farmer's bellow, 'You thieving dog! You cursed, thieving dog!' He thinks any minute there will be the explosion of a blunderbuss, but no. M'sieu, in pursuit of a goose, comes thundering toward him; Jack throws himself upon the bit of rail and this time succeeds in pulling his horse to a halt. Disentangles him. The farmer, still at his door, is still bellowing curses, but is clearly unwilling to trust himself to his darkened farmyard with thieving rebel dogs about. Jack even manages to retrieve the sack of straw.

'You *bloody* idiot,' he tells M'sieu.

The limp, come morning, is worse. And now they have their first outright pursuers, a troop with muskets slung across their shoulders, pushing their way through the bracken on the hillside below.

Maybe a dozen of them, clearing the ground. At night he sees the fire where they have made their camp, and early in the morning, watches as another dozen come to join them, four on horseback. *All this*, he thinks, *all this for little me.* He watches a conversation take place around the smoking remains of the fire. Wonders what the one man might be saying to the other, but to be honest it's easy enough to guess: *You see any sign as you came up?*

No, nothing – he must be behind us. Malignant dog.

That's why you don't bother loading your blunderbuss; because you know these are to hand, already scouring the countryside for Parliament.

We must wait, he tells M'sieu. Let them get ahead of us, then we work a way around behind them. We've done this before. We've befuddled searchers such as this twenty times over.

When he sets off again, M'sieu is still limping.

A shoal of hills ahead, the valleys wooded, the upland bare. The roads run high across the hilltops, unsheltered and unhidden, the trackways low. He thinks how Plumstead would complain at such, which is as close as he will let himself get to thinking of Varney, of his boys, of Pris. The sun rises and he finds a hollow under the plug of a fallen oak, the hollow and the fan of roots and clay big enough to hide the two of them. He brings M'sieu to lie down on the earth, throws his cloak across them both. Munches the last of the rusk from his bag. He was sixteen years old last time he lived like this – him, a horse, hard rations, the road ahead. He feels the years since the way a tree would feel its rings. But he must have slept, they both must have, because when he hears the dogs, he thinks it is Ocker and Todd, from his dream.

In fact, it is M'sieu wakes him, the horse pushing him unceremoniously out of place with his nose. Jack lifts his head to see that wise eye gazing down at him, then hears how M'sieu is huffing in his throat at the barks and whines coming from above. 'Good lad,' he tells M'sieu. 'Steady, steady, steady.' And then into his horse's ear: 'No shouting.'

There's water not so far ahead, he hears it, so he leads M'sieu across this shallow river, up and out of sight, and then goes back to the water and trails his cloak a good five hundred yards along the bank, before balling it up and throwing it into the current. As they breast the rise, M'sieu's head jerking every time he has to use that leg, he hears the dogs down by the stream, barking and baying, and the men with them, yelling encouragement.

It begins to rain. Now, he could do with that cloak; but of the pack that was in pursuit of them, not so much as a yelp. They must be way off the scent. He starts talking to M'sieu, to encourage him: 'We will find a blacksmith, we will get you reshod, and you will rest up, and there will be oats and hay and carrots, and I will change my shirt, and when we tell the boys of our adventures, Pris will – Pris will—'

There was a booklet, printed for the King's own cavaliers: prayers for victory, prayers for those in peril, prayers for the besieged. *Send thy holy angels to be a guard over them. Please God.*

They come up to a crossroads, and at the crossroads, out here in the back of beyond, a toll-house, and a boy sat outside, in the mizzle, ready to take the tolls.

Jack has two pennies in his pocket, his last. 'One for me, one for him,' he tells the boy, pointing at M'sieu. 'Where are we?'

The boy is eyeing the sword tied behind Jack's saddle. 'Looted it,' says Jack. 'Some royalist bastard.'

The boy gives a grin. 'You never,' he says, then, 'You're halfway.'

Halfway?

'This is Halfway,' the boy says, indicating the empty country all around. 'Bristol to London. Halfway!'

Fair enough. Halfway. In which case…

In which case, that town ahead, that must be Newbury. Where they fought twice, and from where, after that first battle, King Charles might have marched on to London, had he not so scrupled to attack the people of his own capital. We in his army, we might die in our thousands, thinks Jack, but march on London? God forbid. We could never have won this war. The very man we fought for, fought against us.

He has not gone one half mile further when he hears the baying of dogs, and sees them behind him, gathering on the road, but fewer this time than last. The horsemen are gone, the dozen infantry too. Did they give up? Go home? He wonders too, if the boy at the crossroads betrayed him, pointed them on. But what difference would that have made: the road is so open, the plain it runs across so empty, they would see him whether they wished it or no. 'M'sieu, forgive me,' he says, as he swings himself into the saddle, 'we must run.' He is putting the plan together even as M'sieu, head jerking with the effort of doing so, gets into his gallop – *that wooded stretch ahead, into the trees, double back, cross our trail*—

They come at him out of the trees, two to one side, two the other, the four men mounted, and the foot soldiers running along behind. In this silent, empty landscape, a furious mêlée: the horses wheeling, whinnying, the stamp of hoof, the huff and pant of the men, the thumping of his heart – one, and he slashes the first man across the shoulder; two, thump, the next, blade through the man's coat; three, thump, the next makes a lunge for M'sieu's bridle. Jack stands in his stirrups and kicks this one off his horse altogether. Comes down into the saddle, makes a grab for a pistol, and there's one of the troopers swinging from M'sieu's reins. He shoots that one in the eye. They are trying to pull him from the saddle, hauling on his boots, his stirrups, his legs. He feels M'sieu bunching and paddling beneath him, sees M'sieu twist his head back, teeth bared, biting and tearing. He knows what these men are trying to do. They want to crowd in upon the two of them until they bear them over, weight of man versus strength of horse, and failing that the man now riding down upon them, brandishing his pistol, is going to put a bullet into him in turn, or one of those others will skewer him from behind. He has M'sieu's reins between his teeth, has his second pistol cocked and ready; he sees the man spy it and wheel away, sighting Jack now along his own outstretched arm. Jack fires. The other horseman does the same. M'sieu bunches his hindquarters, paddles his front legs and leaves the ground.

It is a perfect capriole. At its apex there is the height of a man between them and the earth. The flying kick behind, and he hears the crunch of impact, the cry of whichever man had been standing there; he sees M'sieu's mane whisking through the air, the momentum lifting Jack out of the saddle and almost putting him over his horse's shoulder; the men about them falling back, and M'sieu sees the road ahead, puts his nose forward, stretches his neck and is away. When Jack looks behind it is chaos back there: one horse riderless, men upon the ground. How could the two of them on their own manage all that? He touches M'sieu with his heels, and sees M'sieu's eye roll back, as if checking on him, then the neck stretches out again –

– and then he sees the blood-trail on the ground. The trail that comes with them, that patters alongside his horse's hooves. The gallop slowing. The gallop wallowing. M'sieu like a boat that is taking on water, M'sieu like he is holed.

'No!' Jack hears himself shout. 'No!' He slides from M'sieu's back but M'sieu himself is already sliding, staggering sideways. The blood coming from the hole in his chest is like water coming from a spring. Jack puts his hand to it, and it is so warm it is scalding, you can almost feel the heartbeat in it.

M'sieu is on his knees. M'sieu is on his side. He keeps trying to raise his head, as if in preparation to raising the rest of him or perhaps, in the confusion of death, to better understand what is happening here. His hooves plough the air. Jack holds M'sieu's head against him, against his breast, kissing the forehead, the ears – '*Calme-toi, calme-toi, ça va, M'sieu, ça va.*' He feels a breath thick with drool blown out against his shirt, then another, and then the eye looking into his rolls again and all comprehension, all the tautness, all that fiendish relish, everything held in it goes, all at once, for ever.

He lays M'sieu's head down. He stands. He is mired in gore. He stands with sword in one hand and his old clasp-knife in the other. They are coming at him. He hears another shot, but he is already running forward into them. Reaches the first man, barges him over, puts his knife in the man's neck. A second comes at him, already swinging a blade. Jack goes in under the blow, slides his own sword into the man's ribs between back and breastplate to such good effect that he has to free his sword the way you free an axe from a log. One of the horsemen, it must be the officer, is screaming at his men to stop coming at Jack one on one, but too late, Jack already has his hands – his bloodied hands – on the next, his boot in the man's stomach. No armour for this poor bastard, whoever he might be. He swings his sword up, holds it ready to expose everything in that stomach to the air, looks down. The screams coming from his victim are those of a child. The face is Ned's. Then it is James, one shifting into another as if he is viewing them through water. It is the boy from Runaway Down. On his haunches, scrambling backwards, screaming, terrified.

All strength seems to leave Jack's arms. Why do it? Why

take another life? M'sieu is gone, does he think he can escape his pursuers on foot? This is over. This is done. He lowers his sword, rams it into the earth, stands there as his pursuers come up, as they surround him. Puts his hands atop his head.

He hears the officer dismount behind him, hears the man snarl out, 'You whoreson. You murderous fiend,' and senses the swing of the blow at his skull, but of its landing, he knows nothing.

He comes to in a sort of darkness, light that pulses in and out. His mouth is dry; when he puts his tongue round his teeth he finds the runnels of his mouth are full of blood. At the back of his jaw, the tongue finds raggedy meat and a gap that was not there before. He can open one eye, but not the other. He lifts a hand to the eye, and the hand informs him at once that was a terrible idea, and that the hand, now woken, will make him pay for it. He has to turn his head to squint at it. Three of his fingers have purpled; the segments of each finger swollen like boiled beans.

Someone plucking at his arm. 'Sir? Captain? Fiskardo?'

The light comes from torches on the walls. The pulse is when they flicker in the movement of the air. When he tries to locate the speaker, have them cease their blasted plucking at him, the light whirls. All sense of what is up or down deserts him; he seems to have an insect in each ear.

'Sir! Sir!'

Two dark holes, over his face. No, two eyes. And a voice. 'Sir, quietly, sir, please. You will only bring 'em down on you.'

'B'ing 'ooo?' *That croak, good God, that's me.*

He can see no more of the man who calls him sir, who knows his name, than the eyes and a blur of white, which he realizes at length must be the fellow's shirt. ''Oo're you?' he manages. His mouth feels as broken as his hand.

'Symond, sir. Of Ewelme. A friend to Joseph Cantley,' the voice says. 'I recognized your coat. We were amazed.' The man is whispering. Jack realizes there are others lying round him, silent but watching, eyes wide. 'We thought after so long there could be none of us left.' He casts a glance over his shoulder. 'We are under guard, sir. Best to stay quiet. Save your strength.'

He tries to say *No*, but all he can manage is a 'Nnnnn'. His mouth will only form half-words at best. Half-words. Halfway. *I was halfway.*

A shout: 'You there! Lie back!'

Yes, under guard. With mighty effort he manages a mumbled 'Whe'am I?'

'Reading, sir.'

Reading. He could almost laugh. Reading!

'The old abbey. They brought you in across a packhorse. We thought that you were dead.'

Oh, but I am, Symond. I am.

'They gather us here. They seem not to know what else to do with us. Save your strength.'

CHAPTER NINE

Memento Mori

YOU are desired to Accompany the Corps of
Sir Antony Wyncanton, Bt., of Lincoln's Inn Fields
from Lincoln's Inn to St Dunstan in the West
On Tuesday 20th February 1646;
By Three of the Clock in the Afternoon precisely;
And to bring this Ticket with you.

YES, YES, WE know, the strangeness of the times, but even so – for my Lord Wyncanton's funeral to be organized by his lawyer, rather than his widow? Granted, it was a moiety, the length of time that she and he were married, before the good Lord took his servant to his breast… does anyone know her? No? A most mysterious connection of Sir Antony's, most mysterious indeed. But it must be said, Franklin makes a good fist of the arrangements; all those who should receive an invitation, do; the wine is sufficient without being a temptation; there are those sweet, sandy-grained biscuits from Temple Bar to sop it up; it is all as it should be. And Wyncanton's widow goes from one stranger to the other, accepting condolences, bowing her head, and all in all, behaving exactly as she ought, even if she does prove to be so much younger than her late spouse, and did anyone discover who the two boys are? What relation do they stand in, here?

Wyncanton's *wards*, do you say? One mystery after another. But there, the world is so disordered, we must take such surprises in our stride.

The last of the mourners is gone by eight of the evening, ushered out the door by Moll, standing stern as Hera in her gown of thick black *frizado*, and as warm within it as a cat by the fire, while my Lady Wyncanton must shiver her way through the day in black silk, and is so cold and drained and empty by the end of it that, sat here on her now black-shrouded bed, she does not even have the strength to kick off her shoes.

Everything in the house is shrouded. The tables, the chairs; the windows hung with it. A melancholy black Wyncanton martlet droops on a black-edged flag above the door. My Lady Wyncanton fishes into her bodice for her black-edged handkerchief. She would like to weep.

She does not feel worthy of weeping.

Ned comes to find her, sits beside her on the bed. A recent metamorphosis has lengthened Ned's face, and seemingly overnight lifted his shoulders to where a woman may drop her head upon them, so my Lady Wyncanton does exactly that, and for a little while they sit in silence. Then Ned says, 'It feels like there ain't going to be nothing good nor right in the world ever again.' Pris can hear the twist to his mouth when he speaks, how it distorts his words. Then he adds, 'Pox.'

'Damnation,' says Pris, in reply.

Another silence. What is missing in this world for Ned, Pris knows, is not simply Wyn; it is any news at all, even a single word, of his father. Finally he speaks again.

'Mr Franklin is downstairs.'

God give me strength, thinks Pris. 'What's *he* want?'

'He said a word, when you are ready. James is talking with him. Perhaps we should go and rescue him.'

'Who, James?'

'No,' says Ned, and allows himself a smile. 'Mr Franklin.'

Mr Franklin, again rising from the settle in the hall, and James, hopping down from it. 'We were *d*ebating sequestration,' says James. 'I was asking Mr Franklin, *d*oes he think it right?'

Sequestration. The latest cruelty of the times. It used to mean removing, keeping separate; now it means the taking: of houses, of lands, of possessions, from those who supported Charles Stuart and are to be left without any means of supporting themselves as punishment. Old words must bear new meanings, and all over England families are being turned out of doors and their homes taken away, in some instances demolished, stone by stone. Pris has heard nothing more from Varney, but there they are, on some Parliamentary commissioner's list, so no doubt that will be the next grief to add to all the rest. And how to shepherd the boys through that? 'Mr Franklin,' she says. 'A long day. Shall we end it?'

'If we might, my Lady,' says Franklin, gratefully.

'Come into the—' Her hand falters. All of a sudden she no longer knows what to call this room. Is it Wyn's bedroom still? 'Come in here,' she says, opening its door.

'And if the young gentlemen might also be present?' Franklin asks. 'What I have to say will concern them too.'

Very well. My Lady Wyncanton seats herself at the table in

what had been my Lord Wyncanton's chamber, her back to his empty and black-shrouded bed. Ned sits beside her, his head on a level with hers, then there is a step down, to James, then a step back up to Franklin himself.

'Mr Franklin,' says Pris, 'what is it you have for us?'

'My Lord Wyncanton's will,' comes the reply.

Ah. How foolish of her not to think of that. Pris folds her hands in her lap. *Be still*, she tells herself.

Mr Franklin produces a document from his portfolio. 'It is a simple testament, but perhaps also a surprising one.'

A pit – a small one, but a pit, all the same – opens itself in my Lady Wyncanton's stomach. What now?

'To begin. There are bequests to the household at Goodwins. I will see to the administering of them. There is a pair of paintings, the flower-pieces –' (Franklin nods his head at them) '– they are to go to Sir Theodore, in thanks.' A glance across the table to Pris. 'There is a sum in trust for you, my Lady.' Then he names the sum, and Pris has to bow her head. Once, mention of such an amount would have brought her to tears of joy; now if she wept, it would be tears of shame. Who was that hussy?

Mr Franklin is still speaking. 'We come to all else in my Lord Wyncanton's estate. Which is the lands and house at Goodwins, and the income thereof, and the lease here, of the house in Lincoln's Inn, and its fittings, and some few financial et ceteras. I understand there is a quantity of plate, for example, on loan to Parliament. All of which shall go to his nominated heir.'

Mr Franklin looks over to James. 'Yes?' says James, politely.

'His heir, which is his youngest ward. You, Master James.'

'What?' James says.

'My Lord Wyncanton's heir, Master James. That is you.'

*

'Mr Franklin, this cannot be so.'

'But it is, my Lady.'

She had dismissed the boys from the table, although she and Mr Franklin can still hear them through the door. They seem to be relaying the news to Molly – yes, and there is Molly's squawk in response. Pris thinks she would like to squawk as well. She would like to shriek. She would like to summon Wyn to stand before her, demand that he explain himself.

'But why would he do such a thing?'

'There are some further small requests, which may speak to my Lord Wyncanton's state of mind, I think,' says Mr Franklin. 'For example, he expresses the wish that James might follow him to his own old college, of King's, in Cambridge, in due course.'

She is baffled. 'What of it?'

'Such,' says Franklin, 'would often be the request of a father, for his son.'

It stops her dead. 'His *son*?'

'I understand that in the year of James's birth, there was a hiatus in your presence in London. Lord Wyncanton remembered this. He spoke to me of it. I think it may be he imagined, or perhaps liked to imagine, in his last days, that James might be his child, and you –' (he opens his hands, he lifts them toward her, as if at the simplicity of this) '– the mother.'

'But he is not!' Pris exclaims. '*I* am not. This is – Mr Franklin, this is all *wrong*.'

'Nonetheless. That, I believe, was the basis for my Lord Wyncanton's selection of his heir.'

'But it is nothing but a fancy – there is no truth in it.'

'It may be fanciful, my Lady, but it has the force of law behind it. And even as a fancy, I believe it gave my Lord Wyncanton great happiness.'

A tapping at the door. It opens; James's head appears; then somewhat above it, so does Ned's. 'Mr Franklin,' James says, 'we have a question.'

Mr Franklin stands. 'By all means.'

'What would this mean for Varney?'

'For Varney?'

'For where we used to live.' The two of them are edging round the door, in the same way as they seem to be edging up to the question. 'What was our house before.'

'In what way,' says Mr Franklin, 'do you mean?'

'If Varney was ours, when we were made wards, *d*oes that mean Varney was Lord Wyncanton's as well?'

'Ah,' says Mr Franklin. 'Yes, I follow you. Not his property, but the law would hold that it sat under my Lord Wyncanton's guardianship, certainly.'

A glance exchanged between the boys. 'So can it be sequestered?' James asks.

Mr Franklin is drawing his papers into his portfolio. 'Sequestered?' he repeats. 'Sequester the inheritance of a ward of my Lord Wyncanton's? A man who served Parliament with such faithfulness, and so well? I think not.'

'So is Varney safe?'

'Entirely so, I would say.'

Both of them turn at once toward Pris, but it is Ned who speaks. 'Then can we go back there? Pris, can we just go home?'

Dearest Rafe, dearest Belle,

You must forgive me, sending such a scrawl as this. I will save the full tale till we are face to face, when you shall have all the how and why of it, but I can tell you this: there will be no sequestration, not for Varney. I enclose with this a paper I have had drawn up by a lawyer here, a Mr Franklin, and he says should any more such of Parliament's commissioners appear at the door, this is to be shown them, and they sent on their way.

I have no notion how the roads may be, but I know the boys are in a ferment to be home as soon as soon can be. Please write, let me know if it is safe for us to chance ourselves…

'There,' says Rafe. 'So that is it. They are coming home.' He had stood to read the letter out, now he holds it toward his audience, here about Varney's kitchen table. 'No sequestration. Those are her words. What do you say to that?'

'If Miss Holland says it—' Mrs Mayhew begins.

'Lady Wyncanton,' Rafe corrects her.

The smallest pause. Belle glances at her husband; this shift from one name to the other does not sit as easily with everyone as it does with him, but Rafe seems unaware of this.

'Lady Wyncanton,' Mrs Mayhew continues, 'then we must trust that it is so.'

A mutter from the end of the table, where Old Henty sits, crumbling her bread. 'An' *she* would not have let our silver walk out the house, you may be sure of that.'

THEY DO SO love to talk, these youngsters, to marvel at the size of their misfortune. Hereford gone. Dartmouth gone. Chester gone. Is there any place left, they ask each other, and laugh, because what else can you do? What venture was it, sank the King's fortune into such a pit? Was it Naseby, or was it before? Was it when they did not march on London? Was it when they lost the north? Is it true, all Prince Rupert's luck deserted him, when his little dog was killed, at Marston Moor?

But might those fortunes be restored? Why sure! There'll be a treaty – there must be! The King has not fled to France; he seeks peace with Parliament; he will negotiate – why, surely he will. Jack's companions in captivity talk themselves out of shock at their imprisonment and into hopefulness. They are cheery about everything – the stink from the pit in the corner of the room, their ragged clothes, their dirt-encrusted hands. Get on your tiptoes, look through their single grated window, for the bad old year is done, the new comes forth, soon there will be a green blur round those trees, the half-barrel from which they take their ration of water will no longer have ice around its rim; soon their gaolers will undo their chains and set them marching. And what will happen after that? They are young, this is but a chapter – what next? Some expect release, some ransom; some say they will go abroad; some home, to whatever home might be awaiting them.

'And you, Captain? What will you do?'

There is a woman, he replies. A woman and two little boys. There is no next for me till I have found them.

Their only other topic of conversation is food. Roast pheasant. Cheese! Symond's mother, apparently, makes plum dumplings famed across Oxfordshire. They are bone-thin, all of them. Some have old wounds surfacing on their skin. Jack wants to tell them, yes, that happens. Some cannot complete their sentences. Like old men, their thoughts go wandering. Yes, that happens too. Their gums are ruby red. Their breath is foul; when they speak to each other, they cover their mouths and keep their heads turned away.

And then, inevitably, the fever comes amongst them. This one or that, waking glassy-eyed, greasy-browed, staring at those around them as if no longer able to grasp who or where they are. And then the splash of marks on chest or belly, the wine-stain rash. After that their gaolers will no longer go near them; throw bread in through the door, push in the barrel of water with long poles. The cold holds it off a little while; then the air warms and it moves through them like the rippling edge of a forest fire. 'What is it?' their fellows ask, staring at their companions laid there by the wall, muttering like mad men, whining with pain if you try to sit them up. 'What do we do?'

Close a man's eyes and write his name on his shirt. Those left alive take to memorizing last-will-and-testaments for each other. Some men become the repositories for three or four, then die themselves. If they drop while being marched, the local constables will deal with the body, so their gaolers say, but few of them believe it. No-one is going to touch the body of a man who has died of typhus. All those held prisoner at Reading know is that in that one room in the old abbey, forty of them were confined, and then there were only thirty-three, then twenty-five, then fewer than a score, staggering into Tothill Fields, through the stone gateway of the prison, collapsing across its scrubby yard, and where the morning after their arrival, Lucius Symond wakes befogged and with that wine-stain splatter all across his breast.

Tothill Fields is a ruin. A man could poke his way through its mouldering walls, so the prisoners are held within a palisade, chained one man to the next, with canvasses rigged up to shelter them. 'Come not near me, sir,' says Symond. 'Come not near,' yet the two of them were chained at the foot. 'Are you not afeared?'

'I had this fever when I was sixteen. I never knew of any man who got it twice.' Where Symond lies now, that was Jack, muttering and raving in a hostelry run by a woman called Fat

Magda in the town of Hertzberg, on the border between France and Germany. For four days he had lain as close to the edge of the grave as any man can, without toppling in. He still asks himself why he did not.

That long and wanton road. Did he ever dream that it could be as long as this?

The second day, they are given the sort of blankets you would give a horse, to cover themselves with. He wraps Symond in his, amazed at how long so simple a task can take him, but his thoughts already feel as if someone else is thinking them, as if he does no more than watch himself. Again, when you are starved, it happens. There are rumours that they will be moved from here to other prisons; places more secure: the Marshalsea, Bridewell, the Clink. Of the three, the Clink is apparently the one to avoid.

Symond is murmuring something to himself, over and over again, almost singing it. Jack bends closer. 'Where do we end?' Symond is whispering. 'Where do we end?' He had been flopping and flailing his hand; Jack takes it, and feels the signet ring pressed with desperate fierceness into his own. 'My mother,' Symond says. 'My people, my mother.' Symond breathes his last babbling of playing in Chalgrove Field with Joseph Cantley as a child, and of his mother's kiss when he went off to war.

The two of them have to be unchained, to take Symond's body away. Jack finds he has enough in him to make it to the palisade, the loose chain trailing from his leg like M'sieu with the fence post, before they catch up with him and pull him back. He lands a fist on one of those dragging him to the base of the palisade; then a musket butt cracks into his ribs. The second time he fakes dead himself, and wrestles the chain about the throat of the trooper who comes to investigate. Almost has the man's pistol out his belt. After that, he is chained hand and foot, like a bear awaiting the dogs.

Pest-doctors stalk amongst the rows of prisoners, long gowns flapping at their heels, the beaks of their masks nodding over this man, over that, with the old women, the searchers, in their wake, crowding in close enough to smell the breath, examine the fingernails, see if they are turning black, lift an arm in search of buboes. Only then are the good Samaritans allowed to draw near; they and their bread and their blankets and their offers to get word out to wives and families. Let them know you are alive – at least for now. Send a token to them, so they know the message is true. A name across a piece of paper, an embroidered kerchief. Maybe even this, a signet ring. 'What would you have us do?' this little woman asks. He had watched her nerving herself, these mouse-like scurries back and forth, and then she saw the weight of his chains, and that seemed to bring her forward. Her eyes scan his face, which is stiff with bruising, and the place on his forehead where the butt of the trooper's musket met his head and the skin is broken.

'Symond,' Jack says. 'Lucius Symond, Ewelme. Near to Oxford.'

'Is that you?' the woman asks. She has a way of twisting her fingers together. 'Is that where this should go? Your family? What shall we tell them?'

'No,' he says. 'No.' Speech is effortful, the words must be searched out. His store of them is running low. 'Not mine. A promise. To him.'

'Where is this Symond?' she asks, and he raises his arm in its ragged sleeve and points, where the row of the dead lie under their blankets, naked feet akimbo. He sees how her eyes grow wet. 'We'll see to it,' she promises. 'And you? Your name?'

This tremulous creature in her inky clothes. He tells her. He sees her blink, repeat his name, then watches her scurrying away. There is something of a fog across his vision, but that happens too, once you get to the point where your elbow joint is the thickest place on your arm.

It was out of the fog that he saw the pest-doctor approach.

He had been occupied in taking moody inventory of his hurts (the forehead, new; the sore at his ankle where the weight of the chain drags at the shackle, older; the ache in his leg, oldest of all). The man had bent low over him, the beak of the mask like a probe, looking for some place to insert itself. The red glass in the eyeholes, reflecting the scud of clouds across the sky. Jack could see nothing of who or what might be inside. 'Fuck off to hell,' Jack had growled. His left hand had begun to sing its old sharp melody. 'You've no business with me.'

And then the voice from within the mask. 'Listen to me,' the voice said. The mask gave it a resonance, almost an echo. 'Do you hear me? Listen well. There is nothing for you now. There is nothing and no-one. Your bitch has abandoned you. She married the old man. Your sons, they will call him father now. You have been forgotten. Your life is over.' The figure straightened up. 'I always find you, Fiskardo. I always will.'

He tried to spring forward, as far as a man can, chained at hand and foot. The chains rang out, running through their metal brackets. The pest-doctor stepped back, out of reach. He thought he heard a laugh. Then footsteps coming up behind him, and that inimitable understanding yet again that you are about to receive a blow to the head, and then the blow lands, and that, for a little while, was all.

When he opened his eyes, a sergeant of the guard was standing over him. 'You, you *godless* bastard,' the sergeant said. 'That's the last bit of fucken knavery we put up with from you!'

CHAPTER TEN

My Lady Wyncanton

'We find now to be the time of mercy, but that which is to come to be the time of judgement.'

Michael Jermin, *A Commentary: Upon the Whole Booke of Ecclesiastes*

M*Y GODS PRESERVE me still.*

He has amazed himself. Nothing can harm him, not iron, not steel, not even the tiny arrows of contagion. He can move through the world untouched.

In the midst of life, I am death.

What is more, it seems he has rendered himself invisible, as well as invulnerable. In this disguise, he can go anywhere. He can stand before a wall of tattered posters, all shouting out his name – CARLO FANTOM, AGENT OF SPAIN, WANTED FOR MURDER. INGRAM SKINNER, FOR HARBOURING OF SAME. REWARD FOR INFORMATION TO THE PIGHTLE, CHELSEA – and not one of those crossing the street to avoid him, not one would ever think that this might be the very man sought out so relentlessly, stood there, entirely hidden. One of those from whom all others turn their eyes.

Such had not been his thinking when he tipped the old man into the river. All he had hoped for then was that the old man (so easy a victim, so weak, so solitary!) would have a little money on him. And there had been the fear of contagion, yes, he can admit now, yes, he had felt that, when he first contemplated putting his hand into the pocket of the old man's gown. The heaviness of the purse he found there had astounded him; but then he looked again at the cloak, the hat, the mask, and saw the chance they offered; the chance to hide, to plan how to escape this blasted country altogether, now Hag Place was gone. Now his name and his description were on every wall.

Pest-doctors made their money easily. A house in mourning? Loiter, loiter – someone will throw down money from an upstairs window to have him move on, not paint a cross upon their door. A funeral? Let him hover by the churchyard gate, point with his cane at some nearby tombstone and every last mourner will leave a penny there. A sop to the plague-gods: come not for me! Folk did not even care to have their eyes rest on him. It became almost a game – what could he not get away with? Under the very noses of the men of the Trained Bands (and he knew to be properly wary of them), he had wandered into Tothill Fields. He had loitered around Lincoln's Inn for days. Seeing how he went unobserved, he broke a window in one of the empty houses and moved himself into its attic. He let himself forget the urgency of getting out of England. He began amusing himself by plotting and planning: how first to deal with these loose ends? He had to be careful, of course – as well as the patrols of the Trained Bands by day, Lincoln's Inn Fields was criss-crossed by watchmen all night long. But he too could watch, he could take note – the boys with their nursemaid, the woman herself; one other he remembers from that attempt at capture, a littlish fellow with the look of a lawyer, back and forth, back and forth. Just when he began to find the waiting tedious, there was a funeral. He had followed at a distance, pondering what his first move might be – the nursemaid? The smaller boy?

He would concoct a scheme. He will take them all.

And then, this other. Climbing down out of his carriage, sword at his hip, walking up to the house, ratta-tat-tat on its knocker, and then a yell: 'Niece! Niece! Where are you?'

Niece. A Holland. Another of those who sought to put an end to him. Carlo Fantom leaned forward, breath misting the attic window.

Alack, poor Greville. Not an hour before, there he was, striding into the drawing-room at the Pightle, master of all. 'Bess, I take it not kindly,' he had announced, 'to be so summoned here.' There had been report of Ingram Skinner, sighted on Canvey Island, but it's that other, that bastard Carlo Fantom, Greville wants. One hundred pounds is the reward on offer, on notices pasted up all across the City, and how the devil a man with half his face burned away can have evaded them so long… He had scowled his blackest at the women sat there to receive him – Bess and Mary, like some sort of a committee; Abi all of a twist behind them. 'Any one of you wishes to take over my searchings out, my doings with the Trained Bands, be my guest. I will sit at leisure here.' He folded his arms. 'Well?'

His sister, pressing on her cane, rose to her feet. 'Abi has found Pris's captain,' she announced. 'This Fiskardo. He is amongst the prisoners in Tothill Fields. You wish to be reconciled with her, brother, grand as she is grown, here's your chance to do it.'

Greville's brow had knitted up as tightly as his arms. 'My chance? Mine? Why should this be me?'

'Yours,' said Bess, her tone thunderous. 'You go to Lincoln's Inn, you take this news to her, or by God, Greville, by God, Abi and Mary and I will do it. And we will see how much time my Lady Wyncanton has for you then. This feud of yours, it has cost us too much already. So you go mend it. *Capo*.'

So he had gone, tail between his legs. Ratta-tat-tat. 'Niece! Where are you?'

The door was opened. There stood his niece, in a dusty apron, crates to the left of her, crates to the right.

'And what the poxing blasted fucking hell do you want?' my Lady Wyncanton demands, wholly forgetting herself.

She walked him into the house. 'This is my uncle,' she had said to the boys. A glare at Greville. 'He used to lock me in my room.'

Greville stands with hat in hand. 'Niece, is there a place where we may talk?'

'Here,' says Pris, indicating the hall.

Greville shifts his gaze toward the two boys, then brings it back to her. 'No, lass, in private.'

So she walks him into Wyn's old room instead. Pulls the dust-sheet off a chair. 'Sit,' she tells him. Plucks another dust-sheet away, sits herself opposite. 'Although if you are come to tell me of Aaron, you have wasted your time. I know he is gone.

A Holland, dead in the river at Wycombe. I had all the details of it from Plumstead, long ago.' It is perhaps only the memory of Aaron, like a hand laid on her arm, that stops Pris from adding, *I had hoped it would be you.*

Says Greville, 'I have not come to speak of Aaron.'

'Then what? We are closing up this house and moving back to Oxfordshire, and as you can see, my hands are full.'

He nods toward the door, now closed. 'Those are his boys, I take it? Your captain's?'

'They are. What's it to you?'

'Their father, Pris. He's in London. He's being held at Tothill Fields.'

SPRING IS LATE to Tothill Fields. The rooflines of Parliament House and Westminster Abbey beyond are smudged with greyish murk, the stumpy willows along the riverbank are leafless, the ground so waterlogged planks must be laid across it to make a path up to the prison gate. 'This will not be easy,' Greville had warned her. 'Those few that have been released, first they had the mightiest fines to pay, then there must be promises never to take up arms again. Affidavits. Guarantors. This war may have been fought by soldiers, but trust me, lass, the peace has been taken over by the clerks.'

'I don't care. None of that matters. So long as we get him free.'

He leads her in. The men at the guard post give Pris, in her dusty apron and her hastily donned cap, no acknowledgement at all. What's she? Merely another poor bloody woman, come looking for her man. That is the first shock, that this is clearly a commonplace. The second is that the number of men left here, under those canvas roofs, is so very few. She thinks, *I will see him at once*, but even as she thinks it, she knows that if he were here, amongst so small a number, she would have spotted him – the shape of his head, or the way he would be sitting, and there is no-one who sets off that bird in her heart, and he is not here.

'I'll speak with the guard,' says Greville. And then as if she was a child he was leaving on its own, 'Don't move, don't talk with no-one.'

She waits. She sees a woman sit down with one of the prisoners. The woman unpacks from the basket on her arm first socks and then a scarf, and as she speaks with the man, she swings round the child on her hip, just as if she and her man were at home, before their fireside, and nurses it at her breast. *So this is become life*, thinks Pris. *This is what you do, while you wait for your man's release. But where is mine?*

She hears Greville come up behind her. 'Need to speak with the sergeant.' He peers at her. 'You well, are you, lass?'

'Yes,' Pris answers, composing her face. 'Perfectly so. Where is this sergeant?'

Says Greville, with wholly un-Holland-like outrage, 'In the bloody *pub*.'

The masons who built the abbey are said to have drunk in the Cock and Tabard in Tothill Street, and there is still some ancient coat of arms above the door, faded to almost blindness. She can see Greville is tempted to have her wait outside, beneath it. 'Don't you dare,' she warns him. Besides, inside it is astonishingly well ordered for a London tavern. No-one playing cards, no dicing, no fiddler nor pipe nor voices raised in song; instead men sit in twos and threes, applying themselves to their drink as if under orders to deal with it efficiently.

Greville locates the sergeant; none too pleased to be disturbed. All the same, the man twitches an eye over Pris, up and down, like a reflex he has yet to break himself of, and seems not taken aback at all when Greville puts a shilling on the table at his elbow, then does that business of tacitly forgetting that it's there. Then Greville mentions Jack's name, and the man flares up at once.

'*That* bastard. Oh, we all remember *him*,' the sergeant says, and now those seated round him are animated too.

'Why so?' Greville asks.

'Because the godless devil would not cease trying to escape,' the sergeant says. 'Even manacled. Got his chain about my trooper's neck. Was like to have throttled him.'

'So where's he at now?'

The man eyes the shilling. Greville adds another to it.

'In the Clink,' the sergeant says, with a smack of the lips. 'No more escaping there.' He puts his hand over the coins. 'Not for love *nor* money.'

Greville turns to her a face that says *We've failed* as clearly as if he'd spoken the words.

She strides back into the house as if wearing the seven-league boots of a giant. She feels as if her arms could knock down walls. The pulses of her heart, a battering-ram. Greville, in her wake, is blathering of how he could speak with the men of the Trained Bands and how God knows they owe him, or Wyn's lawyer, what's his name, that Franklin fellow, could he assist—

'Sit there,' says Pris, pointing to the settle. 'Sit and don't move.' She calls for Molly. 'Moll, upstairs. I need to dress.'

'Yes, miss,' comes the blithe reply up the kitchen stairs. 'What is it we are dressing you for?'

Thinks Pris, *I am going to war.*

*

'It's a long time since we fixed you up so, miss,' says Moll. 'Long, *long* time.' She is at Pris's shoulders, twitching every last point of Venice lace to hang as it should. Pris's hair is brushed and curled and pinned, and her every movement brings forth that admonitory *shush!* of silk. A widow's veil awaits her on the bed.

Pris puts her hand on Molly's shoulder. 'Moll, there is a thing I have to do, and I don't know how I am to do it, nor how long it may take me, but while I see to the doing of it, I don't want you here on your own.'

'No, miss,' Molly replies, and knows better than to ask why.

'I want you to take the boys to Bess, in Chelsea.'

'Yes, Miss Pris,' says Moll.

Down she goes. When Greville sees her, he gets to his feet. The boys are sitting either side of him, and when Ned sees her, his face goes through that same expansion of the eyes as Greville's had done, that same registering: a woman who will have no truck with any further foolishness whatsoever. I have my guns out, Bess would say when she was in similar frame of mind. Says Pris, 'We must stay longer here in London.'

'Why?' James wants to know.

'Because I still have business here. So you two, you will go with Moll to Chelsea.'

'Why?'

'Because I say so.'

'But why can't we stay here?'

'Because you would be on your own here, James, and it won't do.'

That small face, tightening in rebellion.

'Demi-Cuit,' his brother cuts in, 'enough. If Pris says we go to Chelsea, then we go.'

And all the while Ned's own face says, *I know full well something is up. And I am scared to think of what it is, because I know there is only one thing it can be.*

'And where is it we two are headed?' Greville asks, as they leave the house.

'Drury Lane.'

THE HOUSE PRIS remembers in Huntingdon, from when she was a tot of four, had a lean to it, as if it was sharing secrets with its neighbours. Its timber bones had been exposed; its plaster skin unpainted. There had been beans and cabbages in its garden; a farmyard over its wall. But this house – this house is not that of a farmer. Its plastering is smooth and white; its upper windows belly outward, like the robes of aldermen. This is the house of a London gentleman, and one of sufficient importance to have men at arms standing at his door. My Lady Wyncanton notes them as she steps down from her hackney; so does her companion. 'Who lives here?' Greville asks.

'My Uncle Nol.'

Greville's mouth drops. 'Girl, you're joking.'

'I am not.'

'Oh, fuckbuggery…'

'And that,' says Pris, 'is exactly why you will be staying here. Remember who I am, Unc. Women such as me, the widows of Parliament's staunch champions? We are hallowed. We can go anywhere.'

She puts up the slide on him before he can voice any further objections. Shakes out her skirts, just as she had in St Martin's Lane all those years ago. It is a very different thing, to wear mourning for real. *You must stay back there*, she tells the creature she was then. *You are me no longer.* Then she takes a breath and walks up to the door. She keeps her eyes down, her pace dignified, she carries herself with all the uprightness she can. She murmurs to the men at arms (their halberds crossed before her), 'I attend on the General. I am expected.'

The halberds are pulled back. The door is opened.

A small room, as you might expect, very plain, whitewashed to make it light, and with one table. From the street, the scatter of conversation. The clerk behind the table stands. 'Madam?' he asks.

'If you would be so good, I am Lady Wyncanton. I wish to speak with the General. General Cromwell.'

'A moment,' says he. Goes from this room into the next, which sounds to be up a set of stairs. She hears the clerk speaking, then she hears another voice. It has not changed at all.

The footsteps return. 'My Lady,' the clerkly young man says. He is very exact. 'My Lady, the General regrets – he remembers your late husband, but the calls upon his time are numerous—'

'Is he up there?' Pris asks, pointing to the door. 'He always liked the rooms where he did his thinking to be up a little way, I recall.' She smiles; she makes sure the smile is bright, but unassuming. 'If he cannot make time for Lady Wyncanton, would you tell him Miss Pris would see her Uncle Nol?'

Again, he goes through the door. Again, the footsteps up the stairs. Again, the murmur of words, then silence, and then a great bark of laughter. 'Bring her up! Bring her in!'

The door is opened once more, but it is held open this time. There are the stairs, just as she had thought. 'My Lady,' the young man says, and beckons her to ascend. More laughter ahead of her as she goes up, and she steps out into a room lit by one immense window, with the man stood before it, holding out his hands. 'By all that's wonderful,' he says. 'By heaven above.'

Another bellow of laughter. He takes her by the hand and pulls her to the light. 'Let me see you.' She puts back her veil. His eyes go back and forth across her face. His own is just as she remembers it – heavier jowled, but her rescuer, her farmer still. Her Uncle Nol. He even has his warts. She remembers as a child how she had made to put her hand up to his face on bidding him farewell, thinking to charm them away for him, as a sort of thank you, and how Bess had knocked her hand down and not let go of it till they were safely on their way.

'I would have known you anywhere,' he says. 'The hair.'

'And I you, sir.'

'By God, this is marvellous. Do we embrace?' And she is pulled to his chest. She remembers this as well – the energy, the passion in his movements. Then she is held away with the same vigour with which the moment before he had pulled her forward. His scrutiny is searching. She remembers those creases on his brow, when he was thinking hard. 'Wyncanton,' he says. 'Parliament lost more than it will likely ever know, in him. But I had no idea he had wed.'

'He was already very ill when he did,' says Pris. 'Very near the end.' Her voice has that teeter-totter. She feels how her mouth has a twist to it, just as Ned's had done. *No, you do not. You do not weep and wail.*

'You mourn him.'

'I do, sir. We were married no time at all, but we knew each other many years. I am grateful for them.'

'God's will,' he says. 'It tests us.'

'You lost your boy, I know,' she says, and now he must look away, out that great window as if the shade of his son was waiting out there in the light.

'Our children are the best of us,' he says, at last. 'But many fathers lost more.'

'Yes, sir.'

'And you,' he begins. 'Are you – have you children of your own?'

'Not of my own, sir, but by default. Two boys. Wyncanton made them his wards, so now they are mine. It was on their behalf I wished to speak with you.' She takes a breath. 'To make appeal.'

'For them? How so?' He holds her by the hand and, as he speaks, leads her to a pair of wicker-seated chairs, there by the wall. They are the only furniture in the room, and she remembers how he liked to have space about him, space in which to stride back and forth as he winnowed and wrestled his thoughts.

He sits with her, the panels of his coat over his knees. 'What can I do for them?'

You do not make flowery speeches with this man. You do not fluff and faff.

'You can release their father,' says Pris.

'Their father.'

'Who fought against Parliament, yes.'

He puts his hands onto his knees – those squared-off, farmer's hands. 'I see,' he says. The creases on his brow return. 'Their father who is where? Their father who is who?'

'He has been sent to the Clink, sir. Jack Fiskardo.'

'Fiskardo.' He leans away from her. 'The discoverer?' The brows drawn together, the large eyes moving. 'Rupert's man. One of those who brought his own soldiers into England's war.'

'He would not try to excuse himself. It is I who ask it for him. For his sons.'

He stands, he walks about the room again. 'We release these men, they take up arms all over again. Their promises are pie-crust.'

'No, sir. He will not.'

'We fight them over and over. If we trust them, this war will never end.'

'We will leave England. We will go away—'

'All the King's men seek to run abroad. And to make war on us again from there.'

'He will not, I promise you. Sir, I was a tiny child when we knew each other. Children keep their promises. I have not changed. You have my word, you will not hear of us—'

'Your word?' More striding about. 'But it is his that matters, missy. What of his?'

She waits for him to come to a stop. She will not press her hands together in front of him as a supplicant might do, but in her head they could not be more tightly palm to palm. 'How does your wife, sir?'

'My wife?' he repeats.

'Mistress Elizabeth. She was as kind to me as you. I always thought of you and she as having a proper partnership between you. A true meeting. I remember one night – it was very late, I should have been abed, but I was homesick, I had crept downstairs, and you and she were there before your fire, and you were talking of how you would take your family from England, to the New World. Your wife was at the fire, with her sewing in her hand, and she listened to your words, then she said most gently, "My dear, you will not."'

He is standing with his hands in his sleeves. His head is down, as if he were hearing her words through his wide forehead rather than his ears.

'There is much force to that female *You will not.* Do you not agree, sir? I think it could stop oceans. Halt landslides in their tracks. It can be so gently said, but it is iron-willed. Why, even great generals abide by it. If it were otherwise, how now would we be here?'

He lifts his head by just enough for her to see the amusement in his eye.

'So that will be my answer too. *My dear, you will not.*'

She sees how he mouths the words with her. She sees that he remembers.

Victory.

Greville throws open the door of the carriage on seeing her. 'Well?' he demands. 'Well?'

She climbs back into the carriage, lifts her hand and strikes its roof to alert the coachman. She has the paper tucked against her heart – the paper with the great spiky signature, and the all-important seal. 'Over the river. We are going to the Clink.'

Along the Strand, past Blackfriars and over the bridge. It is as if time is running backwards, as if her life was a snake with its tail in its mouth. Past Southwark's cathedral. Past the weedy ruins of its one-time palace. Into this narrow street, which is nothing but wall, and then the thick-planked door.

'I hate this place,' Greville says, morosely.

'You don't need to come with me, Greville. I don't need you here.'

'Leave you to do this on your own? Bess would never speak to me again.'

He strikes with his cane upon the door – the door within a door, behind its grille. No answer, so he strikes again. Idle watchers in the street take note. Greville glares at them (and Greville's face was made for glaring) and they go back to their idle watching.

The door within the door is opened. 'Who are you?' comes the demand.

Greville sticks his cane through the grille to keep it open, presents his face before it. 'You know me? You know who I am?'

A surly silence, then, 'Yeah, I do.'

'Then open up.' What it is, in Southwark, to be a Holland.

A grinding of keys. The door is opened.

The first thing that strikes her is the height, inside, of those walls, the narrowness to the sunlight, the depth of shadow it throws across the yard. This cannot be the same sun as elsewhere. In the yard itself, men playing knucklebones, or sitting, smoking pipes, staring at nothing. As they walk in, from every window there are faces squinting down at them – from barred windows up above, or peering from openings at the level of cellars. The gaoler who had opened the door walks beside them. He wears what might once have been worn upon the battlefield, only by maybe four or five other men: breeches that sag down to his calves, a shirt whose sleeves end at his elbows, one shoe darkish, one light, one stocking yellowish, one faded red. ''Oo'd'you want?'

'Fiskardo,' says Pris. 'Jack Fiskardo.' She is tempted, for a moment, to stand there and shout his name, until Jack comes to one of those windows himself.

The man rubs his chin. 'Fiskardo,' he repeats. He looks entirely capable of standing there all day, until of course she comes up with the coin to bring him back to life, like a clockwork manikin.

But it is Greville who presses yet another shilling into the man's hand – bounty so unexpected that the gaoler takes a step back. 'Let's you and I understand each other,' Greville says. 'You fuck others about when they come here. Not me. Not us. Fiskardo.'

'Yeah, but he's below,' the man says. 'Fever rooms.'

'Fever rooms?' The nearest game of knucklebones reacts, the players glancing over their shoulders.

'That's it. Quarantine. Spotted fever. We don't go in an' they can't come out.' The man rubs his chin again. 'You can look in at 'em. Look in at the door.'

Greville puts his hand on the man's shoulder. 'Take us there,' he says.

The way to hell. It begins at another door in the corner of the yard, opening to a spiral stone stair. And a second gaoler, standing guard. '*They* can't come in,' this second gaoler says, levering himself up from his slouch against the wall; bringing his pike with him (rusty-bladed, fanged with wear).

'Greville 'Olland,' says the first, jerking a thumb over his shoulder, and after that, all the way down the stair Pris can hear the whisper coming after them, from doors and passageways: *That's Greville 'Olland, Greville 'Olland.*

There is straw on the stairs, wetness, places you might slip, the smell of earth and stone joining a stink so strong she can feel it coating her skin. The scurry and squeak of rats. She hears voices, weak with misery. This is what it would be like to be sentient within your grave.

The stair stops turning. A small space, lit by the remains of light from above, and then another door, another grille let into it. 'In there,' their gaoler says, standing aside. She looks. She has to stand on tiptoe. She makes out shapes, unmoving, in the gloom. She whispers to Greville, 'I can't see him.'

Says Greville to the gaoler, 'Open this bloody door. Do it now.'

The man heaves an almighty sigh, goes at the door with his keys. Its hinges shriek. She steps in.

The first thing she sees is an enormous humpbacked rat, running along where wall joins floor. Then another, running from underneath something laid there on the floor – no, that is a corpse (the sunken eyes, the caved-in cheeks). Beyond it, two pale shins, feet black with dirt, a blanket pulled up to hide the rest.

Greville has stepped in behind her, sleeve over his nose. 'Pris,' he says. 'There.'

Behind her, against the wall, there is a man lying on his back. Lice sequin his hair and beard; his shirt is rotted away to nothing. His hands lie one above the other at his breast; the flutter of breath in his belly the only sign that he is alive at all, and the only way she would have known that this was him, the tattoos on those hands. Only when she has seen them does she start to recognize more of him – the bump of his nose, the line of his brows. That long mouth. The branching of his ribs. The crater of his stomach, like it had been spooned away. She could weep. But there are no marks upon his skin. There is no rash. She crouches down beside him. She touches his forehead. No fever, either.

'Jack,' she says. Lifts his hand, holds it to her breasts, presses it between them. 'Jack.'

He rolls his head. His eyes open. For a moment he is looking directly at her, found her face and anchored his gaze to it, that ghostly blue; then there is this slow shaking of his head from side to side, and his eyes close again. 'Jack,' she says, 'it's me, it's Pris.' For one terrible moment she thinks she has just watched him die, but then his breathing quickens, becomes a wheeze. 'Can you sit up? Jack, can you sit?' There is so little to him she can lift him herself with her arm beneath him. His head rolls against her neck. Does he say her name? The wing-bones of his shoulders, they are sharp as spades against her arm. She takes the paper from her bodice. 'Greville, this.'

Greville flaps the paper at the gaoler. 'This one is getting out of here.'

'Nah, he can't. Can't do it,' the man says. 'Them put down here, they stay. Quarantine.'

'But this man has no marks of fever. Look for yourself.'

The man shifts from one foot to the other. Scratches at his arse.

'Why has he been put down here?'

'This one –' The gaoler heaves a sigh. 'Look, there's some of them, keep *contending* with us. We put – we put such down here.'

'Right,' says Greville. His voice is heavy with menace. 'Only now, this one gets out.' He holds the paper to the man's face. 'You see that? You see whose name that is? Whose signature?'

'Yeah, but—' Greville is almost standing on the man's toes. 'A'right, *a'right*,' the man says. 'If he can walk. If he walks out of here, he walks out.'

'Then he walks.' For the first time, Greville addresses Jack directly. 'You hear? You are going to walk.' He puts his arm under Jack from the other side. Between them, she and Greville, they get him upright. Between them, they move him to the door. The light falls on his face. 'Christ,' Greville exclaims under his breath.

They walk him forward, feet dragging. She feels Jack roll his head again; it is as if he feels the light. With Pris one side and Greville the other, at a slant, they begin on the way up the spiral. Sometimes he slips – a full-grown man is a shockingly unhandy burden: the legs bend, the feet must be pulled after the legs, the hands bang against the wall, and at every opening off the stairs they have an audience. And still that broken wheeze.

'His breathing, Pris.' Greville sounds horrified.

'It's laughter. I think he's laughing.'

'He's *what*?'

Here is the door to the yard. It opens. They carry him out, and the players of knucklebones scatter at the sight of them. The gaoler falls back. The men at the windows are silent. They are at the door out. They are at the street. Jack's head has flopped sideways, his eyes are closed. The coachman, looking down, begins, '*Oh* no—'

Says Greville, 'Hand us your cloak. A sovereign, and you ever want to drive in Southwark again, hand down the cloak.'

The man lowers the cloak gingerly toward them. Greville wraps Jack up in it as Pris holds him; as he does so Pris hears Greville muttering, 'Don't you *dare* drop off the perch here.'

She gets into the hackney, and Greville pushes Jack in after her. She holds him against her on the seat, his head against her shoulder. The wheezing, the groaning, subside. Is he even conscious any more?

'Now what?' says Greville. 'Now what, lass? Where do we take him? To Bess? To the Pightle?'

'No. His sons cannot see him like this.' But if not to Chelsea, where?

And then she knows. Time running backwards. 'We open up the Leaguer. We take him there.'

CHAPTER ELEVEN

Holland's Leaguer

'... am not I the lady of the manor?
And who shall dare to question me?'

Shackerley Marmion, *Hollands Leaguer. An excellent comedy...*

D*earest Rafe, dearest Belle, my love to all*

Forgive me, but there is business that detains me here. I will write more soon as I can –

'I cannot make head nor tail of this,' says Rafe. He flaps the letter about as he speaks, as if an explanation might be shaken from it. 'They are coming home, then they are not – this is not

Pris. What is this business? Why does she not say? And what is the address she gives in Chelsea? What is going on?' He sighs. True, he and Belle abide here on the friendliest terms of grace-and-favour, but that serves only to have Rafe view his duties as a caretaker all the more seriously. 'Old Abram tells me both the Indian pheasants are no more. He is convinced that they have fallen victim to some poacher's snare. And as if this were not enough, now Topham says he believes Annie is not simply a barrel-belly, but deep in foal. She is doing something he calls bagging up. I have no notion what that means, but apparently it is an unequivocal sign. What are we to do with a foal? I tell you, wife, the trials and tribulations – where do they end?'

'Husband,' says Belle, 'perhaps, if Mr Topham agrees, someone from here might go to Pris and find out what is what?'

WHEN PRIS WAS small, Abi would make up bedtime stories for her of the long-ago family who built Holland's Leaguer. 'Oh, they were fine folk,' Abi would say, stroking Pris's head, as she lay in her bed. 'There was a daddy, who was such a good, kind man, and a mama, who was beautiful, and three little girls.' This while all the riot of the Leaguer at night went on beneath them: a lute, a flute; the slap of dancing slippers hitting the floor; the smash of a bottle; Yellow Katie's parrot-like cackle; or that particular male roar as the first of the mimics made his appearance, in diaphanous himation and with his cock-stand, gilded, underneath. 'One of the sisters could sing,' Abi would continue, lowering her head so that Pris could still hear her, 'and one made flowers out of silk, as pretty as if they had come from the garden. But the littlest one, she was the most special of all. She could do *everything*.'

And what was their name, this wondrous family? Said Abi, 'Their name was Blessedsoul.'

When she grew too old for stories, Pris still used to think of the Blessedsouls, and what they might make of what had been their manor house. The grotto in the garden with the mosaic of mermaids in its pool, clay breasts and scaly buttocks rounded up to loll against or fondle; the summer house with its couches and cushions and the frieze of figures fucking their way round the top of the wall; the menu of offerings frescoed up in the Leaguer's grand reception room, the stick men and women bending, splaying, supine, upright; the old alchemical signs for iron or copper, for her patrons to indicate, was it a woman or a mimic you desired to do this with? And what became of all those who danced and sang and fornicated their way round Holland's Leaguer, in its heyday? Did their ghosts share the Leaguer with the Blessedsouls? Did they wander its chambers, making the cobwebs tremble? And what would they make of this, this room where the planks have been lifted from the window and the shutters opened, and where the man lies on the bed, and the woman sits beside him, hour after hour after hour.

Come back to me. Come back to us. Jack, hear me, please.

He feels so breakable. Raising his head from the pillow feels like holding an egg. Lifting him is like holding a bundle of sticks.

Do you hear me? Are you there?

There are visitors, on top of those that make the cobwebs shed their dust. The ebb tide brings Bess and Mary from the Pightle. Bess who announces (as if this must be the reason for her visit), 'His boys are asking questions.' She stands at the door of the sick-room, taking stock. All the paraphernalia of nursing – the bottles of Portugal water to clean the skin, honey to help the sores heal, lavender to make the room smell sweet, a basket of logs to keep it warm, fresh linens… Her foundling has even cut the ragged beard, clipped away the rook's nest of the man's hair. 'So this is he, is it?'

'This is he,' says Pris.

A lengthy study. 'Was he ever pretty?' Bess enquires.

'No. He never was.'

Bess gives a grunt. 'And yet,' she says, 'I think I see it, nonetheless.'

Mary asks, 'Does he eat?'

'Never mind eating,' says Bess. 'Does he wake?'

They are such a merry company, this roomful of men. They pass his name back and forth amongst them. *Jack Fiskardo, Jack Fiskardo, do you hear me?* Yes, he does, but he wants to be left in peace. He has to plot how to break out of here.

Surprise, surprise, Ancrum is there. I had a clean death, Ancrum says. Snapped me neck.

Ancrum is not so welcome. He feels the words in his throat. You should not be here.

No, says Ancrum. It is you, you rogue, should not be here.

Of course I am here, the voice says. *I will not leave you, Jack.*

He can hear cannon. The boom, then a whoosh like the swirl of water. *Where are you, Jack? Where are you?*

The tide comes pushing up from Rotherhithe, and Mary returns. She brings manchet bread, soft and white, to gentle a shrunken stomach back to life, an urn-full of fresh milk, chicken quenelles, ginger cordial; also, pastilles of liquorice and pulverized earthworm, counted an excellent restorative; hogs' grease, Venice treacle, and a bottle of that new-fangled curative, Mr Wicker's Epsom Salts; so bitter it is as if your mouth has been possessed. 'All from Greville,' Mary says.

Who will no doubt present his bill in due course. 'Where is Greville?'

'Hunting Ingram Skinner. Skinner, and his cutter, the one took Aaron from us. This Carlo Fantom.'

The bottle leaps from Pris's hands. Epsom salts, strewn across the floor.

The tide turns, taking Mary with it, waving farewell from Miguel's wherry. Pris goes back into the house, up its stair, up, up, into the room with the bubbled canvas of Susanna and the Elders on its wall. Yellow Katie always liked a show. She finds the broken mirror propped against its wall, cleans it off, sets it up, sits down in front of it cross-legged, and waits.

It takes a little while. They do not care to be summoned. It makes them surly.

'Bring him back,' she says. 'Bring him back. I know what you want, I know who you seek, I know what you would have me do, but you bring him back first. You bring mine back, or you get not one damn thing more from me.'

SERGEANT-AT-ARMS AT TOTHILL Fields: it's not without its aggravations, such a role, even without folk appearing at your door, demanding the whereabouts of this prisoner, of that. And now a blasted pest-doctor, God above. 'Come you not near me!' the sergeant exclaims, backing up. He contemplates brandishing his flintlock. But the pest-doctor is full of apologies – he has been anxious, declares the voice behind the mask, one of the prisoners, he fears he had seen the early signs –

Which prisoner did you say? Fiskardo?

Indeed. He. He is here no longer?

Fiskardo, Fiskardo – why does everyone ask about Fiskardo? 'Rheumaticks?' the sergeant enquires, kindly, seeing how the pest-doctor rubs at one hand with the other. 'Your man is gone.'

Gone? He is – he has passed?

'Good as. The Clink.'

The Clink. Carlo Fantom stands on the far side of the road, contemplating his next move.

Posters stir on the wall behind his head, a papier mâché of notices as there is every place in London: By Order Of. Information Sought. The King's Secret Correspondence Revealed. The Fall of Bristol, A True Account. The Marvellous Pig-headed Man, To Be Exhibited At Covent Garden…

The few Londoners on the street skirt around him.

You are not there, he thinks, eyeing the door. I know you are not there.

This has gone wrong. Unmistakably, it has. The house in Lincoln's Inn Fields, it is dark. It is as dark and empty as that in which he sits to spy on it. He has miscalculated in some way, but how? How has this happened? How have they outwitted him?

Where might they be? Where would they go? Where does she have?

HE LISTENS TO the blood move through his veins, an underground river through pitch-black caves. *Where are you, Jack? Where are you?*

Here. Here is where but where is here? A sky above him that flaps in and out; and something coming toward him with arms outstretched like wings. And a beak. The beak cracks open; it keeps opening wider and wider, as if it would swallow him whole.

The voice from within the beak says they have abandoned you and you deserve no less, she has married the old man, your sons call him father now and then that sticky-sounding laugh.

He is walking. He thinks he will go on walking for ever. No, he will not, or not this way at least; something is pushing against him, pushing him back. It enrages him, he thrashes against it in a fury. He tries again – no, still his way is blocked, although there is nothing to see. It feels as if there are hands, turning him about, turning him toward a horizon so far away it is barely there at all.

A tiny dot upon it. Movement forward.

Jack, do you hear me? Do you hear my voice? Do you know that I am here?

There is something soft and wet against his mouth. It feels like bread. It tastes like milk. He is ravenous for more. He bites, and hears a yelp, which somewhere deep inside him makes him smile.

Come back to us. Come back to us, please. Wake up, wake up, wake up.

A square of light.

'Do you see me? Do you hear me?'

This will not fool him. This will dissolve, like all the rest.

He lets her sit him up. He lets her feed him, like a child. Then he gets angry, swipes the bowl away. These rages fall upon him without warning, without cause. He sleeps. Awake again. She wants him to get out of bed, to stand. She lifts him and he droops over her. Totters forward. She has a quilt about his shoulders. 'Here,' she says, 'here, by the fire.'

He does not so much sit as meet the floor. She has turned away, her back is to him. He feels dulled by his fury, as if nothing else exists; nothing around him matters, none of it is real. He reaches out his hand for something, anything, and what his hand finds is a basket of logs by the fire.

He will not be fooled by this, by any of it.

But pain is real. Whatever this is, that will show it, how he will not be deceived.

He lifts a log from the basket, puts it into the flames and holds it there.

He hears her scream. It is so real, it startles him. He feels her grip on his arm, pulling his hand back, and oh God in heaven, how it hurts, outrageous pain, as if it has every evil in the world in it. He curls himself about it, and her arms come round him, and then he is weeping, immense unpractised sobs that seem to come up through him from his tail-bone, that hardly leave him space to breathe. He hears himself say, 'My horse, Pris. My horse,' but after that all he can manage is her name – 'Pris, oh, Pris' – as he rocks against her, drawn up into this human reef-knot, and she holds him with one arm about his shoulders and the other about his folded legs, telling him, 'I'm here, Jack, I'm here. I'm here.'

The sobs abate, like the falling waters of a flood. He can keep his breath. He can lift his head and see the room they are in – dots of green at the window, the bed, the quilt pulled round him, and she holding his hand; the char, the blistered mess of it. All the ink and half his history gone. 'I love this hand,' she is saying. 'Please, *please* don't hurt it any more.'

She leads him to the bed, lies him down, lies down beside him, his bandaged hand between them like a swaddled infant. He feels as if he is either just about to fall asleep, or has just woken. His eyes close, then open, on their own. The bed on which they lie has faded tassels hanging loose above them. Leaves scratch the window, the light falls on some faded pattern on the walls. Tumbling blocks. You might paint such on the walls for a child.

'Where are the boys?'

'They're safe. They are with Bess, in Chelsea. Moll is with them. Once you look a little more yourself, we will go there too.'

'So where is this place? Where are we now?'

'This is Holland's Leaguer. This is where I grew up. This was my bed when I was a little girl.'

She has him sit on the bed while she strokes honey onto the sores on his back. When he flinches in anticipation, she tells him, 'Don't fight me, Jack,' and strange to say, after that, all he feels is cooling, ease.

He asks, 'How can you bear to do this?'

'What do you mean?'

'I came back with a bit of battle-dirt on me, and you would scarce let me in the house.'

'That wasn't me. That was some other woman, and she was a fool.'

On her arm, he manages a circuit of the garden. It leaves him damp-browed with effort. His legs tire, his lungs protest; by the end of the day he feels like a puny old man. 'I'm weak as mouse piss,' he complains.

But next time, he manages two. Then three. Small things are coming into flower at his feet. There are glimpses of the river. A bird whirrs across the path in front of them, a length of dry grass in its beak.

There is a room downstairs, large enough to host dozens, has upon its ceiling the remains of a painted oculus, romping with naked nymphs, shaking rose petals down on those below. There is a menu of faded lechery up on the wall so frank that when Jack begins deciphering it, it makes even his face grow hot. 'This is where you grew up?' he asks.

She gives a grin. 'Explains a lot, don't it?'

The fireplace is supported by a pair of satyrs, between whose Capricorn legs rise marble members of pink jasper so erect you could hang your hat on them. Would that his own had such life in it. When he berates himself for this as well, she takes his face in her hands and says, 'Stop. You will be kind toward yourself. You promised me. Jack, you cannot always be invincible. There is grace in knowing when to yield.'

He lies against her breast, listening to her heartbeat, the tiny creaking of her stays. He says, 'I had such dreams of you. When I was in that cell, every time I closed my eyes, I saw you.' But even as he says it, the memory of the dreams is slipping away from him, like water. 'There was a woman who looked like you. I never saw her face but she had hair as red as yours. And three others, very old. It was as if I kept trying to go one way, but they kept turning me about, sending me the other.'

He sees her expression change into something he has no name for whatsoever. 'They did?'

'I know I know them. Where do I know them from?'

She is stroking his head. 'They were dreams, Jack. Only dreams.'

His hair, he realizes, is cropped. 'You've made an Ironside of me.'

'I did. And I hope you weren't saving your beard, for that is going as well.'

She helps him dress. New shirt, new breeches, boots. New buff-coat too. She shows him in the mirror and he has to laugh. 'I look like a ploughman. Like a farmer. Are we making a trip?'

'Yes. We are.'

Now she shaves him.

'Pris, why did I dream you were wed?'

'Because I was.' She is watching the strokes of the razor, not him.

'You were?'

'I wed Wyncanton. Then he died.' She lowers the razor; looks into his face. 'I know, we have to talk of this.'

Her eyes, so close to his, are like looking through the windows of a church. And his boys are in Chelsea, and she is here. 'No, we don't,' he says.

'No, but we do. I wed Wyncanton. He made the boys his wards. Then he died, but he made James his heir.'

'His *heir*?'

'It has kept Varney safe for them. For him and Ned.'

She is rubbing a towel about his cheeks.

'So do we go back there?'

'No. Jack. I made a deal for you. I made promises, I gave my word. I said you would never take up arms again. I said we would leave England. I said your days of soldiering were done.'

He moves her hands from his face. 'No more soldiering?'

'No. You must give it up. You must give all of it up, Jack. Are you angry?'

Give it up. Leave your sword in the ground. How would that be, to leave it there, to simply walk away? How would it feel?

It would feel easy as closing a door.

'Lady, you get no argument from me.'

THIS YOUNG MAN, this country lad, so shy in his manner, so rustic in his dress; he's walked from Charing Cross to get here, but walking seems a deal safer to Toby than riding in a carriage, which might take you anywhere, and in any case, if Mr Endicott's directions can be trusted, this is journey's end. Follow the river, Rafe told him, and you will come at last to Chelsea Church, which you will know for the mighty mulberry tree close by it, so leave the river behind you, up a lane toward what the folk in Chelsea call the King's Road, and you will see it over the trees. The Hollands' house, three storeys, brick, and chimneys either end.

But it is still so very early. Perhaps, thinks Toby, he should make a pause here till it is more likely folk will be awake and welcoming of visitors. He might sit here upon this milestone and rest.

Which is what he is doing when he sees the figure in the lane, under the shadow of the trees.

It catches his attention first of all because he can't make sense of it. That long-sleeved robe, like a cleric's, down to the ground, but then the flat-topped, wide-brimmed hat. It has its back to him, but there is something about the way it moves unsettles him. It looks predatory.

Toby finds he has got to his feet. He follows it into the lane. The figure is headed for the house. Unmistakably, it and he, their goal is the same. It has quickened its pace. Impelled by his sense of unease, so does Toby. The figure is shaking something down from within the sleeve of its gown. The figure moves forward, arm bent. Extending from it, thin as a skewer, a blade.

Back at Varney, if he did see a man moving ahead of him like this, armed and so stealthy, Toby would think at once *Poacher*. And now the figure has reached the gate of the house. It is moving forward, into the garden along the path.

'And this,' Topham had said, as he readied Toby for his journey, 'is a pocket pistol. I do not say as you will need it, indeed I hope not so, but God alone knows what one may find in

London these days, so you take it. It is primed and loaded, so you be sure you do not sit upon it, lad. But you may fire it with one hand, and it will make a goodly noise at least.'

Toby lifts the pistol. It would be unsporting to fire without warning, so Toby is making ready to shout 'Hoi!' when a terrible sound erupts from the ground ahead. It starts with the depth of a chord on an organ, but it goes up and up and up and up, one octave after another, until its yowl is the shriek of demons. At the same time, something drops from the tree above the figure onto its head, knocking away that wide-brimmed hat – something that in its velocity and blackness makes Toby think of catamounts, panthers – good God, could there be such wild cats roaming free in London? The figure gives a shout; it whirls round. The animal (with claws sunk into the figure's scalp) is enormous; it has a tail long as an ostrich feather; it has tufted ears, it has the eyes of Beelzebub, and the figure, hands to its head, trying to shake itself free, reels about and Toby sees its wears a mask, a mask with a beak, like it sniffs out its way, and Toby is so startled, he fires almost without meaning to. The figure cries out and staggers backwards. More noise from within the house. An attic window has come open, there is a woman leaning out. The hideous masked thing is gone, but there is its hat and mask upon the grass. Toby picks them up. The immense black cat is still there, inflated like a porcupine. He is scared to approach it. And the woman at the attic window, leaning out so far Toby fears she may fall from it altogether, that is Moll, and she is calling to him, 'Toby! Toby Dearlove! What are you doing here?'

What is he doing here? Hiding his hand, is what, so that Moll will not be embarrassed by him amongst all these new folk – the woman who takes a tumbler of brandy for breakfast and announces she will go to Rotherhithe; the one who scurries about with her hands all twisted up, saying how they might have all been murdered in their beds; and then this last, majestic as royalty, sat here at the kitchen table, who answers, 'But we were *not*, Abi, and that is what matters.' Using her cane she had eased herself down into her chair. She had held out her hand to him. Her face was like a cliff of chalk, her mouth as red as if she had been sucking blood. He did not know if he should shake that hand or kiss it. It winked with diamonds. 'I am Bess Holland,' the woman said. 'You will know my foundling, Pris.'

The boys (how Ned has grown!) are bouncing round him, demanding news – did Parliament's men come back again? Did Toby shoot at them as well? Were Rafe and Belle at Varney? How was Ocker? How was Todd? And now there is a carriage drawing up outside, so yet more folk, thinks Toby, buttressing himself, but when the carriage door opens, to his relief he sees this is Miss Holland – no, *Lady Wyncanton*, he reminds himself. He knows it must be she even though she has her back to him, for it is her hair. She is helping a man get down from the carriage, a man who seems to unfold himself as he emerges – who is that? Cropped hair, greyish. He gazes up at the house as he leans on my Lady Wyncanton's arm. It is as if he wears a mask composed of features Toby knows, wrapped round his own narrowed head. 'Why!' Toby exclaims, delighted. ''Tis the captain!'

GREVILLE ARRIVES IN such a froth of fury they can hear him before he is even through the Pightle's front door. The pest-doctor's mask awaits him in the parlour. 'Who was this?' Greville demands, striding in. 'Who dared come here, to this house? To our very doorstep? Who would dare?' He stops. He sees his sister is not alone. Sat on the settle, with his arm about one young lad, and another, very much smaller, in his lap, there is a man. A man now getting to his feet (cautiously, like one still not certain that his balance can be trusted). His niece takes the smaller child. Ah, now Greville knows who this must be, although by God, one must do feats of imagination to see in him the scarecrow rescued from the Clink.

'Greville,' says Bess. 'This is Jack Fiskardo.' There is the faintest suggestion of a smile as she says it – yes indeed, Greville. This is he. Shake that hand; think of the fortune behind it.

'I remember you,' Greville is saying. 'You are – much improved, I'm happy to say.'

'I too,' comes the reply. 'And I can tell you exactly who it was came here. His name is Carlo Fantom. This is what he wore when he came visiting in Tothill Fields.'

'Carlo Fantom?' Greville seizes the mask as if it were a living thing, so furious is he. 'This is how he has evaded us? Captain, we have been hunting him for months. He killed our nephew. He menaced Pris. He was hand in glove with the Skinners, damn his eyes.'

'He has taken from me too,' says Jack. 'Mr Holland, I think you and I have common cause.'

CHAPTER TWELVE

Leave Everything Behind

'In Observation the soul sayeth I should do, in Resolution it sayeth I will do...'

William Struther, *Christian Observations and Resolutions*

YOU LIVE ALONG the river, you get used to looking up. Up, to the jetties where your passengers are waiting; up, to keep an eye out for the swing of cranes and hooks; up, to gawp at any particularly fine-dressed folk outside the Thames-side taverns, maybe (once upon a time) even pick a mark amongst 'em for the lifting of a purse; and right as of now, up, to negotiate the gangplank to Miguel Domingo's wherry, moored off Horn Stairs in Rotherhithe Street, to which you bear in either hand one of those cod-cheek pasties, still warm.

'Ah,' says Miguel in welcome, as Bug comes aboard, 'the food of the gods. And what news?'

'So *much*!' says Bug. You might say life for Bug is looking up as well. Since Miguel fished him out the river, he has become a kind of cabin boy (a second-in-command, is how Bug thinks of it) on Miguel's wherry. 'The Hollands, they have put new posters up all over, saying the man they seek has been masquerading as a pest-doctor, and will have a wound upon his face, and the reward is two hundred *guineas*. How many wherries could you buy for that?'

According to Greville, Carlo Fantom should not be able to so much as shit down a jakes, without they hear of it.

'You could always put me out there as bait,' says Jack. He and Greville sit again within the parlour of the Pightle. 'I know we cannot hide here forever.'

Hah, Greville is about to reply. I can imagine what my niece would say to that.

From outside the house, the noise – the considerable noise – of a game of skittles. The captain's boys, it seems, are not a pair to play without dispute. Appeals for adjudication – first Moll then Abi. That shy boy, Toby, looking on. Says Jack, 'I have another idea.'

Which is?

'Take down the posters. Let it be known you are calling off the search. Put it about that you think he is already gone. That he was too cunning for you. Get the word out there. Let him think it safe to make a run for it.'

'I'll tell you this, Captain,' says Greville, considering, 'you may look like someone used you to practise their whittling, but that head of yours still works well enough, eh?' He cracks his knuckles. 'Oh, by God. This 'ud be so much easier if only there was even one more had seen the bastard in the flesh and lived to tell the tale!'

'You will never not do this, will you?' says Pris.

'No,' says Jack. 'That I cannot.'

'And with that I must be content?'

'You must.'

They are out in Bess's garden, Pris with a writing slope on her lap, a letter half composed upon it; Jack with Helen of Troy on his. Helen of Troy's purring is loud as a hive of bees. Jack has to move a little to shift the cat's weight. ('I have always admired a good cat,' said Jack, on making Helen of Troy's acquaintance. 'Yes,' said Bess. 'She knows.') Pris's acceptance of his searching-out of Carlo is a little eerie, tell the truth. 'I cannot leave England, and leave that creature alive in it.'

'We could be in Amsterdam already.'

'And if he follows us there? No, Pris. He and I, we have hunted one another since I was a boy. This ends here. I know I am not what I was. But then, God willing, neither is Carlo fucken Fantom.' He looks over at the writing slope. Oh, that eager pen; its inky trail as much a mystery as ever. 'Who do you write to?'

'To Rafe and Belle. Toby will take it to Varney for me, after we are gone.'

Absently, he rubs at the back of the blistered hand, where the new skin, fine and creased as the petal of a poppy, is itching like the devil. Pris takes the hand and kisses it. The itching stops. How does she do that?

'How are you, sir, today?'

'Greville says I look like I've been whittled.'

A snort of dismissal. 'For Greville, that is eloquence.'

But he does, he knows he does. Every sinew on display. His legs tire, his arms tremble. Also, he is still cropped. Like Samson.

A *halloo* from the garden gate. 'Ah,' says Pris, jumping up. 'Miguel. That is for me.'

'It is? For what?'

'You have your business, Lady Wyncanton has hers.'

'MY LADY,' SAYS Sir Theodore. He advances toward her, leaning on his stick. 'What pleasure to see you again.' Nonetheless, his attention is all on the package Pris holds before her, wrapped up most carefully, tied about and sealed.

'The pleasure is wholly mine,' Pris assures him. 'What happiness, to find you here, your library and indoor garden all unchanged. How does your Angel flower?'

'I would not say she flourishes,' Sir Theodore replies. He gestures to the Floripondio, no longer so little, and housed in a sort of plant-reliquary, of leaded panes of glass. 'I have to keep her under glass for safety's sake and she sulks. But as you see, occasionally she graces us with a bloom or two. When they open, their scent at evening is enough to fill the house.'

'I have brought something more to grace your library,' says Pris. 'Perhaps it will improve your flower's temper, to see herself immortalized.' She hands the parcel across.

'Aha!' says Sir Theodore. He attacks the seal on the string with a paper-knife. A knot beneath it, then another. Yes, my word, most carefully wrapped for their journey to him, it takes all his attention to free them from their packaging.

First one, then the other of the flower-pieces is unveiled.

'They are even more pleasing than I remember,' Sir Theodore says. 'I am most grateful.' He carries them across the room. 'I will hang them here. What pleasure, to have them to rest my gaze upon.'

'I am sure your gaze has deserved them,' says Pris. 'None better.'

'Will you stay to toast them with me?' Sir Theodore enquires. He has a compliment busily composing itself, something about flowers and women's faces, painted beauty and – oh. It seems his guest is making ready to depart.

'Another day, Sir Theodore,' says Pris. 'Forgive me, but I plan a journey, and I am deep in preparation for it. I am taking the boys to Amsterdam, until England is more herself again. Whenever that may be.'

He walks her to the stairs. 'You do me good, madam,' says Sir Theodore. 'It is a welcome change to have a visitor not afflicted by the sorrows of defeat or the anxieties of victory. But then we are fortunate. We are neither of us warriors.'

'Nor are we,' says his visitor, briskly, then to Sir Theodore's delight, lifts herself up to put a kiss on his cheek. 'You have been a most excellent friend to me,' she tells him. 'Good health, Sir Theodore, and many more years in which to enjoy it.'

What an unexpected compliment. Back Sir Theodore goes to his library, flushed with pleasure. A moment more to revel in his new treasures? Yes, he can grant himself that.

He hears the front door close. His kingdom is his own again. He looks from plant to paint, and paint to plant. No – wait. What is this?

Sir Theodore lumbers at speed across the room. He peers into the reliquary. 'Jemima!' His angry shout can be heard throughout the house. 'Have you opened the vitrine? My Floripondio – she has lost a bloom!'

It is so fine a day. Clouds frolic overhead like newborn lambs; the river is wreathed in sparkles. Pris and Miguel Domingo walk to the Strand, where he has pulled his wherry up onto the fine hard sand. 'Where is your Master Barnaby today, Miguel?'

'Ah,' says Miguel. 'He has business for me in Southwark. Where to now, my Lady?'

'Back to Chelsea.' She feels the bloom of the Floripondio in her sleeve, carefully wrapped. 'My business is done.'

THE BEAR AT the Bridge Foot, so called, a famous tavern amongst the many on Southwark's shoreline. Its rooms are free of vermin (at least as much as any place, they are); it has a spacious garden; it has a water-gate, where at the turn of every tide, passengers gather to go down to Greenwich or beyond. It even has a bear – a mournful creature, chained and collared, with fur the colour of peat. Some wag named her Snowdrop, and so accustomed is she to the ways of men, you may feed her from your hand. It also has a landlord fond of a tipple of gin. Not the turpentine-adulterated piss brewed up locally, however, no, the proper stuff, Dutch genever. For how is a man to get through such times as these without a little Dutch courage, eh? And if this comes to him courtesy of that trapdoor in the Dunqerqer's kitchen floor, rather than burdened with the duties and taxes a disapproving Parliament slaps upon it, all to the good. So that is Bug's errand for the day: the delivery of two bottles of the good stuff, in return for which he is provided with a dish of bread and sausage, and a seat in the garden. Here he sits, munching away, swinging his heels, watching the crowd as it gathers like flotsam in the Thames, waiting for the boats to arrive, to bear them away.

Bug looks up.

There at a window above the garden, a man with a hat pulled down over one side of his face. A face that is both curiously pale and oddly blank. Eyes that seem strangely hot.

Bug is gone. Bug is no more than bread and sausage cast upon the ground. Snowdrop sways across, and scoops them into her paw.

All along the river, the tide is rising; the Thames making conversation round the posts of every jetty, every wharf.

Jack lies in the darkness of their room in the Pightle, imagining he can hear it. He used to do this as a tiny child, play in his head the music of a river as it rose and fell, but then the waters were those of the Charente, not of the Thames, and the rise and fall of breathing beside him, that was his mother; not Pris. Pris with her head on his shoulder and all the wildness of her hair across the pillow. Something so sweet-scented in this room tonight – like jasmine, like honeysuckle; stealthy, like them. Softly heady.

The eerie wail of a watchman. And then what he has waited and prayed for, Greville's summons from below: 'Fiskardo! Get yourself down here.'

He unfolds himself from around Pris, bends to kiss her sleeping cheek, tiptoes across the room and eases the door shut behind him.

'We have him,' Greville says, as Jack comes down the stairs. 'He's broken cover. He's at The Bear at the Bridge Foot. No doubt he intends to be away soon as the tide has turned. I have a dozen men waiting outside. We will take him, or it will be the last thing I do.'

He holds out to Jack a sword, its hilt so elegantly curved, its blade inlaid. *NON TIMEO*. 'This was my nephew Aaron's,' Greville says.

Jack takes the sword, tries its balance. 'I ain't meant to be bearing arms, Greville.'

'Don't think of yourself as bearing it. Think of yourself as bringing it along for the show.'

AS THE RIVER rises to its height, would-be passengers leave the garden of The Bear, and flock at its water-gate, waiting for the boats. You want to get an early passage on the ebbing tide: as it falls the waters run ever faster through the bridge, until there is a drop of six feet from one side to the other. 'Shoot we the bridge?' the boatmen ask, and none but the foolhardy answer 'Aye!' Snowdrop watches as the garden empties, until there is but one man left, sat there at that table on his own. You see him by the red glow as he sucks his pipe. Hear his teeth grind on the pipe stem. Hear how he refills his glass, sucking in the wine like he is putting out an inner conflagration. From time to time he lifts a hand, presses his fingers to the eyeball that rages with tiny fragments of glass. How many pipes have there been, how many bottles' worth has he waited here? Where are the boats?

They come, they come, he tells himself. He will wait till the crowd is at its liveliest, pushing its way forward, then he will slide his way amongst them. Get himself out of London, out of this country altogether.

Because he must get out, he knows it. He must cut his losses here. He must get himself back to Brussels. Does he not have Mercator's name to mend his fortune with? By God, yes, he does.

He presses a hand to his eye. He should have run long ago, he knows that now. But he can do it still. He has escaped from worse than this. He has a plan. Even the drunkenness is part of it. Travellers leave a drunkard well alone.

He tilts his bottle to the beaker; the bottle gurgles its last. He throws it from him, to where the bear sits, hears its heavy groan. There will be broken glass where it lies, where it puts its feet, with their great curved claws, and the woman sat opposite speaks. She says, 'Another, Captain?'

He stares at her. He blinks. Where did she come from? He can hardly make her out – she wears a cloak, a hood, a domino. Perhaps she too flees, like him.

'Another?' she repeats. She holds the beaker out to him, brimful. 'It will soothe your pain.'

It looks as if there is something in the glass. The woman clucks her tongue, fishes it out. No more than the white bloom of a flower. 'Drink,' she says. 'Drink. You have time. The tide still rises, the first boats will be another half-hour yet.' And then when he still hesitates, mockingly, 'What, Captain Fantom – are you afraid?'

He takes the beaker from her. He drinks.

Ah, it is good. It is sweet, and fragrant too, but there is a bite to it at the back of the throat. The woman sits back, watching him. Is she reminding him of someone? He wants to ask her, does she wait for the boats as well, will she go down to Greenwich too; he wants to ask because a companion could be a good and useful thing for a man to have. Those watching for him will be watching for a man on his own. Then –

Wait. How does she know his name?

'Oh, I know everything about you, Captain.'

Did he ask that out loud? He cannot remember doing so. He cannot – wait, wait, something is happening here, something is awry –

Her voice comes at him out of the dark. Behind him, he hears the bear rocking itself from side to side, giving a half-whine, like a dog; he hears it snort, sampling the air. With an effort he forces himself to attend to the woman's words.

'Can you not guess why I am here? Can you not guess who sent me?'

He can think of no-one but Hooley. Could it be? Is this rescue?

She leans forward. Her eyes within the domino, they shine. She has laid something on the table. 'Now, Captain, now do you understand?'

A silver wolf. He gapes at it, at her. It seems to – it seems to – it seems to shimmer there, upon the tabletop. Is it his wounded eye, deceiving him?

His wounded eye, he realises, that has ceased to sting.

She speaks again. 'I am here for you, Captain.' She is standing. 'You must come with me. Those who are looking for you, they will be here any moment.'

She is turning her back on him. This is – this is –

The bear growls. It is behind him, it is up against his ear. He feels sweat on his face.

'Come with me, Captain,' the woman calls over her shoulder. 'Come with me!'

The men of the Farringdon Trained Bands, they clank into the garden of The Bear, they clank along its corridors, they kick open every door, they have the crowd waiting at its water-gate back up, single file, against the wall, they have them bring out their papers, they scrutinize every one, and Jack sits in Greville's carriage, with Aaron's sword at his hip, and listens as one after the other the men of the Trained Bands report that they have come up with nothing, not one suspect, no one with damaged face or eye; and from the pavement outside, he hears Greville's increasingly testy response, and quietly as he can, opens the carriage's other door, and steps down, flexing his left hand as he does so. Yes, just as in Breda. *A diviner has his hazel-twigs. I have this.*

I feel you. He had turned. He began walking down the street, away from The Bear. Borough High Street is still full of folk, even as late as this; even with the mist coming in from the river, blurring the lanterns over shop and doorway. Past the taverns: the Tabard, the George, coaches in their yards, disgorging travellers, horses led about... *I know you are here, somewhere, amongst all these –*

And then he sees it. That familiar shape: top-heavy, moving with the rolling gait of the cavalryman. *Carlo!*

Carlo has come up to a crossroads. Beyond it, the size of the buildings diminishes, and then beyond that, nothing. Carlo waits. He is entirely on his own, but it is almost as if he waits for direction. Then, as if he has received them, Jack sees his enemy turn right.

It is all so strange, this. It feels as if he can see everything, every brick in every house they pass, the moss upon the tile of every roof; as if the light illuminating them is shining from his eyes. It is magnificent. He swings his head, left to right, the light falls on everything, the buildings about them, fewer now, thinning out, the open ground, and then the woman, still moving ahead. Where, he wants to ask, where do you take me?

Of a sudden, his heart misgives. It is as if it has been grabbed, clutched, squeezed. It is a horrible sensation. It is like a wound. He has to stop, put his hand against his breast, and for a moment he feels nothing, as if his heart has ceased to beat, and then a thud so heavy he hears himself cry out loud; he must reach out, support himself –

Nothing there. Nothing anywhere. Nothing but barren scrub. He might be on the surface of the moon. He moves forward, and something catches him about the ankle. He looks down, he sees it is a ribbon, half buried in the ground. It writhes about his leg. He tries to shake it off, and hears a crunch – a little cross of sticks, crushed by his boot. Something comes dancing toward him, he has to duck, and it goes dancing away into the night, a petticoat or some such thing. And where he stands is filling with water, the clay trying to hold him, the mist coiling all about. He calls to her. 'Where is this place? Where are we? What have you led me to?'

She turns. She drops her hood, unties the domino, throws it from her, and it seems to fly into the night with wings like a bat. The air is full of shimmer, as if it has become impure. He feels again the sweat upon his face. And her hair – oh God, her hair –

'Do you not know who I am?'

He feels himself step back. Now she smiles. 'You know me, Carlo. You and I have met before.' And then she lifts her arms, puts back her head, so her hair falls all about her shoulders and cries 'See who I have for you!', and he looks about him, wildly, to see who she is talking to, and when he looks back, she is gone. Instead of the woman all there is, is this shimmer, rushing toward him, and he knows no longer what is real, what is not, and he knows what has been done to him: *I have been envenomed, she has poisoned me* –

And then he hears the growl. For one moment of complete derangement he thinks it is the bear, the bear has followed them, but then the growl becomes a word. Becomes his name. There is a man before him. '*CARLO!*'

It takes a moment. The face is thinner, the hair shorter, the man has aged, but the eyes – the eyes are unmistakable.

'You!' Carlo exclaims. '*You!*'

The shimmering has gone. If the woman drugged him, he has conquered whatever she had him drink. He opens his arms, as if in welcome. He's thinking already, *See how worn away he is.* How the man stands, favouring one leg; the unorthodox grip upon the sword - a man whose fingers have been broken. 'I am unarmed,' Carlo says.

'Too bad,' comes the reply.

'You don't look good, my friend,' Carlo calls.

'Nor do you,' comes the reply, then, 'Aaron Holland says hello.'

Aaron Holland? Next moment he hears the blade come at him. He feels the fire of a newly opened cut upon his cheek. Carlo staggers backwards.

'You would not do this!' he protests. 'I know you, you would not kill an unarmed man!'

'A *lot* has happened to me since those days.'

He has to turn to keep his foe in sight. The clay sucks at his boots. He feels the panzerstecher in his sleeve. He has to get his man to close with him again. 'No, you would not do this! An unarmed man? It would not be enough for you!'

'Was my mother armed? Or my father, when you poisoned him? Or my men, when you blew them apart?'

How much he knows. 'Fight me!' Carlo shouts. His voice is no longer serving him as it should. He shouts again, 'Fight me! Hand to hand! Fight me if you dare! If there is enough left of you to do it!'

He sees Fiskardo unbuckle his sword, lift it over his head. 'I will finish you off with my bare hands if I must.'

'Come at me!' Carlo shouts. 'Come at me then!' and Fiskardo's fist connects with the side of his head, all the bones moving one into the other, knocking him almost to his knees. He balls his own fist, punching back. When did he last fight like this? The heel of a hand hits his jaw. Carlo is reeling. He feels the hilt of the panzerstecher drop into his left hand. Another blow, into his gut, doubling him over, left arm bending, and the tip of the panzerstecher comes clean through his sleeve, above his elbow. Let him but free it, let him but close with his enemy again! He grabs at Fiskardo's shirt to pull him close and his feet slide on the wet ground; his weight is enough to pull the two of them down. They are rolling in the mud, but Carlo has him, he is the stronger, it is Carlo who is above, teeth bared, while Fiskardo, arm locked, has one hand braced against Carlo's right shoulder, trying to hold him off, while the other does battle with that now wrapped about the panzerstecher's hilt, that skewer-like blade so razor-sharp it frees itself, slicing its way entirely out the sleeve of Carlo's coat. 'You cannot hold me!' Carlo spits. The arm locked against his shoulder, he feels it tremble. 'Yield!' Carlo snarls through his teeth. 'Yield to me!' and the strangest expression moves across Fiskardo's face, like the passage of a revelation, and the arm holding Carlo off, it folds, and there is just long enough, in the instant before the blade goes through him, before he falls onto the panzerstecher, for Carlo to realize what he has done.

The blade is so swift, so clean, he hardly feels it. And then his enemy pushing him away, rolling him sideways, and he falls, he falls –

The earth receives him like a bed. He lies in water. Above, the stars again. He is lying in an open grave. He lifts his head.

There is the hilt of the panzerstecher, protruding from his right shoulder.

He feels nothing. *I am proof. Nothing can harm me, nothing made of iron or steel –*

He puts his hand to the hilt. He will free himself.

Fiskardo is above him, at the edge of the grave. He reaches down. Carlo feels the silver wolf plucked from the front of his coat. He hears the words '*Wiedersehn*, Carlo.'

And then his enemy is gone.

The water is rising. The ground is so sodden, clay is falling on him from the sides of the grave. But he can still do it, he can pull the blade from his own shoulder, nothing could be simpler! He makes to grab at it again. His fingers slip. No, something impedes him. Something holds his arm, something small. It grips. He tries to shake it away. It is the colour of the clay, but it is not clay, no – it is animate. He feels the dig of a thumb. Fingers. He feels the nails. The water is rising. It is the tide in the river, it must be coming to its height. Now under the water, something has circled his ankle. He tries to kick it away, sending the water surging over his knees, his thighs, but there are more, they grip, they hold –

They are hands. Grey clay-covered hands, grey fingers. They have his shirt. They have his hair. They come up between his legs. He hears himself screaming. The water is filling his ears. He has to clamp his mouth shut, and as he does so, he sees the air again begin to shimmer and against the shimmer he sees the shapes of the three old women, and then the fourth, the daughter, her red hair, gathered here at the edge of the grave, gathered to watch him die.

'SWEETHEART. PRIS, UP, up.' She is so fast asleep he has to lift her before she stirs, and even then it is only to hide her head against him. 'Pris, angel, we have to go.' She feels almost boneless. He lifts her chin so her face is in the light of the candle. Her eyelids flutter. 'Sweetheart, wake up. Do you hear me? Bess is downstairs, Bess and Abi, Miguel, your uncle, everyone. It's time to go.'

He puts his arm under her legs, swings her around to sit. She lifts a hand to her forehead, like a man would if waking deep in drink. Pushes back her hair from her face, blinking in the candlelight. 'I was dreaming,' she says. 'I was dreaming of Crossbones.' She blinks at him. 'I was dreaming of Carlo.'

'No more Carlo,' he tells her. Cups her chin, kisses her. Now she's awake. 'I'll get the boys,' he says. 'I'll send Moll to you.'

He lifts the candle. 'Sweetheart, what happened? Your feet are covered in mud.'

She hears the boys' chatter through the wall, the rumble of Jack's reply. Are they going out through the window again? 'No, James, a boat.' She feels as if she cannot find a level. When she stands, her head swims. None of her limbs seem to belong to her. She looks up at the shelf, the glass where she had placed the flower, but it is empty, and she remembers why, but which was the dream, that world, or this?

She hears Jack chivvying the boys downstairs. *Pris*, she tells herself, *rouse up*. Gets to her feet, and sits back down again, even though she hears the level of impatience for her downstairs rising audibly; she hears Greville proclaiming how his niece is always the last. Oh, but here is Moll. 'Madam, may I speak with you?'

Her maid is twisting up her hands. 'Madam, I know the plan is we go off to Holland, but I must ask if you would let me go back to Varney.'

'To Varney?'

'Yes, Madam. With Toby Dearlove. He ain't much on the eye, I know, but he is brave, which is a great thing in a man, and he is biddable, which is an even greater, and he is fond on me and I find I grow to a fierce liking of him and I do not know how I would do among the Dutch, though I am sure they are splendid folk…' Moll is peering into her face. 'Madam, do you hear me? You look sort of faintish, you truly do.'

'Moll.' She can hardly speak for tiredness. 'Moll, will you ask Abi to come here?'

Molly is gone. Pris seems to swim away somewhere in her head. She comes back only at the sound of that familiar greeting: 'Well, my ducky! What's all this?'

Abi fussing round her, wet cloth round the back of her neck, over her face. 'Abi, I don't know if I'm awake.'

'You're awake, ducky. You used to do this when you were a little girl.'

'I did?'

Abi has had her raise her arms above her head, is dropping petticoats onto her – one, two, three. 'Oh my word, yes. Go all these places in your dreams and when you woke, you'd be like this. All of a daze.'

She remembers none of it. Here come her stockings. Oh, now her feet are clean. Pris peers down at them, frowning. Turns her head to look up at the shelf again. For sure there was something there…

Now her dark skirt and bodice. Abi, lacing her, is speaking again. 'Better now, ducky? Better now?'

Yes. Better. Solid. Flesh and blood.

'Down we go, then, sweetling. One of us has a tide to catch.'

Down she goes, and there they are, Jack and the boys, Greville, Bess, and it is as if she has never seen these people before, yet simultaneously been in love with them all her life. She feels as she imagines a bride must on her wedding day, heartache and hope all mingled together. When she and Moll clasp hands, she finds she is almost speechless. 'Oh, Moll, my letters—' but there they are, Toby has them, tucked into his coat.

James tugs at her sleeve. 'Is Moll not coming with us?'

'No, sweetheart. Moll will go back to Varney with Toby. You will have to make do with me.'

Miguel clears his throat. 'My Lady, the tide. We must go. You have no bags with you?'

'No, we have not,' says Jack. His arm is round her. 'We leave everything behind us. Ain't that so?'

The Thames at ebb. Miguel need hardly touch the oars, the river moves so fast. It is astonishing to see what they share it with – barrel staves and timber beams, saplings torn from the banks. Greville, at the prow, holding a lantern over the water, shouts whenever they come up too close upon some piece of flotsam and Jack leans on the tiller and past it they go. She'd no idea that he could steer a boat.

Here comes the bridge, the noise of the water warning them. 'Aim left, to the north bank,' Miguel shouts. 'The second arch is wider,' and there they go, at a slant, and it is as if the river knows what they try to do; it picks them out and lifts them, carrying them forward. 'Brace yourselves!' Miguel calls back. 'There will be a drop!' James gives a wail of apprehension, which is when Pris discovers that no matter how sharp your own fear, if there is a child with you, you conquer it. She slides from her seat to the boat's sloppy floor. 'James, get down here with me. Ned, you too.' She grips onto the gunwales with either hand. 'I'll hold onto the boat and you hold onto me.'

They are so near to the Bridge that speech is almost impossible. The roar is deafening. Miguel has shipped the oars. He is shouting something at Jack, to hold the tiller steady, do not let it move. Here come the starlings, the dark points breaking the water, and now the water foams, as if they are flying across the top of a jug of beer. Pris, with the boys huddled into her, sees reflections dance across the roof of the arch above and then the prow dips, it plunges down; two walls of water curl about the prow, grey-green and yellow, as if carved from glass. She feels herself lift from the floor of the boat entirely, then bang back down again; they all bang back down; the prow comes up and they are through. There is a small sea inside the boat, sloshing from side to side, but they are through. The boys are cheering. Miguel puts the oars back into the water, and the wherry is again under his control. 'Captain,' he says, 'if you ever tire of soldiering, I will take you on as my apprentice.'

'Thank'ee,' says Jack. 'I will be in need of some new profession, at that.'

It is a quieter journey, the rest of the way. They wring out their clothes, they watch the moon rise. London and its lights and spires falls back behind them, and it becomes so peaceable they can hear creatures on the bank, the plop of rat or vole; far off, a barking dog. 'Where are we headed?' she hears Jack ask.

'The old Dunqerqer,' comes Greville's reply. 'The *Guid Marie* will take you off from there, on the next tide. 'Tis a place we use for such quiet getaways, Captain. There is an old petitioner of ours, caretakes the place for us. Old Josh.' Greville is growing expansive. 'But I should warn you – he likes the place to himself, and odds are he'll be surly. And your boys should be warned – he's a Cyclops.'

'He's a what?'

'Lost an eye. He'd a set-to with Ingram Skinner, years ago. Story is, Skinner relieved him of it with a pickle fork.'

They round the Isle of Dogs. 'Be ready,' says Miguel. 'We look for a light on the north bank. That is where we turn into the Lea.'

There. There it is. Walter Spikenard, like the old year, holding his lantern high, and a young lad with him, like the new, pointing and calling, 'Up here, Miguel! You got water enough!' And there, the riverbank opens, Jack moves the tiller and in they go. Spikenard and the boy walk along the bank, urging them on. They see chimneys, then a roof, then the boy takes the lantern and comes down the bank, showing them where to land. The wherry comes to rest. Out they get, with Jack carrying James and the rest of them squelching ashore as best they can. Ahead, the Dunqerqer, and a man stood at the door who does indeed have but the one eye. Where the other should be, a sink-hole. Pris feels Ned slip his hands into hers. But the boy with the lantern has gone running forward. 'Here they are! Here they are, Old Josh!'

'There you go,' says Walter, urging them on. 'Get yourselves within.'

They do as bid.

It is unexpectedly warm inside; someone has lit a fire. 'D'ye remember my niece?' Greville asks.

'Aye,' says Old Josh. He has a candle in a dish, holds it up to examine her. 'I remember. Bess's wee one, the foundling. You ran off to Oxford.' He swings the candle round until its light reaches Jack, with James in his arms. 'So you are Fiskardo.'

'That's me,' says Jack.

'And these are your boys.'

'So they be.'

Josh Arden holds out his hand. For the landlord of the Dunqerqer this is unheard-of courtesy. Ned and James are staring. It is not just the missing eye – this might be the oldest person they have ever seen.

The hands meet – the one with yellowed fingernails and the fuzz of white fur across its back; the other still bearing the marks of its burns, and for a moment is there – is there –

No. Pris shakes her head. *Little voices, go away.* Old Josh is squinting at Fiskardo. 'I am most glad to meet you,' says Old Josh.

Shooting the bridge has built a camaraderie, especially once Walter uncorks a bottle. The men sit at the Dunqerqer's window, beakers in hand, viewing the river. Old Josh settles Pris in a chair by the fire, with James in her lap, right hand tucked beneath his chin. Ned, she sees, chooses to sit with his father. Child no longer, hey?

'I spent my childhood on a river,' Jack is saying. 'I had a sailboat. It was a fine way to be.'

'There are many sailboats in Amsterdam,' Miguel tells him.

'Then maybe I will get another. God knows, I shall need something to do.'

'No more soldiering, Captain?' Greville asks.

'No,' says Jack, at once, and glances across the room to her, and smiles.

She must have dozed herself, for when she next opens her eyes, Jack is lifting James from her lap. 'Come look,' he says, and, with James still sleeping against his shoulder, leads her to the window. 'There,' he says. Downriver, yet a way off but in first light, that bright expanse of sail. The *Guid Marie*.

Walter is edging to the door. 'Excuse an old man, miss.'

He has an iron bladder, does Walter – all those years standing sentry at the Leaguer will do that for a man – but even so, sooner or later any veteran must take a piss, and at Walter's time of life, the taking takes a while. The *Guid Marie* is off the Greenwich Peninsula before he is done, her crew furling her sails, the flow of the tide upriver bearing her along. It's as he's admiring her stately progress that he sees the shadow flit out of sight round the side of the house. Eh?

Walter follows. There, a man with a pistol levelled in his hand, pointing through the Dunqerqer's window. 'Hoi!' Walter yells. The man spins about.

Ingram Skinner.

He fires. Walter lollops to the door fast as his old legs will take him, plunges through it. 'Ingram!' he shouts. Greville leaps to his feet. Walter is already ramming the bolts across the door when another shot comes through the side window and buries itself in the wall. Fiskardo shouts, 'Get down! Get down, all of you!'

They are on the floor, every last one of them, the Holland girl with the little lad, the older hid beneath his father. Silence outside. Greville lifts himself to hands and knees. Another shot – Ingram has had time to reload. Do they have even a single pistol between them? They do not, nothing other than Josh's old fowling piece on the wall above the fire.

'Walter!' A hiss from Josh. Walter squirms his way across the floor. Two old greybeards, nose to nose. 'Walt, we have to get them out of here.'

Two more shots through the window. The air in the room is beginning to blue with it, the taste of cordite is on the tongue. The little lad is crying in silent fright. Walt sees the Holland girl curve her hand over the boy's head. For the first time they hear Ingram's voice. 'Send them out! The Hollands, send them out to me!'

'Captain!' It is Miguel. 'Captain, the kitchen, it has a trapdoor. We can get out through there. The tide is high enough, we can get out that way.'

Bug lifts his head. 'I can get to the wherry. I can swim around, bring it underneath.'

'You think I'm not in earnest?' Skinner shouts. A thunderous assault upon the door – kicking feet, pounding fist.

'Kitchen,' says Fiskardo, pointing. 'Go!'

Oh my old bones, thinks Walter. More squirming. But Miguel already has the trapdoor open. The Thames laps beneath, and into it goes Bug, with Fiskardo and Miguel lowering him down. The Holland girl, crouched against the kitchen wall, is hugging the boys. Where's Josh?

The daft old bastard, he is still in the other room, pulling his fowling piece down from its rests, bullets running like marbles across the floor. Greville, beside the kitchen door, calls out to him, 'You mad old ape, get yourself in here!'

'Ach, you piece of shite,' comes the answer. Josh has his one eye up at the barrel of his fowling piece, is shaking black powder down it from a powder horn. As much as he gets down it, he scatters more across the floor. 'That son of a whore comes in here, I'll blow the bastard's guts out.' He shakes a fist at Greville. 'Block the bloody door!'

The kitchen's only furniture is its oak cupboard. Walter sees Fiskardo grab one side of it, Greville the other, and they shove it against the door.

The shadow of the foremast of the *Guid Marie* twitches across the floor. Says Greville, 'Does anyone smell smoke?'

Josh Arden does. He sees it too, curling up through the floor-boards. He sees Ingram's grinning face at the shattered window, and fires. Ingram comes in through the door. Old Josh catches a round lead bullet under his heel and goes down like a felled ox. Even in the kitchen, the floor shakes. By now, the bulk of the *Guid Marie*, out in the river, is blocking the light from the window. *Surely to God*, thinks Pris, *someone aboard must see what is happening in here?* Now Ingram Skinner barges the kitchen door, but with Jack and Greville holding the cupboard in place, it will not move. Comes a thunderous knocking from the floor beneath them, at the trapdoor. Miguel hauls it open and there is Bug, in the wherry, soaked from his swim, coxcomb of hair flattened either side of his face. 'You go!' says Jack to Miguel. Ingram, the other side of the door, fires a pistol into it, and a divot of wood drops from the door-frame. Now there is smoke in the kitchen too.

Miguel has lowered himself down into the wherry. 'I will hold it,' he calls up. 'Pass the little one to me.' But James has Pris around the neck and is refusing to let go; if she manages to detach one of his hands, the other latches onto her again, her neck, her dress, her hair. His face is smeary with panic. 'James, we will get into the boat together.' She has no idea how. 'You hold onto me. Hold tight. I will climb down and we will both be safe together.'

James knits his hands round the back of Pris's neck. She sits herself on the side of the trapdoor, the wherry beneath her and black river-water to either side. She tells herself, *I will not think of that*, and lowers herself forward. There is the moment when Miguel must take her weight and James's weight together, and it is enough to send the wherry scooting forward under the floor of the Dunqerqer. Then Bug fights it back into place, rotating the oars, and there is Ned, sat where she had been, then he too drops into the boat. Oh dear God, above the lapping of the waters she can hear the crackle of flame. She hugs the boys to her. It is almost too dark to see; she never knew the river had such presence, such intent. The timbers creak above their heads. She shouts up, 'Jack! Greville! Walt!' but she cannot hear an answer. 'Jack!'

Then there they are. Jack pushes Greville down into the wherry, then drops, himself. Walter, holding his nose, plunges straight into the water. Jack takes one oar, Miguel has the other. Bug is on the tiller. 'Heave, Captain,' Miguel orders. 'Heave!'

Josh Arden comes to, head thumping, smoke in his lungs. He still hears the sound of a pistol shot. He rolls himself over, which is when he finds his hands have been tied before him. Skinner came prepared. He has to get himself onto his knees, then brace himself against the wall to stand.

He staggers across the floor, peppercorns of powder crunching beneath his feet. Ingram is in the kitchen, has knocked out the window and is firing across the river – the river where is the laden wherry, and the *Guid Marie*. The enormous noise of a ship dropping her mainsail: in the wherry Miguel and Jack Fiskardo, Sally's boy, are shouting up to Sant to warp her round, to use the *Guid Marie* to give them cover, and the mainsail is to give her purchase on the wind. Ingram, cursing, is reloading his pistols. Josh comes up behind him. Ingram turns. Josh raises his roped-together hands and slides them over Ingram, to the man's waist. The two of them are face to face.

'You drunken damned old sod!' He feels Ingram's spittle on his face. 'You let me go!'

'Not I,' says Josh. He sees the wherry slip from sight around the prow of the *Guid Marie*. A single flame pokes up between the floorboards. Peppercorns of powder all around. 'Not I. I too had a daughter, Ingram, and Jack Fiskardo is her son. I sinned against my lass as bad as ever you did yours, but I will make good here. We two old sinners, we will go down to hell together.'

The wherry has reached the far side of the *Guid Marie* when the blast of powder takes out the Dunqerqer's front wall. Greville, on his feet, reaching for the net the *Guid Marie* has dropped down her side, gives a yell, loses his balance and falls into the river. Jack grabs the net, holds the wherry close. They must stand up in the boat, Jack showing them how – *hold here, foot here.* Pris puts James's good hand onto the net, steps onto it herself, holding him there. Ned clambers onto it beside her. She tells the boys, 'Hold tight, hold tight,' exactly as if she knew what she was doing here, but it is ridiculous – the ropes, the timbers at her nose, the water all around – there is a *cannon* not a foot from her face. 'Oh God,' she breathes. Then Jack steps onto the net as well, his arms across them all, and the crew on deck starts to heave. The toe of her shoe catches against the edge of a plank. She gives a cry. She feels Jack's arms press tighter against her. She cannot help herself. 'I want a life of cushions,'

Pris wails. Another heave. Another foot higher. 'I want silks, I want rouge – I want no boats, I want no more *bullets*—'

'And you will have it. You will have all the cushions money can buy, I promise you. One yard more, Pris. One yard more.'

She closes her eyes. She hold James tight. Another heave. Ned has raised his head. There are hands on her hands, pulling her in, and there is the deck. She goes sprawling, manages to stand, the *Guid Marie* shifts, she goes down again. The boys are at her skirts, her arms about them. Jack, holding them, is on his knees. Neither one of them seems capable of speech, but speech there is, nonetheless.

'Well now, Jack Fiskardo,' says Mungo Sant. 'Pris Holland. And your boys. I am most heartily pleased to have you safe aboard!'

Miguel and Bug beach the wherry on the far bank of the river, where Walter Spikenard sits, watching the last of the flames dance like the northern lights across the wreckage of the Dunqerqer. Before them, Greville is dragging himself leg by leg through the mud. They can hear him cursing. 'Should we give him a hand, Miguel?' Bug asks.

'No, Master Barnaby,' Miguel answers. 'I think not. This is a new England. Men such as Greville Holland, they must learn to shift for themselves.'

'WELL, THERE WE are,' says Rafe. 'That is Pris's letter. Amsterdam. I suppose I must send something back,' although to be honest the thought of Jack in exile so casts him down, it is hard to think what. 'I suppose I could tell him of our new arrival,' he adds, eyeing the foal. The foal, as if it feels itself the centre of attention, gets to its legs. It is still new enough to rise rump first, frisking that bit of carpet of a tail. So ungainly, thinks

Rafe. Still, Annie seems delighted by it. 'Topham, are they commonly that big?'

'No, Mr Endicott,' Topham replies.

'Then why would he be so?' The foal, as if it knows it is discussed, comes toward him, ears atwitch. It is winning, it cannot be denied. 'Pris always used to say, the two best things about Annie, she was slow and she was low.'

'I think that would be his sire, Mr Endicott,' says Topham.

'Truly? Who would that be?'

'Mr Endicott, a mare will be in foal a year. Think back to the spring last year, sir. The spring before Naseby. The last time the captain was here. The captain and his stallion, Mr Endicott.'

'The captain and – good Lord!' says Rafe, as the pieces fall into place. 'So this is—'

'There can be no doubt about it,' Topham replies. 'This will be M'sieu's foal.'

So there is one thing to share, thinks Rafe, as he goes into the house. He passes the kitchen – oh yes, something else to tell Jack, he supposes, Toby and Moll, although to be honest sharing a house with a courting couple, how very trying it can be. He crosses the hall. He steps over the three-spoked wheel of dog he finds there: Ocker and Todd, with Dash, lying nose-to-nose. He climbs the stair. 'Belle?' he calls.

'In here, husband!'

We should keep this letter safe, thinks Rafe. This and all the other papers, what with me and Belle now being more tenants here than not… He is disconsolate. He enters the bedchamber. 'Belle, do we have a keepsake box? Something of that sort?' He goes into the dressing-room. 'Belle?'

His wife is standing in front of the mirror. She is dressed in the famous yellow satin. 'Do we celebrate?' Rafe asks. The only other time Belle wore that gown was Christmas, for Twelfth

Night. They had been so determined to make merry, whatever the odds; the whole household had perhaps imbibed a little more than they should have done, and here in this very room, in this very bed, he and Belle had lost all their shyness at being in another man's house, and kept the season very well.

'You do look lovely, wife,' he tells her. 'That dress – it suits you indeed.'

'It did,' says Belle. 'But look here.' She shows him. 'I cannot close the waist.' Then to Rafe's amazement, she takes his hands and puts them on her breasts. 'And these feel different,' she says.

'They do?'

'They do. And I am queasy of a morning. The whole of this last week.' Her smile, as she looks up at him, is huge. 'Husband,' says Belle. 'I do believe that I too am in foal!'

NOW WHO CAN be in Paris in the spring, and believe that there is such a thing as trouble in the world? Not Achille de la Tour, as he walks into his office on the ground floor of the Palais Mazarin – modest lodgings, true, and dark, and since the Cardinal rebuilds the palace all about them, somewhat disordered too, but no matter, it is spring. There is his clerk. 'A letter, Monsieur!'

Really. How annoying. Must it be attended to? Where is it from?

'Brussels, Monsieur.'

Brussels? Achille seizes it and slits the seal. He reads. He reads again. He gives a cry of wonder. He looks for a signature, a name. There is none.

It will no doubt amaze you, to receive this, but I write as one intelligencer to another. I wish to share with you a supposition.

I had, upon my service, a Croat gentleman by name of Carlo Fantom. I had employed him to make report to me from England. It was one time a joke with him that he would locate for me that agent of the Dutch known to me, and so I think to you, as 'Mercator'.

It is my thinking now that I was hoodwinked. Carlo Fantom has fallen silent and Mercator has done the same. There has been no trace of him in months. If this is also the case with you, I write to you, to share my thinking that the two men may have been one and the same –

PAST WOOLWICH, PAST Barking Creek, on, on. Past Essex marsh and Tilbury Fort, where Queen Elizabeth rallied her army against Spain; and there the spire of St George's, where Pocahontas lies, who never saw her native land again. 'You will miss England, I know,' says Jack.

She leans her head into his shoulder. Three days to the mouth of the river, where its colour changes, brown to green. To her amazement, Pris has her sea-legs. 'They will have our letters by now. At Varney they will know that we are gone.'

'Then you will write again, and tell them all our doings in Amsterdam. And in Paris too, for we shall go there as well. And St-Étienne, for the boys must see St-Étienne again. And maybe I will even take you to Poitou. Where I am from.' That slow smile. 'Maybe I will. There you are, my Lady. Exile sets one free.'

The boys, at the prow, are leaning out to either side; Ned with a hand to his brother's belt. There is a last lone seagull flying with them, wings white as mica as it tilts, then it is gone. The waters have a chop, a swell. The sea.

'I have this,' Pris says. She holds the silver wolf. 'I didn't know what to do with it.'

Jack takes its pair from his pocket. 'And I have this.'

He sees how she draws back. 'That was his?'

'It was. And I do know what to do.'

He leads her to the rail. Holds out Carlo Fantom's silver wolf, and Pris holds out what for all those years had been Jack's own. Waves cleave away beneath them, forever passing, forever renewed.

'Ready?' he asks, and Pris nods her head. 'Together?'

'Together. On my mark. One, two, three.'

Acknowledgements

This is a book that took the writer into some extraordinary places, none more so than London's 'Crossbones' cemetery. Crossbones has many a guardian spirit, but its historian and champion is Lucy Coleman Talbot, to whom I owe enormous thanks. You can learn more about Crossbones here: https://crossbones.org.uk/. I urge you to do so.

Thanks in the same proportion are owed to Bella Greenwood, for her patience and eloquence and generosity in helping me understand what it is to be as connected to other worlds as firmly as to this.

In Oxford, my guide and squire and fount of wisdom was Samuel Fanous, and my host was Johanna Stephenson. Thanks to them both for their knowledge and kindness and time. Likewise, the staff of the wonderfully atmospheric Turf Tavern, which Jack Fiskardo would have known as the Spotted Cow. 'Varney', the house lovely enough to halt my hero's wanderings, at least for a while, is based on Kirby Hall in Northamptonshire, now in the care of English Heritage. I have played fast and loose with its history and ground-plan, but the inspiration it provided is real. Again, there is more here: https://www.english-heritage.org.uk/visit/places/kirby-hall/

My fellow author Rob Eastaway, mathematician extraordinaire, set me thinking in whole new ways about seventeenth-century espionage; while Dr Jacqui Stanford and her knowledge of the personnel involved in managing London's seventeenth-century plagues led me to Carlo Fantom's stratagem for hiding in plain sight. Thanks to them both.

I first visited Breda back in 2015, as part of its redhead festival, RedheadDays. Its history is striking, the town itself is charming; I earmarked it long ago as a location I wanted to return to, in fiction as I have done in real life. Thanks to all those I met there, redheads or no. Heartfelt thanks too, as ever, to the British Library; to the Rijksmuseum in Amsterdam, the Yale Center for British Art and the Metropolitan Museum of Art in New York for placing on open access the images that grace each chapter here.

The writing of *The Wanton Road* took place over a period where every nightmarishly bad thing you could ever think of seemed to happen all at once. My heartfelt gratitude to Kate Ballard and Clare Drysdale, my editor and publisher, for their patience and understanding, to Tamsin Shelton and Belinda Jones for the safety net of their sharp eyes; to Joe Mills, Ed Pickford and Jeff Edwards for their creativity and empathy; and to my agent, Chelsey Fox, of Fox and Howard. Finally, to family, friends, beloved – thank you.